BROTH

SIS

Adele O'Neill

About *Brothers & Sisters*

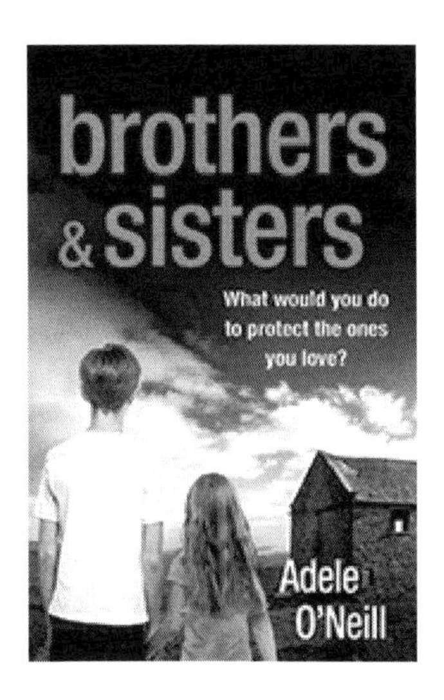

Nothing remains buried forever… What would you do to protect the ones you love?

When human remains are found on Fitzpatrick Estate, Detective Kelly is drawn deep into the complex web of Fitzpatrick family secrets as Timothy and his sister Rose, now in their sixties, are catapulted into the centre of the investigation.

When the pathology report identifies the remains as that of their uncle, Patrick Fitzpatrick, missing from Fitzpatrick Estate since 1970, they scramble to protect their past. What would you do to protect the ones you love?

For Marie and Curly:

To Marie, for showing me that I had something inside so strong,

And to Curly, for teaching me how to use it.

Chapter 1

Monday Morning – 2016

Detective Tony Kelly stretched his arms over his head and pressed his weary shoulders against the black mesh back on his new office chair. Every muscle in his body ached and the unshaven black bristles on his face were an indication of another night spent crouching, crawling and scraping for traces of answers, beside another rotting corpse.

'Ergo-fecking-nomical, my arse!' he said as the padded armrest gave way and clunked heavily to the floor. Nobody flinched, which surprised him, considering it made such a din. 'Who the feck put these together?' No one answered, the four other detectives that shared the incident room preferred not to, for peace sake. He stood and kicked the chair aside; not so forcibly as to attract a response but enough to satisfy his simmering temper. It spun and whizzed before it stopped abruptly, teetered momentarily, and then plonked heavily on its side on the worn carpet tiles.

'Tony,' Detective Louise Kennedy was probably the only detective in their unit that was brave enough to refer to him by his first name. Much like the way a mother would a child, if he was in trouble. 'Do you need some coffee or something?' Her teeth remained clenched as she forced the corners of her mouth upwards and bent her head ever so slightly to the side.

Detective Louise Kennedy's piercing stare and sharp tone left him in no doubt that it was an instruction, as opposed to an offer, the kind of instruction that only a sarcastic friend might get away with.

'No I don't need any fecking coffee,' he paused, 'thank you.' Kelly's bluster was his trademark as were the dark tropical centipedes he had for eyebrows. 'But a chair that worked would be nice.' He kicked it again for good measure, not wanting to relinquish his higher ground just yet.

Louise narrowed her eyes at his sarcasm and shook her head at his childishness. In the seven years since she had first arrived to the station in Kilkenny, he hadn't changed so much as his shirt, never mind his personality, and even though they were equal in rank, he had an unspoken seniority to her in years of service.

Kelly picked up his chair and placed it carefully back at his desk; every movement deliberate and silent. He needed to pull his horns in; he knew that, he just couldn't bring himself to raise his gaze. He could feel her brown eyes boring holes in his head. He shut down his computer and placed his phone in his shirt pocket.

'Maybe, coffee would be nice.' He finally mustered the courage to look back at her, knowing she would not avert her gaze until he reciprocated. 'Would you like one yourself?' He paused for effect and plastered a deliberate false smile across his stubbly jaw. 'Darling,' he added. The sarcasm dripped like molasses from his gritted teeth and a snigger escaped from one of the other desks; Louise couldn't identify which one.

She stood, almost by stealth and scanned the room. She was sick of their feeble joke attempts at her expense, and if the truth was known, she was offended for Kelly also. Being the only female in this division had its drawbacks; being the only other detective that Kelly trusted was an occupational hazard.

'If one other person,' her voice raised slightly, just enough so that no one could mistake the intention in her tone, 'so much as thinks about calling me, "darling", or refers to me as his "work wife", again, I will personally hand you your balls in the same envelope as your P45.' She paused triumphantly. 'Clear?' None of the three other detectives that hid behind their computers looked up, they knew not to. Detective Louise Kennedy was a force to be reckoned with; as headstrong as her male counterpart but infinitely more tactful and correct, she wouldn't hesitate to follow through on her threat, and although she might not have literally handed them their balls, she would have made them feel as though she had, and therein lay her power.

'I'll join you,' Louise said, glaring around the room, daring any one of the three to answer. They didn't – not out loud anyhow. She led Kelly to the break room and closed the door behind them. 'What the fuck?' she hissed at him. 'What's with the hissy fit?'

'Just tired.' Kelly poured two cups from the coffee pot, scrambling for a better excuse to give her. He sipped slowly, buying some time. If he knew Louise Kennedy well enough, he knew that, if nothing else, she was relentless. He sighed heavily and continued, 'I was up at Fitzpatrick Estate for most of the night. Forensics will be finished with the scene before lunch, they reckon.'

'We only caught this case yesterday evening, give yourself a chance; Jesus, give me a chance, would you?' Louise wasn't the type to follow but somehow, since she was stationed at Kilkenny, she found herself content to be in his shadow, it helped that she was secretly in awe of his rebellious nature, even if he was the one who got on her nerves the most.

'Mmm, maybe.' Kelly wasn't convinced. Something was niggling at him. He had stayed at the scene right through the night, accepting copious cups of tea, a wee dram of whiskey and a bellyfull of buns from Marie McGrath, one half of the couple who were the new owners of the Estate.

'Who you interested in?' Louise could tell he was grinding his theories hard to see what flavours remained.

'I want to talk to Timothy Fitzpatrick, landlord extraordinaire.' Kelly had been strategic in accepting the McGraths' hospitality; people talked more over a country cup of tea, he had said to her. 'The McGraths tell me they only bought the Estate four months ago, after years of putting in offers.' He stood against the countertop with one hand lodged in his dark unwashed jeans and the other around his mug. 'From this Timothy Fitzpatrick, one of the original owners, last in a long line of Fitzpatricks, apparently.'

'Should we not be concentrating on the body, identifying that?' Louise topped up her coffee and spooned in another lump of sugar; after the run she did that morning she needed the boost.

'If anyone cared who the body was, we'd already know by now.' Kelly shook his head. 'We need to know how he got there. That's where the key is.'

'Maybe…' Louise said but Kelly interrupted her.

'And why, all of a sudden, after ten bloody years, was it time to finally sell the place – that's why I want to talk to Timothy Fitzpatrick.'

'I take it there's no one on the Missing Persons Register that matches.

'Haven't found anyone yet.' Kelly ran both hands through his black wavy hair and rubbed. Speckles of dandruff spilled onto his shoulders and disappeared like snowflakes landing on wet grass. 'Won't get the pathologist report till tomorrow either, but from the preliminary investigations, the pathologist thinks we should start our search back as far as 1970.'

'I heard that, what's that about?' Louise's frown made a thick line across her forehead, deep enough to do a tyre test with a ten cent coin. At thirty-five years of age, she was beginning to realise that she shouldn't have dismissed her glamorous aunt's advice on moisturiser.

'Something to do with the acidity of the soil, or wetness,' Kelly slurped and sighed as he downed the black coffee. 'Something like that. The pathologist said the conditions…' A waft of his own stale body odour exploded up his nose as he lifted his arms. He looked at Louise and hoped she hadn't noticed. She was standing next to him cradling her mug in her hands. 'The soil conditions sort of preserved the remains.'

'Right, I'll have another look.' Louise dropped her nose into her scarf, creating a barrier between her and the stench. 'Have you not been home yet then?' She stood just to his left a bare sniff away.

'No, not yet.' Kelly's cheeks flushed as he realised she had smelled him.

'You need a shower, Kelly.'

'I know, I know.' His cheeks flushed even pinker.

'Seriously, Tony, go take a bloody shower.'

'If you keep talking to me like that, they'll…' he said quietly, motioning through the break room window at the detectives in the other room. 'If you think "wife" is bad, wait till they start calling you my "mother".'

'More like your daughter. For fuck's sake, I'm half your age,' Louise said.

'Cop on to yourself, fucking half my age.' Kelly sniffed at her remarks, his pride a little dented. 'You're thirty-five, there's a big difference between half my age and twenty years younger than me, or was maths not your strong point either?' Kelly answered, half joking, whole in earnest.

'Jesus, someone's a little touchy,' Louise answered, feigning innocence at her own remark. She was only too aware of Kelly's sensitivity to his age, which was why she was getting such a kick out of tormenting him. 'I was exaggerating for effect,' she began to spell out her intentions, knowing full well that this would aggravate him even more. 'Saying that, it would be more likely that I'd be your daughter, seeing as you are,' she looked away from him, stifling the smirk that was edging her bowlike lips towards a toothy smile, 'twenty years older than me.' She continued as she walked towards the breakroom door, hiding the grin on her face.

He smiled in response, but not while she could see him.

'I've been looking into the McGraths as well, Michael and Marie,' Louise said as she returned to her desk. Kelly followed. 'I'd love to know what possesses a couple in their forties, well, Michael McGrath is in his forties, the wife, Marie is in her thirties, to leave the big city lights and take over an old derelict estate two hours from Dublin. It just doesn't make sense to me.'

'Well, it wouldn't,' Kelly said.

'What's that supposed to mean?' Louise answered. Their exchanges, to anyone a safe enough distance away to observe, were like a tennis match in the Wimbledon singles final on centre court; each equally capable of winning but, more importantly, neither willing to lose.

'You being a city chick and all that.'

The smirk on Kelly's face as he said it bothered her. She could have settled as a beat cop and remained in Dublin with her family and friends close by but she was too ambitious not to pursue the promotion when it came up.

'Says the man who thinks he needs a passport to go beyond the county boundary,' Louise said. She had every intention of rising through the ranks and, unlike Kelly, she was prepared to relocate for her ambition, and besides, two hours south of Dublin to the medieval city of Kilkenny that was steeped in Irish history was hardly the other side of the world. 'And by that token, the McGrath's were city chicks too.' Louise was quick to answer. 'So that just adds to my point.'

'Ah but, farming was in Michael McGrath's blood. You don't know what it's like to want to come home to the land,' Kelly said.

'And neither do you, sure you never left.' She smiled.

'What about you, then?' Kelly wasn't about to let her away with that one. His reasons for staying in Kilkenny and passing up promotion opportunities over the years were his business and while he knew the general consensus amongst his peers was that he was unambitious or disinterested, it bothered him to think that Louise thought the same. 'There was obviously a reason that you left Dublin,' he said. 'Perhaps something you wanted, that you couldn't get there.' Louise nodded. 'Well then, can't we use the same premise for the McGraths?' he asked. 'There was something in Kilkenny that they couldn't get in Dublin, in their case, a farm, a return to Michael's home place, his brother and a better life for their family than they would have had in Dublin.' Kelly smiled smugly; as far as he was concerned, it was that simple.

'I suppose,' Louise answered. She decided to bank the thinly veiled insult about Dublin for later. Even though there were so many similarities between the cities, it was a one-upmanship that they bantered about frequently. Whose city had the bigger castle? Which city attracted the most tourists? Where was the best nightlife? They could tit-for-tat for days about it. Sometimes she suspected that Kelly might be a descendant of *Strongbow* himself when it came to the passion he displayed for Kilkenny and his reluctance to leave it.

'Did you know that they leased the farm before they bought it in January?' Kelly said.

'Yeah, I did, they've been there ten years apparently,' Louise answered.

Kelly wheeled another chair from an empty desk and pushed the new broken one aside. Nobody commented.

'Apparently Michael's a local. He left years ago.' Kelly was cautious as he dragged the new chair towards his desk; he checked the armrests twice. Louise couldn't help but smile. The bolts seemed secure. For the first time, he considered that maybe the bolts on the last chair were tampered with deliberately. He threw a glance around the room. 'He was lecturing in University College Dublin.' He checked his notes. 'Agricultural Science, no less. Came home then, when he had himself a wife and children.'

'And what about the Fitzpatricks?' Louise had brought her coffee back to her desk. She wet her thumb and wiped the droplets from the outside of her mug. Had she been at home, she would have licked them directly off.

'There's Timothy Fitzpatrick, in his sixties, living in Dublin since the seventies. Fitzpatrick Estate was in his and his sister's name up until January this year.' Kelly concentrated on his scrawl in his black notebook, 'There's the sister, Rose Fitzpatrick, now O'Reilly, who'd also be in her sixties, also living in Dublin, and then there's both of their parents up in St. Peter's cemetery.' Kelly had walked the cemetery himself with the intention of reading every headstone until he had found them. Trusting his hunch, he had checked the more ostentatious plots first. There was no way a family with an estate the size of Fitzpatricks' wouldn't have a plot to match it. As usual, his instincts were right. 'There were only the two of them buried up there.' Louise listened. 'Maeve and Liam Fitzpatrick buried within a year of each other, 1986 and 87.' Kelly double-checked the years in his notebook.

Louise scratched a line through the first item on the list in front of her.

'Although, you'd think by the size of the plot, they'd have breed, seed and a generation of Fitzpatricks up there with them,' Kelly added as he leafed through his pages.

'Sure, how else were they going to let people know that they were better than everyone else?' Louise said, watching his hands as they turned the well-crumpled pages. She imagined a tumbling tower of old battered notebooks stacked in chronological order beside his bed with every case he had ever caught, documented in his scrawl; starting with his first notebook thirty years ago and ending with this one he had in his hands. 'There was another Fitzpatrick, you know,' Louise added, realising now that Kelly hadn't discovered it yet. He didn't answer. 'According to the locals, there was a "Patrick", or "Pat Fitzpatrick",' Louise looked across from her notes at his expression. 'Never married, he may have left for Liverpool, in the seventies, I'm told,' Louise added.

'How did I not know that?' Kelly said, raising his eyebrows in disbelief. 'How'd you find that out?'

'I have my ways.' Louise grinned, delighted to get ahead of him. She hadn't verified her information yet, but the old fellas in the local pub were as much an information source as a government census form; small towns with generations of families living in them was one thing that her Dublin City didn't have, but she wasn't about to tell Kelly that. 'Would have been an uncle to your, Timothy Fitzpatrick?' Louise waited for him to reply. She tried her best to suppress a smile that was forming as she watched his notebook ritual of straightening up loose pages, smoothing down the crumples and stretching the frayed elastic band around its middle.

'Well, if he was still alive he would,' Kelly answered. He calculated quickly in his head. 'He'd be in his late nineties. I'll do deaths register, first here and then Liverpool,' Kelly said.

'He's not buried up in the plot?' Louise questioned. She knew Kelly would have been thorough, but when he didn't know he was looking for the uncle, he might have overlooked it.

'He wasn't in the family plot.' Kelly answered. 'Nor anywhere close,' he added. 'I have Timothy Fitzpatrick coming down this morning. I might get a few answers out of him.'

'Right,' Louise said. Every new investigation started for her like a new book. Shiny covers, fascinating blurb and surprising endings, promising gripping detail with twists and turns. She couldn't wait to delve in, crack the spine and devour the clues.

'Grand, I'm going to grab a shower at home and then head back up to the estate,' Kelly said.

Louise pulled back her black hair into a tight ponytail and drained the remainder of her coffee, she rubbed her nose, remembering the body odour from moments earlier.

'You do that,' Louise said.

Chapter 2

Monday Morning – 2016

'Tell me again why I never came to Kilkenny with you before.' Robert admired the rolling patchwork fields as they rounded the last few roads on their journey.

'I honestly don't know.' Tim liked to be honest, but when it came to Kilkenny, Fitzpatrick Estate and anything to do with his past there, it was safer to be silent. That was how it was. There were far too many things left unsaid, and those that were said, hurt deeply. He had never actually told his father or his mother that he was gay, he didn't need to, his father's cutting remarks about his fanciful city ways demolished any chance of acceptance and consequently his visits home were brief and infrequent when his parents were alive. 'It's been quite a while since I've been here myself.' His shoulders stiffened and his hands gripped the steering wheel, almost a little too tightly; Robert noticed. Tim shuffled in his seat and stretched forward over the steering wheel to stretch his back. Long journeys played havoc with his sciatica. 'I really don't like the sound of this Detective Kelly fella,' Tim said. Robert hadn't needed the explanation. 'The message he left was a little…' Tim struggled to articulate what he was feeling; the words he wanted to use were much more vulgar than he would care to admit. 'A little smug, or something, you know?' he added. 'As though, this dead body is something to do with me.'

'They have to talk to everyone, I suppose.' Robert felt for him, he couldn't remember ever seeing Tim this agitated. That first day that Tim had walked into his office, all those years ago, he had known that they were kindred spirits, two peas in a pod. It helped of course that Tim, the young budding architect, needed Robert, the young budding engineer, to make his design work and, for the past forty years, that was pretty much how their relationship had continued to work. 'You know, to rule you either in or out.'

'Mmm,' Tim answered, opting for silence as his response. 'Every year for the past five years...' He stalled at a junction two miles from the estate, while he considered which road he would take. Nothing looked familiar. 'Jesus, everything looks a whole lot different, I'm not sure if it's this crossroads,' he swung his head from left to right, searching for familiarity, inching the car forward, 'or the next, for my left turn. I don't remember any houses being on these roads.'

'Doesn't surprise me,' Robert said, fumbling for his phone. Urban sprawl was one of his pet hates. 'I'll do Google Maps, just to be sure.'

'No, no need,' Tim said. 'It's the next junction I think.' He edged across the road, unsure with his decision but reluctant to rely on a map to get him to his home place. 'What was I saying?'

'You were saying something about the past five years.' Robert was holding his phone at arm's length. 'It really is a sign of old age when your arm isn't long enough to read your phone.' Robert chuckled at his own joke, Tim joined him, albeit tentatively.

'I was saying, these are the tenants, or should I say, the new owners, that have emailed me for the past five years asking me to sell and it was a lot easier to ignore all those emails, knowing that I would never have to meet them,' Tim said. 'You know, this place is cursed. Nothing good has ever come of it.' Tim shook his head, partly to show his disappointment and partly to shake away the memories. 'The last thing I thought I'd be doing when I finally signed the papers to sell the place a couple of months ago was being summoned back here to answer questions about a discovery of human remains. I mean seriously, talk about rotten luck.' Impatiently Tim increased his speed.

'Do you think they'll want to speak to Rose?' Robert asked.

'I hope not, but,' Tim paused, 'I mean, if she has to come back down, she will, I just hope she doesn't have to.' He paused again. 'And what's worse is,' his annoyance danced from his mouth, 'this, Detective Kelly, said in his message to meet him up at the farmhouse, I would have much preferred meeting him in the station. So it looks like I have no choice but to meet the new owners,' Tim paused and drew a deep breath. 'And see the old house,' Tim added, his face darkened at the thought of it. 'The charm of Fitzpatrick Farm,' he sighed.

'You've got that face again. Are you all right?' Robert paused. 'Actually don't answer that platitude. I know you're not.' Robert was sympathetic. 'Do you want to talk about it?' Try as he did, Robert knew that there were some things that Tim could never articulate. Tim's loyalty to his sister, Rose was immeasurable and Robert had accepted that it wasn't Tim's story to tell, whatever the story was. His curiosity through the years had never bettered him, even though he had his suspicions, and today of all days he wasn't going to change that. 'That'll do for now.' Robert rubbed his shoulder. 'We'll be back on the road before you know it; we might even call into Rose on the way back home,' Robert said, trying to appease him.

'That's the start of the land there now.' Tim was relieved he had found his way. Their silver Passat swallowed up the remainder of the road as they reached the next junction, the junction Tim was hoping to meet, O'Connor's Corner. Four police vehicles lined the ditch that bordered the land and a Garda checkpoint flagged them down.

'I'm to meet Detective Kelly at Fitzpatrick Estate,' Tim volunteered the information as the Garda approached.

'What's the name?' The Garda placed his hand on the roof and bent towards Tim's open window.

'Timothy Fitzpatrick.'

'Is that so?' One of the Garda's eyebrows raised slightly higher than the other one, Sean Connery style. 'I suppose, you'll know where you're going so.'

Tim pressed his automatic window to close and drove through the junction under the watchful eyes of uniformed people in high visibility jackets. Rounding the bend, Tim was surprised by the beautifully crafted iron gates swooping from the tall pillars. A large metal plaque with 'Fitzpatrick Estate' engraved, hung from metal rings. It hadn't looked like that in his day.

'Impressive,' Robert stated, as the gates slowly opened to a curvy drive that was bordered by an impeccably groomed, waist-height hedge.

'Pretentious, more like,' Tim answered. 'We only ever called it *The Farm*, never *The Estate*.'

'Those who have money say they don't, and those who don't say they have,' Robert teased.

The drive wound its way up to the gravelled courtyard and stopped at the entrance to the old farmhouse.

'This hill was hell on a bike,' Tim said softly as his engine revved in the wrong gear.

'Bloody hell, it's like Downton Abbey,' Robert exclaimed as the tyres crunched to a standstill to the side of the imposing granite house.

'Exaggerate much,' Tim kidded at Robert.

'Well, maybe not Downton, but you have to admit, it's pretty impressive,' Robert said.

'It never looked like this when I was here, I can assure you.' Tim scanned the surrounds looking for clues of his past, and even though he knew he shouldn't, he scanned for clues of the present. His memory of the farm was far greyer than the technicolour picture that stood in its place.

'Did it smell like this?' Robert joked as the whiff of slurry poured through their open doors.

'Worse,' Tim said. 'It looked and smelled *much* worse.' His voice wasn't jovial this time. His eyes darted to the side of the sheds. He couldn't tell, with the hedges along the pathway grown, whether the cottage below still stood.

'Hello.' Tim quickly turned as Marie McGrath, the owner of the house, approached.

'Timothy Fitzpatrick.' He outstretched his hand.

'Marie McGrath. It's lovely to finally meet you.' She ran her fingers through her greasy hair in an attempt to appear a little more presentable than she felt. The gentlemen that stood in front of her were so well-groomed and handsome, she felt somewhat inadequate in her jeans, fleece jumper and wellingtons. 'You'll have to forgive our appearance; it's all hands on deck at the moment, we haven't had much time for anything, since, well, since everything happened.' She glanced in the direction of the bottom field, drawing Tim and Robert's attention there also. 'Michael is just out on the farm. He'll be in shortly.'

'I think they want to see me below.' Tim was anxious to get closer to the scene. He had no intention of meeting Michael McGrath, if he could avoid it, and even less intention of stepping foot inside the old house, although there was a small spark of curiosity as to what it may have looked like inside.

'Oh, they'll know you are here.' Marie waved towards the activity in the field below. 'You may come in for a cup of tea first.' Marie motioned them to follow her inside. 'The state pathologist is still at the scene.' She spoke as though it was a common occurrence in these parts. Detective Kelly isn't down there yet either, and anyhow, he'll call up here first,' Marie said. Marie's children, Jack and Eve appeared on the steps behind her.

'Will you run down for Daddy, Jack?' Marie pointed towards the sheds. 'Evie, come and say hello.' Both Marie's children hovered around her.

'Oh please, don't interrupt him,' Tim said awkwardly.

'Nonsense.' Marie had a relatively assertive but kind voice. A voice that was familiar with directing children. 'We are delighted to have visitors, aren't we Evie?'

Eve nodded in agreement as she flashed the guests a front toothless smile. Her long curly blonde hair bounced rebelliously across her eyes and with her pudgy hand she pushed it away.

'If you are sure we are not imposing,' Robert said as he threw Tim an uneasy look.

'Not in the slightest, please, Michael is on his way.'

Reluctantly, Robert and Tim followed her as she ushered Evie ahead of her, Jack had run diligently in the direction of the sheds.

'Your boots, Eve.' Marie's voice was firm. 'Leave them outside.'

Eve stopped still. It wasn't the first time she had to be reminded.

'Oops, Mummy, I forgot.' Her eyes were wide with amusement as she giggled at her mistake, then she turned and directed her next question at Tim. 'Do you want to take off your shoes too?' Eve shook her leg to dislodge the mucky boot as she waited for him to answer.

'Oh you scamp.' Marie laughed. 'Our visitors haven't been playing in the fields. Their shoes are perfectly fine.' She mouthed sorry to Tim and led her visitors to the kitchen. 'So, this is your first time back in a good number of years then,' Marie said.

'It is,' Tim answered, resigning himself to the fact that he couldn't avoid going inside. It had been decades since he last stepped over the threshold and his shoulders stiffened as he imagined himself, a teenager again. There had been a reason neither he nor Rose had any desire to be back. 'There hasn't been any need to come down; really, the management company have looked after everything,' he said.

'Well, it's lovely to finally have you both here,' she smiled at Robert, 'even if it is in such bizarre circumstances.' Marie paused, brushing her white shoulder-length hair from her eyes. She didn't want to make a wrong impression, it had taken them numerous years to get Mr Fitzpatrick to agree to sell and she didn't want him to leave, regretting his decision. 'Eve, love, will you pop up and brush your teeth.' She pulled out a kitchen chair and gestured for Tim and Robert to sit down. Robert sat at the head of the oak table and Tim took a chair beside him.

Eve wasn't fooled; she knew her mother wanted to talk about adult things, so she stalled as long as she could.

'How old are you?' When standing, Eve's elbows rested comfortably on the table top and she leaned her chin on her hand waiting for Tim to reply.

'Eve!' Marie exclaimed.

'No it's a fair question.' Tim smiled at Eve across the table, she was beginning to remind him of his niece when she was younger. 'I'm sixty-two, and Robert is sixty-five. How old are you?'

'I'm eight and Jack is eleven. My mum is twenty-one.' She widened her eyes and lifted her eyebrows for effect; she had seen her daddy do it often. Marie shook her head and smiled and even though Eve's charm was hard to deny, she threw a warning look at her daughter to finish up her questions and do what she was told. 'Are you a grandad?' Eve grabbed a freshly baked bun from the cooling rack beside the oven knowing by the look on her mother's face she wasn't going to get away with much more.

'No.' Robert caught Tim's eye as he answered. 'But we are both uncles.'

'That's cool. Where do you live?' Eve sprayed some crumbs from her mouth as she blurted out her questions. She didn't dare look in her mum's direction but she could feel her stare from where she stood.

'Dublin.' Tim could see she was stalling for time and couldn't help but go along with her. 'I used to live here though, when I was your age.' Tim anticipated her response: a wide smile; crumbs filling the gaps where her teeth should be.

'No way!' Eve exclaimed in disbelief. 'In my house?'

'Way,' Tim answered. 'But it wasn't as pretty when I lived here.' He glanced at Marie, hoping the compliment would reach her, as she carried a plate of baked fancies to the old oak table by the double doors. He cringed as he visualised the state of disrepair he had left the place in. He was sorry now. 'You really have restored it so beautifully.' Tim's eyes wandered around the room. He couldn't remember the kitchen ever having as much daylight in it before. 'Was that window always there?' A stream of white light flowed through the slatted blinds, creating dark angled stripes on the otherwise white porcelain floor.

'That was one of the more modern features we installed.' Marie was proud of how the house looked. 'It's such a pretty view from here.' She looked out over the farm and down the hills to her brother-in-law's, George McGrath's farm below. The McGrath's had lived in this part of Kilkenny for centuries. 'That's Michael's homeplace down there'. She pointed down and across the fields to where George McGrath's house stood. 'We tried as best we could to keep as much of the original features, and married them with a bit of modern stuff as well.' She continued to set the table. 'Of course there's still so much we want to do.' She hoped that didn't sound like a criticism to Tim of the state they had found the place in.

'It really is unrecognisable,' Tim said sheepishly. He wondered what she had thought of the place when she first saw it. 'With living in Dublin, I, or I mean, we never really got down that much.'

Marie threw her daughter a final warning look and as Eve left the room, Marie poured some tea into Tim and Robert's mugs, cleared her throat and began to speak. She could tell by the anticipation in Tim and Robert's eyes that they were eager for more information.

'Sorry you were bombarded with all those questions.' She smiled, shutting the door behind her daughter. 'I was waiting for her to leave so that I could tell you, Detective Kelly, he was here earlier this morning and just nipped back to the station for a few things, he said I've to give him a ring when you get here.' She had learned the hard way not to have sensitive conversations in front of her chatty eight-year-old.

'Marie,' Tim was anxious to meet the detective and get back on the road to Dublin, 'if you don't mind, maybe you'll give him a ring there now.' And if he could avoid meeting Michael McGrath, all the better.

'Of course.' Marie patted her head for her glasses and slid them down to her nose. She scrolled through her recent calls and pressed connect when she found the station's number. She smiled at Tim as she listened for the call to be connected. 'Detective Kelly, please.' Her tone was clear and concise, Tim noted as she spoke down the phone to whoever answered. She walked out of the kitchen to continue.

'She seems nice.' Robert spoke softly as the door closed behind her. 'Crazy being back here after all these years, I'd say?'

Tim barely acknowledged his ramblings with a nod.

Robert watched him with sympathetic eyes. 'You can see for miles from this window.' Robert stood by the sink and turned on the tap to rinse his cup. Tim didn't answer. He had never stopped to take in the view when he was a child; he was too busy ducking out of the way of his father's fists. 'Tim.' Robert knew Tim's thoughts were far from undulated hills and idyllic childhood memories. Tim still didn't answer. 'Tim.' Robert spoke more firmly.

'Yes.' Tim shook his head as though trying to banish what was inside of it. 'What, yes, the view, yes it's lovely. Sorry, I was miles away.' It was surreal to think that he, Timothy

Fitzpatrick, was sitting in Fitzpatrick House, drinking tea once more, after all this time.

'You know, I don't think he ever forgave me.'

'Who didn't?' Robert said. He glanced at the door, hoping neither Eve, nor Marie would return too soon. He was eager for Tim to speak to him, talk about how he was truly feeling and he knew that it was a hard thing for Tim to do.

'My father, Liam, the man of the house.' The words tasted like lemon on Tim's lips.

'But sure, what was there to forgive?' Robert said.

'For not being the man he wanted me to be. For letting everything…' Tim paused.' For everything that happened.'

Chapter 3

Monday Afternoon – March 1970

I've grown to hate coming home from school; I'd prefer to stay in the convent with that bitch of a nun, Sister Alphonsus. I still have welts on my left hand where she walloped me with the cane for writing with it. She says that only the devil's children use their left hand and that good catholic girls should write with their right hand, like Jesus intended them to. She says it's the only way that I'll learn my lesson, that and by tying it tightly behind my back so I can't use it. I hate the month of March most of all, mostly because it's lambing season. The season when Tim is ordered out of school by father, even though it's his exam year, and plonked slap, bang, right into the middle of the lambing field until all the lambs are born. He's even made to sleep in the caravan up there, which leaves just me and my mother back here, at the house.

My mother enjoys March most, when my father is either out in the fields or down in the town, drinking. It allows her to pretend we don't exist. Like she's some pitiful widow living alone in the oversized farmhouse.

'Is that you, Rose?' My mother, indolent and dramatic, is only short of fanning herself with feathers and uttering 'woe is me' at the end of every sentence, and it really grates on my nerves. Her voice spills from the mahogany panelled room, scraping the black and white tiles of the hall as it travels towards me and staggers into the kitchen carrying the scent of musty perfumed talc, cigarette smoke and regrets. She would have watched me from her bed as I climbed the drive and rounded the house to enter through the heavy back door. I'm furious that she has asked, there is no one else it could have been. I'm furious that I have to answer her.

'Yes.' The scorn on my face is much braver than the politeness of my voice. It is just as well she cowers behind her door, fearful to be seen, not that she would have seen my face even if she had been standing in front of me. Unlike my father, who says that if I so much as look at him in that tone of voice, he'll teach me how to be pleasant, with his belt, again. I always try my best not to answer him and for the most part it works. My father's belt is like the convent's Mother Superior. When you see her coming, you bow your head and shut your mouth and hope that she doesn't notice you.

'Bring Patrick's dinner below.' Mother's voice wafts from inside her room and I don't bother to answer her. Every word that I have to say to her hurts. She pauses, no doubt to swig the drain that was left in her glass. 'And come straight back.' She warns. I'm not sure what my mother ever did in the house, but whatever it was, she has given up doing it. Which leaves all the, so-called, women's work to me. It's been that way for two years now, since I turned twelve. She has taken the front drawing room as her own, telling my father that her legs can't manage the stairs. It just so happens that the room she has moved into is closer to the drinks cabinet and further from my father's bed but that doesn't seem to matter to him. It's hard to listen to her, not because she slurs and then overcompensates with a pretentious telephone voice, but because, no matter what she does, she just angers me.

I wrap a plate with cold ham, lettuce, tomato and yesterday's bread. I open the back door again and cut across the yard with the tinfoiled plate. The path that joins our house to Patrick's cottage snakes between the sheds and the end of our overgrown herb garden. Tim was ordered to plant hedge clippings along the route last week but they haven't grown yet.

'Is that you?' my uncle says without turning from the sink. He's stood slushing water underneath his armpits with a dirty brown dishcloth, dirty cups and bowls on the sideboard.

'It's me,' I say quickly, embarrassed to see him without his shirt.

'Good girl, what did your mother cook tonight?' He knows well that my mother hasn't cooked in years. I pull back the tinfoil and place his plate on his table. It's easier to show him than to use my words.

'Grand, now like a good girl will you make the tea to go with it, while I get out of these clothes.' He starts to unbuckle his belt in the kitchen and I cringe. It only takes his long legs, three strides to reach his bedroom door. I lift the heavy kettle that has begun to whistle and pour the water into the teapot on the stove. The tea leaves swirl like a kaleidoscope and I have to force myself to close the lid.

'Tea's stewing,' I call in to him as loudly as I can manage, which isn't loud at all. My face is definitely louder than my words.

'Wait a minute.' The jumper he was pulling over his head muffles the sound as he talks to me from his bedroom next door.

'Mother says I've to come straight back or my dinner will get cold.' The hairs on my arm stand taller as though they feel a chill. The chill hasn't reached the rest of me yet. I try to cover them but the sleeves on my school blouse are an inch too short.

'It's already cold,' he says. 'Salad.' He smirks as he waves towards the plate as if he has figured out a maths problem that no one else could. I steal a look at him from under my fringe. 'Anyway, you may wait for the plate.' He settles at the table and so does the smell. I think of a smart remark, just like I did when Sister Alphonsus caned me, but I don't say it. Sometimes it's just not worth it.

'Sit down.' He points to the bench beside him. I do as I am told. My nostrils flare as the smell of him seeps inside of me, engulfing me in the rancid odour of the farm. 'The salad is lovely, tell your mother.' He slurps as he speaks, and spits of saliva land on the table in front of him. I'm not sure whether he is being sarcastic or not, but I am sure that the salad is not lovely. Discreetly, I cover my nose and my mouth and concentrate on the smell of the carbolic soap from my hands instead.

He pauses slurping and peers at me from the side. 'You're growing to be a lovely girl just like your mother.' He picks up the chunk of ham in his filthy hands and tears a massive bite with his yellowed, unruly teeth, caveman-like. I wish he would use his fork. I take deep breaths, my stomach is about to chuck out the paltry soup I had at lunchtime in school. I hate having to wait for the plate. 'She doesn't come and see me anymore,' he sneers. 'Your mother,' he clarifies, and even though it's not a question, I know by the squinting of his eyes and the derision in his statement that he is waiting for a reply.

'She's not able,' I say. My voice is weak, something I despise my mother for.

'So I hear.' Patrick takes a crust of bread and wipes his plate clean. He folds the slice in four and places all of it in his mouth at once and I feel sorry for the bread. 'Sure, you're the woman of the house now.' He hands me the empty plate, presumably to wash it. I slide from the bench as quietly as I can, as though by being quiet he might not notice me. He follows me to the sink and stretches over me with his mug. The smell of him does nothing to ease the nausea I'm feeling and my stomach turns over almost three times. His arm brushes across my chest and I freeze.

'What are these?' He turns me slightly with his large filthy hand on my shoulder and he flicks at the front of my blouse as though there is a stubborn insect resting on my front. I notice the black lines of dirt framing his fingernails as he points to my chest. My blouse is tight now around my chest and for the first time this year I regret not asking for a new one. I can't breathe. My face must have told him so because my words couldn't.

'Ah don't be shy, Rose. Come over here and sit beside me.' He speaks every word slowly as though he is speaking to Mr Patel in the corner shop in town. I hear the floor groan as he retreats back across the tired floorboards. It doesn't sound half as loud as the silent groan echoing inside of me. Instinctively, I shuffle my legs so I can turn the rest of the way. I don't like the idea of him being behind me. My wellies squeal like captured piglets as they rub against each other and I keep my hand on the sink for balance. It's time to leave, I decide and I manage to take the plate without looking him in the eye and stoically make for the back kitchen door. There is no way I am going to sit beside him like he wants me to.

'Rose.'

I freeze with one foot on the threshold as he calls my name. I draw a breath deeply into my lungs and glare at him, ready to run.

'I don't think your father would like to know that his little girl, Rosie, is growing up, do you?' He says. 'He'll take the belt to you.'

I watch him from behind my fringe and can see his beady eyes narrow menacingly. I can hear my heart beating inside my head. My lungs feel as though Sister Alphonsus has made us do twenty jumping jacks so that she doesn't have to put the heating on. I am drenched in worry as a swell of panic washes over me. I don't know which to dread more: my father's belt or my uncle's hands. I decide to take my chances with the belt and push my voice out in front of me.

'He'll take the belt to you more like.' It turns out my voice is as brave as my face after all. I stand, poised to leave and hold the wet plate to my bosom as my shield. He remains at the table and suddenly the silence of the room is filled, decibel by climbing decibel, as his whimpering snigger transforms into a thundering laugh.

'Well then, our meek and mild virgin, Rosie's, got her brother's balls.' Patrick stands and the old oak table screeches as it scrapes across the sticky timber floor.

I edge closer to the door and have decided that I will throw the plate, if I have to.

His sinister grin stretches from one side of his face to the other and the malice inside of him drops like grains of gravel in the quarry. 'Feisty,' he says as he bites the side of his bottom lip and puts his hands in his trouser pockets.

'What's it to you?' My voice cracks a little but my face doesn't; it means business, even if I am terrified.

'We'll see how long you can be brave for, Rosie.' I hate it when he calls me that. Tim is the only one allowed to call me Rosie. He pauses a moment and then retakes his seat but keeps his hands in his pockets. His feet stretch under the table and out the other side. I notice the kettle simmering on the stove and consider pouring it over him but I don't. For some reason, I say in my head that a watched kettle never boils. 'Your mother never fought back,' he spits. His words drip with arrogance and gratification. I suspect his ego couldn't help but tell me.

The handful of courage I had moments ago escapes through my small pale fingers and I clinch the damp plate closer to my body. It's a minute before I realise the indentation it makes on my chest. My uncle is a long man with long lean muscles that stretch from his thick country neck to his bulky calves. The vessels in his neck pulsate like worms crawling underneath his skin. The shaking in my knees has migrated to my hands and my voice follows suit. My mind hurries to my departure and I'm afraid to use any more words.

'That shut you up, you little prick-tease.'

I can feel him staring at me but don't come out from behind my fringe. I steal a look in his direction when I know he has blinked. Beads of sweat leak from his hairline across his forehead and bring with it the day's muck from his face in grey streaks. I wish he would take his hands from his pockets and wipe it away, but his eyes close momentarily and languish there before they flicker. Then his breathing quickens and deepens. I can see more beads of sweat escape from his upper lip and he lets out a quiet groan, slow and low like a bull. I run.

The plate is still wet and I rub it on my chest as I hurry across the mucky yard and up the path to the house. We have loads of these plates, big and small, cups, saucers, teapots and bowls; all neatly stacked in the dining room dresser. There was a girl from the village who used to do the housework for my mother, but even she doesn't come here anymore. The plate looks fancy with rust-coloured swags and gold trimming along the edges. Fine cracks spread at funny angles from the centre. '*Wait for the plate,*' I repeat in a deep mimicky voice. I want to march back to my uncle and throw the plate at him. Or better still, smash it over his head. I wish I had done it. I wish I was braver.

The March sky looks electrically orange and leaves just enough light for me to make out a shadow across the field. I concentrate hard to see if it's the cattle, my father or Tim. My boots are heavy with wet sticky mud lodged in the grooves of the soles, refusing to scrape away. I hesitate on the spot as the shadow moves closer. It might be Tim but it might be my father, so I make for the house as quickly as the heavy boots allow.

The yard is abandoned and the farmhouse looks dark. No doubt my mother is still in her bed. I push the heavy back door and place the plate on the table. I wished I had smashed it, into shards and smithereens. I shake my boots loose and pick my way in my stocking feet past the dresser and out into the hall in the darkness. I stall outside her door and listen. She has disappeared into a cloud of gin mist and I expect we won't hear from her till tomorrow. 'Thank God,' I whisper and I climb the old staircase to my room.

Nothing is the same when Tim is lambing, the farmhouse is even emptier, if that's possible. The darkness is greyer and despite the spring warmth, the bitter chill becomes a blizzard. Night-time creeps sluggishly through the shutters and tomorrow feels as though it will never come. I turn the heater on and sit huddling my legs on the carpet in front of it. The isolated burn on my face does nothing to spread the warmth to my body, so I shift to my side as though grilling a piece of toast, one side at a time.

I hear footsteps on the stairs and quickly turn off the gas and jump under my covers, even though I'm still dressed. I close my eyes tightly and open my ears. I listen for the creak of the second last step. Tim knows to skip it.

'Rosie.' I hear my name outside the door and I lift my head half an inch from my pillow to listen. Pillows are noisiest in the silence and the sound of cotton shifting underneath my ear drowns out the sound of the voice. I'm not sure who it is. I remain stuck in this position. My back is to the door when a sliver of light shoots along the carpet and snipes lengthways on the wallpaper. I hear the squash of the carpet pile underneath a boot, and then another and then another. A dark elongated shadow sweeps across my bed and spans itself diagonally across the curtains. I can tell from the shadow that I'm about to feel a hand on my back.

'Rosie, you awake,' Tim says softly.

I begin to breathe. The barrel of my body underneath the covers shrinks as the air leaves my lungs, relieved.

'Tim, I wasn't sure if it was you or not, I was pretending to be asleep.' I flick the blankets down and sit beside him on the edge of the bed.

'You okay?' Tim says and I nod yes.

'I didn't think you'd be able to get back tonight.'

'Father has gone down to the pub, says he'll be back in an hour.' We both smirk, knowing full well that the whiskey will tell him to do otherwise. 'Patrick, I'd say will go too, I don't see any lights below in the cottage,' Tim says. 'Mind you, that fecker is so mean he is probably sitting in darkness.'

'Good,' I say.

'Where's she?' Tim asks, nodding out to the landing and down the stairs.

‘I haven’t seen her. She called out of the room when I came home earlier, but there’s no sound now.’

‘Good,’ Tim says.

‘Tim,’ I think about telling him about Patrick but hesitate. I don’t want to waste any time. If the past few weeks are anything to go by, Tim’s time is so precious. ‘Em, what about the lambs?’ I manage instead.

‘They’ll be grand. Nature can sort itself out.’ He walks to the heater and realises it’s not turned on. ‘Let’s go back down to the stove, I’m starving and freezing.’

We abandon the room and quietly creep back downstairs so as not to wake my mother. The last thing either of us wants is to have to listen to her.

It’s unusual to see Tim looking so untidy and unclean. He is normally so well put together. His clothes smell and are covered in an array of coloured stains. He catches my nose wrinkling in disgust.

‘Sheep’s blood,’ he teases, knowing that my constitution is far weaker than his.

‘Is it nearly over?’ I ask hopefully.

‘It is, Rosie; why else did the auld fella think it was okay to leave. He wouldn’t have risked losing any money on the last few lambs or, God forbid, one of the ewes,’ Tim says and ruffles my hair. He stops short of telling me that they will let the ram back in soon. I lean away from him and smile; it was so good to have my big brother back. ‘Have you eaten?’ Tim says while he tries to dislodge an acre’s worth of soil from underneath his fingernails.

‘No.’

‘Rosie. You have to look after yourself, I told you that. No one else will around here.’

Our tones are hushed.

'I know, I just wanted to go to bed, that's all. It's lonely here without you.'

'Has, she, eaten anything?' He nods toward the front of the house where my mother is.

'Not that I know of, she shouted out to me to bring Patrick's dinner below,' I say, unable to look him in the eye.

'I told you before, not to go near that old bastard, Rosie, he's not a good man.' Tim turns so quickly from the tap that dollops of water splash across the floor. 'Seriously, Rosie, don't go near him.'

'I have to bring his dinner down; otherwise you know there'll be trouble,' I answer.

'The bollox can starve, Rosie. Don't. Go. Near. Him.' His lips are closed and angry. 'If you have to go down there again, come and find me first. It doesn't matter where I am.' He held my chin up in his hands. 'I fucking mean it. Do you hear me?' I nod yes and playfully punch his arm away. 'That's my girl.' He keeps looking at me as though he can make me hear it louder if he stares. He returns to the sink and I pour us some tea. 'The sooner the better I get these exams over with and we can get the hell out of here for Dublin.' He has said this before and I know he has a plan, I just don't fully understand how it is going to work because I have two more years left. If I leave school, I'm afraid that Sister Alphonsus will come looking for me. But I suppose I don't need to understand if Tim does.

Chapter 4

Monday Afternoon – 2016

Michael replaced his phone in the breast pocket of his overalls. His warm breath formed a bubble of fog in the early morning March sky. 'Marie says that Timothy Fitzpatrick is up in the house and has Jack not found me yet?'

'Oh.' George nodded, almost disappointed. 'I thought it was news.' George McGrath was seventeen when Michael had been born and he had taken the job of being Michael's big brother very seriously all his life.

Michael leaned on the metal gate and watched the forensic team trample back and forth across the bog. The white and blue tape left nobody in any doubt that they were to venture no further and the blue screen prevented them from catching a glimpse of the action, as tedious as the forensic investigation was. Uniformed Gardaí stood motionless, afraid to smile at their posts.

'Those white suits would be a grand job for painting wouldn't they?' George said.

'Jesus, George, seriously,' Michael whispered as he watched the forensic team return across the gorse ditch, dressed in white, hooded suits, zipped to their chins.

'They would though,' George said; his signature smirk growing gently on his face. His bachelor lifestyle had been greatly enhanced when Michael took over the farm next door to his. 'It'll hold you up, though. They won't let you dig here now until they've done a thorough search.'

'Don't I know, this bloody delay now is going to cost me a fortune?' Michael sighed. He looked around at the hired machinery lying idle. Fitzpatrick Estate, as a working dairy farm, yielded a modest income for the McGraths and for years it had been his dream to develop the house and the farm, but it was Marie's plans to develop the farm for agri-tourism that was going to help sustain the family in the long run, especially with the help of government grants.

'Do, you know who it is?' George spoke under his breath. 'The body, like.'

'Jesus, of course I don't know.' Michael couldn't help but be amused. In the forty-six years that Michael had known his older brother, he had never known him to waste any words.

'I just thought maybe it was one of them bankers that fleeced you on the loan.' George laughed, he had a way of grounding every stressful situation with a hearty laugh that made Michael worry a little less. 'But, you know, if you did…' He glanced at the men and women in uniform, making sure they couldn't hear his hushed words. He lifted his cap and scratched the crown of his head. 'You know yourself.' He lifted his eyebrows suggestively.

'George, seriously.' Michael slapped his brother's back and shook his head. His brother's loyalty was indisputable. He knew that if he had needed it, George would have been the first to give him an alibi.

'Sure, I'd do jail for you,' George said. 'There's no point in you going in to Mountjoy and me at home here looking after Marie and the kids and both farms.' He scratched the side of his ear and scrunched up his face. 'Be fecking easier in jail.'

'I'll tell Marie you said that.' Michael laughed. 'She is dead right about you, you know.'

'What's that, then?'

'That you're too fecking mean to get a wife.'

'Ah, sure she's a genius all together.' George was terribly fond of his sister-in-law and although he wouldn't admit it, he loved the way she designed the inside of his house for him and the new clothes that she had bought for him suited really well. 'It won't be long before the rubberneckers are up from town, they'll have the tape stretched out on the road like they do in that C.S.I,' George said. 'That'd be grand, wouldn't it, C.S.I Kilkenny.'

'I'm more bloody concerned about how long this is going to hold us up.' Michael sighed. 'Let's leave them to it; are you coming up to the house then?' Michael's boots squelched as he turned from the post they had taken.

'I won't. The less I have to do with that Kelly character the better,' George said, turning towards the jeep he had parked a short distance away from the marshy field.

'I'll walk then.' Michael closed the driver door behind George. His dog, Charlie, sat obediently at his side. 'Try and clean off the boots on the way and walk Charlie back up,' he said. The wet fields at the bottom south corner of the farm had left mounds of muck on the soles of their boots. 'Marie will eat me if I walk more muck inside.'

'Right then,' George started the engine and drove slowly towards his farm.

Michael made his way back up to the house. By the time he reached the back door, Jack had found him and most of the muck had disappeared. He knew by the car parked in the courtyard that Timothy Fitzpatrick was still inside.

'Hello gents, you're very welcome.' Michael stood six foot tall in his stocking feet. It was more than his life's worth to come in with his boots on, regardless of who was visiting. He extended his hand to Robert first. 'I'm Michael,' Charlie went straight to his bed underneath the table.

'Nice to meet you, I'm Robert.' Robert gestured to Tim who stood equally as tall to greet the man of the house. 'This is Timothy Fitzpatrick.'

'Lovely to meet you Mr Fitzpatrick, after all these years.' Michael took Tim's hand firmly in his.

'It's Tim, call me Tim,' he said, struck by the man who stood in front of him. 'Lovely to meet you too.' They were still shaking hands when Marie returned.

'Oh good, you've all met.' Of all the weeks for something like this to happen, this was the worst, with the children at home for the Easter break. She was looking forward to packing them off to pony camp in the morning, the less they were around the events on the farm that week, the better. 'Like a good boy, would you go up to your room and tidy up and keep your sister occupied until I call you.' Her instructions didn't need to be repeated as Jack bounded dutifully up the stairs. She closed the kitchen door behind him. 'Detective Kelly is already on his way up, the station told me.' She looked at her husband and the two men in her kitchen. 'The pathologist seems to think he has everything he needs. They'll be finished down there shortly.'

'Have they any idea who it is?' Tim was careful with his words. 'Has anyone been missing from the area or anything?' Marie gathered fresh mugs from the cupboard and poured steaming black coffee from the percolator. She had finished her call to the station some moments before and had stayed in the hall considering the information and how she might deliver it.

'Well, there is no actual information yet but there is a lot of talk about.' She was stuck for words to finish the sentence. She didn't want to be part of the local gossip-mongering. She reconsidered her response. 'What they did say to me is that the body appeared to have been…' She shook her head again as though disassociating herself from the information. 'Like it was preserved or something, something to do with the acidic levels in the soil profile or maybe it was the lack of acidic levels, I'm not sure what they meant.'

Michael glanced at his wife. It wasn't like her to be unsure of anything, let alone, lost for words.

'The body could be years old, is what they are saying. The land is more like a bog down in that corner.' She looked to Michael for reassurance. 'They're saying that the fact that it is so wet is what could have preserved the remains for so long.' She looked at Tim to gauge his reaction. The first thought that she had when she heard the gossip from her friend in the station was to thank God that the body wasn't from their ten years there, the second thought was to wonder about the Fitzpatricks and the involvement they might have had.

'The drainage is, terrible,' Michael offered. 'That's why we were digging it up in the first place. I had a group of lads down there working for me.' He poured himself a mug of coffee from the pot. 'There's talk from the fella that dug him up.' He spooned sugar into his mug and stirred. 'I'd say he got the fright of his life when he pulled that up in the digger,' Michael said. 'It was definitely a man; he said the skin looked tanned, preserved almost, even his clothes were more or less intact.'

'The officer, the one I was just talking to, said they will be finished with the scene at the end of today and that everything else can be investigated in the labs.' Marie shrugged, interrupting her husband's unscientific ramblings. 'Even uttering the words "scene" and "labs" feels peculiar.' She looked at both Tim and Robert's feet. 'I don't suppose you brought any boots with you.' They both shook their heads. 'I'll root you both out a pair; you'll need them if you are going down to the field.' Marie hurried towards the mud room. 'I won't need any Marie, thanks, I'll leave that bit to Tim, if that's okay?' Robert said.

'Sure.' Marie answered and left to get one pair of boots for Tim.

'I'll go outside and wait for the detective.' Tim followed the hallway to the old front door. The hallway seemed much smaller than it used to. The same chessboard black and white tiles adorned the space but even they seemed smaller. The door to the drawing room was closed, he noticed as he opened the front door. He watched as Detective Kelly parked his car.

'Detective Kelly, I presume,' Tim greeted the plain-clothes man from the steps of Fitzpatrick House.

'That's me.' An athletic arm extended to meet Tim's. 'And you are?'

'Timothy Fitzpatrick.' Tim didn't like him already. He was brash and righteous, Tim could tell.

'Well,' His squinty eyes focused on Tim's face. 'Good of you to come down.' Kelly held Tim's gaze for the same awkward time he held his handshake.

Tim nodded silently.

'We,' Detective Kelly inhaled deeply, then exhaled slowly, 'might take a walk.' He let go of Tim's hand and looked in the direction of the field.

'Sure.' Tim looked back down the hall to see if Marie was coming. 'Marie tells me I'll need boots, though.'

'She's right.'

Tim wasn't sure whether the pause in each of the detective's utterances was a speech impediment or a deliberate attempt at unnerving him.

'Here we go, these should fit.' Marie handed Tim some boots. I'll mind your shoes here for you. She scooped up his loafers as he stood out of them on the step. 'I'll leave you to it so.' She stood back inside her hall and watched as both men walked across the court yard towards the field.

'So,' Kelly's boots dragged across the yard, scuffing every stone. 'You're,' he exhaled slowly again, 'the famous Timothy Fitzpatrick.'

Tim cringed. 'What do you mean?' He was careful with his tone. He didn't want to antagonise him.

'Well, I'm told, the Fitzpatrick name is pretty famous in these parts.' His arm extended, gesturing the farmhouse and fields. 'Generations of Fitzpatricks living on this land,' Kelly said. 'That was until you left. Local Legends.' Tim was sure the last part was meant sarcastically.

'I don't know about that.' Tim had never used the Fitzpatrick name to his benefit, quite the opposite. 'As far as I know, I'm the only named Fitzpatrick left and I haven't lived here in nearly fifty years, so I'm not sure quite what you mean.'

'Forty-six.' Detective Kelly was precise. He hadn't needed to pause. 'It's not fifty years, it's forty-six.'

'I didn't even know the exact length of time,' Tim mentally calculated the years since he had left. 'Forty-six years.' He repeated.

'But you, were still the landlord,' Detective Kelly answered. 'They still have the grand big sign up on the gates with the Fitzpatrick name on it.' Tim had never seen that sign there in his day; it was obviously a choice by the new owners to keep its original name.

'Fitzpatrick Farm was what I knew it as, the Estate bit is a new addition,' Tim clarified. 'And yes, I was the landlord up until the beginning of the year.' Tim was beginning to understand the rhythm of Kelly's speech. He decided it was a tactic. 'But I sold it to Marie and Michael McGrath.' He was deliberate in saying Marie's name first. 'They've leased the farm for the past ten years.' He knew that none of this information was new to the detective but volunteered it anyway.

Detective Kelly climbed over the concrete stile expecting Tim to follow.

'I see.' Kelly turned to wait for Tim to climb down. 'You were,' Kelly's pauses made Tim impatient, 'seventeen when you left.' Tim nodded in response. 'Went to Dublin for college.' Tim nodded again. It was like a thwarted version of *This Is Your Life* with no big red book and no Michael Aspel. 'And never came back,' the detective finished.

'Well, I did come back; just not to work the land. Farming wasn't for me,' Tim said hesitantly. He didn't want to have to explain his lifestyle choices to what seemed like a cross between Mr Bean and Colombo, the handsome version, Tim noted reluctantly.

'No children, of your own?' Kelly said. The boundary tape fluttered gently just in front of them.

'No, what has...' Tim paused before he finished his sentence. 'Why do you ask?' His tone was forcefully polite.

'Just wondered.' Kelly zipped up his coat. 'You kept the farm for so long, maybe you were keeping it in the family for a reason? Maybe something you wanted to keep private?'

'No reason,' Tim exhaled, he was growing increasingly uncomfortable at Detective Kelly's line of questioning. 'Anything else I can help you with, I need to get back to Dublin.'

'Ah, yes, to your sister Rose.'

Tim's eye's narrowed as he considered his response. There wasn't much these days that would have Tim wanting to punch a man but today he felt like throwing a right hook at Detective Kelly's jaw, but he didn't. His shoulders broadened as he stretched up to his full size. 'Can I ask, why do you mention Rose?' His brows furrowed as he tried to relax his breathing and uncurl his fists.

'You told me yourself that you had no children, so I presumed the reason you were in a rush to get back was for Rose.' Kelly remained unfazed. His style of interrogation was to burrow deeply under the skin. 'I'm just trying, to get a picture of what went on, you know, in these parts, all those years ago.' Kelly stretched his neck to the side and pushed his shoulders down. His vertebrae cracked. 'Help me understand why there is a man lying in your ditch, and nobody, for forty-six years, knew anything about him.'

'Well, first of all, it's not my ditch, hasn't been since January, and second of all, I don't know anything about a man lying in the ditch. I'm sorry I couldn't be of more help to you.' Tim extended his hand to bring the encounter to an end. Kelly took it but didn't shake.

'One other thing, before you leave, is your uncle still alive?' He continued to clasp Tim's hand as he waited for the answer.

'I don't know,' Tim said succinctly. He had been waiting for that very question.

'Would your sister know?' Kelly asked.

Tim pulled his hand away and clenched his fists at his side. His heartbeat quickened once more. 'I doubt she would,' Tim said slowly. Kelly already knew his weak spot and both of them knew it.

'And why is it that you don't know where your own flesh and blood is?'

'I was a child when I last saw him; I don't know anything about him and my parents never spoke of him since he left.'

'Oh, he left, did he?' Kelly kept agitating. He thought if he rubbed hard enough, the stain would come out.

'I don't really know when he left, nobody ever heard from him again.' Tim fought hard to tame his temper but a smidgen seeped out. 'Good riddance to him,' he said.

'Well now, aren't they very strong feelings for a child to have about your own flesh and blood?' Kelly paused; he was a master at reading a reaction. The gaps that his stuttering left, gave him more answers than his words. 'How old did you say you were when he left?'

'Seventeen.' Tim forced his gritted teeth open to answer, already regretting having said a word.

'A child you say, some would say a man?' Kelly raised his eyebrows to match the raised pitch in his question. 'Or have I been fooling myself all these years?'

'I was seventeen. He left. That's all I know.' Tim hadn't the patience to continue.

'And the Estate was left just to you,' Kelly pulled his notebook from his back pocket and unsnapped the worn elastic band. 'Tell us this much,' he looked up at Tim, 'nothing for your sister?'

'The Farm was left equally to both of us.' Tim spoke clearly and concisely. 'What has that got to do with this?' he asked impatiently.

'Just establishing who had the title to the land,' Detective Kelly paused. 'Seeing as it was you who did all the business, you know, with the lease and the agency.' He paused again. Tim wondered how he had his information and why the sale of Fitzpatrick Estate was of such importance to him. 'And then with the sale of course.' Tim didn't answer him. 'Did you ever consider that your uncle might have had a claim in it, or still may?' Kelly looked to the forensic dig site and then back at Tim. 'If he's still alive that is.' Kelly paused to read Tim's reaction. 'Maybe it wasn't yours to sell in the first place.'

'I can assure you, that all is in order, in relation to the title of the land.' Tim was reluctant to elaborate but felt obliged to. 'According to my father's solicitor at the time, they had my uncle declared dead after he was missing for seven years. As far as I know, my father's solicitor would have dealt with all that. It was my father's to leave to me and...' He hesitated before he mentioned Rose's name. 'And my sister.'

'Oh, so he is dead then?'

'Like I said, I wouldn't know.' Tim cleared his throat. 'And neither would Rose, she was only fourteen when he went missing.'

'I see,' Kelly said.

'Well, Detective, as I said, I must get back on the road to Dublin. You have my number?' Tim said, knowing full well that whatever there was to know about him, Detective Kelly seemed to know it already.

'I do, I have your number,' Kelly said.

Chapter 5

Monday Evening – 2016

It was six in the evening before Robert turned his car onto Pleasant Street. Like the tide washing in, darkness had crept unnoticed over the city and street lamps glowed amber, crafting a haze in the evening drizzle. As soon as they had turned off the motorway, bumper-to-bumper traffic had created chains of red dots as far as the eye could see. They were both relieved to be back.

'Home, sweet home,' Robert said, for want of a better thing to say. While neither of them were fans of small talk and platitudes, he felt the silence needed filling.

Tim plodded down the granite steps of the Victorian townhouse to the garden-level entrance; that was where Brandy was.

'I had better let Brandy out. I can hear her whimpering.' Tim doted on the dog; both of them did. 'I'd say she thought we were never coming back.'

Brandy was scratching on the tiled floor, eagerly wagging her tail and dancing on all four legs when Tim walked in.

'There you go, darling.' Tim opened up the French doors to the paved courtyard outside and the dog raced out, bounding with excitement.

Robert poured them both a drink and they followed her.

'Clever girl.' Brandy rolled in happiness as Tim dragged his chair underneath the canopy to avoid the drizzle. 'Calm down, you crazy dog.' He laughed softly as the rusty-red dog barked with happiness. 'What a day?' Tim finally confessed.

'Indeed,' Robert answered. 'I'm going to order in for us.' Robert glanced at Tim.

Robert's engineering coupled with Tim's architectural expertise had dragged the old Victorian villa kicking and screaming into the twenty-first century and their sleek, stainless-steel and gloss finished kitchen didn't really see much activity, other than the opening and closing of the wine fridge and the hiss and gurgle of the coffee maker.

'Yeah,' Tim said. He shook his glass realising it was already empty. 'I could eat.' He walked into the kitchen, wiping his feet on the mat, and poured another glass of red wine, Robert followed. The whitewashed walls from the courtyard blended seamlessly with the clean lines inside. The open plan of the garden-level area made their home very functional.

Tim took his refilled glass to his armchair. The furniture in the living area was pristine and dark oak bookshelves punctuated the open plan ground floor. The oversized rug softened the porcelain tiles and gave Brandy a place to doze in the afternoon, just as the sun peeped in through the front room window.

Robert finished placing their order and put his phone on the cream Silestone countertop. He turned off the lights in the courtyard and gently nudged the sleeping dog with his foot. 'Come on Brandy, let's get back in.' The temperature outside had lost all of the day's warmth and the dampness made the chill even more noticeable. 'You better not be wet.' Robert scolded the dog as she reluctantly returned, barely lifting her head to acknowledge him. There was nothing like the smell of wet dog to put them off the Chinese food he had just ordered.

Robert headed to the sofa, taking the bottle of red wine with him. 'Are you going to tell Rose tomorrow?'

'What am I going to say to her?' Tim said. His sigh was heavy. Rose and Tim had no secrets, but as her big brother, he still felt the need to protect her.

'Don't be overcomplicating it; it is what it is. They found a body on the farm that you both used to own, simple as that.' Robert knew Tim had a tendency to overthink things, especially where Rose was concerned.

'I swear, the whole idea of selling it was so we would be done with it once and for all.' Tim swigged from the crystal glass. 'You were there; we drank to finally being free of it. And now this, I just can't believe it, it doesn't seem fair.'

'I'm sure the body that has been lying in the ditch for the past forty-six years will echo your feelings of fairness,' Robert said. Tim didn't respond.

'It's just that, ah, it's hard to explain.' Tim sat back in his chair and sighed even deeper.

'I know,' Robert said. He had heard this sentence before. 'But, if I may say so, I love Rose, just as much as you.' His hands were animated and he could tell that Tim was about to throw in a 'but'. 'I know, I know, I didn't grow up with you guys, and I know that it is not your story to tell.' Robert was using all the answers he had heard Tim utter before. 'But sometimes, I think you might underestimate her.' Robert sat forward; he was passionate about what he was saying. Rose was as much in his life as she was in Tim's. 'She is a strong sixty-year-old woman, Tim; I think she is more than capable of handling it.' Robert's eyebrows rose involuntarily. 'You don't have to keep protecting her.' In the early days, that comment would have sounded jealous, as though Robert envied the special bond that his lover had with his sister, but now, all these years later, it was as genuine and heartfelt as could be and Tim knew it. Robert understood that neither Rose nor Tim had any good memories of Fitzpatrick Estate, the detail as to why, he was still unsure of. He knew that Tim would tell him in his own good time, but he had his suspicions.

'Nothing but misery ever came from that godforsaken place.' Tim exhaled slowly and spoke with his head in his hands. The resentment he felt for Fitzpatrick Farm sparked across his skin making it prickle.

'You've said.' Robert rubbed his chin, the scratch of his day-old stubble felt comforting on his hands. It was a sensitive subject and Robert knew to tread carefully. 'Or you could look at it like this: it made you both, who you are today.' He topped up Tim's glass from the bottle. 'A pedestal to stand on, rather than a noose around your necks,' he suggested. 'And I for one am glad you are who you are.' Robert lifted his glass and chinked it with Tim's.

Tim knew he was lucky to have him.

'I know, I just can't help thinking of it.' Tim stretched his neck and shoulders and exhaled deeply. 'She said a long time ago that she never wanted anything to do with the place again and I don't blame her.'

'I know, but you may tell her what's going on, there's a chance that it'll make the national news. She's bound to recognise it.'

'I will, I just didn't want to have to stir up old memories for her. I'll tell her tomorrow.' Tim had understood her reluctance to have anything to do with Fitzpatrick Estate. They had both made a promise, and they had kept it. 'I still don't understand why that Kelly fella asked me to come down. He didn't ask me anything he didn't already know.'

'I'd say he just wanted to cross the T's, as they say,' Robert said. 'With the property having changed hands so recently, I suppose he needed to include you in the file as well.'

'Maybe. I could have punched the smug little bastard though when he mentioned Rose.' The long day and the wine were gradually taking their toll on his fighting spirit, loosening his tongue and allowing his imagination to run back to those dark places. Places nobody wanted to visit. 'The nerve of him, even to mention her name,' Tim said. 'She was only fourteen, Robert. How the hell could she have had anything to do with a body ending up in the ditch, seriously.' Tim's breathing became faster. 'She doesn't need this hassle, none of us bloody well do.' His grasp tightened around his wine glass. 'Seriously, all we thought of was getting out of the place, how could we have known anything that was going on?' Tim said. Robert knew it was rhetorical. 'What sort of a halfwit was I, though seriously?' Tim shook his head in disbelief.

'You were the same halfwit that every other seventeen-year-old boy was. It was the seventies, Tim, for Christ's sake.' Robert shook his head. 'I don't remember what was going on when I was seventeen and this detective Kelly is not going to be able to use anything you can or can't remember, when you were only a boy, against you,' Robert said. 'You can't be held responsible for your father's failings, Tim, or your mother's for that matter.' Robert knew enough to know that the dark memories of an angry whiskey-fuelled father and a reclusive alcoholic mother was the foundation upon which their disdain for Fitzpatrick Estate had grown, but Tim had spared him the detail of the depravity thereafter. 'You did what you could, you got out and you brought Rose with you,' Robert added. 'End of.' Robert was considerate and patient, he thought he knew the depth of Tim's pain.

'That's just it though.' Tim's voice was quiet. 'It's not end of, it's just the beginning of, and that little bastard Kelly, thinking he knew everything about me, about us. The fucking cheek of him.'

'You should talk to Rose, maybe try and get some closure for you both. Ask her how she deals with it, you know the memories and everything. It might help you.' Robert remained facing forward. He had suggested this to Tim on several occasions over the years. It seemed, as close as both Tim and Rose were, they had never spoken of what happened since they had left.

'The only thing I want to know is whether or not it is Patrick, and if it's not, where the bastard is or where he went that night,' Tim said. 'That's the only closure I need.' Tim was stone-faced in temper, as he was every time he allowed himself to think of him.

'Have there ever been any sightings of him?' Robert was curious, in all the snippets of Fitzpatrick history he had heard over the years, the disappearance of Rose and Tim's uncle had barely been mentioned.

'Not that I know of.' Tim shook his head. 'The most the investigation showed up at the time was the complete lack of interest anybody had in his disappearance.' His tone was flippant.

'I see,' Robert said. 'That's unusual.'

'According to the locals, and my father actually,' Tim added, his memory of any conversation he had at the time of his uncle's disappearance was as clear as day, 'he had been bragging all night in the pub about what he would do to his girlfriend when he got home.' The disgust was palpable in Tim's voice. 'And he was talking about getting the boat to

Liverpool because the women in England were much more his type.' Tim shook his head.

Robert's curiosity piqued.

'They looked for him for a couple of weeks after, but no trace of him ever showed up.' Tim coughed, the wine had gone against his breath. He cleared his throat. 'Bloody coward.' The adrenaline raced around Tim's body and made his tongue sharper and his breathing faster.

'Do you think it's him?' Robert questioned.

'No.' Tim shuffled in his seat. 'Oh, I don't know. I just don't know,' he added. 'Maybe I should talk to my solicitor.'

Even though it might have been the sensible thing to do, it sounded odd to Robert that Tim would think a solicitor was necessary. He leaned against the brown leather arm of the sofa and thought for a moment. He closed his eyes trying to squash the suspicions that were sprouting in his mind. He grew concerned that the nightmare of Fitzpatrick Estate was even more of a nightmare than he had imagined and if the years of whispered memories and guarded histories were about to come tumbling down around them, spilling out in the open for everyone to see, he needed to know everything, whether it was Rose's story or not. His love for Tim was unquestionable but he couldn't help if his hands were tied.

'Tim, if there is more, which we both know there is,' his expression was determined, 'you need to tell me, do you hear me?' Robert's seriousness was unusual. 'No matter what.' He fixed his eyes on Tim's. It was a phrase that had become somewhat of a mantra between them, a phrase that had given them both strength to be who they were, to be in love with each other, regardless of what anyone else had thought or how unequal society had seen their love. 'No matter what,' Robert repeated.

'There's no "no matter what's" to worry about, Robert. Trust me,' Tim answered. 'I just need to be sensible here, that's all,' he explained. 'If you had seen this detective guy today, you'd be doing the same thing, for some reason, he has it in his head that there is more than meets the eye to this story, and I can tell you now,' he reached across and took Robert's hand, 'there isn't, okay?'

'Okay,' Robert held his gaze. 'I need to know everything though, there might not be a "no matter what", but there is more to the story and we need to discuss it, okay?' Robert finished.

'Agreed,' Tim answered. 'But I want to talk to Rose first, tell her that I am telling you everything, once and for all. I owe her, you and her, that much,' he explained.

'But speaking of solicitors,' Robert said, 'didn't your solicitor want to speak to Lizzie, in relation to the trust and transferring the monies?' Since they had sold the Estate four months ago, both Rose and Tim had decided, neither of them wanting anything to do with the money from Fitzpatrick Farm, that the proceeds would be placed in a trust for Lizzie, Rose's only daughter and the apple of her uncle Tim's eye.

'I think Rose was waiting for her to come home, tell her about the trust and then have her go into the solicitor to have everything signed off,' Tim added. When he spoke about his sister, he always referred to her formally as Rose, but in his head, she would always be his Rosie.

'Yeah, or you both could take a trip to London, to see her, speak to her in person there, maybe.' Robert's suggestion made sense. 'You could bring the documents with you?' Robert added.

'Yeah, maybe,' Tim said. 'It might be a good idea.' Tim wasn't sure. It would take some convincing to get Rose to agree, and besides, he thought, maybe it would be better to be around, he couldn't rest easy knowing the detective would be looking for him.

'How do you think she'll react.' A smile spread cross Robert's face. As much as he treated Rose as his sister, he most definitely treated Lizzie as his niece. 'When you tell her about the trust?'

'I'd say, she'll faint.' Speaking about their thirty-three-year-old niece brought the first smile to their faces that day. Their smiles were interrupted by the sound of the doorbell.

'Chinese,' Robert declared; their conversation paused until they ate.

Tim took a breath, contemplating his next move, he didn't know what to expect and that worried him even further. Some secrets were never meant to be told.

Chapter 6

Tuesday Evening – March 1970

As soon as I hear the crunch on the gravel outside, I know it is my father. I watch him from the corner of my eye as I stand at the sink, washing and rewashing the crockery so that I don't have to move. I pinch my lips closed as though making sure no words fall out.

'I presume your mother's asleep?' He sits at the table and unlaces his boots. I can tell he's tired by the groan his bones make as he lowers himself down. Our normal exchanges include a cursory acknowledgement of the woman down the hall. He doesn't refer to her as his wife, just mine and Tim's mother. The conversations we have after he drinks, however, are entirely different. Those are the ones I hide from.

'I think so,' I answer and lift the kettle to fill it. A bowl sits on the sideboard, waiting for me to pour his soup. I have already cut his bread and softened his butter. I hate the smell of Oxtail soup. I hate the idea of it too.

'Did you bring some soup to your mother?' he says. I often wonder does he, my father, actually care. It might appear at times that he does, but then, like when he is full of whiskey and rage, I know he doesn't.

'I did.' I don't elaborate by telling him that she upturned it in a gin-fuelled stupor and scalded herself. It was funny, until she flung the bowl at me for laughing. I fill his bowl and place it in front of him beside the bread I had already buttered. I wipe the smile from my face before he sees it. Just in case he wants to bring it up in conversation with me later. It doesn't take him long to finish and as soon as he wipes the bowl clean with his bread, I take it to the sink to wash it. I fill the quietness that falls between us with the sound of the tap running and the squeak of the Delph as I rub it dry. I'm relieved when I hear Tim at the back door because if I rub the bowl any harder I'm afraid that the rusty swagged pattern will come off. I'm also relieved because if both Tim and my father are both back at the house at the same time, it means that all the lambs are born, which means that Tim can come back to the house. My father mumbles something at Tim and then he throws the keys of his Ford Cortina at him.

'Won't be long, Rosie,' Tim says. My father gets up to leave and Tim follows outside. He has been driving tractors for years and now my father is letting him drive the car. Tim says when we move to Dublin we'll get our own car. I'm not sure how we'll pay for it, but I think Tim has a plan. I make sure to leave the kitchen spotless. My father doesn't like to come home to an untidy kitchen. I learned this the hard way and only a fool doesn't learn from their mistakes, so he says every time it happens. Sometimes I don't even have to make mistakes to learn a lesson. Apparently, it's all for my own good. Tim says, that my father doesn't know any better, that he is angry because he can't understand why our mother has ended up so useless and in his own warped way is making sure, with his fists and his belt, that we don't go the same way. I think that of all the things he could create a fuss about, a clean kitchen shouldn't be one of them.

'Rose.' I shut my eyes and sigh as soon as I hear her. Fire races up my spine and explodes out my ears. The sound of her voice is infuriating. I stifle my annoyance and try to tolerate her calling.

'Yes, Mother.' I walk towards her room and stand outside the door on the chessboard tiles. The old front door must be painted shut, I think, as I study the perimeter of the frame. I don't ever remember it being open. The first room as you enter, or the last room as you leave, depending on what way you look at it, is the drawing room. She has been holed up in there for nearly two years now. Emerging only under cover of darkness and gin, like a squirrel just to gather and retreat. Her bed stands freely in the centre of the room flanked by a Queen Anne chair on one side and a lamp table to the other. A rainbow of small coloured tablets sit in brown plastic tubs on the lace doily cloth. Her clothes hang haphazardly on the back of the door and from the picture rail that circles the room. I don't like going in to her as much as she doesn't like me in there. 'Do you want tea?' I ask.

'Is your father gone?' she says, ignoring my question. I presume she is standing at her window looking at the tail light of the car as it leaves and it always irritates me when she asks a question I know she knows the answer to.

'Yes,' I answer.

'Did he eat?' she says.

'Yes.' I study the frown on my face through the hall mirror. I stretch my face and show my teeth. I shrug as I notice how small my clothes have grown on me. I could have asked for money to buy new ones, but it was easier not to.

'Did you bring Patrick his?' she says weakly from behind the door. I imagine her shuffling from the window across the carpet to the door, afraid of what's on the other side.

'No.' I sigh deeply. 'I'll bring it down now.' I imagine a conversation with her where I tell her what Patrick said the last time I was there. I grin at how ridiculous the notion of talking to this woman as a mother is. As if, I say to myself.

'Rose.' She pauses. 'Don't wait around. Come straight back.' I don't answer her but I notice in the mirror my eyes are squinting and small. 'Else, he'll be up here looking for it.'

Silently, I mimic her, wagging my head and mouthing her words. I clench my fists and nod my head in anger at her weak attempts to talk to me. I amble back towards the kitchen, making sure to take one last look at my scorn in the mirror. I practise my scowl. I visualise my mother standing at her bedroom door, waiting to hear me leave and I deliberately take my time. There is small satisfaction in it, but satisfaction none the less. I know she listens till the house is silent before she leaves her room and I enjoy making her wait for me. I wonder should I wait till Tim returns like he warned me to but decide not to. I remember my reflection with my last year's blouse and decide to wear my duffle coat.

*

It's nearly twenty minutes since I arrived at the cottage. I don't have a watch, nor can I see a clock, but I'm good at guessing time. It's a trick I have never told anyone about, but it can be used anywhere, at home, in school, wherever. If there was a competition in time guessing, like when you have to guess the amount of jellies in the jar, I'd win. I have a list, you see. A list of things that I like and it takes sixty seconds for me to name them all. I usually go through my list three times when Sister Alphonsus gets a hold of me. That's not so bad. But now, since Patrick has a hold of me, I've done my list twenty times. He has had me for twenty minutes now.

I'm forever learning lessons. I'm learning that people say things for a reason. And most times they like you to figure the reason out for yourself. So not only do you have to listen to what is being said, but you have to figure out why they are saying it. I can figure it out now, but I think it's too late and now I have to learn my lesson the hard way. Lessons are hard work. It would have been easier if my mother had said why she wanted me to come straight back or why she didn't want Patrick coming to the house, easier if Tim had said why I was never to come down to Patrick's cottage alone, but they didn't and now I'm learning the hard way. I'm learning that my scorn and my wit is no match for his depravity. I'm learning that kicking and scratching doesn't help. I'm learning that if I concentrate on my list, I can dull the hurt.

'Jesus you're a strong young one, Rose. That'll teach you to answer me with cheek,' Patrick utters smugly as he emerges through the bedroom door, zipping up his fly and buckling his belt. He lifts the kettle and prevents it from whistling.

I stand at the bedroom door, afraid to move any further. My thin spindly legs are like jelly underneath my school skirt. My eyes hurt from fixing them closed. I can't stop shaking. My whole body is numb.

'Good girl, Rosie,' Patrick says. He has his back to me, standing at the stove.

I lean against the frame unsure how much longer I can stand. The smell of him lingers inside my nose. I look towards the door but am afraid to move, afraid to pass him by.

'It's okay, Rosie.' His smarmy remarks make me want to cry. 'I'm only teaching you how to grow up.' He notices me shaking and starts to walk towards me with a mug in his hand. I flinch and he sees it. 'You see, you can't be like that when the boys come calling. Shaking with fear won't get a girl married.'

He turns away from me and sits at the table. His legs stretch in front of me. To move past him I'll have to step over them and I don't think my legs could do it. I shuffle to my right, closer to the door. I can feel liquid trickle down my legs and I think I've wet myself. 'I did the same for your brother, showed him how to grow up, what to do to the girls.' He sniggered. 'Mind you, I don't know if it did him any good.'

I'm not close enough but with every word he utters, I'm reminded of the repugnant odour from his breath and the escape I imagined moments earlier with my list alludes me. My stomach gurgles and gags. I can feel a lump at the back of my throat, so big that I'm afraid the air won't get through, but I'm determined not to let him see me weakening. He looks at me, looking at the door and I'm afraid of the look in his eyes. My body is torn and weak and my hair has fallen out of its clip.

'And there's no point in telling anyone, no one will believe you, there's no evidence, nothing to show that you were here,' he threatens. I glance at the dinner plate on the table. 'Besides, if you do, I'll say you were a right little goer.' He sniggers.

Faintly, I edge again one more inch to the door, away from the support of the frame. Blood drains, drip by drip, from my head and the contents of my stomach erupt from my mouth in repetitive reaches, taking every ounce of bile, oxtail soup and crusts of bread I had in me. I'm hoping that the remnants of his assault inside of me come out too.

'Jesus Christ Almighty.' Patrick jumps upright to avoid splashes of yellow on his boots. 'You stupid little bitch,' he says. 'What did you do that for?'

*

'Mother,' Tim calls from outside her door. 'Where's Rose?' Tim doesn't wait for her to answer and rushes up the stairs. 'Rose,' he calls, becoming anxious with the silence. He bounds back downstairs to find the kitchen empty. 'Fucking hell,' he says and bangs loudly on his mother's bedroom door. 'Mother, where's Rose?' She doesn't answer him. Tim turns the handle and bursts the door open. 'Mother.' Tim speaks slowly and loudly. 'Where is Rose?' His mother sits at the side of her bed whimpering. Her once pink dressing gown drapes on her bony shoulders and extends down her legs, opening slightly to expose her shins.

'Dinner.' Her voice is barely audible. 'Patrick's dinner.' Her lips are dry and sore. She clenches her dressing gown closed. She's not able to look her son in the eye.

'You spineless bitch.' Tim's anger propels him towards her and she cowers away. He swipes the empty bottle on the dresser and holds it aloft. 'You know she shouldn't be down there on her own.'

'Tim, no,' she snivels. 'I told her to come straight back, I did.'

'You useless piece of shit.' He steps away reluctantly. 'If he has done anything to her, I'll kill him first and then you.' He leaves, slamming her door on its hinges.

The cattle's drone sounds deep and distant as he hurries past the sheds. Outside the cottage he notices Patrick's boots on the step. He moves impulsively towards the window to the side, still clutching the glass bottle in his hand. Tim crouches lower to look through the half-drawn curtains. The wireless standing on the table in the corner is surrounded by mountains of papers precariously piled. The brown velvet curtains to the front of the room have been carelessly pulled across, scantily covering the bare night outside. A taste of bile rises rapidly from his stomach as he hears the door open. He freezes to the spot.

*

'You little bitch,' Patrick shouts as I make a dash for the door. A pool of sick remains on his kitchen floor and he slips in it trying to stop me. I slam the door behind me. I'm glad. Glad he can't catch me and glad that he is lying in it. I'm nearly away up the path, past the bushes and close to the sheds when I stop running. A rustling back at the cottage makes me turn around. I focus and through the trees I'm sure I see Tim's silhouette. Anxiously, I run back to him.

'Tim, No!' I cry quietly. 'Not like this, Tim.' My eyes dart to the cottage door. 'He'll kill you.' My heart thumps wildly in my chest, making me breathe shallowly, every breath shorter than the last. 'Please, Tim, don't,' I whimper.

'Rosie, what are you doing? Go back to the house now,' he whispers through his closed teeth. His grip stiffens around the neck of the gin bottle and even though my seventeen-year-old brother is not in the habit of being violent, instinctively, I know what he intends to do with it. His face is etched with fury and his muscles supersaturated with adrenaline. I can't tell by the glassiness in his eyes if he is full of sadness or full of rage. I decide its equal measures of both. I panic; I don't want him to get hurt as well, or worse still, to end up dead. I stare at him uneasily.

'Please, Tim, no, come back with me now. I need you.' I place my hand on his jaw, almost frightened by its sharp edge. I pull at his arm to follow me, but he doesn't. His eyes seem black and his body feels like stone, solid like a wall. I bury my face in my hands and for one breathless second, sobs escape from my core. Tim is startled by the sound.

'Shhh.' He glances hastily at the cottage door. 'Come quickly.' He leads me quietly from where we stand. 'Before the old bastard hears us.' We pace the pathway back by the sheds and return across the yard. 'He won't put his hands on you ever again. I can promise you that.'

'I'm okay,' I plead, wrapping my arms around my body, I'm feeling cold. I close my eyes and will away the burning pain inside of me. But it doesn't work. 'Please, Tim, leave it so.' I can't stop the stream of tears washing down my face.

'What did he do to you?' Tim stops me from walking and places his hands on both my shoulders so I stand squarely in front of him. He towers over me. I don't have any words. I don't know what to call it. I know that Patrick grunted and groaned and I know that it hurt. 'Jesus, Rosie.' Streams of tears flow quickly now and he wraps me in his arms before I can see his. I don't need to say any of the words; he can hear the answer in my eyes. 'I'll kill him, with my own bare hands. I swear, Rosie.' Tim is exploding before me. White lines of anger stripe across his face like war paint. His nostrils flare and his chest inflates. He paces back and forth in front of me, chewing the inside of his mouth. The trickle continues slowly like a snail on the inside of my legs. I wonder where my father's shotgun is. I worry that Tim will find it.

'Tim.' He stops in his tracks and comes to me. His tightened expression loosens momentarily as his eyes meet mine. 'I need to get home. I want to clean myself.'

'Yes, okay,' he says and takes me by the hand. He squeezes tight. We have never held hands before and it feels odd but reassuring. He walks me to the back door. 'I'll be in shortly.' He angles his arm to encourage me inside without him.

'No, Tim, don't leave me on my own.' I know he's planning on going back and I don't want him to. 'I'm afraid,' I say. He softens and has no choice but to come with me.

'Just answer me one question.' He sits me down on the kitchen chair and closes the door to the hall. We both suspect my mother will be listening from behind her wall. He hunkers in front of me and lowers his voice. 'Has he done this to you before?'

I shake my head, unable to meet his gaze, mortified at what has happened and even more mortified to have to talk about it to Tim.

'I need to know, Rosie. I need to know.' He notices my discomfort but insists on me answering anyway.

'No.' My voice is low and raspy. He grabs the blue and white stripped tea towel and dries my face gently. He stands up and leans on the table. The stillness of the evening jars with the chaos in our lives.

'Look at me.' He pulls my chin upwards with his hand. 'He will never touch you again. I can promise you that, here and now.'

I believe him and I'm worried, I wonder if it would be easier to endure my uncle than to watch Tim do battle with him. I feel shame.

'Never again,' he repeats.

We take a moment for it to sink in. My body feels battered and bruised and the tops of my legs feel swollen and tender. My hips feel dislocated. I pull myself upright, feeling every muscle contract on my way. My legs are too shaky to hold me so I sit back down. I can feel wetness in my knickers.

'I need to wash, Tim,' I say quietly. 'Help me upstairs.' I stretch my arm over his shoulder and he walks me to my room. As we pass my mother's door we exchange a glance. We both know, without uttering a word, that she could have stopped it. Neither of us is surprised that she didn't.

Chapter 7

Tuesday Morning – 2016

Snatching a second look and catching her breath, Marie lunged for the television remote. 'Jesus, that was quick.' She spoke at the television as images of their Estate flashed across the screen while the brunette newsreader spoke.

A collection of reporters and journalists had descended on their little sleepy enclave purposefully, looking to unfold the shady mystery they imagined of the forty-six-year-old remains in their two-minute or two-column segments. The cheekier ones had jumped her gates and knocked on her door; the more respectful ones only intruded by phone. As a consequence, her electric gates remained firmly closed to stop any rambling reporters calling at her door. It was a plague of story grabbers that had descended upon them.

'Where's your daddy?' Marie said urgently as Jack spooned the last few clumps of his scrambled egg into his mouth. She scooped her long blonde hair and looped it in a messy bun on top of her head. The old raggedy grey oversized T-shirt she wore for sleeping in had seen better days.

'He's gone over to the sheds, I think,' Jack muffled, with his mouth full and his eyes half shut. He was like a carbon copy of his daddy, with big brown pools for eyes and blond curls flopping uncut around his ears, he was already taller than her and only eleven years of age.

With the volume still on mute she studied the images, scanning for evidence of their life.

'Will you run over for him, as quick as you can, good boy?' Marie turned up the volume to hear the narrative. 'How the bloody hell did they get that?' she said out loud at the image of their new black jeep leaving through the electric gates. She couldn't make out who was driving.

She jumped to the window and peered outside, paranoid that reporters were still hovering around her property. Conscious that she was barely dressed, she pulled her T-shirt longer to cover her bare legs.

'Can I have two plaits instead of one?' Eve jumped down from her seat. 'Fiona always has two and she said that my mum is no good at doing plaits, so I want two plaits please?' Eve rooted in the drawer for matching bobbles and a brush while she spoke. Her wavy blonde hair was a warren of knots and a nightmare to tame, a little bit like herself.

'What, yes, sure.' Marie was distracted as her hands began to shake. She heard the words, 'Murder', 'Michael McGrath' and 'Timothy Fitzpatrick' all uttered in quick succession as she tried to catch up on the storyline. She wondered what else they knew. She couldn't decide whether to increase the volume or to press mute. She opted for mute, just until little ears were out of hearing distance.

'Or will I have one plait, do you think?' Eve was undecided. She didn't want Fiona to think that she was doing it to copy her, although it had become quite fashionable to have two French braids at pony camp and she didn't want to be the only one without. 'I think I'll have two,' she decided.

The back door opened and Michael rushed inside.

'What's wrong?' Michael's normally sallow skin was flushed red from his run. Panic was etched on his face and his boots were still on. It was the same panic that Jack mimicked, as he ran in behind him. 'Are you okay? Is Evie?' His questions were as short as his breath. Slowly, his breathing settled as he looked from Marie to Eve and back to Marie again, reassured by seeing both of them.

'We're fine.' Marie winced as she realised how worried he was. She might have given Jack the wrong impression. She should have known better than to spook him, he was such a sensitive little soul. 'Did Jack tell you there was a problem?' Marie said, her forehead scrunching apologetically. In the fifteen years since they married, Michael had never known her to be dramatic; as a matter of fact she was usually quite the opposite, a stoic, 'everything will be just fine' type of girl that wasn't frazzled easily. It didn't matter that she was ten years younger than him; she was still far more mature than he ever was. 'We're both fine,' she repeated reassuringly.

'Jesus, Marie, I thought something had happened,' Michael said, sighing with relief. He cleared his throat, thinking about the potential of things going wrong. He couldn't have coped if anything had happened to her, or the children. He looked at her, grateful, she was okay. Standing barefoot in his old, oversized grey T-shirt, no make-up, she looked vulnerable, younger almost. 'I just got the wrong end of the stick,' he said, aware that his last response might have been snarky. 'You normally don't send Jack running for me,' he explained, trying to justify his reaction, his breathing just about normalising. 'I was in the middle of the milk count.' He hadn't got the numbers freeze-branded onto the tail end of the cows so was trying to remember the numbers from the cow's ear tags. When he was interrupted by Jack, he ran disregarding where he was at in the count and now, everything would have to be re-done.

‘I could hardly run across the yard like this.’ She held out the frayed hem of the T-shirt, his old T-shirt, and smiled. ‘It’d give the lads a heart attack,’ she said.

It was the most unflattering she could possibly have looked, but yet he couldn’t take his eyes off her. She hadn’t the body of the nineteen-year-old student that she was when she first wore it, but that was still who Michael saw when he looked at her.

‘I really think you should burn that thing,’ Michael said laughing. ‘How long have you had that tattered old T-shirt?’ he said.

Marie didn’t answer, to her it was sentimental, a piece of their history, a remnant of her young carefree student days; the days when she fell in love with him. Marie looked at him purposefully, changing the subject with her eyes. He followed her gaze to the news story on the screen and he realised why she needed him in the first place.

‘Okay.’ He signalled his thumb towards the lounge at the front of the house. ‘I’ll just check the thing, in the front room?’ he suggested carefully, not wanting to draw Eve or Jack’s attention. Closing the door behind him, he turned the news channel on but he was too late. The report had just finished.

‘Come on guys, you’ll be late for pony camp.’ Marie shooed the two children towards the door. ‘Helmets,’ she scanned their hands. ‘Boots,’ she glanced at their feet. ‘Back braces, good.’ She slapped Jack’s shoulder, ‘And lunch.’ She kissed them both on the top of their heads. ‘All set, guys.’

‘It’s over,’ Michael said, returning through the heavy double doors to the kitchen. ‘We may catch it on playback. I’ll run them down now.’

‘Come straight back here, Michael, will you? I’ll put the kettle on.’ Eve and Jack jumped into the jeep. ‘Close the gates behind you, though,’ she reminded him. She didn’t want any other roving reporter calling, especially since she hadn't had time to get dressed yet.

She looked around the kitchen at the clutter of cups, milky spoons and the half-full bowls of cereal on the countertop and began to clear away. She adored their home and had painstakingly invested all of her time, effort and energy in restoring it. Every stroke of paint was done by her fair hands or by Michael's. It had been a labour of love, for both of them, and Marie had fallen in love with the old house, just as she had fallen for Michael all those years ago. Her mother-in-law's influence had definitely worked to their benefit.

Marie sat at the kitchen table and pressed rewind. It was shocking to hear her husband's name in the same sentence as 'murder'. 'Sensationalism,' she spoke out loud at the television. 'Bloody hacks,' she added. It was the same type of journalism that required the morals of a loan shark and the cunning of a poker player, she thought.

'Well,' Michael said, returning through the back door ten minutes later.

'Nothing new,' she sighed. 'But they know your name, mentioned Timothy Fitzpatrick as well.' She paused. 'Which is why, I suppose, they are showing images of the house and you leaving through the gates' She shook her head. 'And that you only bought the house in January.' She shook her head. 'Trying to suggest that you had something to do with it.' She rewound the image to play for a third time. 'That's outrageous.' She sighed again.

'Ah, don't let it get to you,' He poured himself a mug of coffee from the machine. 'You know more than most what they are like,' Michael said.

'They are trying to create a story out of nothing.' She lifted her mug. 'Me too.' She held her empty mug out for him to pour. She had lost count of the amount she had already drunk and she wasn't even dressed yet. 'Trying to influence the audience, vilifying you because you happen to have a nice house, a nice jeep,' Marie said, repeating her frustration. Her heady passion for investigative journalism and student activist days had long since waned, however she was more worried that, in their digging, they might uproot more than just the details of the body. Her mind flicked to the secret her mother-in-law had told her, a secret that Michael didn't even know existed. She needed to protect it; she needed to protect her family. 'They should be reporting the facts, not influencing the audience with cleverly orchestrated images and subliminal suggestions, the bloody politicians do enough of that.' This was the same type of sensationalism that she baulked against, the type of journalism that made her turn her back on the industry, leave her job in the national newspaper behind and move to Kilkenny to start her family. *There was no place to tell a story unless you could sell a story,* her editor had said to her.

'You're worse, for getting bothered,' Michael said, shaking his head. The passion in his wife had never taken much to ignite. He shifted in his seat so he could touch her, connect with her. There was something so attractive about her when she was fired up. Was it the curve of her jaw or the conviction in her voice or the sense of goodness that shone from her? He studied her. Maybe it was the way she pursed her lips in determination. He couldn't decide.

She smiled and leaned into him, just like she always did.

'You're cold,' he said; his eyes twinkling with mischief. 'I think I'll warm you up a bit.' Michael had as much desire for her now as he had the first time he'd said the very same phrase to her.

'Upstairs,' she suggested, afraid that George McGrath might just wander in the back door and see much more than he bargained for on a Tuesday morning.

'I've a farm to see to, Marie, I can't just drop everything on a whim.' Michael smiled, his eyebrows raised in anticipation. 'Just for your, pleasure.' He couldn't have denied the appeal of her, even if he wanted to.

She made her way across the kitchen tiles; her painted toes creating a flash of ruby red colour with every step. He watched from behind as she took the first step of the grand staircase, the mahogany bannisters just tall enough to cover her chest.

'Here then.' She crossed her arms across her body, lifted the old grey T-shirt over her head by its falling hem and flung it back towards him, she was naked underneath. 'Now, I'm even colder,' she said, smiling diffidently.

Michael traced the outline of her body with his eyes and stood slowly to follow her, not breaking his gaze.

She began to move, slowly at first, step by step; her hand on the rail as she climbed the steps. His long legs strode across the floor and as his pace quickened, she sprinted up the stairs, her hair falling in tangles down her back; her bare skin creating a kaleidoscope effect as snippets of her body flashed through the carved posts of the staircase. He took the steps, two by two.

The high ceilings of the entire upstairs made the bedrooms feel quite majestic and Marie had been steadfast in restoring the historic details perfectly, from the brilliant white snowflake centrepieces to the charming elegance of the cornices; it had cost a fortune to restore properly.

Marie ducked under the scattered sheets that lay in crumples across the four-poster bed and waited for Michael. The duvet draped from the foot of the bed to the floor in the same position that they had left it earlier.

Michael dropped his clothes, his stone-coloured work clothes blending with the deep tones of the mink-coloured carpet, creating a camouflage effect.

All his life, having grown up on the farm next door, Michael had felt compelled by the appeal of Fitzpatrick Estate, taking every opportunity in his youth to make sure it wasn't crumbling too fast or too furiously. He lamented its decay on his frequent visits home from college and watched as the once beautiful sash windows flaked and crispy patches of paint fell like autumn leaves to the ground, swirling around in the winter winds. He often wandered through the fields watching the brambles strangle the grasses and commandeer the hedges. He ventured through the old farm buildings and every time he did, he mourned. What was once the grand old house on the hill was deteriorating in front of his eyes, season by season, year by year. He wished then, while he watched the rotting roof sag with the weariness of neglect, that he could rescue it.

'I still wonder how I got so lucky.' He pulled her into him and she kissed him.

'Do you mean that about me, or the house?' she said, her hand on his chest as she lay against him. She couldn't help but giggle at his deliberate hesitation. Since she had known him, he had spoken wistfully about his plan to restore the old, grand house on the farm next to his and as soon as the inheritance from his mother's estate had come through and the opportunity to first lease and then buy Fitzpatrick Estate had presented itself, he had never looked back. He pounced at the chance to buy the old derelict farm and restore it to how it should have been. Although Marie's plans for the place didn't stop there and with applying relentlessly for agri-tourism grants from the local council, they were finally in a position to develop it into a working farm retreat with holiday chalets for the thousands of tourists that visited their medieval city. That was until the body was discovered.

'But did I tell you how much I love this house?' he answered, his smile stretching across his face. Her skin felt so soft against his calloused hands. Clean hands were one of her demands, he was always sure to wash them if he wanted to put them anywhere near her.

'No, do tell,' she said, her cold skin rapidly warming with the heat of her husband's body against her.

'I love how elegant it is.' He ran his fingertips under her eye, faint lines showing the amount of times she had laughed and the amount of times she had cried. 'How it blends the new and the old together.' His fingers continued across her cheeks and pushed her hair back on her shoulder. 'I love the way, it's so classy.' He kissed her shoulder. 'And clever,' he added.

'Really, a "clever" house?' She laughed at his descriptions.

'I love how strong it is,' he said, his arm around her back with his large hands stretching nearly its full width. 'Like nothing, no matter how bad, could knock it over.' He grinned.

'I'll knock you over in a minute if you don't stop talking about the house,' she answered, feigning outrage. His double meanings were not lost on her.

'I love that, even though it's old,' he said. She slapped his chest. 'Or getting more mature,' he said, grinning. 'That it is finding new ways to be, evolving and changing to meet the needs of the family that lives inside of it.' He placed his hand over her heart. 'Like a guru of agri-tourism house.'

She couldn't help but laugh at his ridiculousness; she knew he was running out of words to use.

'Careful,' she warned him. 'There are those houses that might be ten years younger than others,' she said and winked at him.

'That it's still the only place, in this entire world, I've ever wanted to be and nothing else, nowhere else, compares to it,' he said, his hands held her tightly.

Marie knew how much he loved the house, how much of his life he had spent dreaming about owning it and how much it had meant to him to be finally in a position to fulfil that dream. She knew that it was his one wish, his driving force, to return to Kilkenny and take over Fitzpatrick Estate and she had been happy for it to be her dream also. Little did Michael know that the force behind his love for Fitzpatrick Estate was rooted far deeper than his appreciation for the old architecture and his love of the land.

'I love you too,' she said.

They had reclaimed the downtrodden overgrown farm and transformed it, allowing it to breathe again, filling it with freshness and newness, even gave it a slightly grander title of Fitzpatrick Estate. He loved the house then and now, ten years later, even with every cent he was owner of gone and a dead body buried in his land, he loved it even more. And he couldn't explain why.

'Still though,' Michael continued the earlier conversation, 'I'd love to know where they are getting their information from,' he said; his arm extended across both pillows. Marie's hand rested on his chest.

'So would I.' Marie was equally as concerned. 'God knows, there are too many busy bodies down in that town, it'd be hard to blame it on just one,' Marie said.

'I don't like the idea of them using my name, though. Seriously, if they only checked out a few facts, Google will forever now have a link to my name and this bloody story.' He sighed.

‘Mmm,’ Marie’s thoughts were the same, but even more concerning were the thoughts of what else the reporters might uncover. She knew only too well how deep they were prepared to dig. ‘That’s how they draw you out.’ She lifted her head and rested it on her hand. ‘They make the public believe something by suggesting it, not actually saying it, mind you, so we can’t sue them, and then they tell you they are doing you a favour by getting you to do an exclusive interview, to tell “your side of the story”.’ She reached to the bedside table to grab the remote. She wondered was it too late. ‘I want to see if anyone else is running it. I might have an idea of how to stop this circus in its tracks.’

‘What are you cooking up now?’ Michael asked, rolling to his side of the bed.

‘I’m not sure.’ She had an immense love for Michael and a desire to protect him, just as his dying mother had asked her to do, she had no choice but to do it. ‘I might have an old contact who could bury this from getting any bigger,’ she said, considering her options. It wasn’t the most ideal of situations but she decided it was the better of two evils.

Chapter 8

Tuesday Afternoon – 2016

'Afternoon, Dearest.' Rose hadn't needed to put her glasses on; she recognised Tim's ringtone from the first note. He had been her rock all her life and now, especially since her beloved husband, Matt, died a little over a year ago, and her only daughter, Lizzie, working in London, he was irreplaceable to her, as was his partner Robert.

'You do realise "dearest" is a term of endearment, Rose, and I'll thank you not to use your sarcasm on me this fine Tuesday afternoon, not today anyway.' Tim spoke drolly. He could picture her where she sat in Matt's armchair by the back patio doors.

'What can I do for you, brother dear, is that better?' she asked impishly, even after all these years, she couldn't help herself when it came to teasing her older brother. 'Where are you?'

'At, home,' Tim said. 'Working,' he added. He hadn't been able to concentrate on any project and had decided to work on his current project at home; Robert had joined him there. 'I was going to come out and see you this evening. I want to talk to you about something.'

Rose could sense a difference in his voice. 'Okay,' she said suspiciously. 'Can I have a hint?' It would have suited Rose to have an evening alone. Her dizziness was increasing, particularly more so in the mornings and her energy was nearly non-existent. If Matt was still there, he would insist on her seeing a doctor, which was why she had made an appointment with the doctor and subsequently got a referral to the hospital. She hadn't wanted to say anything to Tim and Robert until she knew more.

'No,' he answered, unapologetically.

'I see, it must be good so.' She laughed. 'Is Robert coming with you?' Robert and Matt had been the greatest of friends, they had to be, considering Rose and Tim always took each other's side, especially when it came to winning at their regular poker games. Rose and Matt's plans to travel following both their retirements as teachers had always included Tim and Robert flying in to meet them at whichever far-flung destination they had decided upon. But like a thief in the night, Matt's cancer robbed them of their chance to follow through on their plans together.

'No I won't let him.' Tim was brash but loveable. He threw Robert an apologetic glance.

'That's a pity.' Rose was as skilful with her witty one-liners in return.

'I'll be out around seven, don't cook, we'll order in.'

'Okay.' Rose was grateful. She knew that otherwise she would have needed to find the energy to get to the supermarket; there wasn't even a crumb in the cupboards. A takeaway would help that problem.

'Did Lizzie phone as usual last night.' Tim had already texted Lizzie, and knew the answer, but asked Rose anyhow.

'She did. She's grand, she seems to like this guy she's dating, but still a bit homesick, if you ask me.'

'You would say that.' Tim had picked up the same discontentment in his niece's voice but didn't want to add to Rose's burden. It was no secret that working in recruitment wasn't Lizzie's profession of choice, not any more. 'What are you like, she's fine, having the time of her life in London, she is.'

'Maybe.' Rose wasn't convinced. 'Well, I'll see you later then.'

Tim hung up his phone.

Rose sunk into the sumptuous mink velvet armchair and snapped open her book. This was her favourite spot, just after lunch, where the sun slanted through the French doors in her kitchen. She hadn't finished the first page of her book when her phone buzzed.

> St Vincent's University Hospital: Your appointment at 11:20 at the Neurology Unit on Friday has been cancelled. Please contact the hospital on Ext 352 to reschedule. Thank you.

The timely reminder of her pending diagnosis caused havoc with her concentration. She didn't have the heart to continue with her book so she dialled the hospital number instead.

'Neurology department please.' Rose was pleasant and patient as she spoke to the hospital's switch. The friendly voice that received her call made her smile. 'Oh, hello, it's Rose O'Reilly here. I've just received a text cancelling my appointment on Friday. I was really quite eager to see the doctor as soon…'

'Oh good, Ms O'Reilly.' The receptionist had prepared herself for the barrage of complaints following the generic message that the clinic had sent. 'You're one of the first to respond.' Rose shifted in her seat. 'You see, the consultant Mr Tomkinson has had to change his surgery days. He is expecting that the junior doctors are going out on strike. So he wanted to reschedule everyone in advance.'

'I see.' Rose was endeared by her eagerness but anxious none the less. It had worried her enough to attend the doctor in the first place and complete the battery of tests they had suggested. Her appointment on Friday was necessary for her to understand what it meant.

'I can actually fit you in today, if it suits. Normally, he's not here on a Tuesday but he's here now.'

Rose shivered. As eager as she was, she wasn't sure that she was ready.

'I can fit you in just before five. If that will work for you?' Rose looked at her watch; it was already ten past four. 'Otherwise the next available appointment is in three weeks.'

'Okay.' Rose's voice didn't reflect her anxiety. 'No time like the present, I suppose.'

It was the insidious nature of this illness that bothered Rose the most. There was no intense pain, or rash or obvious culprit. She would have preferred those. Whatever it was, it hid inside her, taking over by stealth under the cover of darkness, when she wasn't looking. It crept, inch by inch, and now a mutiny seemed to be going on between her brain and her muscles, rendering her far less capable than she was comfortable with, it was time to see about it. She put on her coat and her shoes, grabbed her bag and made her way for her appointment.

*

'Rose O'Reilly,' she announced herself to the young receptionist behind the counter. She suspected by the brightness of the receptionist's smile that she was the friendly voice on the call earlier.

'Oh great, I have your file right here. I'll bring you straight in.' The receptionist walked slowly, clutching the brown file to her chest. Rose followed. She announced Rose's name as she entered the doctor's office and handed him her file.

'Ms. O' Reilly, please,' he waved his arm across the desk and pointed to the chair on the other side of it. 'Take a seat.'

Mr Tomkinson was a pale, sincere-looking man with wiry grey hair. He looked at Rose from his notes over the top of his glasses. He had taken his suit jacket off and it was hung neatly on the rack behind the door.

Rose let out a little sigh. She wasn't sure herself if it was from relief. She studied the consultant as he studied her file. His eyes darted across the graphs and notes that were fixed inside a binder. It was obvious from his demeanour that he wasn't the most social of beings. A book had been written about her, she noticed, as the wallet of medical information was organised into different sections, denoted by different coloured papers and various degrees of X-rays and prints. He looked at her over his glasses that balanced on the end of his nose, as though confirming some detail in the dossier. She watched his intense eyes scan the data and input it into his brain.

'Well then,' he started as he fixed his attention on her. Rose noticed she had been holding her breath as she exhaled slowly. 'Tell me what your concerns are?'

'I feel…' Rose tried to find the words. 'I feel as though I'm drunk, most of the time, I suppose is the best way to describe it.' She looked at her hands and stretched her stiff fingers. They were ghost white. 'It's as though my body won't do what my brain is telling it. You know, it might take me an age to get moving in the morning, as though my muscles won't wake up,' she explained.

Mr Tomkinson nodded and rechecked a scan in the blue tabbed section of her file.

Rose spoke and tried as concisely as she could, to explain what she referred to as her increasing inability to do everyday things. 'I have an overwhelming fatigue at times.' She shook her head. 'And rigidity in my muscles, like they're frozen.' She waited for him to write on the page. 'And I'm always dizzy, especially in the mornings.' She watched as he wrote his shorthand account of her longhand explanations. She stopped short of explaining how she felt, intuitively, that something wasn't right. She suspected he was a man that worked only with facts and that intuition wouldn't count for much in his diagnosis.

'Hop up here, till I have a look.' He walked towards the bed in the room and waited for her to follow. It was his tactful way of observing how well she could walk. He waited, patiently for her to lie flat on the bed and then gave her various instructions to move her limbs.

Rose watched soberly as her left leg disobeyed. It lay there, oblivious to her brain screaming at it to move in sync with her right. She could tell by his murmurings that he had seen what he had wanted to see and returned to his desk, making sure to assist her from the bed. As he scribbled, she smoothed out her clothes and went back to her seat.

'Your symptoms are very suggestive of a disorder of the nervous system. We are possibly dealing with a degenerative disease. The possibilities include, Motor Neuron Disease or Parkinson's Disease,' the doctor said. 'The presence of upper and lower motor neuron signs in a single limb is strongly suggestive of some of the neurological disorders.'

Rose sat silently in her chair, anxious that she might misunderstand.

The doctor paused as if giving her time to absorb the information. Rose inhaled deeply as though bracing herself. 'There is no definitive test as such; instead our diagnosis is primarily based on the symptoms and signs we observe.' He paused again. 'I propose we do a full neurologic examination at regular intervals to assess whether symptoms such as muscle weakness and spasticity are getting progressively worse.' Rose sat silently as he flung the words and descriptions across the desk at her. 'I suggest you come back and see me in four weeks.' He pushed his glasses back up from their position on the bridge of his nose and continued to scribble.

'Mr Tomkinson,' Rose's voice trembled, 'are you confirming that it is one of these diseases I have?' She wasn't sure if she had understood. He had said the words so flippantly.

'As I've said, there is no test to confirm it. However, we have done tests that rule out other options.'

Rose's hands shook and minute droplets of sweat formed on her upper lip creating a shimmer.

'With that said, all indicators at the moment, given your age and your symptoms, would make this diagnosis the most likely. But we need to observe you for longer.'

The shaking migrated to Rose's legs and travelled rapidly up her spine.

'There are some medications that, given a chance to work, have a certain efficacy with one or other of the diseases we are looking at. This is another way that we can identify, the exact nature of what we are dealing with.'

'Okay.' Rose was waiting for him to continue. He opened her file to the yellow section and scribbled furiously for two minutes, filling half a page. Rose fumbled in her bag for a bottle of water, to no avail. Her tongue stuck to the sides of her gums.

'I'm giving you a prescription.' He handed her the yellow page. 'You should start to see a difference in as little as ten days.' Rose read it as though she would understand what it meant but she didn't. 'Particularly with the dizziness and low blood pressure.' He clarified. 'And I will see you again in four weeks. Have you any questions Mrs O'Reilly?'

'No, I don't think so. I don't know.' Rose was dazed. She stood up, retrieving her bag from the floor beside her chair.

'If you would like to email later, if something does occur to you, or if a family member would like to contact me for further details, my contact information is in the pack,' he spoke softer now. 'A nurse will speak with you outside.' Rose knew he was eager for her to leave. 'My secretary will arrange for your follow-up'. Rose couldn't speak; she merely mustered the ability to acknowledge him by nodding as she left the room.

Chapter 9

Tuesday Night – March 1970

I watch Tim's expressions as we whisper. I'm pleading with him to calm down, to listen to me. We sit, perched on the top step of the back stairs. Stairs we never use. They're furthest away from my mother's room, my father's room and the back door. We used to play here when we were younger. It was the most secret place to be. I'm washed and freshened from my bath and I'm wrapped warmly in my dressing gown. I made him promise not to leave me and Tim is very good at keeping promises.

'Why didn't you tell me, Rose?' The tears still haven't dried in his eyes and the jagged edge of his jawline still hasn't softened despite his wearisome wait for me to emerge from the bathroom. 'How could I have missed it?' He didn't know the answer the first time he asked it and he still doesn't know six hundred times later. His voice wavers with every question.

'I don't know,' I answer, because I don't. It seemed easier to endure my uncle, than to confront him. 'I don't know,' I say again.

'Oh, Rosie, my poor Rosie.' His head falls into his hands as though chopped from his shoulders. His legs reach the third step from the top, mine are on the second. 'Are you…' he cleared his throat; I could tell he was awkward. 'You know, sore?'

'Not anymore,' I say, even more embarrassed than him. His words are as stuck as mine and a cloud of silence floats over us and lingers for a while. I twist the fleece belt of my dressing gown around my fingers, over and over again. I watch as the blood bunches at the tips, angrily elbowing to flow, and then gushes back down the length of my fingers when I let go.

'I'll never let him touch you again.' He knits his arm through mine, blanketing my small hand with his and squeezes. 'We have to get you out of here.' His voice reminds me of a film and I can't remember the name to tell him. Anyway, Tim doesn't like films, not like I do, especially not the musical ones I watch. He likes books. I draw my knees to my chest and huddle. I trace the swirls and curls of the brown and orange pattern on the stairs with my eyes and follow it, till the darkness at the bottom obscures it. I trace it back up and back down, again and again, counting the swooshes along the chain. There's twenty-seven on the way down and twenty-eight on the way up, I don't understand it.

'What you thinking?' Tim follows my eyes.

'I was sick, you know,' I say. A gentle smirk rolls up my cheeks as though I had achieved something. 'All over the kitchen floor,' I add. I glance at Tim and my smirk is contagious. 'It was brown and orange and all sorts of gunk.' Both of us giggle. 'Just like the carpet,' I say, pointing downwards. Our smiles swell on our faces. 'He slipped, on my sick, trying to catch me.' We laugh, not loudly but heartily and it feels so good. As if we are happy.

'That's my girl, always have the last laugh.' Tim unravels his arm and wraps it around my shoulder. I lean against him and we're safe, for now. 'It won't be long, Rosie.' He squeezes me too tight, I suppose his energy has to go somewhere. 'Till we're out of here,' he says.

‘How though?’ It doesn’t feel possible to me. I have resigned myself to waiting and counting my lists until they’re dead, my mother, my father and especially my uncle. I never thought for one minute that there was an alternative.

‘Don’t worry about it. I have a plan.’ Tim says this all the time and I nod, just like I always do.

‘What plan though?’ I ask. He doesn’t answer. ‘Father won’t like it; he’ll have no one to work on the farm with him.’ I worry that Tim’s temper will get him into trouble. Only the holes in the walls know how angry he is.

‘Don’t worry about him, Rose; he’s not worrying about you. Don’t worry about any of them, they’re not worth it,’ Tim says. His voice is low. Our smiles that imagined Patrick slipping in my sick have evaporated and left in their places are rigid lines across our faces. ‘Either way, I’m not leaving you here. You can come with me.’

‘But what about school?’ I say. I still don’t understand him. Sister Alphonsus will come looking for me, I think. ‘And what about mother?’

He looks at me as though he doesn’t need to answer. ‘We’ll figure that bit out later, but you are not staying here.’ Tim is definite. He ruffles my hair and says I should get some sleep. I don’t feel sleepy, but I do what he says. Tim looks at his watch and then back at me. ‘Come on, let’s get you to bed.’ He insists and stands to walk me to my room. I go with him, carefully hopscotching on the landing so as not to creak the boards.

‘Tim.’ I’m under my covers and Tim is standing at my window. He checks his watch again. He doesn’t answer. ‘Tim,’ I call again.

‘Right, you ready to sleep.’ He turns and leans across my bed.

'I think Patrick did the same to Mother, Tim,' I say, my voice so quiet, I wonder does he hear. He doesn't respond. 'Did Patrick ever do that to you?' I ask.

'It doesn't matter anymore, Rosie, the only thing that matters now is what we do next,' Tim says. His eyes tell me, yes.

'Tim, don't go back out, promise me.'

'I'm only going back up to the ewes to check, before Father gets home, as far as he is concerned I'm still up in the caravan.' He tucks my eiderdown tightly around me. 'I won't be long,' he says. 'Actually, wait a minute.' He darts from my room and returns seconds later. 'If anyone comes in to your room, even if its Mother, blow this as loudly as you can, I'll leave your window open, I'll be able to hear you.' He hands me a whistle and I clasp it to my chest.

'Tim, come straight back.' I deliberately don't add, 'Please'.

'I promise,' he says and then he is gone.

The house is in darkness except for the amber glow from the lamp that Tim left lighting my room. I often listen at night, trying to separate the layers of sounds that create the silence: the hum of the heater, the rapping of the rain, the gentle breaths. The harder I listen, the louder the lullaby, and tonight the lullaby keeps me awake.

A soothing breeze sneaks through the window and brings with it the smell of the wet night outside. The rain tap-dances on the window sill like Ginger Rogers and Fred Astaire. That's exactly it; I say to myself, that was the film Tim sounded like. The curtains rise and fall to the rhythm of the gusts and I can hear the wetness of the stones underneath Tim's fading steps outside, gradually disappearing. I'm waiting. Waiting for Tim to not break his promise.

*

Tim's bicycle whirred down the hill and clanked across the cattle gate at the bottom. He stopped still, focusing his eyes on the road ahead of him. Dozens of hawthorn bushes lined the crooked road into town and the asphalt glistened under the drizzle of the moonlight. He had watched and waited patiently for his Rosie to recover and now, with her safely in her bed, he wore a determined expression on his damp face as he pedalled into the blackness in front of him. It hadn't taken him long to reach O'Connor's Corner, only two miles later, and he dismounted his bicycle.

O'Connor's Corner always remained the landmark by which they would give directions to the house. It was the last junction used to point the direction of their land. The old house at O'Connor's Corner had lain derelict with weeds and greenery slowly creeping through the windows and doors. It was a perfectly secluded spot for Tim to wait for his uncle to pass. The clouds crept slowly across the moon, dulling the light from the sky. He stood motionless in the niche of the old stone wall.

As the footsteps grew louder so did the beating of Tim's heart. He felt each individual pulse drive the blood through his veins, carrying with it the strength to fight.

'I want to talk to you.' Tim stepped from his hiding place at the side of the stone wall.

'What the…' Patrick paused and noticed the rock in his nephew's hands. 'What the fuck are you playing at?' His words, laced with venom and whiskey, zigzagged out of his mouth.

'You bastard.' Tim stepped closer to him, squaring his shoulders and inflating his chest. 'I know what you did to Rose, you spineless piece of shit.' The words spewed from Tim like lava erupting from an awakened volcano.

'Ah, the lovely Rosie,' Patrick said, mocking his nephew. 'Sweet little Rosie.' Patrick watched as his nephew drew himself up into his shoulders. 'So you found a pair of balls after all,' he said. 'Your sister fought harder than you. Fucking pussy,' Patrick said.

'Make you feel like a big man, did it?' Tim's anger was about to bolt. His adrenaline had peaked and it needed to go somewhere.

'I'd say she liked it just as much as you did,' Patrick answered.

Tim lunged for him then, knocking him to the ground, his youth and soberness giving him the upper hand over Patrick's staggering strength. He buried his boot, over and over again, in Patrick, drawing blood from every orifice on his face.

'You,' thump, 'will not,' thud, 'lay,' bang, 'a hand,' thunk, 'on her,' thud, 'ever,' thwack, 'again.' Tim stopped and stepped away, scared of the strength he found within himself. He watched his uncle writhe, bleeding, on the wet asphalt road. Blood oozed from his eyes and his ears, and the swelling was almost immediate. Patrick's eyes flickered and rolled in his head. Tim hauled him upright into a sitting position by the scruff of his neck. 'The next time you so much as think about touching Rosie, or anyone else for that matter, I won't stop, do you hear me?' Tim shouted. Patrick groaned. 'The only reason I don't kill you is because it would be too easy for you.' Tim, winded by his exertion, gasped for air. He shoved Patrick back to the ground. 'If you are on Fitzpatrick Farm tomorrow morning when I wake up, I will make sure, that everyone,' he spit a ball of saliva on the ground. 'And I mean everyone,' the words spilled from his lips in bitterness. He hauled Patrick upright again, slapping his face to look at him. 'Will know how much of a pervert you are. And I don't just mean what you did to Rosie.' Tim hauled Patrick's battered body sideways from the road. 'I don't care, you bastard, not any more, I'll tell them what you did to me too.'

Tim stepped away backwards from Patrick's frightened whimpers and groans. If he had learned anything, it was not to turn your back on him. He watched as his uncle attempted to right himself. He hoped he had done enough. He pulled his bicycle from the hedge and set off for home. He wasn't sure how long it took Patrick to get to his feet behind him.

Chapter 10

Tuesday Afternoon – 2016

'Rose, hi, I'm Nora, the nurse.' A tall willowy lady, wearing green scrubs appeared as Rose left Mr Tomkinson's room. 'I'm going to take you over to this room here.' She stood in the sterile passageway and guided Rose across the room. 'We just want to check a few details on your file and check your blood pressure and a few things. Is that all right?'

Rose nodded her consent. She was feeling fragile. The combination of the shocking news coupled with her low blood pressure had conspired to drain her of her ability to refuse, even if she wanted to.

'Get that into you,' Nora instructed kindly as she placed a sweetened cup of tea and two ginger nut biscuits in front of her. 'It's all a bit much to take in at first,' Nora said sweetly.

'It is a bit,' Rose agreed and sipped her tea. It had been a while since she had sugar and it tasted sickly-sweet.

'Is there someone I could call for you, you know to explain anything?' said Nora.

'No I'm fine,' Rose said, stoic to a fault.

'Is there anyone at home?' Nora was opening her notes and produced a form. 'There are just a few things I need to get for your file if you don't mind answering a few questions.'

'No, I'm a widow.'

'How long is your husband dead?' Nora was pleasant and even though her questions were personal they weren't probing.

'Just a year,' Rose said.

'Tough year for you.' Nora smiled comfortingly and pulled an information leaflet from Rose's pack. 'I'll explain the medication to you too, it can be hard to get used to, but once you get into the rhythm of it you won't even notice.' Nora continued to fill in her form. 'And how many children do you have?'

'Just the one.' It was a question Rose could never get used to answering. 'Lizzie, she's thirty-three.'

'Oh that's marvellous, any grandchildren?' Nora was skilled at conversation. She liked to get a picture of her patients' supports, but did it in a non-intrusive way.

'No, not yet,' Rose said as she sipped her tea.

'Bring this pack home and have a read through.' All the details were bound in a red plastic folder. 'My number is in there as well as Mr Tomkinson's email, so if you have any questions that can't wait till you're back with us, just ring up or email. There is an answering service if we are not here. We could be in theatre or anything. Like today.' Nora held the front of her scrubs out for demonstration. 'Make sure you tell your daughter and give her a read through. It'll give her a chance to absorb it too.'

'Okay, thank you, Nora.' Rose was grateful for her time, but there was no way she was going to bother Lizzie with this; the first thing that Lizzie would do would be to pack up her life in London and race home to look after her and she didn't want to worry her, not yet anyhow.

'Have you far to go?' Nora's calmness went a little way to ease the chaos that Rose was feeling.

'No, not far, I'm just up in Kilternan.'

'Ah, a mountain woman, they're made of good stuff. I'm a Wicklow Hills woman myself,' Nora said. 'Takes a lot to knock us over.' Nora winked, Rose smiled. 'Take your time now, going home, there's no rush.' Nora helped Rose up even though she didn't need it, not in Rose's opinion anyhow.

'I will, Nora, thanks, I'm going to ring my brother before I leave. Thanks again.'

Rose exited through the clinic door onto the main concourse of the hospital and took a café seat to dial Tim.

'Hi Tim, how are you?' Rose spoke deliberately cheerfully, trying to mask any giveaway signs in her voice.

'Great, looking forward to later, I'll wait for the traffic to ease and get on the road about a quarter to seven.'

'That's why I'm ringing; I think I've a cold coming on. I think I'll give tonight a miss if you don't mind and we'll rearrange for later in the week.' She spoke through her nose to bolster the fib she was spinning.

'No way, Rose O'Reilly, you're not standing me up.' Tim was determined to see her tonight. Rose needed to be told. If Tim's suspicions were right, that weasel of a detective would do his best to drag her in to the investigation and she needed to be prepared.

'Genuinely though, I really am coming down with some…'

'No worries,' he cut in, reluctant to lose the opportunity, 'I'll still come out and check on you and bring you some dinner.' It wasn't something he could tell her over the phone, he was sorry he had to tell her anything at all, but by the way the investigation was stacking up, something was urging him to warn her, before it was too late.

'If you're sure.' Rose would have preferred not to see Tim, she needed to process what she had just been told, but with her brother's perseverance, there was no reasonable way she could have avoided his visit. 'See you later, then.'

'Where are you? It sounds noisy.' Tim was surprised that Rose wasn't at home tucked up on the sofa as she normally would have been with a cold coming on.

Rose froze, unable to think of anything to say and her silence concerned him.

'Rose, where are you?' he asked again, laughing nervously waiting for her answer.

'I'll tell you later.' She couldn't bring herself to lie. 'I'm okay though,' she added, knowing that she had sounded strange.

'Well that's a load of crap,' Tim snorted as he tried to figure out where she was. He could tell she was hiding something.

'Okay,' Rose said. 'I'm actually at the hospital. Don't worry though; it's just a check-up,' Rose was quick to add.

'A check-up for what, wait, what hospital?' Tim raised his arm, getting Robert to notice him. He had just settled on the brown leather sofa and kicked his shoes to the side. Tim stood and jerked his head towards the door and Robert understood. He patted his pockets, searching for his keys and found them in the bowl on the radiator shelf. Robert reached for them and hurried out to the car.

'I'm in St. Vincent's. It's just a usual thing. You know blood pressure and things.' Rose tried to minimise his concerns. She had no intention of discussing what she didn't understand herself, especially not over the phone.

Tim repeated 'Vincent's' so that Robert would know where they were headed. He pulled on his shoes, leaving the laces untied.

Robert mouthed, 'Okay.'

'And how'd you get on?' Tim said as he headed out the door, his house was only ten minutes away at most; he kept her on the call.

'Oh, grand, I've to come back again next month.'

Robert drove as efficiently as he could, avoiding tailbacks by taking the bus lane.

'I see, and are you feeling alright in yourself or why did you go in there?' His questions were a deliberate attempt to stall her from leaving.

Robert sped on the inside, there wasn't much that would make him break the rules, but Rose was one of them.

'Oh yes, fine, I had just been in with the GP and he had set up this appointment for me, so I took it. Nothing to worry about,' she added, her voice pitched a smidgen too high. 'Anyway, I'll fill you in later, if you are still insisting on coming out.' Her attempts at nonchalance fooled no one. 'Mind you, if I thought I could convince you, I'd tell you to leave it till tomorrow.' Rose hoped for a miracle.

'Nope, you still have to eat, so I'll bring us something,' Tim said as Robert weaved the car through the waiting ambulances into the set-down area. He unclasped his belt and jumped out of the car.

'I best go, Tim. I want to get out of town before the traffic gets heavy.'

Tim nodded to Robert knowingly; they hadn't needed to discuss what to do next.

'What was I going to say to you,' Tim stalled the conversation as though trying to remember something to tell her and he raced inside. He stood at the door and surveyed the hospital lobby. He noticed the information desk in front of him. He was thinking on his feet.

'Actually.' The solution just dawned on him. 'Could you do me a favour, are you anywhere near the information desk there before you leave.'

'Em, why?' Rose looked across the lobby. It was like Connolly Street Train Station on a Friday evening. Hundreds of patients, visitors and staff milled around the area.

'I was going to send a card to a pal of ours that's in for a knee replacement. Would you ask them what ward John Cannon is in for me, so I can make sure the card gets to him?' He smiled, hoping his ruse would work.

'Okay.' Rose had thought his request strange, but obliged anyhow. 'I'll just go check now, do you want me to ring you back with it?'

Tim noticed her silver hair pulled back into a clip as she slowly turned from the busy lobby area in front of the shops. He ended his call. He watched her as she took the phone from her ear to check if they were still connected. She walked closer and realised the man that was standing at the desk was Tim.

'What on earth?' Rose was in disbelief. 'What are you doing here?'

'We were just outside, when you rang, so Robert just turned in.'

'Oh, Tim.' Rose's eyes began to water, she didn't know how he did it, but somehow Tim always seemed to be in the right place at the right time.

'Let's get you back home, you can tell me on the way.'

Rose patted her tears dry.

'Where'd you park, I'll drive,' Tim said.

Gladly, Rose surrendered her keys.

'How is it, you always know where to find me?' she asked.

'I'm your big brother, I'll always find you'. Tim answered.

Chapter 11

Tuesday Evening – 2016

The weather had been diabolical all day and the grey, damp Kilkenny streets were illuminated by bumper-to-bumper red brake lights. Detective Kelly parked his car in his usual spot and made his way to the office.

'Right, I'm back.' He threw his coat over the back of his chair and sat at his desk. 'What's up?'

'Just been talking to the coroner's office,' Louise answered across their desks. 'They've confirmed, it's Patrick Fitzpatrick.' She raised her eyebrows waiting for Kelly's response. 'They're contacting the next of kin to release the remains tomorrow.' Louise had phoned Kelly as soon as she had finished the call. 'Cause of death,' Louise picked up the yellow Post-it note that stuck to her screen and read, 'subdural haemorrhage from blunt force trauma to the head. Catastrophic brain injury, they said.' Louise paused to hear Kelly's reaction.

'I could have told them that,' Kelly said. 'What else?'

'Secondary to that, he had cirrhosis of the liver, which made him very vulnerable, they said, not sure if they meant physiologically or psychologically.' Both Kelly and Louise smirked. In their line of work, dark humour was exactly what they needed to get through the working day, even if the Inspector might have called it *irreverence*. 'And there was vomit at the scene. Most likely a physiological response to the brain trauma, they said.' Louise re-stuck the note to her screen. 'Only the victim's blood, no one else's.'

'Forty-six-year-old vomit, nice.' Detective Kelly was raring to investigate. 'Nothing else?'

'Nope, it's amazing what is preserved in a bog,' Louise said.

'But no indication of anyone else at the scene.' Kelly checked again. 'No "frozen in time" footprints to go with their "frozen in time" vomit?'

'Nope.'

'Any idea of what could have caused the trauma?'

'Nope, could have been an assault, or equally could have been a fall, given the fact that he had so much alcohol in his system.'

'Right so, I think I'll go for my dinner You coming?' He asked. 'We'll go down to the Brasserie on Castle street.' He added.

'What time is it?' Louise turned her watch on her wrist. The strap was loose and her watch always fell to the side. It was nearly seven. 'I might as well,' she answered. Kelly's offer sounded a great deal better than the lunch left-overs from the hot counter in the garage on the way home.

'So what are you thinking now?' Louise had waited until their order was taken before she asked. Given that they had both ordered steak and chips, she knew they would have plenty of time to discuss before the food arrived, especially since she had asked for hers to be well done. 'Definitely looks suspicious.' She grabbed a slice of tomato bread from the basket and covered it in butter.

'I'm not sure.' Kelly poured two glasses from the bottle of red wine that sat at their table. 'We can rule Michael out anyhow. Seeing as he was only born the year the victim died.' He took the glass in his hand and swirled the liquid around.

'I had a chat today with the solicitor who completed the sale,' Louise said. Kelly wasn't the only one with a hunch and Louise's had led her to wonder about the timing. 'He didn't tell us anything we didn't already know, but he did mention, which I'm sure he wasn't meant to—'

'Jesus, woman will you just get to the point.'

'All right.' She shot a warning look across his bow. 'Everything in the sale was above board and they did complete all the necessary documentation in relation to declaring the uncle missing for seven years, presumed dead, etcetera, etcetera.'

'And?' Kelly's impatience was about to explode out of him like a bull in a cage.

'The farm was severely undervalued by the Fitzpatricks. Actually, the solicitor reckons by about half the market value.' Louise was delighted with her discovery and Kelly's intrigue in her discovery was written all over his face. 'Although, he did say, when you took factors such as the property market, the recession and the fact that the farmhouse was completely derelict when they first took over the lease, that it wouldn't be beyond the realm of possibility for the value to be so low.'

'That's very bloody interesting.' Kelly tore a mouthful of bread with his teeth and chewed. 'Very bloody interesting indeed.' He grinned. 'I presume Michael McGrath knows he got a bargain then, he's no fool.' Kelly's eyes squinted as he plotted.

'Well, the estate agent said that given the cost of the remedial works that Michael undertook, the low purchase price was justified, at least partly,' Louise said. 'But yeah, I'd say he thought he hit the jackpot when they agreed to his offer.'

‘I think we might have to talk to Michael after all.’ He washed down the bread with a mouthful of water. ‘Before I talk to Tim again.’

Their meals arrived and Kelly had his devoured in minutes. Louise tried to ignore his slurping and slopping as he gobbled his way through his steak.

‘You’ll get indigestion.’ It wasn’t the first time Louise had said this to him. ‘You’re eating those Rennies like they’re Smarties.’ He didn’t respond to her. ‘Anyway, where did you go earlier?’

‘Bloody hell, Louise, the cops wouldn’t ask me that.’ Kelly feigned offence. It was peculiar how they could work so intuitively together and yet be completely oblivious to each other’s personal lives.

‘That’s not an answer, Kelly.’ Louise was using her best interrogation voice. She gulped another mouthful of wine.

‘What’s it to you, where I go on my time off,’ Kelly said. He topped up her glass again. He was both delighted that she had noticed and pissed off that she thought she had the right to ask. If he had wanted her to know what he was doing, he probably would have told her.

‘I’m just interested, is all,’ Louise said and spooned another bite into her mouth. She stopped short of telling him that for the past while she had noticed a pattern in his movements and, for some reason, on Tuesday afternoons, for the past number of weeks, he was unreachable, nowhere to be found. ‘It’s just, I tried ringing you and your phone was off, that’s all, no big deal.’

‘Oh, leave a message the next time.’ He avoided the question that she was trying to ask and, for some reason, he felt bad for not confiding in her.

‘It’s just that I didn’t know if I was to cover for you or if the Inspector knew you were off, that’s all.’

‘Don’t you worry about me, I’ll let you know if I need anything.’ Kelly winked at her, surprised by her interest. ‘All you need to worry about is this case, the quicker we get to the bottom of it, the less you’ll have to put up with me.’ Kelly smiled.

‘Well if that’s not incentive for me to solve it I don’t know what is.’

Louise’s responses were always sharp and humorous; it was what Kelly liked about her most. If he was twenty years younger, he decided, he would have married her for her wit alone, it was just a bonus that she was as gorgeous as she was.

‘I’m going to go back up to the station, do you want a lift home?’ Kelly said once they’d finished eating. They shared many a meal together and, if the truth be told, Kelly enjoyed it. Not that he’d admit it to her. He had taken her under his wing since the day she arrived at his station and never once regretted it. It had helped of course that one of the first things she did when she arrived was to put one of the other detectives in his place with a quick-witted retort. He had admired her for that, that and her ‘take no prisoners’ attitude.

‘Yeah, but you should go home too.’

Kelly had taken only one glass of wine from the bottle, discreetly topping up her glass as they talked. The three glasses of wine were beginning to tell on her. Her normally stern expression had softened and her movements were less regimented and clumsier.

‘I will, I’ll drop you first.’ Kelly took her by the hand and steadied her to her feet.

‘What time is it?’ Louise rotated her wrist, looking for the face of her watch. Her skinny wrists were dwarfed by the oversized titanium. It was like watching a dog chase his own tail.

'Eight thirty,' Kelly answered. He reached for her hand and righted her watch. 'I don't know why you use that bloody thing. It's far too big for your tiny wrists.'

'It's sentimental, I told you.' Louise leaned on him as he walked her outside.

'Mental is right.' Kelly opened the passenger door and watched her flop ungracefully onto the seat. He insisted on driving her even though her apartment building was only five minutes away. Besides she had needed that time to rummage in her bag for her keys. 'You need to sleep. I'll ring you in the morning, make sure you wake up,' he said.

She leaned over and kissed him on the cheek. 'You're a good man, a good, good man.'

'I've been called worse, I suppose.' Kelly smirked at her softness. It wasn't a side he got to see that often, but when he did, he enjoyed her. The third glass had given her just the right amount of rose tint that she needed to look at him with.

He watched her as she fumbled out of the car and walked towards her building. Making sure to see her safely inside, Kelly made his way back through the stonewashed streets and parked outside the station for the third time that day. He patted his pockets and popped out another Rennie. His dinner had sent his insides on fire. He needed to catch up on the few hours he had been off for earlier that day. He smiled as he remembered Louise and her interest in his whereabouts.

Taking two steps at a time, Kelly was back on the office floor in moments. He was itching to make a phone call and was quick to dial the number and wait for it to be answered.

Chapter 12

Tuesday Evening – 2016

'I swear this day couldn't get any worse,' Tim said as they both shuffled, downtrodden, through Rose's back door. 'You go inside; do you want tea or something stronger?'

The drive home from the hospital to Rose's house had been filled with snippets of information, punctuated with disturbing silences. Rose for the most part had been stoic in her accounts and Tim had been silent and patient.

'Tea,' she answered resignedly. As bad as her day was, Tim didn't want to compound it by telling her about Kilkenny. That'll have to wait, he decided.

'Well, I need something stronger.' He rummaged through the knife drawer looking for a bottle opener. 'I'm not terribly fond of these new screw cap bottles, pulling a cork from a full-bodied red makes it more of an event,' he spoke to the empty kitchen. 'I'll open this one.' He showed Rose the bottle he had pulled from the rack. 'This one suits me.' He smirked to himself. 'Flighty, fragile, and prone to obstinately weedy flavors, it says.' Tim handed her a steaming mug of black tea as he rattled off the description on the side of the bottle. 'Speaking of "weedy flavours", remind me to give Robert a call, he'll be up to ninety.'

Rose managed a smile on her pale face.

‘Well, what’s going on?’ Tim looked at Rose. He had been patient as he drove her home, had accepted that there was bad news and now he wanted the detail.

‘I haven’t been feeling great lately and I had been in with the GP. They sent me in to the neurology department for more tests.’

Tim was relieved; he was waiting to hear oncology.

‘And what are they saying?’ Tim’s voice was low and deep.

‘Well nothing really, I told you already, they are just doing tests.’

‘What sort of tests?’ Tim said.

Rose shrugged lethargically.

‘Well, what are your symptoms then?’ Tim concentrated on her face as he tried to read her expressions.

‘Mostly just tiredness, a complete lack of energy.’ She paused. ‘I’m always very dizzy in the mornings, so much so that it takes me an age to get going.’

‘What else?’

‘It’s in my muscles; they just won’t work properly for me.’ She was reminded of the stiffness in her hands and stretched them both in front of her. ‘It’s as though my body just won’t do as it’s told. My muscles have gone rogue,’ she snorted, attempting to lessen the seriousness.

‘I see.’ Tim was listening intently. ‘And what are the possibilities?’

‘Well, he’s mentioned Motor Neurone Disease or Parkinson’s. Like I said, they don’t really know; they are going to monitor me and keep testing.’

Rose glided her feet into her slippers. She pressured the inner corner of her eye with her middle finger in an attempt to control the beads of tears that were queueing up to escape. Her beautiful brown eyes misted and glazed. Tim took one deep, long breath. He could read her eyes like a book; they had always told him what she was not saying. He had seen these sad eyes before and the story behind them didn't have a happy ending.

'Thanks so much for showing up at the hospital today. How is it that you always know when to show up?' Rose said sniffling.

He stood almost a foot taller than Rose and drew her up into his arms. 'I told you, I'll always find you, you're my baby sister.' Tim's voice cracked as he uttered the words. 'Whistle or no whistle.' He joked. From the information she gave him, he feared the worst and struggled with himself to hold his resolve. 'It's not one bit fair, Rosie.' He wiped his own eyes on his shoulder. 'I'll get us both a brandy.' Tim decided as he broke away from the hug.

'It's the waiting,' she said when Tim returned with the drinks. 'The waiting to die. I won't do it.' Rose was resolute that she wasn't going to be anyone's burden.

'There are a few high-profile people as well, with enough money to throw at anything, and if they haven't been able to find a cure, or even a successful treatment, what hope do I have?' Rose was pragmatic and knew she hadn't the energy to climb the mountain that rose in front of her.

'Like who?' Tim queried.

'Well, it depends on the diagnosis. There's Michael J. Fox or Stephen Hawking and loads of others. All at the mercy of one of these bloody conditions.' Rose's frustration was beginning to turn into anger. 'And there is not one thing that anyone can do about it,' she exclaimed.

'Well, Stephen Hawking revolutionised physics, we'll just have to find you something to revolutionise too.'

Rose was grateful for his wit.

'Failing that, maybe we'll get a DeLorean and go back to the future and discover a cure,' he kidded. 'Seriously though, it matters that you just don't give up.' Tim was almost forceful in his statement.

'Just one rule,' Rose spoke decisively. 'No one is to know, I need time to think. Agreed?' She raised her eyebrows waiting for his response. Tim nodded.

'By no one, you mean Lizzie?' Tim clarified.

'For now, anyway.' Rose answered.

'Is it okay if I tell Robert?' Tim asked. He had already texted him a brief update when he was pouring the brandy.

'Sure, but let me get to grips with it first, okay?'

'But, don't leave it too long, I think you should tell Lizzie soon.' Tim was forceful with his suggestion.

Rose didn't answer for a while, she didn't feel able. It took a further two brandies in silence before she found her words.

'You know what.' Rose closed her eyes.

'What?' Tim drained the brandy from his glass.

'I've had enough, enough of being at the mercy of someone or something else.' She shook her head slowly. Tim tried to think of anything worthwhile to say but he was as angry as her and just as stuck for meaningful words. 'Tim, thanks for listening, I really am just tired. Don't mind me.' She looked at her brother and felt sorry for burdening him. 'I might just have an early night, it'll all be better tomorrow.' Rose tried but failed to reassure him.

'You go on up.' Tim stood and pulled her upright. 'I'll lock up and let myself out.'

'Okay, good.' It suited Rose for Tim to leave. 'If you don't mind, I will then.'

'Grand.'

'Thanks Tim.' Rose kissed her brother on his cheek.

'Goodnight, Rosie.' Tim watched her up the stairs. 'What about your prescription, where is that and I'll pick it up for you in the morning.'

'It's on the table in the kitchen, beside my keys.' She held the bannister to balance herself where she stood. 'Oh Tim, was there something you said you wanted to talk to me about.' Rose remembered their conversation hours ago and called down from the landing.

'No, not at all, it's not important, I'll check on you tomorrow.'

'Okay. Goodnight Tim.'

'Goodnight Rose.'

Tim locked the back doors and set the alarm. He rounded the house and walked towards the stone-faced wall, waiting for his lift. He leaned against the wall and sunk his hands into his trouser pockets. He pulled out his phone and noticed the missed call.

'Christ Almighty,' he muttered to himself when he saw Detective Kelly's number on the screen. 'Is this day ever going to end?' He hesitated before he pressed the button to return his call.

'Detective Kelly, Timothy Fitzpatrick.' He cleared his throat. 'I've a missed call from you.'

'Mr Fitzpatrick, yes, I'd like to speak to yourself and your sister,' Kelly paused. 'In person.'

'I'm really not sure what help we can be.' Tim considered telling him Rose was unwell and then decided against it. 'And I'm not sure I'll be able to get back down to Kilkenny any time soon.' Tim sighed heavily and rubbed his face.

'I've a few more questions; some other information has come to light. I might take a spin up your way, day after tomorrow, Thursday.' Kelly was determined, if Timothy

Fitzpatrick wouldn't help voluntarily, he would find a way to force him. He didn't say that though. 'Why don't you come in and see me in Harcourt Street Station, Thursday at two.'

'Is that an invitation?' Tim's tone was curt.

'Sure that's all it is, save you coming down to Kilkenny.' Kelly was eager to speak to him. 'I'll need to see your sister, Rose as well,' he added.

Tim didn't speak, he didn't trust himself to. He thought about the anguish he had seen in his sister's eyes and hated Kelly for wanting to create more for her. His head was buzzing. He was starting to think of ways to put this intrusion to an end. The last thing he expected to have to deal with right now was this.

'I see.' Tim couldn't manage anything else.

'You know what, Detective Kelly; I'll come in and see you on Thursday. I really just want this nuisance to go away. We have other things to be dealing with right now.' Tim made a mental note to phone his solicitor first thing in the morning. He'd bring him with him if he needed to.

'Right so.' Kelly yawned. He decided he'd make Louise come to Dublin with him too. She could interview the sister. 'I'll see you both at two then on Thursday.'

Chapter 13

Wednesday Morning – 2016

Lizzie pulled a pillow from underneath her head and flung it across the bed at Lucas. 'Oh my god, who on earth is ringing at this time on a Wednesday morning.' She didn't open her eyes to check where the pillow had landed.

The phone rang again.

'Seriously.' She groaned. Lucas's phone had been responsible for disturbing Lizzie's sleep more than once in the past six months. She was beginning to question whether or not it was a good idea to date a reporter that would never pass up any story that came his way, regardless of the time it happened at. 'Turn it off,' she grumbled and turned over in his bed.

'Sorry.' Lucas hauled himself upright in his bed and pawed the bedside cabinet, feeling for his glasses. 'Its work, I'd say.' He much preferred being at his apartment to hers, not just for the fact that it was closer to the city but because he needed to have access to his computer when a story came through.

'No shit, Sherlock.' Lizzie's Irish accent always made him smile. 'Seriously, you need to get a job that allows you to sleep at least a couple of hours at night.' Lizzie turned in the bed, making as much noise with her hawing as the phone. 'And me,' she added. Since she had met him nearly six months ago, they had settled into a comfortable routine together, meeting each other's friends, staying over in each other's apartments, and sharing most of their evenings together, but the twenty-four-hour nature of Lucas's job was the one thing that Lizzie complained about.

'Actually…' he squinted in the half-light of the morning sun that was sneaking through the blackout blinds, making sure he was right. He checked the clock: 7:30 am. 'It's not me.' Smugly he flopped back onto his pillow. For once, her interrupted sleep wasn't his fault and he knew how much she loved her sleep.

'Oh.' She groaned. She reached for her phone as quickly as she could, forcing her eyes to focus on the screen. 'It's Tim, oh my God! There must be something wrong.' It wasn't unusual for Tim to ring, as a matter of fact, they were in regular contact. It was Tim she told first about the night she had met Lucas and how he had shared his cab with her. It was Tim who she described their second date to and how he had brought her flowers and it was Tim who had heard of how he had made her feel. Tim was her confidant and from everything she had told him, Tim knew she was falling in love. But the last time she had an out of hours phone call, it had been to tell her that her dad wasn't well, that had been before she met Lucas.

Her hands shook as she tried to dial his number.

'Tim, what's wrong?' she said.

'Nothing love, don't panic, did I wake you?' Tim answered. Hearing the croakiness of her voice, he realised he had woke her up. He had waited till half seven deliberately, expecting that she would be making her way to the station at that time. 'I didn't mean to scare you. I just presumed you'd be on your way to work,' Tim said apologetically.

'Oh,' Lizzie's breathing began to regulate, her heart had skipped a beat; actually her heart had skipped several, with the fright. 'I'm…' She paused as she looked around Lucas's impressive fourth floor apartment. It was only a twenty-minute walk to her offices on Jermyn Street from here. It was a pleasure not to have to use the train. 'Yes, I'm just about to leave.' she fibbed. As close as she was to Tim, it wasn't really the thing you discussed with your uncle on a Tuesday morning while sleeping in your boyfriend's bed.

Lucas stretched and swung his legs to the side. 'Coffee,' he mouthed.

She covered the phone with her hand and mouthed 'Sorry' back to him.

He shrugged in response, early mornings were never a problem for him.

'What's up, Tim?' Lizzie pulled herself together. She hauled herself back against the velvet headboard and tucked the crisp white duvet back around her and listened.

'Well, there's been a few developments,' Tim said and while he wanted to reassure her that Rose was okay, he couldn't bring himself to tell his niece a lie. 'With Kilkenny, and that's what I was ringing you about.' He hoped that the Kilkenny story was enough to distract her from thinking there was something wrong with her mum. 'I'm not sure that the news would make the London headlines,' he sniggered, knowing Lizzie would appreciate his discreet reference to her new romance. 'But there's been a discovery.' He paused for a moment to make sure she was listening. 'Of human remains, on the land in Kilkenny.' He paused again, waiting for her reaction.

'Human remains, like a body?' she said, shaking her head at the absurdity.

Lucas returned just in time to hear words he could relate to. As a freelance crime reporter, these were supposed to be his type of phone calls. The very ones, that Lizzie complained about. He nodded at her for more detail.

Lizzie pulled back the covers and waved the steaming mug Lucas had given her under her nose. She could taste the aroma before it even touched her lips. Gratefully, she sipped, savouring the deep russet loveliness of the Nespresso. Lucas had good taste, she decided, and not for the first time.

'And the thing is, because we used to own the place, your mum and I have become "persons of interest" apparently,' Tim said.

'You're kidding!' she answered. 'Persons of interest,' she repeated.

Lucas's interest piqued further; this sounded right up his street.

'No. Afraid not,' Tim said. Lizzie could hear the seriousness in his voice. 'The thing is, I was hoping to try and cheer your mum up a bit with, maybe, a surprise visit from her one and only, that's if you were up for it.' He scrunched his cheek in anticipation of her reply. The unusualness of his request was not lost on her.

'I don't see why not,' she answered trying to sound nonchalant. 'I'm sure I could arrange a few things in work this morning.' Mentally she checked her work to-do list. Recruiting C-Suite Executives for wealthy corporations was what she did and both the client and the busy executives that she was trying to recruit had been booked in her schedule for weeks now. It wasn't going to reflect well on her to have to rearrange at this late stage.

She watched Lucas as he stripped off for a shower. The glass shower wall clouded with the steam and he disappeared behind it.

'When were you thinking?' she asked Tim.

'I was thinking maybe a long weekend, maybe this weekend, if it suited you?' Tim said. He didn't want to alarm her by insisting she come as soon as she could, but that was what he wanted.

Lizzie detected the hopefulness in his voice. She was sure there was more to his request than he was letting on.

'I do have a few interviews lined up for one of the big accounts, so I'll try and get as many of those out of the way tomorrow and then try and get an early flight on Friday, would that work?' If Friday was time enough, she wouldn't compromise herself in work too much; give her boss less to complain about. She only had two appointments on Friday morning and she was confident he would cover her. 'I'll have a look at flights and let you know.'

'Don't tell your mum, though,' Tim said. 'It'd be nice to surprise her,' he added.

'I won't,' she answered and hung up the phone.

'What was that about?' Lucas said, when he came out of the shower a few minutes later. He pulled the blind up, revealing a grey damp sky, sprayed deodorant under his arms and wrapped a towel around his waist.

'A body apparently, found on the old farm that my mother and uncle used to own,' she explained. 'And before you ask, no you can't have the exclusive.' She smiled; she knew exactly what he was thinking.

'Well, what's the point in sleeping with you if you won't give me the exclusive on the family murders?' he answered. His smile stretched wide on his face. 'Seriously though, what's the story?' His curiosity got the better of him. 'A murder in the family?'

'All I know, is that a body has been found,' Lizzie answered; she was as perplexed as he was. 'Google it, see if anything's up yet.' Lucas was already opening his laptop. Lizzie had called him an Apple nerd when she first realised just how many

Apple gadgets he owned. 'I think I may head home for the weekend, see what's going on for myself,' she said. 'That was my uncle Tim, he reckons I should go and cheer Mum up a bit.' It was in saying it out loud that she confirmed to herself that it really was a strange request.

'Really?' His eyes were focused on the screen. 'Do you want me to come with you?' Their relationship hadn't progressed to the 'meet the family stage' yet, but her family did know that she was dating someone that she really liked and Lucas had already told his parents about her too. Lucas had to admit that Lizzie's family were beginning to sound quite interesting. He scanned the words looking for the story. His laptop or one of the many other gadgets, was never too far away from him. 'Tools of the trade,' he had said when she mentioned it. 'Kilkenny?' He asked as he scrolled through the Google answers.

She nodded to confirm. 'That's the one,' she said. 'Don't go drawing anyone's attention to it though?' Lizzie warned, she knew how the world of journalism worked from her many questions and observations of his lifestyle over the past six months. 'If you start asking questions, the other reporters will start asking questions about why you're asking questions, if you know what I mean,' she said. She had seen it happen before where as soon as a reporter with Lucas's calibre expressed an interest in a story, the whole industry followed. You didn't get to have fancy apartments so close to the city by being mediocre. 'I'm hopping in the shower,' she added, she needed time to think, she had a feeling that there was more to Tim ringing her this morning than he was letting on.

It had only taken Lucas fifteen minutes to find all the necessary details he would need to make a decision to follow a story. And from his brief investigation and strategic online searches, this was a story he could write and do well from, he decided. 'Shit,' he said out loud as images of the old, but beautifully kept country house rolled across his screen. His story spark was well and truly ignited and the familiar thrill of the elusive exclusive took hold. 'There's definitely more to the story than meets the eye,' he said to himself, craning his neck towards the bathroom door to see if Lizzie had heard him. He shook his head and looked surprisingly at the detail.

'What did you say?' Lizzie emerged, showered, dressed and dried, rooting for her shoes. 'Did you see my....?'

'At the fridge in the kitchen,' he answered. He remembered because he had tripped over them earlier when he was making the coffee. Lucas's professional attention to detail carried through into his personal life and every inch of his own apartment reflected it. He had a photographic memory when it came to detail. He liked order; he liked to know where everything was.

Lizzie smiled her thanks.

'There's more to this story than meets the eye, you know,' he said again, keeping his attention on his screen.

The smell of Chanel No. 5 wafted around the room as Lizzie rushed by, spraying her neck and dabbing her wrists.

'What do you mean?' she asked, this time rooting for her phone.

'It's beside the bed, where you left it.' He sighed, exasperated at how disorganised she was. 'I was saying, there is a story in this, you know?' he said, testing her reaction. He would love to cover it, but not until he knew for sure the angle he was going to take. In all the years he had been an investigative journalist, he was sure that no matter what the storyline was, there was always more to it, wasn't the statistic that eighty per cent of murder victims knew their murderers?

He was compromised for the first time in his career; his intuition was telling him to proceed, but for the first time ever, doubt niggled at him, that maybe he might lose something, or more precisely, Lizzie, if he did.

'Well, yeah, I know,' Lizzie answered, stopping this time to talk to him. 'But…' She hesitated. They hadn't been together long enough for her to be in a position to ask him to make sacrifices for her, or had they? She wasn't sure where they stood. She rotated the phone in her hand, flipping it back and forth nervously, thinking about how to say it.

'But what?' he answered, deliberately allowing his screen saver to power on.

'What's on the screen?' she asked, her eyes flicking over his shoulder, sensing he was hiding something. His laptop sat open on the glass-topped table that was positioned in the walkway from the living to the bedroom. The only other items on the desk were a notepad, a pen and a mouse.

'Just research,' he said, taking his hands away from the desk, as though by removing them he didn't look guilty.

'Show me,' she said, sensing his reluctance. Her earlier mood darkened.

'It's just work, Lizzie, that's all,' Lucas said. He pushed his mouse, showing her the screen. A picture of Fitzpatrick Farm was in the largest window.

'Is that…?' She studied the country house that dominated the screen.

'Fitzpatrick Estate,' Lucas finished her sentence. 'Do you not recognise it?' For a moment he thought he had found the wrong information, he hadn't had a chance to verify. He would do his fact-checking when she left for work.

'I was never there; I don't know what it's like,' she answered, scanning the rest of the pictures as she spoke. She tried to decipher his writing on the notepad as she stood over him.

'Seriously,' he said, he found it hard to believe, 'you were never here, in this stately home, the home of your family ancestors?'

'No,' she answered.

'Have you even seen a photo of it?'

'Nope,' she answered. It had never occurred to her that it was something she should have asked more questions about, not until now. 'Is that the body?' she asked as she noticed what looked like a photo of a bronze statue curled in a foetal position on the grass.

'Eh, no,' he answered, reluctant to explain. 'It's actually, eh, a photo of a Russian pilot.' He looked from the screen to Lizzie and back to the screen again. 'Sergeant Lazerov, I think. He was a pilot in the Second World War.' He breathed deeply, trying to figure out what he would say next. He could tell by her expression that she didn't understand. 'Like I said, it's just research.' He reached to touch her hand and she didn't pull it away. 'It's just that like our friend here,' he pointed back to the photo of the pilot, 'the body in Kilkenny had been there for some time, preserved by the acidic conditions of the soil, apparently.' What he didn't tell her was, that as a journalist, to mention the Second World War, however remotely relevant, in any story would almost guarantee a national headline, if not an international one, he just needed to weave it into relevance if he wanted to make some money from it. 'He was found in 1998, I think,' he added.

Lizzie didn't know how to react. She knew he had a profound sense of curiosity, that was what made him a brilliant journalist, she supposed, but it just seemed a little too close for comfort that Lucas would even consider getting involved in a story about her family, she had seen what he had covered in the past and she didn't rate her mother or uncle Tim as the type of people he would have reported on before.

'I better get to work,' she said, looking at her watch, one eyebrow raised, not knowing what to say next or, for that matter, not knowing how to feel.

'Are you, okay?' he asked but didn't wait for the answer. 'Are you coming back later?' He stood up, holding both her hands in his. He had a feeling he had blown it.

'I'll ring you,' she paused. 'Later,' she added, unsure of what she would do. 'I just want to...' She stopped speaking as his phone rang. He pulled it from his jeans and looked at the screen. It was an Irish number, he noticed, so did she. 'You had better take it, it might be important.' She couldn't help sounding annoyed. She grabbed her bag and left, hearing him answer as she closed the door behind her.

Chapter 14

September 1970

If a person is missing it means they are not able to be found. At least that's what my dictionary says. And that makes sense, because it is nearly six months since my uncle has vanished into thin air, like a wicked wizard, evaporating in a puff of smoke, and nobody is looking for him. Not the Gardaí, not my mother and especially not me. Tim says he's not coming back, but he doesn't say why; I sometimes wonder if he knows something I don't but don't ask him. Patrick's cottage still stands down the path from the house and his clothes still remain flung across his chair as though he is just down the fields. My father doesn't look for him either, as though he already knows he can't be found.

Somehow the burn of the September sun has turned the fields golden with the weight of the rays beating down on them and our house shimmers in the sunset up on the hill as though a light from heaven is trained on it. Microscopic grains float and dance across the countryside in the evening breeze and I sit on my perch baking and dehydrating in the meadow waning with the heat but I leave my jumper on, I'm afraid to take it off, afraid of what is underneath From this angle I can see the world. It's my place to be.

I watch the combine as it treks, inch by inch and row by row, swallowing up the golden grasses, then spilling them out crumpled and cut to sunbathe for a day on the ground, drying and shrinking to be collected again tomorrow. There is a certain satisfaction in watching the progression and I don't want to leave till I see the field clear despite the discomfort I'm beginning to feel. I'm waiting a lot lately, waiting for summer to be over, waiting for Tim to leave for college and waiting till I figure out how I can go with him.

My arms and legs weaken so I move to get comfortable. A swell of pain spreads across my stomach and I hold my breath willing the pain to leave me but it doesn't. I turn on my side, desperate for relief but it doesn't work. My muscles tense and the pain expands from my stomach to my back, violently. It shoots between my legs and finally washes away. I draw the deepest breath I can find in the airless dusky air, stunned by the sudden assault.

There are only two rows left, I notice. Tim will be finished soon. I drag myself upwards to stretch the pain away when I'm attacked once more. This time the pain strengthens and wallops me with its might, forcing me downwards on the ground, back to where I just lay. A vice-grip tightens around me, ripping my stomach from the inside out. Nothing I do makes it better. The pain escalates and I wish I was dead, not because I can't bear the pain but because, I think I know what the pain means. Then in an instant, like a tidal wave, it falls and retreats once more, leaving destruction in its wake; a tsunami of violence.

'Tim,' I cry as loudly as I can manage but my voice falls short of reaching him, like a paper aeroplane losing its direction and crashing to the floor. I curl sideways, unable to move as the wave brutally washes over me again, battering me with its spray.

The long grasses rustle, waving wildly as though calling for help but the rhythm of the rotating barrel and scythe continues only ten feet away.

'Tim.' The pain forces me to cry. I still can't move, he still can't see me. My insides are being wrenched from me like nothing I have ever felt before. I reach inside my pocket, searching, and then I find it. I wait for the next tidal wave to pass and muster what air I have left, and blow, as hard as I can, and he hears me. He said he would.

'Rose.' He finds me, distorted on the grass. 'Jesus, what is it?'

'Oh Tim.' The sinews of my neck protrude as I clench my jaw. 'Something's inside of me.' I force the words from the roof of my mouth. I feel the wave approaching, gaining momentum as it arrives, intensifying and multiplying the attack from before. A fire shoots from my spine to between my legs and I roar out loud, viscerally.

'Rosie, Jesus.' Tim panics, unsure of what to do. The honeyed fields stretch for miles and we are closer to McGrath's house than we are to our own. 'Can you walk?' he stutters.

'No,' I shake my head. 'I don't think so.' My body is buckled, bent out of shape.

'You're too warm,' he says, pulling at my clothes. 'Water, we need water,' he decides and darts back to the combine for his flask. Moments later he is back. 'Here drink this,' he says breathlessly as he returns. 'It will cool you down.' I manage to sip it in between the onslaughts. 'Take off that jumper,' he says, tugging again at the oversized jumper I wear. I let him pull it from my body, catching his shocked expression as his eyes land on my belly. 'Rose,' he says, more scared than I have ever seen him before.

The swell inside my tummy is large now and I hide it underneath my clothes. And even though I had hoped that I was wrong, my small waif-like body has grown to accommodate the baby growing inside of me. I was waiting, waiting for Tim to go to college and waiting to escape. Waiting for it to be over. Once again the cramp paralyses me and I hold my breath and wince.

'McGrath's is just there, we've got to get you there, isn't Mrs McGrath a nurse?' His arms scoop me up like the bucket on his tractor and I manage to hold on to him as he runs, bursting through Mrs McGrath's back door.

'Jesus, what's the matter?' Pushing back a chair from the table, Mrs McGrath jumps to my side. Tim places me on my feet and my insides erupt, spilling in puddles across Mrs McGrath's kitchen floor. 'Oh, Rose, my love.' She looks at me sympathetically. 'Get her upstairs, Tim, quickly,' she warns.

'I'm sorry,' I sob, ashamed as Tim places me on her bed.

Mrs McGrath has a quiet voice and a sympathetic manner. She is a slight woman with hair gathered in pins to the back of her head. 'Your baby is coming, sweetheart, I'll be with you but you've got to be brave.' Mrs McGrath already makes me feel better, even though I feel the worst I've ever felt. She quickens her movement and instructs Tim to go outside. Before he does, he looks at me and I can see his eyes glisten with tears, just like mine. Mrs McGrath spreads newspapers on her bed and removes some of my clothes. I do my best to stifle my sobs as I'm swept away with agony and when Mrs McGrath tells me to push, I do, feeling the tidal wave wash out of me, tearing me from my insides out and bringing with it a sensation of relief.

A wail erupts from the bed, piercing, shallow and wet and I realise it's not from me. It's from the four-pound baby boy screeching wildly in Mrs McGrath's blood-covered hands.

'A little boy,' she says, wrapping him in a towel.

I can't move, I'm frozen with fear and silence stills us all.

'It's all going to be okay, Rose, you'll see,' Mrs McGrath encourages me and places the bundle on my chest. 'I'll just fix you up.' She smiles.

'I can't go home. Father will kill me with his bare hands.' I have waited silently and finally my words form and slink out of my mouth.

'Shush now pet, we'll figure something out,' she says. Her hands are soft and kind and she rubs the baby's back as he lies on me. She uses the baby's towel to wipe my eyes. Her eyes study me and the baby and I can tell she's uncomfortable about something.

We both hear a commotion outside. The voices sound strained.

'I'll just be a minute, Rose.' She takes the baby and lays him beside me. 'While he's sleeping, you should close your eyes. Your body needs to recuperate,' she says before she creeps out of the door. I am mesmerised by the perfectly formed baby that lies by my side. I speak to him softly and I think by the way that he opens and closes his eyes that he can hear my voice. I am amazed something so precious has come from something so bad and warm tears prick down my cheek.

*

'What do you mean it's none of my business, you are in my bloody house, boy?' Mr McGrath was in the kitchen shouting at Tim.

'It's okay, Thomas, it's okay,' Mrs McGrath calms the men with her arrival. 'I'll explain everything,' she warns her husband with a look. 'In a moment.'

'Is she okay?' Tim says impatiently.

'She is,' Mrs McGrath reassures him. 'Where's George?' she asks her husband.

'He'll be back in minute,' Thomas answers.

'Okay, I need you to send him back out, think of something for him to do,' she speaks calmly, giving most of her instructions with her eyes. 'Tim, you have some questions to answer.' Her voice is stern, almost accusatory.

'Can I see her?' Tim asks. Thomas looks at his wife for an explanation but she doesn't give one. 'She's sleeping, as soon as she wakes up,' she says, answering Tim. 'Tim, go into the front room, would you?' She shows him where the door is. 'I don't want George asking questions about why you are here.' Thomas lifts his hands in confusion as Tim follows her instructions. 'Thomas, will you make some sweet tea and toast and bring it up to the bedroom, as soon as you send George back out.' Thomas nods, still confused. 'I'll be up in the room waiting for the tea, Thomas, and Tim, I'll be down to you as soon as I make sure they're okay,' she says.

*

The baby is awake and his black eyes flicker open every few seconds as though the room is too bright. His mouth opens and closes like a bird waiting to be fed and I am amazed at his instincts to search for my breast. I am stunned, in awe that something so beautiful, so fragile and small, could be because of something so awful. Is that the way it's meant to be? His skin hangs on his body like it's his big brother's shirt that he will grow into. He whimpers so silently. I hold him tightly, afraid that he will fall.

'There's something spilled on the kitchen floor.' Mrs McGrath stalls on the stairs when she hears her son's voice. 'I nearly slipped on it,' George says loudly.

'Just throw a few newspapers on it George, would you?' she calls from the step, waiting to hear him do it.

'Actually George,' Mr McGrath says from the hall, 'you may round up the mares in the top field. The wind is to be strong enough tonight and I don't want old Fitzpatrick up here tomorrow complaining of the noise they were making.'

George protests but leaves to do as he was told.

'Thank you,' I manage as Mr McGrath brings me a tray.

'I'll be out in a moment,' Mrs McGrath tells him. He doesn't speak, not to me and not to his wife.

'You get that into you, Rose, you need your energy.' She stands by the bed. 'I'll be back in a minute.' I can hear hushed tones outside the door and strain my ears to listen but they move, back downstairs.

*

'What's going on, Tim?' Mr and Mrs McGrath find Tim in the front room.

'I don't know.' He shakes his head in as much disbelief as them. 'I was out cutting, I found her in the grass, I didn't know…' He couldn't say any more. A ball of tears form in the corner of his eyes.

'You didn't know she was pregnant?' Thomas asks, his voice more harsh than his wife's.

'I swear.' Tim sits with his head in his hands. He hides the snot and tears that have erupted behind them.

'Are you the baby's father?' Thomas queried, suspicious of the seventeen-year-old in front of him.

'What, Jesus Christ, no.' He stands and paces the room. 'Christ no, what do you think I am?'

Mrs McGrath is reassured by his reaction.

'Why come here then?' Thomas is direct. He was reluctant to give old Fitzpatrick a reason to fight with him. 'Has it anything to do with George?' His own son George, the same age as the young man that sat before him in tears. He walks to the window, looking out for his son, his temperature rises slightly. 'Is that why she came here, I'll break his fecking neck,' Thomas exclaims, looking at his wife. 'Do you think George… do you think he's the father?' Anger bubbles underneath his skin. 'I swear to Jesus, I will strangle him.'

'No it's not George,' Tim answers. 'At least I…' Tim pauses. 'I don't think so.' Tim wipes his face in his sleeve and looks Mrs McGrath in the eye. He begins to count his fingers, the fifth of March will forever be etched in his memory, that was six months ago, the day that bastard Patrick got a hold of his Rosie. Why didn't he see this before, why didn't he know? But six months, would that make sense?

'It did cross my mind too about George,' Mary says, looking at her husband and then back to Tim. She can see his lips as he mouths the months while counting them on his hand. 'That little baby is not full term, you know, he'll need a doctor, so will Rose.'

'What do you mean?' Tim answers.

'The baby is only four pounds, he definitely wasn't the full nine months. She's lucky, he survived.'

'Is she?' Tim clamps his hand across his fore head. 'Would he be six months or so, I mean three months too soon?' Tim knew the answer to his own question, he just needed the nurse to tell him it was possible.

'That's probably about right, three months premature, I'd say.' Mary watches as her answers seem to anger him and confirm what he is thinking. 'Which would make sense, seeing as no one noticed her growing belly. As I said though, I'm only a nurse, we need to get them a doctor.' Her eyes roll upwards to where Rose and her baby lay.

Tim's fists clench by his side. 'She can't go to a doctor, she can't.' Tim states clearly, hoping that Mrs McGrath will heed his wishes.

'Why?' Mrs McGrath pushes for an answer.

'Well, my father will kill her, for one.'

'And two?' Thomas interjects.

'They'll find out who the father is, and nobody wants to know that, least of all the child.' Tim's eyes fill with pain.

Chapter 15

Wednesday Morning – 2016

As soon as Tim left his solicitor's office, he dialled his sister's number. 'So how are you feeling today?' he asked.

Rose had expected his call, following her revelations the day before. But she had no idea that Tim was calling for something entirely different. 'I won't be running any marathons, I don't think, but I'm not too bad,' she reassured him.

'So, nothing's changed then.' Tim was quick.

'Not funny,' she answered him, shaking her head in pretend disapproval. There was a sense of relief in having spoken to him, but then there always was when she shared her burdens with him. She sidestepped the washing that she had just folded and took a seat in the garden through the open patio door, knowing that Tim's calls usually lasted a while. 'I'm not sure these tablets are going to work for me though. My legs were jerking all over the place last night.'

'You have to give it time, Rose,' he said, comforting her.

'To be honest, I'm looking forward to having some time for myself,' Rose answered.

'Point taken.' Tim grinned. 'You haven't lost your sense of sarcasm then, I see.'

'I didn't mean it like that.' She smiled, knowing he wouldn't have taken any offence even if she had. 'But if I see or hear much more of you, I'm going to have to charge you rent,' Rose finished.

'Well actually, I'm going to have to come out to you again, today.' Tim winced as he continued his sentence. 'I got your prescription filled.' He hesitated, unsure whether to tell her the other reason he was calling to see her. 'And there's something we need to go over.'

'Is there something wrong?' Rose panicked. 'And you've got work.' She glanced at the clock; it was just turning ten.

'Not as such, I've just been in with the solicitor and we need to talk.' The beauty of running their own architecture and engineering firm meant that Tim had the flexibility to suit himself and with everything going on this past couple of days, he couldn't concentrate anyway. 'And Robert is keeping everything running in the office. I'm on email if they need me.'

'I see,' Rose said.

'I'm on my way out to you. We'll talk then.' Tim paused. 'I'd prefer to have the conversation, face to face.'

'Okay,' Rose answered, somewhat nervous by the secrecy. There was usually only one subject that had them talking in hushed tones and guarded secrets and that was Kilkenny, Rose was worried and Tim's mention of a solicitor did nothing to ease her mind. She spent an anxious half-hour waiting to hear Tim's car pull up outside.

*

'Wow.' Rose sat fixed to her sofa listening to Tim. 'Of all the things that I thought I was going to hear today, that was not one of them.' She shook her head. 'Unbelievable,' she uttered, barely able to comprehend the detail of what her brother was telling her. Let alone what the discovery and the forensic investigation might uproot for them. 'An actual body, preserved by a bog, of all things, on Fitzpatrick Farm. I just can't believe it.'

Tim looked up from his hands. His black framed glasses perched on his nose as he scratched his two-day-old beard.

'Who is it?' Rose was dumbfounded. 'Do they know?'

'It's not confirmed, but...' He scrunched up his forehead and exchanged a worried glance with Rose's surprised one. 'They are dating the body to around forty to fifty years ago and this Detective Kelly is asking a lot of questions.'

'Unbelievable,' she uttered again. She was shocked to the core. The dread of the past and everything that Fitzpatrick Farm was to her fourteen year old self crept silently inside her, stiffening her back and clenching her stomach out of shape. She had buried those memories in the deepest recesses of her brain but now, with Tim's revelation, she was catapulted right back to 1970 and the reason why she had to leave.

'I swear, Rose, you couldn't make this stuff up. Now, this guy, Detective Kelly, who wants to speak to us tomorrow by the way, is a bit of a jump-up, if you know what I mean, full of his own importance,' Tim said, almost relieved to have spoken about it. 'He is poking around in the history of the farm, which they have now renamed the Estate, by the way, and for some reason is fixated on why we left it all behind us,' Tim explained miserably. 'I don't know if his questions are relevant, but he is definitely leaving no stone unturned.' Tim looked at Rose's hands as she wrung them on her lap. He noticed, now that he knew there was something to look for, the paleness in her skin and rigidity in her muscle tone. Her hands looked cold. He wondered how he hadn't spotted it before. 'What a week,' Tim said. 'What a bloody year.' His shoulder's sagged, almost defeated. 'He is working off the theory that it could be...' He stalled before he said his uncle's name, he hadn't uttered it in so long, and it felt bizarre.

Rose was a mile ahead of him; she had already deduced the timing and thought to herself that it was too coincidental. 'Patrick,' she said, only just tolerating the vile taste that saying his name had left in her mouth, it was a name she hadn't allowed herself to speak of, in the forty six years since she had left. 'There's obviously no trace of him anywhere else.' She shook her head, her calculations added up. 'Not in Liverpool like father said?' she questioned Tim almost a little too harshly.

'Apparently not,' Tim answered, not taking offence from her tone. He understood how difficult it was for her.

'But father insisted at the time, that Patrick said he was going to Liverpool, he had been spouting off all evening in the pub?' Tim nodded, he didn't need to be reminded of the details, he remembered all too well. 'Was that not the case?'

'I don't know, Rose, I don't know.' Tim blew out the remaining air in his lungs as forcefully as he could manage. 'They won't confirm anything yet, but it seems that it is the case, to me.'

Rose moped for a while quietly, glancing sideways at her brother. Her chest tightened, the anxiety causing her breaths to shallow. She calmed herself as best she could to continue. 'And you've been back down to the house, the land?' Her eyes were wide with wonder. Questions that she promised herself she would never ask bounced inside her head like a ten-year-old on a trampoline. Long, locked-away memories were jumping to the fore.

'I have,' Tim confirmed. He knew what she was thinking; he also knew she wouldn't ask. 'Robert was with me,' he added.

Rose looked at his face, trying to extract even one ounce of detail of what he had seen, or what he had thought about when he saw it. His face looked older than she had remembered it to be, the tiniest of wrinkles spread from his eyes to his temples, and from his mouth to his jaw, like hairline fractures on his skin, evidence of a lifetime's worth of stress.

'That's what you wanted to talk to me about,' Rose just realised. 'In the hospital yesterday, sorry, it's only dawning on me now.'

'Mmm.' He nodded. The stillness allowed them time to think. She sat imagining the difference that forty-six years would have made to everything she had left behind.

'Rose, talk to me.' Breaking her train of thought, Tim reached across the coffee table and held her hand. 'You had enough to deal with yesterday. I didn't want to put this on you too. That's why I didn't say anything.'

'It's okay, Tim, really, I'm fine,' she assured him. 'I get it.' She hesitated. 'Did...' she paused, afraid to ask the question. Forty-six years of keeping a promise had made it almost impossible for her to break it. 'Did everything look...' she swallowed hard and looked deep into Tim's soul waiting to feel his answer. 'Did everything look okay?'

'It did, Rose, everything looked okay.' He knew it was the answer she needed.

'Okay then.' She drew her shoulders back, as though readying herself for a fight. 'We can see this, Detective Kelly tomorrow. We have nothing to be ashamed of.' She looked at her older brother and saw him as a strong seventeen-year-old once more.

'The questions might be a little harsh, just so you know.' Tim had been armed with a briefing from his solicitor. 'There are two detectives on this case, Detective Kelly and Detective

Kennedy; I've only met Kelly yet,' he added. 'For some reason, Detective Kelly is hell-bent on figuring out why we left Fitzpatrick Farm.' Tim rubbed his face. 'As though, that's going to help him solve this case.'

'We keep our promise though, okay, for everyone's sake, right?' Rose insisted. 'We haven't come this far to have everything dug back up…' She looked at Tim, almost smiling at the bad choice of words. 'You know what I mean,' she said.

'Right,' Tim agreed.

'Do you think we should tell him the rest?' Rose wasn't the type to wallow in her past and didn't relish the thought of rehashing her childhood to satisfy this Detective Kelly's curiosity, but if it was reason he wanted, well, that was reason enough.

'No. I don't know,' Tim said again. He wasn't sure that revisiting the hidden history or raking up secret memories was going to help anyone. 'Rose, don't let him walk all over you, you know. It's your business, not his, remember, it's just helping him with his enquiries, we are not under suspicion or arrest. Okay?'

'Okay and the solicitor?' Rose asked.

'He reckons it might be a bad signal to send, if we show up all lawyered up. He says to ring him if we want him, or want to check a question with him and that he can get to us if needs be.'

'Okay then,' Rose agreed. But, for the second time in as many days, she felt as if her world had been turned upside down.

Chapter 16

Wednesday Morning – 2016

'Hi Lucas, it's me.' Marie paused to give him a chance to think, it had been years since they had spoken. 'I was hoping to run something by you, I sort of…' she stumbled a little with her words. 'I eh, need your help?' Her voice sounded like it had always done, he recognised it straight away.

'Wow, there's a sentence that I would never have thought I'd hear you say again,' he said. She could hear him draw a deep breath and swallow. 'Actually, I think the last thing you said was that you never wanted to have anything to do with me ever again, if I'm not mistaken.' A phone call, after nearly twenty years of silence from Marie, was the last thing he had ever expected.

'Lucas, we were only kids,' she said, expecting something of a backlash, seeing as they hadn't been in touch since college. 'It wasn't like that, Lucas, and you know it,' she said. 'Us getting together would have been a massive mistake.' He didn't answer her. 'I didn't want it to ruin our friendship, which I suppose is the biggest irony,' she said, her voice trailing off.

'Anyway, we've all moved on, I suppose,' Lucas said, trying to appear unfazed. It wasn't every day that the one girl that broke his heart phoned him out of the blue. 'I presume you're married and living in a mansion with a load of children, and you've probably written your novel by now,' he added, trying to sound funny. While they were in university together, Marie wasn't just a crush for Lucas, she had become an obsession, an itch that got right under his skin, an itch that he couldn't scratch. He had been devastated when she didn't feel the same way about him.

'All true,' she said, 'Bar the novel bit.' She giggled. 'You?'

'Oh, same,' he replied. 'Bar the married bit, and the children bit, oh, and the living in a mansion and the novel bit.'

'I've been keeping an eye on your career,' she said. 'Very impressive. I knew you'd do well.' His reputation had elevated him in the industry, making him the standout journalist of the year for his hard-hitting investigations.

'Thanks,' he paused. 'What about you?' he asked, not really wanting to know the answer, he had thought about her from time to time and wondered if she had stayed with him, that older man that she had left him for. He wanted to ask her if she had married him, but didn't.

'Well, left the job in the *Sunday Independent*,' she said. She always worried how it might be perceived, especially by those that she went to university with.

'I see,' he said. He had already known she hadn't been there for years, he had wondered why she left. 'Why did you leave?' His voice felt like stretched elastic.

'Life changed, Lucas, that's all. Got married, had two children, Jack who's eleven and Eve who's eight.' They both fell silent waiting for the other to speak. 'Lucas,' she said finally, 'I have a bit of a problem and I need someone, you know, who knows the business, to kill a story for me, or if not kill, at least bury it.'

'What you do, murder someone?' he said, trying to sound as though he was laughing.

'No, not me, but there has been a murder and well, it's complicated, I need to know that you'll do it.' She was reluctant to elaborate, she needed his assurance that he could help before she confided in him.

'Are you in trouble, Marie?' Lucas said. He stood from the desk and paced around the floor. He refreshed his laptop screen and checked his notifications, no new murders reported, although he wouldn't pick up the Irish scene as quick as his Irish counterparts. He typed, 'Dublin Murder.' Five showed up, he scrolled as quickly as he could, searching unsuccessfully for a connection to Marie. The coincidence of hearing about two Irish murders in the space of an hour wasn't lost on him.

'No, not as such, Lucas, it really is complicated.' She sighed heavily and searched for the best words to use. 'It's Michael, Lucas.' She cringed as she spoke her husband's name to him. Old wounds were the hardest to heal. She imagined Lucas holding his breath at the mention. 'A body has been discovered, and well, the local media are bandying his name about suggestively…'

'Did he do it?' Lucas interrupted, he listened intently for her giveaway signs.

'Of course not,' she said and laughed nervously. 'It's just that it, the body, was found on our land and well, you know the way it goes, now every time it's reported…' she cleared her throat before she said his name, 'Michael, is in the image behind the headline.'

'Michael,' he repeated. Michael, the guy she had left him for in college. A lecturer in Agricultural Science, he was the reason they never spoke again, she picked Michael over Lucas and he had never forgiven her for it.

'Yes,' Marie sighed. 'Michael.'

'*The* Michael,' Lucas repeated. He took his phone from his ear.

She could hear him faintly, she was sure he said, fuck.

'Lucas,' Marie said. She knew he wasn't listening. 'Lucas.'

'Yes. I was just looking at something on the computer.'

'I married Michael, Lucas,' Marie said, her voice almost apologetic.

'Marie, that was, what, nearly twenty years ago, water under the bridge,' Lucas said, attempting to sound like he didn't care. It pained him when she hadn't felt the same way about him but it had sickened him that she had chosen Michael over him and even though he had moved way past his obsession with her now, at the time, he had wanted to die. 'Look, I'm glad it worked out for you,' he continued. 'As you said, we were only kids.'

'The thing is, since I left the paper, I have no contacts over here in journalism.' She could sense the tension in his voice but wanted to focus him on the task in hand. She knew it would have been hard for him to open old wounds, especially where Michael was concerned but he was the best in the business and she desperately needed his help.

'And you want my help?' Lucas said, still disbelieving that she was on the other end of the line.

'You could say that,' she said, thinking of how she left. 'I need someone with a bit of clout to kill the story, or at least the angle they're going with.'

'I don't get it though, Marie.' Lucas would have done anything for her in the past, she was his everything, then; he wasn't sure about now though, and he definitely wasn't sure about why it was so important to kill a story that would die its own death anyway, particularly if there was no substance there and besides, the fact that Michael was involved was making him less inclined, to say the least. 'I don't really know what I can do,' he said.

'Lucas, look, if you are worried that Michael is the murderer, he's not, he has a cast-iron alibi, he wasn't even born when it happened.' She sighed. 'I just don't want my kids googling their dad's name and coming up with murder on the same page,' she said.

'When was the murder?' Lucas couldn't help but be curious.

'1970's, they think,' she answered.

'In Kilkenny?' he said. What are the chances? He thought to himself.

'Yes' Marie said.

'And how, do you and...' he hesitated, finding it hard to say Michael. 'How do you guys fit into the picture?' He walked towards his desk and scribbled down some notes.

'Michael is from here, born and raised on the next farm up,' she said. 'We've been here, leasing the land, for the past ten years, and now, just recently, January in fact, we finally bought it.'

'Jesus Christ, Marie, you weren't joking when you said yes to living in a mansion.' He studied the picture of the grand house on his screen.

'How do you know where... What do you mean?'

'I'm looking at your house on my computer screen right now.' Lucas zoomed in on the picture of Fitzpatrick Estate. The grandeur of the house suited her, he thought wistfully as he admired the beauty of its exterior architecture.

'You are really... that was quick,' she said, shyly. 'Oh my God, don't tell me that the story is out already.' She panicked. She couldn't understand why something so rural and local to Ireland would have hit the headlines in the UK.

'I just have a radar for this stuff,' Lucas lied. He wasn't about to explain that he just happened to be sleeping with

Lizzie O'Reilly, a member of the family that appeared to be equally implicated in the murder. Not yet anyhow.

'Look we are really just caught in the crossfire here, is there anything you can do?' Her sigh was heavy, Lucas could hear her desperation.

'I told you he wasn't for you, you should have listened to me,' Lucas said, grinning. His humour had always been the same, which is why they were such close friends in the first place. 'I'm still not one hundred percent convinced that there isn't more to it.' He read her like a book.

'That's the complicated part.' She sighed. 'It's not the fact that they will pin the murder on Michael, it's what they'll rake up when they go rooting.'

'I'm listening,' Lucas said, he grew worried at the tone of her voice.

'I'd much prefer to speak to you in person, it's too…

'Let me guess, complicated,' Lucas answered for her, already searching for flights on his screen. 'Marie, can I ask just one question?'

'Of course.'

'Does Michael know you are ringing me?

'No.'

'Leave it with me, then.' He smiled. 'I'll see what I can do.'

Chapter 17

Wednesday Morning – 2016

'My Jesus, that's some report.' Detective Kelly slid a bound copy of the preliminary autopsy report across to Louise. 'There now, Detective Kennedy, broken jaw, cracked skull, this fella was seriously kicked to death. We don't need any bloody hearing to prove that, surely, it's an open and shut homicide, even if it was forty-six years ago.'

'And frozen in time for us all to study it, mad altogether.' Louise nodded her head. 'And you honestly think this Timothy Fitzpatrick guy has something to do with it, he's just so…' Louise scrunched up her cheeks, searching for an apt description. 'So, not the type.'

'I don't know if he did the kicking, or the leaving him for dead for that matter, but I'm sure there's something he's not telling us.' Kelly swivelled on his chair, thinking. 'Yeah, there's definitely something.' He chewed the end of his biro; he couldn't quite put his finger on it but he knew he was close. 'We'll know more tomorrow when we sit down with them, I suppose.'

'Maybe.' Louise paused and rubbed her temple hard. 'Maybe not, though.' She'd had a splitting headache since she woke and scrutinising photographs of a forty-six-year-old corpse did nothing to settle her stomach. She was close to passing out with the heat and she could feel Kelly studying her from across the desks, willing her to admit she was hungover.

She shouldn't have opened the second bottle of wine when she got home last night, she thought. Being weak was not something she would confess to lightly but the thought of travelling two hours to Dublin that evening was grating on her. 'Do we really need to go up tonight, though?' Louise asked.

'Well, no *you* don't'. Kelly answered. 'But that's when I'm leaving', even if he hadn't wanted to travel tonight he would have done so, just to torment her. He could tell by her grey pallor that she was suffering. 'You could make your way up in the morning, if you preferred'. Kelly said, knowing she wouldn't.

'No, I'll go.' She answered. 'But I want it on record that I'm not happy about it.' She flicked her eyes across him and smirked. 'I am not one for taking advantage of expenses and overnight allowances, like some'. Her expression suggested indifference and he smiled at her in response. Normally she would have been the first to jump at an overnight opportunity, especially if it was in Dublin. 'As long as you drive'. She added, knowing he would have insisted on the exact same thing.

*

With Harcourt Street Garda Station across the road, the Camden Court Hotel in Dublin was a familiar spot to visiting detectives. It was close to seven p.m. when they pulled into the car park.

'I'll never sleep tonight now; you shouldn't have let me sleep so long,' Louise said jokingly as they made their way to their rooms. 'We may hit the town in- spots, wear me out a bit,' she giggled.

Kelly smiled. He could have matched her energy level just not her enthusiasm for barrelling into some overcrowded, overpriced pub in the city centre. He was more into eating a well-cooked meal, in good company with a few drinks and then bed.

'A hangover will do that to you,' Kelly said, he had been waiting for an opportunity to slag her off about it all day and with her falling asleep for the entire drive to Dublin, it was the first time he'd had the opportunity.

'Shut up,' she said, the sleep in the car helping her to normalise. Kelly had used the back of his fingers to gently slap her awake and she had berated him for it. 'Jesus there is nicer ways to wake a sleeping beauty,' Louise had said to him.

'When I see one, I'll be sure to wake her with love's true kiss,' he'd sniggered.

Louise sleeping for most of the journey had left Kelly with more headspace to think about how he was going to get inside Timothy Fitzpatrick's version of the truth and he thought he had a plan. Her gentle snoring had made him glance at her more than once on the trip, but it was her top slipping slightly from her shoulder that turned his glance into a lingering look. He had looked; knowing that he shouldn't, at her milky-white, pale skin and wished he could have touched it.

'Right, 206, this is me.' Kelly slid his card into the receiver. 'You're next door.'

'Grand. See you downstairs, in say…' she looked at her watch, spinning her wrist to catch the clock face in the right position. 'Eight okay for you?' she continued. 'Or is that too late for you OAPs?'

Kelly was already gone.

He took a quick shower, checked his emails and it was still only seven thirty. He grabbed his phone and made his way downstairs to the bar. He was debating whether or not to tell Louise he was early, but decided against it, ordered himself a beer and took up a sofa in the lobby to wait. Scores of sumptuous sofas were dotted around the open area, separated by leafy plants in oversized ceramic pots. He could see the appeal to the many different types of person that milled across the marble. There were business types, family types and everything in between. He could tell by the shoes of most what their intention in the city was. As he was sure the staff could tell that he was one of the team from Harcourt Street Station. He'd have a swim, he decided, in the morning, early, before Louise was even awake. He would have been there right now if she hadn't suggested they meet up. He leaned back on the sofa and took the first swig of his beer. He took his phone from his pocket to ring her, when he heard her voice.

'Well, I hope you have had a cool shower to douse those sexy thoughts.' It was definitely her voice but he couldn't make out where it came from. Kelly was fixed to the spot as he listened. 'As if you need reminding,' Louise said then. She had arrived at the bar earlier than Kelly, and when there was no sign of him, she took the opportunity to ring her sister. She found a sofa in the lobby and dialled Alex's number. Kelly moved silently, craning his neck to find her. She was silent, no doubt listening to her caller. 'Ugh, please too much information, Alex. Keep your sordid information to yourself.' Louise's voice sounded louder this time, almost girly, he thought. 'I can't, I wish I could, but I'm here with a colleague.' He heard regret in her voice. 'Well, what time does your gig end?'

Kelly wished he knew who she was talking to. Whoever this Alex guy was, he decided, she sounded close to him. He hadn't thought about it before, but he supposed, a good-looking, successful girl like Louise was bound to have a boyfriend. The pangs of jealousy he felt took him by surprise and he couldn't understand why the thoughts of him and Louise being together, had never crossed his mind till now. He had always treated Louise just like a friend, some would say, much to Louise's annoyance, like family, but she was someone he was comfortable with, someone who didn't play any games and that, in Kelly's book, was a rarity.

'I know, but I am back up in Dublin next weekend, we'll get together properly then.' Kelly was sure that the intention of the get-together was anything but 'proper' by the tone of Louise's voice. 'You could just come to my hotel room after your gig, stay with me here?' she said. Kelly's hernia was about to burst out of his gut. 'No, I'd say Kelly will have gone to bed by then, so you won't have to meet him.' He would be mortified if she knew he had heard her.

Listening intently, Kelly's jealousy was overflowing. Afraid to move, he listened to the entire conversation. He hadn't realised it till now, but he was yearning to be with Louise. The office banter with her was the highlight of his day, not because of her witty one-liners, or her ability to reduce a grown man to tears, but because there was something more to her, genuine and sincere, and Kelly was falling for her.

'Oh and Alex, will you bring me in some underwear. I'm sure I left some there for occasions such as this.' She giggled. 'I was so hungover earlier, I've forgotten almost everything, and I won't have time to go out shopping.' He could hear her laughing. 'I'll be knickerless tomorrow,' she said and laughed loudly.

Kelly's face flushed at the thoughts of it. The image of Louise knickerless was impossible to shake.

'I could imagine bringing Kelly into Marks and Sparks to buy lacy underwear,' Louise laughed. 'Although you are probably right.' Louise had confided in Alex about how she felt about Kelly, and Alex's suggestion that underwear shopping with her colleague might just be the bomb that Louise needed to put under him, either that or a neon sign saying, hey I'm into you. 'Okay, Alex. See you later. Love you too.' Louise unzipped her bag and dropped her phone inside the pocket. She lifted her empty beer bottle and click-clacked across the marble floor of the lobby in the direction of the bar, to order a second. It wouldn't be long before Kelly was down, she thought and she was glad, now that the journey was behind her, that they were back at The Camden Court Hotel. She was looking forward to it. She was sure to keep to beer though; she wouldn't be as hungover on that.

Kelly, finally able to move, stretched his long lean legs. He shook his head; berated himself for thinking that he had any kind of rapport with Louise and took out his phone to text her. He glanced across the lobby and followed her path inside the bar door. He was too uneasy with what he had just heard to be able to face her. The thoughts of her, his Louise, spending the night with this Alex guy made him want to leave. He gulped back the remainder of his beer; wiped his mouth with the back of his hand and composed his text.

Inside the bar, Louise waited till the barman looked in her direction and held her beer bottle up to signal another. '208,' she said to him when he handed her the bottle and he put it on her tab. She found a table, away from the TV's and pulled out her phone. She could have taken Kelly to see Alex's gig, but she didn't want to, she was looking forward to having a quiet meal with him instead, and besides, she was still feeling a little tender and needed a quiet night, and Alex's gig was guaranteed to be anything but. A chance to have dinner again with Kelly was far more appealing.

Kelly deleted the third attempt at a text to Louise; he couldn't find a way of saying what he wanted, not without offending her. He picked at the label on his bottle, leaving a mess on the glass coffee table in front of him.

> Won't make it tonight. Catch you in the morning for breakfast, 8 a.m.

He pressed send. He'd go for a swim instead, he decided. Maybe order some room service. Let her wait on her own for her booty call.

Louise lifted her phone to read his text. She sat up straighter when she read his blow-off. 'Shit,' she muttered under her breath, she was disappointed. She shook her bottle to check how much was left; she had barely taken a mouthful. She tutted and left the green, long-neck bottle standing back at the bar. She hadn't the heart to sit there on her own and headed back to her room. If the truth be told, a good night's sleep was just what she needed, as disappointed as she was. She kicked off her boots and sat on the edge of her bed. Opened her phone and responded. She climbed out of her clothes, leaving them where they fell and flopped into her bed, not giving anyone or anything a second thought.

With each length of the twenty-metre pool, Kelly grew more agitated and consumed with jealousy. The annoyance that he had hoped to wash away with relentless lengths of the swimming pool hadn't budged. If anything, the cold water coupled with the adrenaline coursing through his body had intensified his jealousy, so he abandoned his usual gruelling training schedule, dried himself off and returned to his room. He wasn't in the humour to do anything else.

He stalled outside her room as he walked towards his own and listened, wondering if she was alone. Afraid to find out, he continued past and slipped inside his own door, his imagination doing far more damage to his mood than reality could. He couldn't understand why he hadn't realised before, realised that he liked her, in fact realised that he wanted to be with her. Had she, he wondered, or was it all in his head.

Back in his room, he took a towel from the rack and rubbed his wet hair, drying away the excess water that had gathered on the tips of the strands and kicked off his flip-flops by the bed. He reached for the remote, flung his legs across the sheets and punched his pillows into place behind his back. He was going to have to leave the volume on all night, he thought, the last thing he wanted to hear was any comings or goings in the room next door. It was then he noticed the message on his phone.

> Can't believe you stood me up! Pity. See you in the morn. Lou X

Kelly read and reread the message four more times. He couldn't decide what she had meant. He had never seen her sign off as Lou before, and the kiss, that was a first. He wondered did she intend the message for him, he couldn't decide and he surely wasn't going to be able to sleep. It was going to be a long night.

*

The next morning, Louise looked at her watch for the second time in as many minutes. It wasn't like Kelly to be late. In truth, it wasn't like him to have stood her up last night either, so she intended to have a go at him, that's if he ever showed up. They needed to be in the station in forty minutes. And if at all possible, she wanted to be there early, so she didn't have to run the gauntlet of ex-colleagues milling around the common rooms up there.

'There you are, what's the story?' Louise was buttering her toast when he arrived.

'No story.' Kelly was cool as he answered her.

She looked at him, not afraid to hold his gaze. 'What happened to you last night?' she asked, the early night had done her the world of good and she was fresh and sharp.

'Just something… something came up.' He didn't elaborate and poured himself some tea.

'Something happen?' Louise was perplexed, he was unusually quiet.

'Nope.' His expression was like a neon sign, a flashing annoying light that was telling her something was off. 'Just had a few calls to make, had a swim and went to bed, you do anything?' he continued.

'Eh, no, had an early night,' she answered. She could tell that he didn't believe her. Irked by his attitude and confused by his responses she immersed herself in thoughts of work instead. 'Right then, want to talk strategy, about the case?'

'Of course,' he answered. The open neck on her blouse had caught his eye. Her skin looked soft underneath it. He wanted to reach across and touch it, he wondered had Alex done so, last night. He didn't hear the question she had asked him.

'Hello, Kelly, calling Tony Kelly, what the fuck is the matter with you this morning?' She waved her hands at him dismissively.

'What, eh, sorry, I was just thinking about something.' Kelly tried not to be as obvious and adjusted his expression. He stared past her shoulder, from the dining area out to the lobby. Dublin was looking mighty bright and shiny through the floor-to-ceiling windows. He screwed his eyes shut and waited for his vision to reset, he was sure he had just seen someone the very same as Louise in the lobby even though she was sitting in front of him. He opened his eyes and fixed on the woman again, waiting for her to turn so he could see her once more. He looked startled when she turned and walked towards them. 'Eh, Louise.' He looked at Louise and then at the woman walking towards them. Louise turned to follow his stare.

'Oh, my God,' she exclaimed and jumped to her feet, Kelly followed.

'What are you doing here?' Louise asked her excitedly.

Kelly stood behind her, confused.

'Oh, I feel bad about last night; I just wanted to catch you before you head to work.'

Kelly was stunned looking at both of them.

'You needn't have, I told you I was fine,' Louise said to the woman, hugging her again.

Kelly moved back to his seat, wondering what the hell was going on.

'Oh, em, let me introduce you.' Louise pulled the woman by the hand over to their table.

'Kelly, this is my baby sister.' The women looked at each other; the family resemblance was striking right down to their smiles. 'Alex.' Alex extended her hand to Kelly. 'Alex, this is

Tony Kelly,' Louise said. 'Here sit down and have some brekkie with us.'

'Alex,' Kelly reached out his hand, 'your sister,' He looked at Louise. 'I didn't realise.' He shook his head. He scoured his memory looking for a mention of her sister. He vaguely remembered her talking about an Alexandra, how stupid had he been not to make the connection. If it had been a case he had been working on and missed an obvious clue like that he would have never lived it down. 'I think I remember a sailing story with Alexandra or something last summer?' Louise smiled that he remembered. 'Lovely to meet you Alexandra,' he said, relieved to find that the Alex, Louise had been talking to on the phone last night was her sister.

'You better call her, Alex.' Louise glanced sideways at her sister. 'She's only Alexandra when she's in trouble.' Both sisters smiled.

'I didn't know you guys had plans today?' Kelly said.

'Well, if you hadn't have stood me up last night, you might have.' Louise was curt in her reply; Alex could sense a frisson of tension between them.

'You stood her up too.' Alex cringed as she looked at Kelly. 'So did I, I was supposed to come over and spend the night with her, but it was after three when we finished up the gig and then we went to an Early House,' Alex said, apologising to Louise as she explained.

Kelly felt awful; he scolded himself for his stupidity in silence. It hadn't occurred to him that Alex could be a girl, let alone Louise's sister. He felt like a right prick now, and not to mention the opportunity he had missed at the chance to spend the night with her.

'I'm...' he hesitated. 'Don't mind me, Alex,' Kelly smiled tautly, embarrassed at how he must have looked to Louise.

'I'm going to go and let you girls catch up.' He shook Alex's hand again. 'I'll see you over there, Louise, there's no rush, not meeting the Inspector till lunch.' He placed his hand on her shoulder as he left. He took his phone from his pocket and sent Louise a text.

> Sorry, didn't get a chance to explain. No need for you to come in early, why don't you leave it till one and we'll get our strategy together then for the interviews.

Louise didn't answer him, but Kelly was expecting that, at least he had called that one right, he thought.

Chapter 18

September – 1970

'Who is the father, Tim, you need to tell us,' Mary McGrath probes, a little softer than before.

'I can't. I'll take her away, to Dublin with me, nobody need know anything. I'll look after her.' Tim walks towards the door, desperate to leave. 'I'll be leaving for college in a week when I get the cutting done, I'll bring her with me.' He sighed. 'And the baby.'

'No, Tim, you can't, please relax, sit down, we'll help you.' Mary's words don't get through. 'She can't go anywhere Tim, not tonight, she's too weak.'

'I can, I'll bring her to college with me. I'll help her look after the baby, we'll do it together.'

Thomas blocks the door. 'It's okay, son, let your sister rest, we know it's not your fault.' Thomas's voice is less severe, almost as sympathetic as his wife's. 'We know the auld fella is a bit of a bully,' Thomas says, referring to Tim and Rose's father. 'Sit down; we've all had a shock, but none as much as the fourteen-year-old girl up in the bed.' He places his hand on Tim's shoulder and walks him back to his chair. He keeps his hand on his shoulder as though he needs to keep it there for balance. 'Mary, maybe the chap would love a cup of tea.' He lifts his eyebrows at his wife to follow his lead. 'Now, with the women out of the way, talk to me, Tim, man to man.' Thomas takes the chair opposite him, sensing he is about to get through.

'I don't know,' Tim shrugs, reluctant to tell him.

Thomas pushes a little harder. 'We'll help you, you know, you just have to say, we won't breathe a word.'

'I don't know if she even knew she was pregnant herself.' Tim pauses. 'It wasn't her fault, you know, he took her, he…' The corners of his mouth reached down towards his neck and air raced shallowly through his lungs.

'Who? Your father?' Thomas asks.

'No, he's never… he only… he's just angry.'

Thomas can't be sure but from what he can understand, Tim wasn't blaming his father, not for anything more than being violent anyhow. 'Who, Tim, who did this, if not your father?'

'Patrick, it was that bastard, Patrick.' Tim's eyes fill with sadness. He drops his head into his hands and cries. 'He had her,' Tim says. 'He raped her.' It is easier for him to say the second time but still, Tim's shoulders collapse over his chest as the air from his lungs escapes, carrying with it every ounce of hurt and disgust he had stored.

Thomas has no words to comfort him, because there are none. 'Does your father know?' he asks.

'No.' Tim lifts the arm of his T-shirt and wipes his eyes. 'We could never have told him, he would have killed Rose, or me, and then he would have killed Patrick.'

'And your mother?'

'She wouldn't have done anything even if we did tell her,' Tim says. Thomas can hear the bitterness in his voice. 'You know my mother hasn't been well?' Tim says.

'I do.' Thomas doesn't elaborate as to the rumours about how Maeve Fitzpatrick was suffering with her nerves or about how nobody would blame her, having to put up with the muck savages of Fitzpatrick men.

*

Mrs McGrath gently pushes back the bedroom door.

'I'm awake,' I say weakly.

Mrs McGrath smiles. The baby is fast asleep in my arms, swaddled in a dark green towel. The room is dimly lit and in the darkness of night I can see out to the starry sky and the round full moon through the opened curtains. Fat salty tears bounce down my cheeks.

'Oh now, sweetheart, it's okay. You don't need to cry. It's all going to be okay. It hadn't taken Thomas long to tell her what Tim had told him in the front room downstairs. We've been speaking to Tim, he's explained everything,' Mrs McGrath says gently. 'Did you know the baby was coming?'

I shake my head. 'Not really,' I mutter desperately. 'Well', I hesitate. 'Not at first but then, I didn't know what to do.'

'You had no one to talk to'. Mrs McGrath affirming that she understood and hot tears well inside my eyes. 'You poor darling'. Mrs McGrath's voice is soft and kind which makes me want to cry more.

'Do you think you will be able to look after him?' Mrs McGrath asks.

'No,' I sob. 'I don't know'. Ever since I realised I was pregnant, I have spent my time wishing it not to be true, I hadn't got as far as wondering what I would do next.

'Well don't you worry, Thomas and I will see what we can do to help you. Are you ready to see Tim?' she says, smiling.

I nod, embarrassed.

Mrs McGrath opens the door and Tim walks in, he looks at the baby and looks at me, then he sits by my side, holding my hand. We both watch silently as Mrs McGrath opens the bedroom door and leaves. We hear her footsteps on the stairs and the sound of muffled voices from the good room downstairs.

*

'The baby is only tiny. Four pounds, maybe five at the most,' Mary says to Thomas, waiting for a reply. 'We can't send her back up with him. Fitzpatrick will kill her.'

'I know, but what choice do we have, Mary?' Thomas says.

'We can help them get to Dublin maybe, get out of that hellhole up there.' Mary runs her fingers through her hair, exasperated. 'They've... well Rose especially, has suffered enough at the hands of those godforsaken Fitzpatrick savages.' Mary's voice breaks. 'Just as well that, Patrick, is gone missing, otherwise I'd go down myself and strangle him,' she finishes.

'Our hands are tied though, Mary, it is not our decision to make,' Thomas says reluctantly. 'We can help them with money, but what will Rose do when Tim is in college? How will she hide from the schools. She has two years before she can leave.'

'Maybe I could mind the baby for her?' Mary suggests.

'Get real, Mary, how could you mind the baby and they all the way up in Dublin,' Thomas answers. 'What about those mother and baby homes, are they still going?'

'No,' Mary shakes her head. St. Columba's County home would have been the closet but if the rumours were anything to go by, Mrs McGrath would have no part in placing anyone in the care of the nuns up there, and definitely not a sweet, fourteen year old girl who found herself pregnant through no fault of her own. 'What if we kept the baby…' she pauses. 'As our own?'

'Don't be ridiculous, Mary, you can't just take the girl's baby, and anyway the doctors would know that he wasn't yours, wouldn't they have to check you…' he draws circles in the air with his hands, 'and everything?' Thomas panics.

'What's the alternative, Thomas?'

'I don't know, Mary, but seriously, what would you say, oh by the way, I brought a new baby last night, here it is.'

'Don't be smart, Thomas, I'm trying to figure it out as best I can,' Mary answers. 'And besides, it's perfectly reasonable to have people think I have had another baby, I'm only forty years of age.'

'Forty years of age and not pregnant for the past nine months,' Thomas says.

'But that's just it, the baby is premature, which could be why I haven't told anyone yet. I can say the baby arrived three months too soon.'

'And what about when the doctor wants to check you?'

'I won't let him, I didn't let him check me on George and he was fine with it, considering I am a nurse.'

'I don't know, Mary, and what about the future? When Rose comes back looking for her baby, what will you say then?'

'She won't.'

'You don't know that.'

'No, but I do know that that child, those children, up in that bedroom have had a lifetime of sorrows in a handful of years and it will only get worse for them if we do nothing.'

'I don't know, Rose,' Thomas shrugs his shoulders in desperation. 'I don't know.'

*

Tim sits gazing at the baby with tears shimmering in his eyes. I doze comfortably with him by my side as darkness tiptoes through the window.

'I may go back up, otherwise Father will want to know why the combine is sitting idly in the field.'

'I'm sorry, Tim.' I can't look him in the eye.

'Don't, Rosie.' He holds my face in his hands. 'None of this is your fault, do you hear me, none.' He stands, afraid to touch the baby. 'I'll come back. Mrs McGrath says you can't leave yet. I'll wait for Father to go out and come back up for you then, okay?' he says.

'Okay,' I say. I want to ask him about his plan but I'm afraid of the answer. I'm afraid that Tim's plan won't work, not now with a baby.

The door opens and Mrs and Mr McGrath sneak in.

'We just wanted to talk to you before you go, Tim, if that's okay?'

'Sure.' Tim says, looking at me. He is conscious of the time and afraid of what they need to say.

'We've been thinking, we've had a chat downstairs, and we want to help.'

Tim and I listen.

'If you want, but only if you want…' Mrs McGrath looks at her husband's face as though she's waiting for the final confirmation, 'we can rear the baby for you.' She pauses, knowing the weight of what she is saying. Her husband pats her hand to continue. 'We can keep the little mite.' She rubs the baby's back and smiles, neither I nor Tim speak and she continues. 'Of course, we would have to get you to promise to never speak of it again, and I mean promise.' She looks at Tim first and then back at me. 'The baby would be reared as a McGrath and would never know...' she clears her throat, 'how he was conceived.' She looks at me for a long time, there are tears in her eyes. 'For the baby's good, but also for yours, darling.' She lifts my free hand and rubs her own cheek with it. 'Tim,' she turns slightly so that she sees him more clearly, 'you are going to college and Rose here still has two more years in school. If she disappears, they'll look for her. The state will send someone to your house and all manner of trouble might arise out of it.' She looks at our expressions, trying her best to understand them. 'I don't mean to frighten you, really I don't, but how do you think you can survive in Dublin without any money. Tim, you'll be a student, in student digs, how will you keep Rose?'

Tim shrugs.

'There's another bit to the plan, our way of helping if you like,' Mrs McGrath looks at her husband who nods his head. 'The school, where I went, it's a boarding school, and if you like, Rose, I can arrange for you to finish off your two years there, but only if you want to.' She pauses. 'I could explain it to your mother, that it's a scholarship, full-board and tuition. The letters would come from the school. You would only have to come home at holidays or weekends, or not at all, if you preferred.'

'I don't know, Mrs McGrath, could I talk to Rose alone?' Tim says.

'Sure. But listen, it's only if you want to. Do you understand?' Thomas says as he walks his wife from his room.

Chapter 19

Thursday Morning – 2016

Tim and Rose followed the uniform Garda to the meeting room just off the outer office on the ground floor. They had spent most of the previous evening sorting through their memories together, searching through the locked vaults of time, filtering the information that they felt comfortable talking about.

Rose was anxious. Tim pulled a conference chair from the table and gestured for her to sit down. He was too tense to sit himself. It didn't help that the windows were closed and the room was airless. He poured himself water from the cooler and waited.

'Right then,' Detective Kennedy entered the room, followed closely by Detective Kelly. Louise could tell by the reaction of both the Fitzpatricks' faces that they weren't expecting her. That gave her a little rush. 'Rose Fitzpatrick, I presume.'

Detective Kennedy's face was friendly, unlike that of Detective Kelly's, Rose noted.

Tim finally took a seat.

'It's O' Reilly,' Rose corrected as she shook Louise's hand.

'Of course, sorry about that.' Louise smiled. 'Would you like to follow me?' she instructed.

'Sure,' Rose answered.

Tim stood to follow also.

'Timothy, we'll stay in this room.' Detective Kelly could make out Tim's unease with the separate interviews and was a little satisfied with the outcome of his plan. 'We like to conduct the interviews separately, hope that's okay?'

Tim had no choice but to consent and nodded discontentedly.

'Right then, let's get going, Timothy.'

It suited Tim that Kelly only knew him as Timothy as opposed to Tim, although he would have preferred Mr Fitzpatrick, it was definitely a power play on Kelly's behalf not to use it. Half expecting him to remain standing so that he could be taller than him, Tim was surprised when Kelly took the chair opposite him across the table.

'I can confirm that the body is that of your missing uncle Patrick Fitzpatrick, but I think you already knew that.'

'I didn't.' Tim had decided to answer politely and not elaborate, he was off to a good start. 'Not for definite.'

'The coroner will be contacting you later. They are releasing the remains, you know, so you can give him a burial. I'm sure you'll want to give him a proper send-off.'

Tim was sure he could taste the bitterness from Kelly's words. He didn't answer.

'Can you describe the last time you saw your uncle?'

'I can't really remember.' That was Tim's first lie. 'I suppose, I must have seen him that day out with the lambs, but I'm not a hundred per cent sure, it was nearly fifty years ago.' Tim was conscious of the same question being asked of Rose and how she might answer it. He had advised Rose to use the 'nearly fifty years ago' reference that his solicitor had told him to use. They had also decided to be truthful about the abuse, but only if there was no other way to explain something.

'You didn't see him back at his house or back at your house that evening?'

'Like I said, I can't really remember, it's fifty years ago,' Tim said again.

'Forty-six.' Kelly liked to be precise. 'Did you see him go out that evening?'

'No,' Tim answered succinctly; that was the truth.

'What's your recollection then of what happened that night?' Detective Kelly had honed his interrogating skills to a fine art. He prided himself on being able to draw the deepest secrets from anyone. He knew Tim would be a difficult nut to crack, but he wasn't going to let that stop him.

'All I remember is my father, Liam, going out to the pub, my mother, Maeve, in her room, Rose in her room and me in mine. I presume my uncle went to the pub, but I didn't see him go there, or after that, for that matter.' Tim sipped from the white plastic cup of water, squeezing the sides just enough for the plastic to rattle. It was hard to resist the urge to repeat the noise, much like clicking the top of a pen. His tongue had gone a little dry. 'As far as I knew, he had gone to Liverpool and I never questioned it.' Tim ran his fingers through his hair. 'I never had any reason to.'

'How'd you know that, Liverpool?'

'My father said it. I remember him telling people at the time that Patrick had gone to Liverpool, that's all.' Tim drew a deep breath.

'Tell me about your father?'

'What do you want to know?' Tim paced his answer; his measured reply at odds with the chaos that had formed a knot inside his gut.

'Did Liam and Patrick work well together, did they get on?' Kelly wanted to push for more but he was finding Tim a little hard to read. He could almost see the cogs turn over behind Tim's eyes as he considered every word.

'They did, I suppose. I don't really know.'

'And what about your mother, Maeve?'

'What about her?' Tim asked.

'Did she get on with Patrick?'

'My mother wasn't well, she barely left the house for the two years before Patrick went missing so,' Tim shook his head, 'I don't know, I can't remember, really.'

'And your mother and father passed, in 1986 and 1987,' Kelly turned the page over in front of him.

'Yes,' Tim answered. 'Mother was first, and then my father the year later.'

'So, your uncle was certified missing, presumed dead, while your father was still alive. It was your father's solicitor who handled the proceedings?'

'Yes.' Tim held himself from elaborating. His solicitor had advised him to, it was best to only answer what was asked of him.

'Unusual theory don't you think though, that a man, your uncle, just walks away, from a fortune to take up a life in Liverpool, and convenient for your father too that he didn't take his fifty per cent share with him.'

'He wouldn't have seen it that way, he would have seen it as double the work,' Tim said. He could hear his father's complaints in his memory.

'Would your father have killed Patrick?'

'I have no idea.' No, is what Tim really wanted to say but he knew that if he was sure about that fact, Kelly would presume he had known who did.

'Would he have had reason to kill him?'

'I have no idea.' Everybody, had a reason to kill Patrick is how he would have liked to answer.

'And you didn't question it either when you inherited the whole estate, were you not worried that your uncle could come back and claim what was rightfully his, or maybe if he had children of his own? Or did you know then…' Kelly paused for the accusation to sink in, 'that he wouldn't be coming back?'

'Like I said before, that was all arranged by my father's solicitor, in my father's time.'

'Yes, you did say.' Kelly silenced himself deliberately. It was usually the gaps that gave more information than the questions. He watched as Timothy's frown grew across his forehead. He was waiting to ask his next question. 'Do you need more water?' Kelly watched as Tim drained the last droplet from his cup, clicking the plastic as he squeezed.

'No,' Tim answered even though he could have drunk a gallon in one gulp.

'Can you explain to me though, why you place such little value on the Estate?' Kelly was leading nicely to where he wanted to be.

Tim shrugged. 'The Farm was valued for the market at the time,' he answered. That was Tim's second lie.

'You have to admit, it looks peculiar, you selling up for nearly half of what it's worth and four months later the *forty-six*-year-old body of your uncle turns up in your ditch?'

'I suppose it does.' He paused. 'And it's not my ditch, by the way,' Tim confirmed. 'We didn't need the money. We decided to sell. That's the sum total of the reasoning.' Tim would have finished off his statement with the phrase 'that's not a crime', had his solicitor not briefed him not to. 'Our agent took into account the remedial works that the McGraths had undertaken; when they first leased the farm, the farmhouse was derelict.'

'Can I ask, what you did with the money?'

'I don't see what that has to do with the investigation?' Tim answered, reluctant to give him an answer, not because he had anything to hide but because it was none of Detective Kelly's business.

'Okay, that's fine, if you don't want to answer, there must be a reason, and that's fine. We'll find out another way.' Kelly pushed just enough buttons to rise Tim's temper another degree more. Tim whipped off his glasses and rubbed his eyes. 'I wonder is your sister doing okay, in her interview, without you.'

Kelly's insinuations were hard to swallow.

'I'm sure she's fine.' Tim used every restraint, not to react to him.

'Are you sure there is nothing else that has slipped your mind?' Kelly asked, intimating his disbelieve and wrapping it loosely in a veil of false concern for him. 'Maybe I'll give you a moment to have a think on your own.'

'Look, Detective Kelly,' Tim wished he didn't feel so constrained with his answers. He would much rather have said, 'the bastard got was he deserved,' or something along those lines, but telling Kelly about the fight would only prop up his, already circumstantial, case. He wasn't about to confess to giving Patrick the hiding that he deserved. He wasn't to know that his uncle had lain in the ditch all these years. He just presumed that he took off, like he warned him. If he had have known that he was lying in the ditch, he might have celebrated it. 'I want to see justice done, as much as you do.' He was trying to say the words that he needed to say to get Kelly off this merry-go-round. 'I wasn't close to him, none of us were.'

His eyes flickered in the direction of the next room. 'But none of us had anything to do with how he ended up in the ditch. And that's…' He stopped before he uttered the next phrase, he remembered 'the truth' being on the list of things that his solicitor had told him not to say. 'That's all I know,' he said.

'That'll do for now.' Kelly jotted down some more thoughts in his notebook and placed it firmly in his back pocket. 'I'll organise some tea to be sent in to you.' Kelly stood, stared at Tim for a moment and spoke again after a short pause. 'Give you a chance to see if you can remember anything else.'

Kelly texted Louise as arranged and they met down the hall in another room.

'Well, what do you think?' Kelly said.

Louise sat agitated on a grey plastic chair that was bolted to the ground feeling worn out from the detail she had just heard.

'That wasn't pleasant.' Louise rubbed her eyes and pushed her fringe to the side. Straggles of black hair had escaped from her ponytail and fell in wisps down the sides of her face. Kelly looked at her expectantly, waiting for her to elaborate. 'It's no wonder no one missed him or reported him missing all those years ago. He raped her, as a child of fourteen years of age, Kelly.' Louise, shook her head and glared back at him. 'Did you send some tea and coffee into them?' she asked. She was feeling sorry for Rose.

'I did,' Kelly answered. He paused for a moment. 'How'd she tell you that?'

'As agreed, I asked her when was the last time she saw him. She said in his cottage around dinner time on the day he disappeared. He had raped her when she brought his dinner down to him.' Louise knew she was telling the truth.

'Did she say if Timothy knew about it?'

'She says she told him afterwards,' Louise answered.

'Well then, there's your motive.' Kelly was almost celebrating. 'Big brother to the rescue, finds his pervert uncle and kicks him to death for touching his baby sister. Timothy never mentioned anything.' He pulled his notebook from his back pocket and wrote some more notes. 'But he wouldn't, would he, points the finger directly at him.'

Despite Louise's hard outer shell, she was a compassionate girl, and Rose's story had wrenched on her.

'Makes sense.' Kelly paced the room over to the window and back. 'What doesn't make sense though, is why bury him on the land, right under your own nose?'

'Or, you have to ask, if you knew there was a body buried on your land, why sell it, why take the risk that it would be discovered by someone else?' Louise said matter-of-factly. That was the part she couldn't understand. 'If Timothy Fitzpatrick, or Rose for that matter, knew that the body was buried on their land, the last thing they would do is sell it, surely.'

'True, it doesn't make sense that you'd take that risk.' Kelly flicked through the tattered pages. He was getting further away from what he wanted to hear.

'Rose mentioned the father, Liam.'

'What did she say?'

'Well he was a bit of a bully himself, prone to take out the belt when it suited him. But as far as her father was concerned, Patrick had most likely left for Liverpool, he had been mouthing off all night about it.'

'Timothy said something similar'

'Apparently, Patrick was prone to disappearing, wasn't unusual for him to end up in a nearby town on a drinking binge and not come back for a few days. She used to hate it, she said, because it meant that Tim had to work more on the farm, and she was left on her own.'

‘Mmm, it does feed into the “nobody batting an eyelid” when he disappeared theory,’ Kelly conceded. ‘Do you think they’ve stewed enough.’

‘I do,’ Louise answered.

‘Actually, before we go back in, did you ask Rose why they sold Fitzpatrick Estate so cheaply?’

‘I did, she just said she had no interest in anything to do with it. She said, once she left Kilkenny, she never looked back. She didn’t even keep the money for herself. Put it in a trust for her daughter,’ Louise checked her note. ‘Lizzie is the daughter. She works away most of the time, mainly based in London, around the same age as myself.’

‘Before, we go back in,’ Kelly scratched his head. It was a move she saw him do on the rare occasion when he was nervous. ‘Did your sister get off okay?’

‘Yeah.’ Louise was waiting for something more than a polite reference to her family. As he said himself, he didn’t do small talk.

‘Well, I just wanted to say, I’m sorry for being a bit of…’ He paused and Louise interjected.

‘A bit of a prick.’ She shrugged her shoulders. ‘Or arsehole,’ she offered. ‘For standing me up.’

‘Yeah, I deserved that.’ He smiled at her brashness. ‘But I was going to say a bit “off” earlier, but yours work just as well.’ He was delighted to see that she smiled. ‘And I’ll make it up to you later, I’m bringing you for dinner, right. I want to explain to you what happened.’ He raised his eyebrows slightly, narrowly escaping another onslaught.

‘I can’t.’ Louise was glad he had made an effort to make amends and was interested in hearing what he had to say but couldn’t break her plans. ‘I’ve told my sister, I’ll meet up with her later, around eight,’ she added.

'Good, perfect,' Kelly answered. 'I'll take you out for something at six and then your sister can meet you at eight, that way we are all happy.'

'Okay then,' Louise said. 'We may go back in.'

'Enjoy your tea?' Kelly asked Tim when he re-entered the room.

'Thank you.' Tim nodded and placed the cup back on the tray.

'Just a few more questions and then I think we have everything we need for now. The money from the sale…' He opened his notebook on a blank page, as though he was reading from notes that he had already taken.

'Yeah,' Tim answered.

'Lizzie O'Reilly, your niece, she did very well out of it.' Kelly was working on a hunch that if Rose wanted nothing to do with the fortune, Tim might have felt the same.

'And?' Tim answered, one of his eyebrows cocked higher than the other.

'And you gave yours to Lizzie as well,' Kelly took a guess. His statements were far more effective at times than actual questions could be and this was one of those times.

'What's that got to do with it?'

'Just trying to get a picture, that's all.' Kelly took some notes. He didn't know yet if it was of any relevance, he'd decide that later. 'Did you kill your uncle?' Kelly asked in an attempt to shock him.

'Of course not,' Tim answered.

'Do you know who did?' Kelly cleared his throat.

'No,' Tim said. One thing was for sure, Patrick got what he deserved and if Tim did know what had happened to his uncle, he sure as hell wasn't going to tell Detective Kelly about it.

Chapter 20

Thursday Evening – 2016

Lucas's research and investigation in to the case had grown massively since he had last spoken to Marie and in other circumstances, he would have jumped at the chance to cover the story but something about this case felt a little too close to home. As much as he wanted to redeem himself with Marie, he was more interested in showing Lizzie that he was prepared to walk away from a story for her. It was to do with her family after all, and once stones are uncovered, it would be very hard to cover them over again. He dialled Marie's mobile, now that he had saved her number.

Marie checked she was alone and pressed to answer.

'Marie, hi,' Lucas started. 'The thing is, I'm not sure I'm going to be able to help, I really don't think you need me digging around on a story like this, I think it'll go away by itself.' He wasn't about to tell Marie that the more he considered how his involvement might have impacted on Lizzie, the more he was reluctant to help.

'Oh, please Lucas, I really do need you to cover this.' Marie grew anxious. She had hoped that he would jump at the chance on the merit of the case alone, she didn't want to have to tell him the rest of the secret and the real reason behind why she had contacted him.

'Look, you know as well as I do, that with the story as it stands, it'll be dead in a day or two,' he said.

'Lucas, there is more, and I really wanted to talk to you face to face about it.'

He could hear the panic in her voice. 'Marie, if there is more to the story, or if you are afraid of something getting out, you can tell me.'

'Oh, Lucas, I don't know, I'd just feel better looking you in the eye, it's very sensitive stuff, please you have to come.'

'You need to tell me what it is.' Lucas exhaled, his intention to tell her no was rapidly fading and the desperation in her voice left him no choice.

'Is this line secure?' she asked him.

'Jesus,' he laughed nervously, 'conversations that start like that either end up in Scotland Yard or the graveyard. What type of trouble are you in, or should I say, is Michael in?' He sat back at his desk and clicked on his pen. He kept an eye on the time, he was conscious of Lizzie finishing work soon and he wanted to meet her, he didn't like the idea of her being unhappy with him. 'No, no one is monitoring my calls, not that I know of anyhow.'

'Will you come over then, if I tell you?' Marie pleaded.

Lucas agreed. It was a halfhearted promise that he hoped he wouldn't have to follow through, not if he wanted to show Lizzie how much she meant to him.

Marie drew a deep breath and proceeded to tell him all that she knew; the details of the letter, the instructions from her mother in-law and the reason, the real reason, why she didn't want the press to dig too deeply.

If her story hadn't been compelling before, with the gaps well and truly filled in, Lucas knew now he had no choice but to help.

'Jesus,' Lucas said. 'And he has no idea?' He was incredulous that Marie was the only one who had known.

'No, and the last thing we want is for some rogue reporter finding out and telling Michael.'

'The thing is,' he rubbed his head, 'I'm going to pay the price for this personally and I only hope that she will understand when it's all over.'

'Who?' Marie said.

'My girlfriend, Lizzie, who just happens to be the daughter of Rose Fitzpatrick.'

*

Sheets of rain plummeted from the sky and bounced from the footpaths like a scene from *Singing in the Rain*, but it was far from dancing that Lizzie felt like doing. She stood outside her offices on Jermyn Street and waved frantically at the passing cabs, ignoring the ringing from her bag. Every single cab was full.

'Damn it,' she said, dodging the muddy spray as she jumped backwards. Her fitted Diane von Furstenberg dress would be ruined if it got any wetter, she sighed. The blazer she wore over it barely covered her, so she retreated back inside the doorway and waited for the rain to ease. Tumultuous dark clouds blustered across the sky, making London seem even greyer and angrier than it normally was. She reached into her bag and rooted for her phone. As she suspected, the missed calls were from Lucas. She cleared the backlog and zipped it back inside. He could wait, she was nothing if not strong-willed, like her mother, her father would have said.

Lizzie couldn't quite put her finger on exactly what it was that she was discontented about, not just today, but in general. Since she had moved to London, she had always missed home, but lately the homesick feeling had felt a little more raw. She couldn't exactly blame her job, it was good, as was the money, but she wasn't enjoying it and even though she had moved up the corporate ladder, there just wasn't much satisfaction in it for her. She tried to remember if there ever was. She was sure she liked London at some stage in her career, didn't she? Maybe she was just bored or maybe it was because of missing home. She couldn't decide and the more she watched the rain plop in massive droplets around her, the more her memories faded to Dublin, of her mum and her dad and how she missed him.

Peering outside the shelter of the doorway, she glanced up and down the street, the rain was easing, only slightly, but every cab was still whizzing by. In spite of her tailored dress and high-heeled shoes, she decided to make a run for Piccadilly station; it was then that a cab pulled up to the kerb.

'Oh,' she waved, attracting the driver's attention. 'Great,' she said out loud, claiming the cab as hers. She reached across for the door and jumped in.

Lucas was inside.

'What are you doing here?' she asked; she wasn't sure if she was grateful or infuriated and even though, since she left him on Wednesday morning, he had attempted to phone her numerous times, she hadn't spoken to him. She shook tiny droplets from her hair and brushed the wetness from her legs. The windows steamed up.

'I knew it would be impossible to get a cab down here, so I jumped in one outside my building and thought I'd collect you,' he said.

Lizzie flicked her fringe vigorously and tiny droplets sprinkled down her face, it was impossible to fix it without a mirror.

'Did you not see my calls, I was afraid I'd miss you.'

'If it hadn't been raining so heavy, you would have,' she answered. She didn't elaborate on whether she had seen the calls or not. As a matter of fact if she hadn't met Lucas, some six months before, she wondered would she have made the decision to leave London by now and return home like she wanted to; he had been the only thing she had wanted to stay for. But the excitement that she had felt since she had first met him had been dampened and in its place a seed of discontent had begun to sprout. He had let her down, just as London had, she thought. Both he and London had lost its appeal.

'Will you come back with me, we'll order in,' he said, hoping that the monotonous day that she spent in the office had softened her.

'Piccadilly, please.' She ignored his pleas and instructed the driver to take her to the station. 'I need to get home and pack.' She looked at him for the first time since she sat in the cab. It had been a long day. 'My flight is in the morning,' she clarified.

'I'll make sure you get home, in time,' he said, pleading with his eyes. 'I promise,' he said.

'Okay', she answered not returning his gaze. Lucas confirmed his address to the cab driver before Lizzie had a chance to change her mind.

The stale stench of the cab had blended with her wet clothes creating a vacuum of vomit-inducing odours and Lizzie had never been as relieved to pull up outside Lucas's building. Her waist-length hair was plastered to her head and she was sure, even though she couldn't check, that her mascara was likely to be running down her face.

'After you,' Lucas said as he opened the apartment door.

She nodded and forced a smile. 'I'm just,' she had toyed with the idea of continuing her silent treatment but couldn't do it, 'going to get out of these,' she said, turning to look at him. She wasn't the type to play games, what you saw was what you got with Lizzie. 'We can talk then,' she reassured him. Lizzie's voice was soft, defeated almost, as she slinked inside the bedroom.

Without responding, Lucas continued to the fridge and pulled out a chilled bottle of wine. He gulped the first glass standing by the pale grey granite countertop before he poured one for her. Topping up his glass, he made his way to the sofa, placing both the full wine glasses on the table in front of him. He watched the daylight fade through the impressive windows from where he sat and the city lights glowed a warm amber through the haze of the raindrops.

'Here,' he said, handing her a glass when she came in; his second glass was already half-empty. 'Or do you want something warmer?' he asked, as she patted her hair dry.

'No.' She sipped a mouthful. 'This is just fine.' She sat beside him on the cream couch. 'This okay?' She motioned towards the gear she was wearing; his sports shorts and sweatshirt.

He nodded; she looked extremely gorgeous in his oversized clothes.

'Listen,' Lucas cleared his throat; he had rehearsed a few approaches and was going with his best pitch. If he had learned anything in journalism it was that he needed to know his audience, pitch the story exactly right. 'I know you think I was taking advantage of the story, which I sort of was,' he said. She watched as his hands moved animatedly when he spoke. 'But, all connections aside…' Her forehead scrunched, warning him to be careful with his words. 'I mean…' he fumbled for a quick second. 'I have a contact from years ago, that has actually asked me to cover the story.' He knew by her expression that she didn't believe him. 'In a sympathetic way, sort of. If you know what I mean,' he said, struggling to find the words.

'Cover a murder story in a sympathetic way,' Lizzie repeated, her tone disapproving. 'I don't get what you mean.'

'It's an old friend, a girl I went to college with,' he said, knowing that it sounded far worse than it actually was.

'Perfect,' Lizzie said, sighing deeply as she considered what to do next. 'So you won't not cover it for me, but you will actually cover it for her,' Lizzie said. 'Is that what you are saying? she asked.

'It's not like that, Lizzie, its different, I mean…' he stumbled through his explanation. His promise to Marie prevented him from telling Lizzie the truth, for now at least, and now more than ever , not only for Marie and Michael's sake but for the Fitzpatricks' as well, there was no way he couldn't get involved.

'That's fine, Lucas.' Lizzie uncurled her legs from under her and rose from the sofa, her bare feet sunk into the deep pile rug. 'I think I'll get that cab now,' she said. 'Can I get these to you, another time?' she asked, her strong voice sliding lower as she pointed to the clothes she wore. She could understand his enquiring mind wanting nothing more than to follow a lead, investigate and report, what she couldn't reconcile was how odd she felt that he didn't consider her first, whether or not she wanted him to cover it, and secondly, and the worst insult yet, that he'd do for some other girl what he wouldn't do for her.

'No, Lizzie, not like this, wait till I explain,' he said, desperate for her to understand.

'No need,' she answered. 'It's okay, I'm not overreacting, I'm just…' She paused. Her thoughts were flipping inside her head. She'd had enough of London and everything to do with it. 'I'm just going home to pack,' she said and left slamming the door behind her.

Chapter 21

Thursday Evening – 2016

Kelly had carefully selected his shirt for the evening. Accustomed as he was to casualwear, he wore his best blue casual shirt and a clean pair of jeans. Louise was used to seeing him dressed down, especially in the evenings, so tonight would be no different. After his quick shower and a brush of his teeth, he grabbed his phone, wallet and key card and made his way to the lift, pausing briefly as he passed Louise's door. 'Fecking eejit,' he muttered to himself, only too aware of the mess he had made the night before.

Louise rooted in the bottom of her Ted Baker make-up bag. She was convinced she had thrown a tester-size perfume spray in yesterday when she'd packed but she couldn't find it. She upended her bag and all its contents on the bed. 'Aha!' she said to herself. 'I told you I had brought it.' She caught her reflection in the desk mirror and laughed. She sprayed the perfume sparingly onto her soft powdery skin.

Kelly checked the clock over the bar and ordered her a beer as he saw her coming. True to form, she was twenty minutes late, he was already on his second beer.

'I hope I kept you waiting,' Louise quipped when she found Kelly at the bar. He appreciated her joke, but threw her an exasperated look anyhow. 'Shall we eat, I'm bloody starving.'

They walked towards the dining area and were shown to their seats.

'You look...' Kelly paused trying to find just the right amount of compliment without sounding too cheesy.

'Lovely?' He pitched the end of the word as though it was a question.

She smiled at him. She knew he meant it.

'Well,' Louise had devilment in her eyes and she had every intention of making Kelly work for his forgiveness, 'what's the explanation for the shitty behaviour last night?'

Kelly shook his head in response. 'Jesus,' he laughed, he supposed he shouldn't have expected anything different, 'would you give me a minute, to order?' He tapped her menu across the table, trying to get her to focus on her food.

She called the waiter by lifting her hand. 'We'll have two steak and chips, well done, and two more bottles of that beer.' She pointed to the beers that Kelly had brought to the table. 'Now,' she smirked at his reaction, 'food is organised, tell me why you were a prick?'

Kelly exhaled and rubbed his face. A black shadow of stubble had spread across his cheeks and chin. There was something mesmerising about the girl, he thought, she blew him away. 'Well,' he laughed, sensibility had abandoned him, 'If you must know,' he couldn't believe he was about to confess to her, 'I was annoyed.' He shook his head at himself, knowing he was putting his head in the lion's mouth but happy to do it anyway, 'I was annoyed because—'

'Two beers.' The waiter placed the beers in front of them. 'Would you like a glass?' he asked Louise.

She was growing impatient; she was very interested in what Kelly had to say. 'No thank you,' she almost barked. 'And neither does he.' She forced a smile on her face, compensating for her sharpness.

'Okay.' The waiter left, not sure if he had offended her or walked in to an argument, either way, he would be careful the next time he had to approach the table.

'You were saying,' Louise urged Kelly to continue.

He took the third bottle and gulped, gaining courage to speak his mind with every swallow. 'I was saying…' He stopped and gazed at her and she didn't look away. Her eyes sparkled with mischief. She wasn't typically beautiful, in the false-eyelashed, fake-tanned, footballer's wife kind of way. It was something far more elusive that she had, that was what made her so attractive. 'Right.' He drew a deep breath. 'I was jealous.' He exhaled as he said it. He played with his napkin on the table, avoiding her gaze. He peeped up at her and she was smiling. He took another gulp from his bottle, and then another. He continued until it was empty and held it aloft so that the waiter could bring another.

'Jealous,' she repeated; she contorted her face, trying her utmost to suppress the grin that was rapidly spreading from ear to ear. 'Of what?'

The waiter returned swapping the empty bottle for the full. 'Would you like some tomato bread?' he asked, to which neither of them replied. They remained looking at each other until he left.

'I overheard you talking to Alex, I thought *she*,' he coughed, 'was a *he*.' He threw his eyes upwards. 'I heard your plans for Alex to come to your hotel room and, well, you know what I thought.' He looked up at her. '*Her* obviously now being your sister, I realise, it was a girly sleepover thing not a man coming to sleep with you kind of thing.' He gestured his hands, knowing that he was rambling. 'And I was green with jealousy at the thought of it.' He put down his bottle, rubbed his hands on his face; the clamminess left a shine on his cheeks. He held her gaze; he couldn't tell how she was reacting. 'There I said it.' He squinted, cringing with embarrassment.

'Kelly, I don't know what to say.' Louise was utterly stumped. She was thrilled he had the same feelings for her as she had for him.

'That's a first.' Kelly felt somewhat lighter than he had in years.

'Very funny,' she whispered. 'Talk about bolt from the blue.' She looked across at his shirt and noticed he looked well. 'Or bolt from the man in blue,' she managed.

'Don't say anything, no need; I'm sure I'll get over it.' He swigged from his bottle, throwing his eyes around the room. She knew he was embarrassed. 'Beer goggles,' he quipped.

'It's just that…' she spoke softly; she knew how hard it must have been for him. 'I have a policy, a rule that I'll never be with anyone from work.'

'That's fine, don't worry about it,' Kelly said. It was cringeworthy, having admitted his feelings to her and then, even though part of him expected it, to be turned down.

'So, it's a good thing,' she reached across the table and touched his hand with hers. 'It's a good thing,' she waited for him to lift his eyes, 'that I have a bit of a reputation for breaking the odd rule here and there.' Her eyes danced in his direction, her smile grew even larger on her face. 'Even my own rules.'

'What… what did you say?'

'I said it's a good thing that, if the reason is good enough, I am prepared to break the rules.' She deliberately spoke with a drawl, mimicking him for being slow on the uptake.

'Really.' Kelly couldn't believe his luck.

'Really.' She smiled; she looked around for the waiter, telling him they had changed their minds. 'Let's go somewhere quieter,' she suggested.

Kelly looked at his watch. His time with her was limited. He couldn't believe what was happening.

*

Just before eight, Alex popped the card in the slot to illuminate Louise's room. The housekeeping team had already drawn the curtains and Louise's clothes were draped messily across the backs of the upholstered chairs. The room had been serviced but there was no mistaking that Louise had been here. Some of her jewellery lay tangled on the dresser and a half-squeezed bottle of moisturiser slouched on the desktop. Alex checked the clock; it wasn't like her not to show up.

*

'You know what's funny?' Next door, Louise disentangled herself from Kelly's clasp.

Kelly lifted the sheet that barely covered them both. 'Eh, no,' he said, smirking, eyeing her naked body next to his under the tunnel the sheet had created.

'Behave, I didn't mean…' Louise playfully sighed and pulled the sheet back over them. 'I mean,' she turned his jaw towards her so that he could look her in the eyes, 'I think it's funny, that we can work with each other, every day,' her finger traced the black and grey hairs that curled on his chest, 'and get on so well.' Kelly shrugged as though that was a matter of opinion. 'Behave, we do get on well.' She slapped him gently. 'I mean,' she opened her eyes wider; she needed him to know that she was serious, 'it's just that we spend all this time together and we barely know anything about each other.'

'We do, we know loads,' Kelly answered. He ran his hand gently over the curve of her hip to her ribcage and back to park his hand across her waist.

'Oh really, you didn't even know I had a sister called Alex,' Louise exclaimed.

'True,' Kelly answered. 'Well what do you want to know, then, shoot.'

'I don't know, what do you want to tell me?' she asked. There were so many questions swimming around her brain.

'There's nothing to tell, what you see with Tony Kelly is what you get,' he said.

She lifted her head from where she lay in the crux of his arm and pushed herself upright on the bed, folding her legs in front of her, and pulled the sheet up over her chest and tucked it around herself.

'Although, if you must know, my legs don't fold like that,' he joked. She continued to look at him, unsatisfied that he was taking her seriously enough. 'I have a feeling though,' Kelly scooched himself up in the bed, placing a pillow behind his back, 'that there is a question that you would like to ask me.'

'I just want to know more, more about Tony, that's all,' Louise said.

'Just ask, and it really feels weird when you call me Tony, I keep thinking I'm in trouble.'

'Well, where do you go every Tuesday afternoon, for instance?' It had been a question she had wanted to ask for months. She wondered at times could it have been AA meetings, but then she never really saw any signs of that, and besides, she was his drinking buddy so if it was AA it wasn't working.

'Really, that's what you want to know.' He smiled at her curiosity. 'Not what my politics are, what the meaning of life is to me, or how much money I have saved.' He ducked as she swiped at him.

'I'm only interested because you won't tell me, and I think you won't tell me because there's something to hide.' She worried that there was something more serious she was missing.

'I've no problem telling you about Tuesdays.'

'Well?' Louise waited.

'On Tuesdays, I spend the afternoon with Annie. Annie is my girl,' Kelly said. 'We normally stay together for the entire afternoon and evening and then I bring her back home. She loves to come to my house, sometimes we cook, sometimes we order in, that's what we do,' he explained. 'It depends on what she feels like.'

'What?' Louise's forehead scrunched. 'Annie?' She shook her head at her own stupidity, how could she not have known. 'You've a daughter?'

'Nope. No children,' he said. 'Annie is my sister, Louise,' Kelly explained, he realised from the shocked expression on Louise's face that she didn't quite understand.

'Your sister?'

'She's my girl,' Kelly smiled as he imagined Annie saying it; '*Tony's girl*' was how she always introduced herself 'She has Downs and a few other issues, lives in a care home, just outside of town.'

Louise didn't know what to say, tears pricked just inside her lids and her eyes grew wet. She had never imagined this side of him before. 'Oh Kelly, that sounds just so sweet.'

'Well now you know why I didn't tell you, I needed you to think that I was hard-ass.'

'Is that why…' Louise stopped herself, it really wasn't fair for her to demand so much personal information, or was it?

'Is that why, what?' Kelly asked.

'Well, I always wondered why you never left Kilkenny, didn't put yourself forward for promotion.'

'Well, first of all, I did go for a promotion, but they gave it to that bollox, McCarthy.' McCarthy was their station inspector based in Kilkenny. Neither of them had any love for him. 'But yeah, I'm not interested in promotions outside of Kilkenny. I'm all the family that Annie has, so I'll be there as long as she is.' He picked up her hand and kissed it.

She reached over to him and kissed him on the lips and he grabbed her closer. She knew what it was like to have a sister she loved so much; she felt the same about Alex.

'Shit, Alex', she exclaimed. 'What time is it?' She stretched across to the bedside table for her watch. 'I must go.' She said hurriedly.

'Okay, I don't know if I can take my hands off you though.' Kelly pulled back the sheet and sat on the edge of the bed. The last two hours had been bizarre but wonderful.

'I'm sure you'll manage.' Louise reached for her blouse that was lying on the floor. She giggled as she threw it over her head. 'We need some food, I don't know if that waiter will serve us again though.' Kelly wasn't sure where to go from here and it was possible that she didn't either.

'Alex will be looking for you,' he said, pulling up his jeans over his boxers and reaching for his watch from the bedside table.

'Do you…' She hesitated for a moment. She had been looking forward to spending time with her sister but couldn't bear not to be with him. 'Do you want to come with us, for a bite to eat?'

'Are you sure?'

'Yeah, she'd love to meet you.' Louise was confident. 'Properly, I mean.'

Kelly stood buttoning up his shirt; it was slightly crumpled so he smoothed it out.

'She might put you through your paces though,' Louise warned. 'She was always the tough one,' she added.

'She, was the tough one, Jesus Christ,' Kelly quipped.

'Tell me again what you said you were thinking about all week,' Louise teased as she reminded him of his whispered confessions earlier in his bed.

'Actions speak louder than words.' Suggestively he joked, 'I will show you later what I was thinking about.'

'See you in an half an hour then.' Louise kissed him goodbye. 'For dinner, I mean.' She smiled and took the short walk to next door.

Alex embraced Louise tightly. 'Where were you, I was worried.'

'What did you do, pretend you were me at reception and get another room card?' Louise already knew the answer. They were forever pretending to be each other over the years.

'Did you wear that to your meeting?' Alex noticed Louise's casual appearance and dishevelled hair.

'Eh no.' Guiltily, Louise smiled. 'I've just been inside, in Kelly's room.' Louise scrunched up her eyes as though bracing herself for an attack. When Alex didn't speak, she continued. 'Apparently, he has similar feelings for me as I have for him.' Her voice was jittery with excitement.

'Have you lost your mind, Louise?' Alex exclaimed.

'Shush, he's next door.' She glared as though there was a chance that Kelly could hear her through the solid wall.

'Louise!' Alex whispered. 'You work with him,' She laughed loudly at her sister. 'And wait till Dad hears his age.'

'He's only fifty-five,' Louise pleaded.

'Only?' Alex repeated.

'I know, but we've talked it all through and it really isn't an issue.'

'How do you know this is not just some fling for him?' Alex was protective of her sister's feelings.

'Well you can see for yourself, we've to meet him in half an hour.' Louise plonked herself down on the edge of the bed.

'I'm not going to dinner with you and Mr Loverboy to play gooseberry. I'll be happy here with my room service, thank you very much. You go and enjoy yourself while your only sister is all on her own in your hotel room.'

'Okay then.' Louise knew she was kidding. 'Did you bring my underwear?'

'Don't tell me you were, actually knickerless for the day.' Alex flung the clean pair of undies at her sister.

'No,' she winked, 'just for the past hour.' She jumped up from the bed and raced for a quick shower.

Chapter 22

Thursday Evening – 2016

Kelly waited patiently in the lobby of the Camden Court Hotel. The past days had been the most bizarre of his career and, if he was truthful with himself, the most bizarre of his life. He positioned himself on the first sofa he found so that Louise couldn't miss him when she arrived, not this time; the velvet seats were well-dented and the cushions unplumped. A smattering of empty glasses and torn crisp bags were scattered on the smeared glass table in front of him; no doubt the remnants of a family with small, sticky-fingered kids.

If there was one thing Kelly was sure of it was that, after Annie, Louise was the most magnificent person in his life, with her no-bullshit approach and tough, try-me attitude, he was well and truly taken with her. What he wasn't sure of though was did she feel the same? Sure, they had spent a blissful two hours together, but it wasn't just the age gap that put her well and truly out of his league, she was an absolute stunner as well. He wondered if it would work in real life, back in Kilkenny. He looked at his watch again.

'I'll clear that for you now.' A smiling waitress busied herself with clearing his table; she looked tired, worn off her feet. Her once crisp white blouse showed evidence of a day's work, clearing tables and scraping plates for those that didn't have to. Strong liquor aromas and flowery scents from the number of vases dotted around the lobby filled the air. 'Now,' the waitress smiled at him, 'can I get you a drink, sir?'

'Just a beer, please,' he answered, somewhat embarrassed to ask her to do more. 'When you get a minute,' he added and smiled as though trying to make his order seem less demanding.

He clenched his teeth together and breathed deeply. He could still smell wafts of Louise's perfume up his nose and when he closed his eyes, a spike of arousal shot through him like a dart, imagining touching her smooth, fragrant skin. It had been a while since he'd touched someone like that and, my God, it was worth the wait. With each blink, every angle of her naked body flashed across his eyes. He found it hard to believe what had happened. Louise Kennedy naked, in his arms. Maybe the lads back in the station were more copped on that he gave them credit for, in fairness, they saw it coming. He looked at his watch again; she was more than twenty minutes late but that was no surprise.

Louise was nervous as she and her sister rode the lift to the ground floor. She was excited to see Kelly again, providing that was he still wanted to see her. She opened her mouth but couldn't find the words to use it. In all her time, either training for the force or working in it, she had never allowed herself to get close to any of the lads, *never*, despite the many offers, but Kelly, he was different.

'Jesus, what are you like?' Alex's voice interrupted her thoughts. 'Calm yourself, would you.' She giggled incredulously. She could tell by the snaps of breathing and heavy sighing that Louise was in panic mode.

'Oh fuck, Alex, what have I done?' Louise whispered, even though they were on their own. The seeds of doubt had grown into brambles and began to strangulate her. 'He is probably regretting everything.' She stretched her neck and closed her eyes. She rubbed her face in anguish, forgetting about the mascara that Alex had made her wear.

'Jeez, Louise.' Alex smiled, her eyes were wide seeing her sister so shaken. As corny as it sounded, Alex knew the age-old phrase which they'd used in their childhood would make her laugh. 'What's got into you?' Alex shook her head, her normally level-headed, don't mess with me sister, was a mess, a big, hot, dithery mess; she had rarely seen her like this before. 'My God, girl.' Alex reached into her bag, looking for a tissue to fix her face. 'You are, so, over-analysing this, seriously.' She spat on the tissue and dabbed the streak of mascara that Louise had rubbed under her eyes. 'Just go with it. What's there to worry about, you guys like each other, you just slept with him for Christ's sake, I guarantee you, he's not regretting a single thing.'

Catching her breath, Louise settled herself, patted her cheeks and waited for the lift doors to open. 'I know, I know. Just a wobble.' She flashed her sister a winning smile. 'I'm grand,' she said, her words sounding much braver than she felt. 'And Alex, follow my lead with him, work with me, will you?' Louise was anxious that her sister's lack of tact might embarrass Kelly and she didn't want her to frighten him off. Not yet. 'He takes a bit of getting used to,' she warned.

'Don't worry; I won't say anything about the two of you supposedly professional detectives shacking up in a hotel when you are supposed to be working,' Alex teased. 'And I definitely won't say anything about the fact that he is twenty years your senior and if the inspector found out about it, he would be discharged,' she paused, 'Dishonourably.'

Louise threw Alex an exasperated look as the lift doors opened. 'We're not in the Army,' she answered, laughing at

Alex's deliberate attempt to joke with her. 'Behave,' Louise warned, knowing full well what her sister was capable of.

With his eyes fixed on the lift, Kelly downed the last mouthful of his beer. The doors opened and Louise and her sister stepped out. He cleared his throat and wiped his mouth with the back of his hand, the thrill of seeing her again making him smile.

He walked towards them and smiled. 'Ladies, I hope I didn't keep you.'

Louise enjoyed his sarcasm. 'No, not at all.' She flashed him an intimate smile and immediately they both relaxed. 'Shall we eat?' She threw Kelly an embarrassed look as they both remembered the way they had behaved with the waiter in the hotel restaurant before they had skipped back to his room. 'Maybe we'll try the Italian down the road?' she suggested; she felt too awkward to return.

'I'm easy,' Kelly answered, he was happy to go along with Louise's suggestion.

'So I've heard,' Alex answered. She flicked a look at the new man in her sister's life and waited for him to react. It was sort of a litmus test she set for him; his answer would dictate whether she was going to like him or not.

'Alex.' Louise shot a warning look at her younger sister, she had expected her to put him through his paces but she hoped that maybe they could sit down and eat first.

'No, it's a fair observation,' Kelly smirked. He knew he had his hands full, one smart-mouthed, quick-witted woman was hard enough, but two. He laughed helplessly at what he had in store. 'Your sister will attest to the fact that I am, actually, quite "difficult".' He had a hunch that if Louise had ever complained about him to Alex that the word 'difficult' would have been used. 'And in fact, I'm actually quite, eh, taken, with your sister, and couldn't believe my luck when she felt the same way about me, and believe me, nothing about your sister is easy either.'

Saying Louise wasn't easy had won the argument for him, maybe Alex was going to like this Kelly fella after all.

They arrived at the restaurant after a short walk. 'Shall we go in?' he offered, unsure whether he should have opened the door for them.

'Let's,' Alex answered. She smiled at her sister and they took the stairs to the basement level bar, waiting for a table.

'That's my phone,' Kelly said. He pulled his phone from his pocket and baulked when he saw the Inspector's number on the screen. 'I'll just take this outside,' he added, scrunching up his face. 'Louise knows what to order for me.' He grinned. It was their first private joke in front of Alex and Louise enjoyed its timing as much as Kelly did.

Kelly found a quite doorway on the street and redialled the Inspector's number. 'Inspector, Kelly here, sorry I missed your call.'

'We were scheduled for a six p.m., Kelly. It's now eight.' Inspector McCarthy wasn't happy to have been kept waiting. 'I've a function to go to.'

'Things just got delayed and I got waylaid trying to tie up loose ends,' Kelly explained to him. He left out the detail that the real reason why he missed the scheduled conference call was because he was tied up under the sheets with Detective Kennedy and that was a detail that no one in the station would ever know. Not for his own benefit, he would have loved nothing more than to be able to say that Detective Louise Kennedy was in his bed, proud that she thought that he, Tony Kelly, was good enough, kind enough, clever enough or even sexy enough, for her to like him, but no, no one at the station would ever hear it from him, he had far too much respect for her to do that, the lads would never shut up about it.

'And, do we have a case?' the Inspector grew impatient.

'We have motive, we have circumstantial evidence, we can place him in the vicinity.'

'Why aren't we arresting him then?' His voice thundered down the phone. 'This is dragging on, Kelly, where is Detective Kennedy on this?'

'She feels the same, sir.' Kelly couldn't be anymore vague. He was buying time. 'But we do just want to rule out Liam Fitzpatrick and Maeve Fitzpatrick. They were both alive and unaccounted for at the time of Patrick's death. They would have had motive too by the same token.'

'That's bullshit, Kelly.' His patience was wearing thin but more importantly to the Inspector, he wanted the glory of announcing the arrest in the forty-six-year-old murder case at the function he was attending that night. 'I need an answer now, I'm going to be hounded by the press.'

'Can we just have till tomorrow, sir, we should be a little clearer then.'

'Fuck sake, no, Kelly, what is wrong with you, man, you have the bloody murderer in your sights.' There was no glory in charging the deceased bodies of Liam and Maeve Fitzpatrick. It was far more newsworthy to have a living suspect. 'I need to see you and Kennedy tonight. I'll be back at the station around midnight. We'll talk then. Right.'

'Right,' Kelly said. He didn't know how he was going to get out of it. 'I'll see you then.' He dropped his phone back into his pocket and paced to and fro on the footpath. 'Fucking typical,' he muttered under his breath. 'Of all the fucking times.' He shook his head and kicked a crisp packet from the pathway in front of him. There was no way out of it. He would have to tear up the road, get back to Kilkenny, miss out on spending the night with Louise, just when they were getting together, and put up with McCarthy posturing once more. 'Stupid prick.' He looked around him hoping no one was in earshot of his mumbling.

He walked inside to tell Louise and stopped on the top step. He watched as the sisters smiled and laughed and whispered, it was a side that he had rarely seen in Louise, a side that she didn't have the comfort of showing in work. It really was a lovely sight.

He stood back from view, pulled out his phone again and composed a text. He'd leave her to enjoy her night with her sister, he decided, and he would make her excuses to McCarthy and she could catch up with him in Kilkenny in the morning. There was no point in her night being ruined as well as his.

> Louise, sorry, need to leave for Kilkenny, will explain in the morning. Tell Alex I said goodbye.

He pressed send, raced back around the corner to the hotel, gathered his clothes from his room, checked out and made his way to the car to get on the road to Kilkenny. If he had told her in person, she would have insisted she came with him and that wasn't what he wanted for her.

If he called McCarthy a prick under his breath once, he did it one thousand times.

Chapter 23

September 1970

It's been an hour since the baby has arrived and he is hungry and loud. I hold him and his busy little arms and legs thrash wildly when he is not bundled tightly in his blankets. Mrs McGrath says it's because he thinks he is falling. I think it's because he wants to thrash. He has realised that he can move and he is doing it, plain and simple. His red face has faded and in the subdued amber half-light from the bedside table, he now looks milky-white. The square brown alarm clock reads 10:16 p.m.

Mrs McGrath crumples up the newspaper that she had spread and underneath there is a red chenille bedspread with flowery patterned swirls and curls that frame the edges.

'Let's get you freshened up,' she says and takes the baby from me and places him in a cocoon she has made from pastel stripy pillows on an armchair facing against the wall.

'Okay,' I answer, embarrassed.

She walks me towards the bathroom and reassures me that no one will come in. A waft of white musk hits me when I open the white painted bathroom door. It smells delicious. 'Everything you need is there.' She points to a neatly folded pile of clothes, a brand new bar of soap and a folded blue towel. 'Take your time, and give yourself a really good wash,' she says as she makes circles with her hands around the front of me. 'When you are ready, then come back in,' she says and closes the bathroom door behind me.

When I return, dressed and fresh and clean from my musky soak, I watch as Mrs McGrath uses a sponge and a yellow basin to wash the white stuff from the baby's head. She talks to the baby as though he can hear her. She tells him that she is giving him a 'sluice.' Mrs McGrath looks at the baby with loving eyes; she looks like the kind of mother that has so much love to give, a generous caring soul, the absolute opposite to my mother.

'Mrs McGrath.' My voice is weak, unsure of itself. The clothes that she has given me smell like lavender.

'Yes, darling.' Her voice is strong, confident, the type that would make you feel safe.

'I was thinking.' My wet hair leaves a patch on the back of the oversized jumper I am wearing and Mrs McGrath places another, dryer towel around my shoulders. I feel cold and sit at the edge of the bed, shivering.

'Yes.' She continues to busy herself, swiftly washing and then drying the baby, area by area, from top to bottom.

'Can I give him a name?' I say, afraid to have said something I shouldn't have. I see a quick sliver of worry dash across her face. She pauses for a moment, unable to look at mine. 'If that's, okay,' I add.

'Do you want to?' she says. Her eyes are only for the baby and they smile for him. She rubs his skin with oil and the baby seems to like it. The corners of her mouth meet her eyes as she coos at him. I think the baby feels as safe as I do.

'I think he should have a name, maybe, so he knows if we are talking to him,' I say.

Mrs McGrath doesn't answer. She folds a terry cloth like a triangle and decides that it is too big. 'Just a minute, love.' She places my hand on the baby's belly and puts a towel over him. I stay in that position until she returns.

I look at the baby and ask him if he is okay. He squirms and I pat the towel around him tighter.

'Here we are,' Mrs McGrath announces as she brings back a smaller cloth. 'This will fit better.' She takes charge again and folds the cloth around him and fixes it with a pin. She finds the smallest white Babygro from a black sack of baby boy clothes and she dresses him. 'Now, my little treasure,' she says and kisses him on the cheek.

'Mrs McGrath,' I say again and she looks at me.

'Yes, Rose?'

'How about Michael?' I say, nervous but determined. I'm sure she doesn't know how to respond to me.

'For the baby?' she asks and I nod my head, still slightly afraid to say something wrong. 'Let's see,' she says and she places a blanket and folds it in a triangle in front of me. I am beginning to realise that there are a lot of triangles. She takes the baby and swaddles him tightly inside. He looks like a caterpillar with just his face exposed. She cuddles him closely and then returns him to my lap. 'What do you think, Michael, do you like that name?' she says to the baby and then smiles at me. I know then that Michael would love to have a mother who cares so much. Mrs McGrath's eyes fill with tears and she looks at me. 'Michael, it is.' She leans towards me and kisses me on the head and then she kisses Michael. 'You know, Michael is my father's name,' she says.

'Oh!' I say.

She looks at the clock and then back to me. The clock reads a quarter to eleven and I realise she is anxious about the time. 'I don't mean to rush you, but I would like a doctor to have a look at him soon,' she says.

'Why?' I ask.

'Just as a precaution, he is a very small baby and he might need to be seen to, just to make sure,' she says.

My stare wanders from the bundle in my arms to Mrs McGrath and then back to the powder-blue blanketed bundle on my lap. I study his nose, his closed eyes and I listen for his whimpers. His tiny breaths make his little nose move ever so slightly in sync with his rising chest. 'Michael,' I whisper, wondering does he hear me. 'It's me, Michael, Rose.' I have been thinking and thinking and have been unable to decide, up until now. 'Mrs McGrath,'

There is silence in the room as she stands watching me from the end of the bed. I can tell that her heart is beating faster than it normally does, from the way she is breathing. As I speak she makes her way to sit on the bed's edge.

'I was thinking…' I say. Her eyes are bright in the darkness of the room. 'That maybe…' I look at Michael and his eyes flicker, looking for me, and then they close again, 'if it's okay with you, maybe I could go to your school in Dublin.'

'If that's what you want, darling,' she says, hoping I mean it.

'I do.' I manage.

Mrs McGrath can't find her words so she nods, smiles and strokes my face.

'Will you…' I look at Michael and back at her. I think it's an imposition to actually ask her if she will look after him. 'Is it okay?' I say.

'It is, darling, he'll be one of us, and I promise you that.' She wipes away the tears that are streaming down her face, then, as she giggles, she takes the edge of the blanket and wipes away mine. 'And I can say…' she swallows hard, 'I can say that both my sons were born on my bed.' She tries to read my reaction, but there's none, not yet anyhow. 'That's if you want.'

'I do,' I answer her. My eyes turn to the baby. 'Hello, Michael McGrath, welcome to your new home.'

Chapter 24

Friday Morning – 2016

If you can meet with Triumph and Disaster
And treat those two impostors just the same…
If you can fill the unforgiving minute
With sixty seconds' worth of distance run,
Yours is the Earth and everything that's in it,
And – which is more – you'll be a Man, my son.

Rudyard Kipling

The sun had risen and in the sparkling of the dew, the grass woke gently with the breeze shaking off the moisture from the night before. There was always a moment, before the world was awake, that it was peaceful and poignant, Rose thought contentedly. Maybe there was a silver lining to sleepless nights. She topped up her cup from the pot of tea she had made earlier; it was exactly how she liked it, tar.

All night she had tossed and turned with more questions than she had answers to. How did Patrick Fitzpatrick end up in the ditch? Who had put him there? Why didn't anybody search for him in 1970? It was a testament to the type of man he was, she supposed. Tim had said they would have to bury him, but she didn't want to return to Kilkenny, she had always promised she never would. What would happen to Tim?

She opened her notebook and placed it on the table. Beside it, she put her silver Cross pen, a present from Lizzie. She had reached for it in the early hours as her legs jerked and her mind jumped, both afflictions disturbing her ability to close her eyes. Scribbling her thoughts, she realised, had been therapeutic and once she had started she had found it hard to stop. It hadn't been her intention to structure her wishes in these letters, but in the early hours of the morning, she had a brainwave; sleeplessness had its moments. She wrote four letters in total.

Retrieving her laptop from the living room, she booted it up and made her way into the kitchen. Her handwriting these days barely legible; she set about transcribing her scribbled notes onto her computer. The dexterity in her hands had long since been replaced by rigidity. Her muscles misbehaved in ways she couldn't explain, betraying her commands. The events of the past few days were a stark reminder of how wrong everything could be. This was her chance to give her side of the story.

The kitchen was cosy; Matt had painted it in a duck-egg blue – her favourite colour. The cupboards were antique cream and suited the classic feel of the house. Various photographs of happier days adorned the walls and the sideboard to the rear of the room. She smiled as she could hear her husband's encouragement in her head. It was days like these that she missed him the most, her rock, her heart.

Before she began to type, she studied the meticulously calligraphed, black ink letters, curling eloquently through the words of Rudyard Kipling's poem on the front of her notebook, it was her favourite piece. As she reread her notes, she tried to type, wiping away the tears as they fell. She had decided, sleeplessly, that it was time.

Dearest Lizzie, she began. The late-night scribbles proved difficult to read but she persevered until she had written for her daughter her wishes for her future. She allowed her hand to type what her heart wanted to say. When she had finished she sat still and silent, satisfied that she had said everything. It had been wonderful to express her feelings as freely as she had. Building on the sense of relief she was feeling, she started another.

Dearest Michael, she began. The words for the second one proved a little more difficult for her to find. When she had finally finished and typed the last kiss, she sighed with relief, feeling the pressure that she had been carrying all these years evaporate like the condensation on the morning window. The letters, she decided, would be confined to her solicitors for safekeeping. Only to be read on her instruction, or on her death. She folded the printed papers and placed them beside their envelopes. She lingered, knowing that the next time they would be opened, they would be in her children's hands. She pulled out two more envelopes and left them ready on her desk.

She stared at the mug in her hands and considered the next words she would use. She imagined it being read and the impact it would have. Words flowed and her fingers typed as though they had a mind of their own. With every sentence, an ounce of torment lifted till eventually she felt weightless, floating almost. It hadn't taken long to fill the pages and with her third letter written she left it to the side, addressed the envelope to *Detective Kelly* and then began to write the fourth, this would be the easiest letter of them all.

Dearest Tim, she began and within minutes her thoughts about her brother cascaded onto the page. She read over all four, folded them in three and placed each of them in an envelope and sealed it. She was sure that it was time. If she was fearful at all, it wasn't because people would finally know her secret, but rather the consequences of people not knowing what was in them. Rose's conscience was clear and, as far as she was concerned, justice had been done, maybe not in the traditional way, but it was done none the less. She took the four envelopes and shuffled them in her hands, one for Lizzie, one for Michael, and on the third envelop she wrote, Detective Kelly and the fourth for her brother Tim. She placed the envelopes by her keys on the hall table and made a mental note to root for Tim's whistle, to go along with his letter.

By the time Rose had showered and prepared herself for the day, she was exhausted. Everyday tasks were becoming harder and harder and she was beginning to feel incapable. She would have loved nothing better than to take a stroll in the woods but she knew her muscles would let her down. She resigned herself to drift from room to room, touching the ornaments of her life and making a cup of tea instead.

There were many years when she didn't use the strength that she had been born with and now, for the first time, she regretted it. The current state of her health and the hassle with the Estate helped her put things into perspective. She was confident that the letters were the best thing to do. Adjusting to her illness had been hard for Rose but the heaviness in her legs was no match for the heaviness in her heart. She picked up her phone and scrolled for her solicitor's details. Taking a deep breath, she dialled the number. He'd have her wishes safely in his keeping, providing there were no distractions, by the end of the day.

*

Tim sat poised in the set-down area on Friday morning outside the arrival gates at Dublin airport. He dutifully ignored the amplified message that repeatedly warned him that the area was for set-down only. There was an art to airport pick-ups and Tim was determined to master it. Timing the collection perfectly, Lizzie emerged pulling two bags behind her.

'Hi Tim. I told you I'd get a taxi.' She hugged her uncle tight and he lifted the first bag into his boot.

'What on earth have you got with you?' Tim said as he lumped her second bag on top of it. 'It is just for the weekend, you know,' he added.

'Actually, I'm here for the week,' she answered. 'I realised, when you rang, that I haven't taken any leave at all, let alone been home in months, so I took the entire week.' She didn't elaborate about the growing discontent she was feeling for her life in London, nor her tentative plan to come home for good in the near future. 'I'm not going back till next Sunday,' she said. *And that's just to hand in my notice*, she added in her head.

'Well, I'm glad I decided to collect you now, seeing as you have so much stuff with you,' Tim said. 'I've been tracking your flight on the tracker app so I knew you were ahead of schedule.'

'I know, I barely had time to get my seat belt on and we were already descending,' Lizzie answered, grateful to be home.

Tim pulled out gently and they set off.

'So, she has no idea that I'm coming home,' Lizzie questioned.

'None,' Tim answered. 'She'll be delighted though. She misses you,' he said.

Lizzie knew enough to know that Tim was up to something but she was patient enough to wait for him to tell her. She was excited to be home.

'Sweet Jesus!' Rose gasped as she opened the heavy front door. Unsure whether her legs were wobbling from rushing down the stairs or from the shock of seeing her daughter, Rose needed to sit down. 'Oh my God, I can't believe it.' Her heart thumped. Her pale brown eyes widened. 'What on earth is going on?' Stunned, she looked at Tim and then reached for her daughter's hand to steady herself. Lizzie squeezed her hand tightly in return and led her mother back towards the kitchen. A sense of excitement infected Rose as she regained her thoughts and her steadiness. 'Ah, Lizzie,' Rose pulled her daughter in for a hug. 'It's so good to have you home again.'

Rose opened the double living room doors and led Lizzie and Tim inside. 'This is such a surprise; I presume your Uncle Tim had something to do with it?' She threw a knowing look at her brother and Lizzie caught it. Once Lizzie had been settled and the pleasantries were out of the way, Rose began to talk.

'Right, there are two things.' Rose wavered slightly as she placed herself opposite Lizzie in the armchair. Tim sat forward showing his support. Easing her daughter into the information was her strategy. Lizzie was childlike as she sat on the couch. 'I've been a bit worried lately so I've been to the doctors to check it out.' Lizzie inhaled deeply and held her breath, this wasn't the news she had anticipated and she didn't know what to expect next. 'What they've said is I might have a condition, a neurological disorder.' Rose explained as succinctly as she could. The details could come later, she thought. There was no sense in bombarding her with minute detail. 'There are no definitive tests to determine what it might be, but the medical team has mentioned, Motor Neurone Disease and Parkinson's as some of the possibilities.'

Lizzie looked to Tim, his gaze resting softly on his sister. He hadn't said anything, but it was obvious to Lizzie that he wasn't hearing this for the first time. His breathing remained steady and his body was unmoved. There was strength behind his eyes, willing his sister to be strong. She looked at her mother and noticed her furrowed brow. Her dancing eyes still piercing behind her thinning lashes, now glazed with a coat of tears. Instinctively, Lizzie reached for her hand, noticing her draw a deep slow breath. She pressed her hand tight. There was a hopeless quality in her mother's voice, forlorn at the bleak expectations for her future.

'I'll be with you every step of the way, Mum. Always and forever.' Her own eyes beginning to glaze, Lizzie moved to sit beside her mother. She wrapped her arms around her small body and let her tears flow.

A lump rose in Tim's throat as a symphony of sobs and sniffles swirled in the atmosphere.

'And before either of you say it; it wouldn't have helped if we had known any sooner. There would have been nothing we could have done then, just as there is nothing we can do now.' She rubbed Lizzie's back from where she sat. 'I've started on a myriad of tablets and drugs so maybe they might be able to help me cope in some way. But in the meantime, it's business as usual.' Rose was firm. 'I'm not bad yet. Just a little slower that's all. So we'll play it by ear. Okay my lovely.' She was attempting to smile. 'I'm going to make a drink.' Rose dragged herself forward in the chair and pushed herself into a standing position, steadying herself on the sideboard. 'Who's for tea?' She made her way to the kitchen before they answered. It was then that she remembered the letters. She rushed to the hall and placed them carefully inside the console table's drawer. The solicitors could wait till Monday, she decided. For now, even though she wouldn't have asked her, she was happy Lizzie was home.

Stillness had settled comfortably in the back garden as Rose looked down the lawn. A tiredness had taken hold and she felt sleepy. The lack of sleep last night and the stress of the past week had taken its toll on her.

Tim came in to the kitchen.

'Now, do you feel better that she knows?' Rose wasn't sure yet, so didn't answer. Tim noticed her rubbing her hand. 'I know you're probably going to give out to me for getting her to come home, but, well, I just thought that you could do with seeing her', he raised his eyebrows slightly not knowing what she was going to say. 'And she could do with a little break', he added trying to deflect from his intentions.

'It's fine, Tim, really', her smile was small but genuine, 'actually, it's more than fine, I'm glad she's here', she glanced at the door making sure that Lizzie hadn't heard them. 'I really do miss her so much', she whispered, her eyes tearing up.

'I know you do, Rosie, I know', he patted his pockets looking for a tissue to hand her and when he couldn't find any he pulled a sheet of kitchen towel from the roll, folded it and handed it to her. 'Will I bring in the tray?' he offered.

'No thanks, it's all in hand,' Rose answered. Her determination and resilience was never as evident.

'It's all in hand,' Tim repeated as he laughed at the poetic irony. The pun was unintentional.

'When are these tablets supposed to start working?' Rose directed her attention to her hands, drawing Tim's focus there as well. Her frustration was unmistakable.

Tim held her cold hands in his as he spoke. 'You need to give it time.' Tim moved to hug his sister, feeling her small waiflike size in his arms. He noticed that she had lost weight. She was fading before his eyes. 'Come on, let's get back in.' Tim said. Rose wiped her face and brushed her hair from her eyes. She straightened herself up and brought the tray from the kitchen to the living room.

'There's one other thing,' Tim said. Rose cradled her mug in her hands, hoping that the heat might help the pain. Lizzie froze; the fear was etched on her face. 'As you know, your mother and I grew up on a farm, an Estate, they are calling it now, in Kilkenny.'

'Yes,' Lizzie's brow scrunched, she hoped that this was the news about the body, the reason she had come home in the first place, she wasn't sure if she could take any more surprise announcements.

'Well, there's good and, well I won't say bad, but more sort of, nuisance news, attached to this one,' Tim reassured. 'Well, neither of us have any love for the place.' Tim looked at Rose and Lizzie followed his glance. 'We decided to sell it, just at the beginning of the year.'

Lizzie watched the expressions that her mother and her uncle shared and tried to decipher them.

'This is the good news part.' He smiled. 'We, your mother and me, we've put the proceeds of the sale in a trust for you, to get you started in life.' Tim's eyebrows rose. 'It's a substantial amount; we want you to set yourself up with it.'

Lizzie looked at her mother and then back at Tim, speechlessly.

Tim paused and drank some of his tea before he continued. 'It's had the same tenant in now for nearly a decade. And this tenant made an offer to buy,' he looked at Rose again, 'and we accepted,' Tim said. 'Just at the beginning of the year, there.'

Rose remained silent; she was unable to speak.

'I honestly don't know what to say,' Lizzie shook her head incredulously.

'It's decided. Both Tim and I are fine financially. Maybe buy a house, travel the world. Whatever you want. It's for you, for your future.' Rose's voice broke as she wondered how much of her daughter's future she would be around for.

'It's settled. The solicitors need your bank details to do the electronic transfer,' Tim added. 'But that's about it.'

Lizzie felt relieved when she heard the news and very quickly felt guilty for even thinking about finances when she had just been told about her mother's illness, although, she thought, having money meant that her move home from London was infinitely more possible.

'And the nuisance part?' Lizzie asked.

'The body that they dug up…'

'Yeah.'

Tim's voice began to weaken and he cleared his throat. 'The thing is, it happens to be the body of an old uncle of ours, who went missing in the seventies.'

'Seriously,' Lizzie answered. The Fitzpatrick family history had been sketchy at best, when she was growing up and it had never occurred to her to ask if she had any more relatives that she hadn't known about. She knew about her grandparents but they had died when she was very small, this was the first she was hearing of her mother's uncle.

'Seriously,' Tim said. 'Which is why,' he looked at Rose's pale face, 'both your mother and I are still involved in the investigation,' he said. 'Us being the only ones still alive who would have known him,' he added. 'So now that they are finished with the autopsy, it's down to us to have to bury him,' Tim said.

Lizzie could tell by Tim's tone that this was something he didn't want to do and she was curious as to why. 'What was his name?' she looked at her mother to answer but Tim interjected.

'Patrick.' Not wanting to waste his breath on mentioning his name, Tim exhaled as he spoke.

'This is just bizarre, crazy' Lizzie said.

'I know, love', Rose spoke softly.

'When, then?' Lizzie asked, 'when is this funeral?'

'Tomorrow,' Tim answered.

'Funeral's tomorrow,' Rose confirmed.

'And do we even know what happened to him, who killed him, who killed Patrick Fitzpatrick?' Lizzie asked.

'No'. Tim answered, afraid to meet his sister's gaze.

'We'll probably never know'. Rose added.

Chapter 25

Saturday – 2016

Tim pulled up outside the old country church, Rose could barely remember it. Despite the morning sunlight a cold crisp breeze, the kind that would cut you in two, whipped around them and Rose shivered. Vaguely, she pictured herself here as a child, but she couldn't remember the specific occasion or event. The small church, by the looks of it, could hold maybe one hundred people, and even though it was small by Catholic Church standards, it was still too big for the event it was hosting that morning, surely no one else would show up?

'Apparently these gates only get opened for funerals and weddings,' Tim whispered to Lizzie as she walked by his side. The black wrought-iron gates were held open by metal hooks that were fixed to the stone ground. 'It costs extra,' he said, a disapproving smirk flashed across his face. Lizzie nodded her response. It was just one of the gripes on a very long list that they could fault the Catholic Church in Ireland for. 'Mind you, there's only the four of us, it was hardly necessary, seeing as the graveyard is in the grounds,' Tim added, he could hear Rose and Robert's footsteps behind him. 'Okay?' He turned and waited for Rose to catch up.

'Fine,' she answered. 'Let's just get this over and done with,' she added. 'And, Tim,' he stopped and looked at her, 'thanks for taking charge, you know, for arranging everything.'

He smiled his response. Had it been possible he would have had Patrick cremated, burned, just as he deserved, but to return with the remains to the crematorium in Dublin would have only prolonged the entire event. It was much easier to phone the local funeral director and have him arrange everything. 'I expect, we will be over and done with in no time,' he reassured her, knowing how difficult it was for her to return.

Rose frowned, she had dreaded the idea of it; getting in and out as quickly as possible, so that she didn't see anyone she wasn't meant to, was her focus. They walked towards the old wooden arched door across the weathered grey slabs. They were just in time.

As much as Rose didn't want to be in Kilkenny any longer than she had to, she knew that she wouldn't have been up to a return journey that day, so they had booked themselves in to Lyrath Castle to spend one night. It was a treat, a way of compensating for having to be there and go through the motions in the first place. Tim knew, as well as Rose did, with such a high-profile case, that if the next of kin weren't even bothered to show up for the funeral, questions, the type of ones that they couldn't answer, not without consequences anyhow, would be asked.

The oak coffin stood in the centre of the aisle and Rose couldn't bear to look at it, she drew a deep breath through her clenched teeth. The coffin and its contents did nothing to ease the invisible fury that burned like hell inside of her.

'May he rot in hell,' Tim spoke quietly in her ear. She reached for his hand and he for hers. 'I can't tell you how angry he makes me feel.' She patted his arm. The charade was taking its toll on both of them.

A waft of incense filled the small space and a subtle bell indicated the priest's arrival on the altar. Avoiding the attention from the pulpit, Rose focused her gaze on the beautiful interior of the church. The bright morning outside filtered through the stained-glass windows, throwing chasms of colour and sparkles of light across the dull stone floor. She followed the lines towards the ornate statues, both larger than life, that stood on either side of the altar; like sentries guarding the tabernacle and other sacred ornaments. Seven bronze lamps hung from the newly restored ceiling, reflecting the sunlight as it bounced and ricocheted around the high spaces. Tim reached for her clenched fists on her lap; he didn't need to speak.

A gust of damp air rushed in and around the church, as the heavy door clunked open behind them. Curious, Rose turned, glancing in their direction; instinctively, she knew it was him, she knew it was her son, Michael. She had never allowed herself to imagine seeing him again, she had kept true to the promise she had made to Mrs McGrath but now, with him a mere two feet away from her she had to restrain herself from throwing her arms around him and holding him just like she had done before she left him.

She remained silent, unable to speak. Her heart began to race, the thump so loud, she feared that everyone in the church could hear it. Her mouth was as dry as sand as she swallowed hard. She opened her bag and clenched her hands around a plastic bottle, her fingers turning white; she handed Tim the bottle and he opened it for her. The congregation could hear the whispering apologies as Michael, Marie and George McGrath took the row behind them.

'You okay, Mum?' Lizzie whispered, noticing her mother's pale face. It was as though she had seen a ghost.

Rose wasn't able to speak, she opened her mouth but there was nothing in there. She nodded and shrugged, vague memories and hidden feelings jousting their way to the front of her heart.

Tim could feel Rose tense beside him, like plaster of Paris stiffening around a limb. He had a feeling he knew why.

The sound of the Angelus bell resonated from the small but perfectly engineered steeple as they wheeled the coffin outside. Wrapped in her Catholic guilt and draped in her sorrow, it took Rose by surprise when the handful in the congregation stood, solemnly waiting for her to follow, as though she was to be commiserated with.

'Rose.' Tim waited in the aisle and dutifully she followed, afraid to look in Michael's direction. Tim linked Rose's arm for the short walk to the graveside, her feeble legs tired and unreliable, finding every step a chore. He squeezed her arm, both of them connected in their shared thoughts. She was afraid to look up, afraid to meet his eyes. Every single day, since she had left her baby, she made a wish for him, a wish that he was happy, a wish that he was kind, a wish that he would never have to know the awfulness that had brought him to life in the first place. She had kept the secret, like Mrs McGrath had asked her to do and it had worked. He had been loved, he had been taken into Mrs McGrath's home, into her heart but most of all, he was safe, safe from the horrors of her past.

*

Out of the corner of her eye and over the shoulders of those waiting to offer their condolences, Rose watched as Michael spoke to the woman he was standing next to, his wife, she presumed. She felt weak with nervous energy. Rose drew a deep breath, savouring every snippet of fresh air she could, in an attempt to settle her nerves; she couldn't believe that she was standing across from him.

'How are you doing?' Tim asked.

'Holding on,' she said. 'Barely.' She exhaled slowly as she saw Michael McGrath approach. 'Tim.' Her voice wobbled.

'Ah, Michael, very kind of you to come, thank you.' Tim extended his hand. The undertakers lifted the coffin onto the wooden posts that straddled the grave and threaded through the lengths of sturdy belts to lower it.

'Not at all,' Michael shook his hand, looking him in the eye. 'You remember Marie, and my brother George.'

Rose stood wide-eyed beside him. She felt as though her skeleton was dissolving inside of her like wet chalk, as the little strength she had left seeped out through her toes.

'Michael, this is my sister, Rose.'

She snapped at the air grasping whatever air she could find, as though she was about to go under.

'Rose,' Tim cleared his throat, 'this is Michael McGrath.'

She mustered a feeble amount of strength to shake his hand.

'His wife Marie,' Tim continued, Rose forced a smile. 'And Michael's brother, George. You might remember him from years ago,' Tim added. He continued to link Rose's arm while he made the introductions, he didn't want her to collapse, not in front of everyone.

'I'm so sorry for your loss, Rose. I hope you guys are holding up,' Marie said, smiling gently at both of them.

'Of course, it's very thoughtful of you to come, though, you really shouldn't have,' Tim said, knowing Rose wasn't able to speak. The glare of the sun bounced from the white marble cross causing all but Rose to squint.

'Really awful, what happened,' Marie continued. 'Were you close?' she asked sympathetically.

'Well, em, we were only children, really.' Rose's voice broke as she tried to answer her, grateful for the priest as he tapped the microphone and silenced the gathering at the graveside.

Chapter 26

Saturday Morning – 2016

Louise leaned against the car, looking back towards the congregation at the graveside. Not wanting to appear disrespectful, she checked if she could be seen and then pulled out her phone. The funeral had been a tense, but quiet affair. Sometimes in times of grief, people talked more than they needed to. But no one had offered anything and now it was over, she was heading back to the station.

'Jesus Christ,' she muttered to herself as she scrolled through the number of missed calls and messages, all of which, bar one, were from Kelly. She had texted him earlier, avoiding having to talk to him, and told him that she would go to the funeral. She had been so pissed off at him for leaving her in Dublin without a proper explanation that she refused to answer any of his calls.

'You rang.' Louise yanked her seat belt around her and started the engine of her car. She had a good mind not to answer at all. She craned her neck sideways, pulled out on the empty road and made her way back to the station.

Kelly swung around on his office chair and placed his elbows on his desk. 'Hey,' he paused, he could hear the annoyance in her voice. 'Why haven't you answered me, I've been calling you since yesterday.'

'I've been busy.' She was short with her answers, she was trying as best as she could to avoid a fight.

'I see.' Kelly didn't realise she had been so pissed. 'I was a little worried about you.' He shot a look around the office to make sure he wasn't overheard. Since he had left her in Dublin, he hadn't had a chance to explain to her why.

'Well, no need, I'm fine.'

'Are you pissed, Louise?' It was dawning on Kelly that he had done something wrong, but what, he wasn't quite sure.

'Nope.' She exhaled loudly.

'Okay.' Kelly shook his head, he couldn't understand why she was so curt. 'I think he's looking for a bit of publicity, you know, with all the attention this one is getting,' Kelly quipped but Louise remained silent.

They all knew the attention that the station would receive in the media for solving a forty-six-year-old case, especially with the likes of McCarthy loving the idea of being interviewed by television. But Louise was still not convinced that arresting Timothy Fitzpatrick was the right or, more importantly, the just, thing to do. Kelly could hear the tension in each of her sighs.

'Apparently there is some freelance reporter covering it from the UK as well,' Kelly said, regurgitating everything the Inspector had told him, nearly word for word. He really had had an earful of McCarthy and was losing patience with the case for that reason alone.

'Mmm,' Louise answered. 'There was a hire car parked there all right. Male, in his thirties driving it,' Louise said. 'Although, he appeared to be the only one, I'd have thought the crew that were hanging around the Estate would have followed the McGraths to the church,' she added.

'So the McGraths were there?' Kelly said, flicking back through his notebook, looking over the notes.

'Yes and what appeared to be Rose's daughter,' Louise answered.

'And what about the interaction between the McGraths and the Fitzpatricks, anything, you know, familiar between them?' Kelly asked.

'Not that I could see.' Louise took her turn for the station car park and parked in her usual spot.

'Louise, are you sure you are okay?' He wanted to talk to her about what they had shared together, he wanted them to have private jokes and connect like they had in Dublin, and he couldn't understand why she was so stand-offish. He shook his head, knowing there was no way he was going to get to the bottom of her apparent annoyance, over the phone.

'Yeah,' she said, her voice a little softer. 'I'm fine.'

'Are you still at the funeral?' he said. He wished they were back in Dublin, wrapped in the sheets in the Camden Court Hotel, that was the only type of electric tension he wanted between them.

'I'm outside the station, I'll be in, in a sec,' Louise answered, reaching across to the floor of the passenger side for her bag.

'Wait there.' Kelly grabbed his wallet from his jacket on the back of his chair. 'I'll come to you.' He raced down the rubber-covered stairs, two steps at a time. He wanted to be able to touch her, look her in the eye, and he knew he wouldn't have the peace of doing it inside the station.

Louise sighed deeply and drew in a lungful of air. She wiped away the crumbs that her garage-bought breakfast had left on the passenger seat and crumpled up the white paper bag. She leaned into the back seat and grabbed a plastic Tesco bag to use as a bin. She was in the middle of scooping up day old empty water bottles and week-old plastic sandwich cases when the passenger door opened.

'Louise.' The side of the car shifted as Kelly's weight flopped onto the passenger seat. 'What happened?' He shrugged his shoulders and opened up his hands in despair. He had thought that what they had in Dublin was special. A quick flash of her naked body in his hotel room sparked through him as he glanced at her, her gold chain, the same that she had worn when she was underneath him, sat delicately on her clavicle, just inside her crisp white blouse. He could nearly taste the almond flavour from her skin again. If he wasn't so worried, he would have enjoyed the flashback and the joke he had made then, about being allergic to nuts.

'Nothing happened,' she insisted but he didn't believe her. They sat in silence for a time.

'You know McCarthy wants to go for that arrest today, that's why he called me back.' He looked towards the second-floor window where the inspector's office was tucked.

Louise didn't follow his eyes, she didn't need to, she listened as he explained. She reached back and placed the bag she had just filled on the back seat.

'Tim has motive, no alibi that we can verify, and even a financial gain in the long run, everything adds up to manslaughter, we'll go for a straight-up arrest,' Kelly said. He had deliberated on it long enough. Louise couldn't look at him. 'But we need to execute today, so McCarthy says, anyhow.'

Louise remained silent. Something didn't feel right and for the first time in her professional career, her head was overruled by her heart. She filled her cheeks with air and exhaled slowly. She shifted slightly, pointing her knees towards him and sighed, one of her many faults was her compulsion to cut the bullshit and call each and every situation as she saw it, no matter how uncomfortable it might have been and today, she felt, was one of those days. 'I can't do it, Kelly.' She drew in a deep breath, paused and continued. 'And I don't want you to do it either.' They both glanced at the white painted masonry building across the car park.

'You want me to not arrest a suspect because, why, you don't think he did it? Louise knew that his question was rhetorical and didn't answer him.'

'Well, if you had a heart, Kelly...' It came out an awful lot harsher than she had intended it to.

It had only been two days since she was lying naked in his arms, he couldn't believe that they had drifted so far apart, he had even planned to tell Annie about Louise the next time he saw her. 'If I had a heart.' The hurt from her remark cut deep.

'Look, I didn't mean it like that.' She placed her hand on his thigh and squeezed. 'Just stall the Inspector for a day.' She wanted to say 'or two' but didn't push it, she knew he was at his limit. She needed him to see her side of Timothy Fitzpatrick's story first.

'Are you hearing yourself, are you for real?' Kelly ran his hand over the stubble on his face. He couldn't believe what she was saying. He unclasped his hand from his jaw and placed his head in both his hands. 'Since when do you make a call like that, Louise, seriously? I just don't get you, Louise, fuck's sake,' Kelly said.

'Well, neither do I,' she said. She could hardly expect him to understand if she didn't understand herself. Rose's statement, how she had described what had happened to her when she was only fourteen had impacted her in a way that she couldn't understand. It wasn't as though she hadn't been exposed to harrowing stories before but the way that Rose spoke about her brother Tim, how he had saved her from the horrific events that they had endured, had made her pause. Did she think Tim had motive to kill the uncle? Yes. Did she think that arresting him for it was the right thing to do? No. And that was why she had asked Kelly for more time. 'Kelly,' the resignation in her voice made him lock his eyes to hers, 'I can't explain this one, I know I have no right but,' she knew she was taking a risk asking him to compromise himself professionally but she felt compelled to, 'could you just stall, tell the Inspector that we are ruling out another line of enquiry before we make the arrest.' She held her breath waiting for him to answer. 'Let's just grab a bite to eat, talk over the case, just once more, I want to be sure, we haven't missed anything. Can we just hold off for an hour even?

'Okay,' Kelly said.

She looked away not trusting the stinging feeling that was creeping in to her eyes and exhaled a sigh of relief.

Chapter 27

Saturday Morning– 2016

Standing opposite Michael, across the grave, with Tim holding her upright, Rose studied her secret son from behind her sunglasses. He looked like the man she had imagined him to be, handsome and happy, and even though she felt she had no right to, she felt proud, proud that she and her son were both strong enough to have endured their ordeal. It amazed her that something so precious was born out of something so horrific.

She pictured Matt's face, her wonderful husband, whose kind eyes, strong hands and powerful words had told her this day would come. The day, when finally, her eyes would meet her secret son's and she would know, with all her heart, that everything, absolutely everything she did for Michael, had been the right thing to do and she did because she loved him. She wished that Matt was with her, she wished that she could tell him how right he had been. His patience with her regrets and reverence with her sorrow had allowed her to grieve, to mourn the son that she had never known. He had told her that she was to be proud of it, proud of what she had done for him. She wanted to share it with him, her soulmate, the love of her life, she wanted Matt to be here and look on Michael with her and share in her pride. She looked to the sky and hoped that he could hear her thoughts.

'Rosie,' Tim tugged at her arm again. 'You okay?' he whispered.

'Yes, fine.' She gave him a reassuring smile.

'You were a million miles away. Michael is on his way back over.'

'Okay, thanks.' Rose stiffened her grip on Tim's arm.

'It was a really lovely service', Michael said, reaching Tim's eyes first.

'Thank you so much for coming,' Tim said as he shook his hand.

'God, it was the least we could do,' Michael answered, 'It's terrible the whole thing,' he said.

Rose looked at him with tears welling in her eyes.

'You must be driven mad with the media presence at the gates to the farm,' Tim said. 'I've caught a few snippets of it on the news.'

'Actually, it's died down a fair bit, to be honest. I expected more of a turnout this morning,' Michael added. He had been pleasantly surprised to drive away from his front gates and find the media had moved on, 'In turnout I mean with the media, not the funeral,' he added awkwardly, conscious that it might have sounded like a criticism. 'Actually,' he continued, drawing his wife into the conversation, 'Marie here, wondered,' he nodded his head in his wife's direction, 'well, we both did,' he conceded, he knew his wife's intentions were good, 'if you'd like to come back to the house, you know for old time's sake?'

He looked almost childlike, Rose thought, vulnerable even. She dabbed her tears behind her glasses relying on Tim to speak for her. She studied the lines on his skin and the warm hazel colour of his eyes. He was tall, the same as Tim, but Michael was much more muscular, built to work the land. His black suit hung stylishly on his broad frame as though it was tailored for him and the shine on his leather shoes reflected the bright midday sun.

'We couldn't impose, like that,' Tim answered.

'Nonsense,' Marie offered. 'Would you like to, Rose?'

Rose caught Tim's eye and let him know that she was okay. It was more than that though, she wanted the opportunity to be with him and if it meant going back to Fitzpatrick house, well that was what she was prepared to do.

'It's just that, I've promised Eve and Jack that we might have visitors…' Marie continued.

'George has just left for them, they were in a neighbour's for the morning,' Michael added.

'I told them that you might come up to the house for tea, that maybe Mr Fitzpatrick and his guests might come up too.' Marie raised her eyebrows in anticipation. She knew by involving Eve and Jack in the equation, it would be a hard invitation for Rose and Tim to refuse. Having Rose Fitzpatrick, or O' Reilly as she was now, in Kilkenny was exactly the opportunity she needed to follow through on her mother-in-law's plan.

'I suppose that'd be okay,' Rose said, surprising herself and by the expression on Tim's face, him too. 'We have Robert and Lizzie, with us though,' she said searching around for either one of them, 'they are here somewhere.' She shrugged.

'Of course, all welcome,' Marie said. 'Nothing fancy mind, but Eve and I did a little baking,' she added.

'Okay then, Fitzpatrick Farm, it is,' Rose announced; much to Tim's amazement. 'Or Estate, I mean.' She remembered the new title the McGraths had given it but despite the new name, to Rose it was still the same place and the thoughts of going back to the house filled her with dread.

*

Lizzie read the text for a third time, shut her phone off and zipped it back inside her oversized bag. She could barely believe it. She hesitated before she lifted her head, knowing from the three sentences he had sent her that he was watching her, waiting for her to speak to him.

> I'm in Kilkenny, I need to speak to you. It's not what you think.

She didn't answer. Since she had left him in London she had wondered what he would do and his text had answered it. She backed away from the gathering and placed her back against the graveyard wall. Keeping her head low, she replayed the sentences in her head.

'There you are,' Robert said.

'There I am,' she said, her smile not quite reaching her eyes.

'Your mum is wondering where you got to.'

'Just answering some emails.' She patted her bag. 'I need to make a call though.' She looked expectantly at Robert. 'Can I borrow the car keys?' she asked; her voice shaky.

'Sure, they've just to do the shaking hands bit, but then I think I overheard your mother arranging for us to go back up to the McGraths' for tea,' Robert said, unsure of the arrangements himself.

'Okay,' she said distractedly, darting her eyes across the road. She knew Lucas would be waiting to catch her on her own.

She hurried to the car, clicked the fob, opened the car door and sat in it. Moments later, she watched him in the rear-view mirror approach the car. He bent to look in the passenger window and she motioned at him to get in.

'It's good to see you,' Lucas said and reached across to kiss her. He was dying to hold her, continue where they left off before any of this Kilkenny stuff had interfered with them. Lizzie rebuffed his attempt. 'Listen, I know, this seems as though I'm like a vulture circling overhead, but it's not like that.' He cleared his throat. 'I'm here for a different reason, I promise you,' he said, watching Lizzie scan her mirrors. 'There are no other reporters,' he said. 'If that's what you're looking for.'

'I'm not,' she answered abruptly, not meeting his gaze. 'And I don't know why you're saying that, as if it's a good thing. Seeing as you are the only one low enough to cover a funeral,' she added.

He didn't take the time to explain that had it not been for him, the reporters would have been all over the place. 'Where's your old friend then, the one you dropped everything for?' the thoughts of Lucas's old girlfriend from college had been forefront on Lizzie's mind.

'It's complicated, Lizzie' Lucas sighed, 'but I can assure you it is not what you think, and she wasn't exactly my girlfriend'. It had been odd for Lucas seeing Marie arrive earlier, with her husband in tow. For a time in college they had been inseparable, the best and closest of friends and Lucas had ruined that with his jealousy, he knew that now and if he was honest, he knew that then. This was his chance to make amends with Marie and show her that it was her friendship that he had cared about most.

'And I'm not here to cover the funeral…' he hesitated. 'I mean, it's not like that.'

'So you're not here to write a story about the forty-six-year-old murder of one of my family members?' She asked.

'I am but…' he said.

She didn't let him finish. 'So what then?' She looked in her rear-view mirror and saw the small crowd dispersing.

He wasn't able to answer her, not concisely anyhow. 'Can I come see you in Dublin tomorrow, before I head back, I'll explain then,' he pleaded, he placed his hand on the door handle, waiting for an answer.

'I won't be in Dublin,' she said sullenly. 'I'll be here, in Kilkenny in the morning.'

'Okay, good then.' He watched the crowd approaching through the mirrors. 'Just do one thing for me, please.' He opened the door and placed one foot outside. 'Just answer my call in the morning and I'll explain everything then, please.'

'I'll answer the phone,' she said, 'that's all I can promise.'

'Lizzie, I'm so sorry about all this, I really am, I'm not doing what you think I'm doing, I promise you.' He couldn't have been any more sincere but couldn't find better words to articulate what he felt for her. He smiled and left the car before the others noticed.

'Lizzie, you okay?' Tim spoke as she climbed out of the car a couple of moments later.

'Sure, fine,' she said. She glanced towards the silver Volkswagen Golf, the hired car that Lucas got into. 'Grand.' She hesitated. 'Eh, everything okay with Mum?' she asked, changing the subject, she couldn't be sure if anyone had seen Lucas leave; she'd have some explaining to do if they had.

'She's actually fine,' Tim said. 'Surprisingly,' he added. 'And she's arranged for us all to go to the McGraths', apparently.'

'That's fantastic.' Lizzie had never been brought to Fitzpatrick Farm before and was eager to see where her Mum and her uncle had grown up. It would have been a shame to be so close and not have seen it.

Chapter 28

Saturday Afternoon – 2016

Since Lucas had arrived in Kilkenny, Marie had been on edge waiting to tell Michael what she had done.

'I was anxious about this morning, were you?' she asked Michael as they made their way back to their car. She didn't wait for him to answer. 'I thought more people from the town would have turned out to see what was going on?' she said, trying to work in the conversation about Lucas. She needed to explain. 'It was unusual not to have more photographers and reporters there, don't you think?' she offered.

'Yeah, maybe,' he said.

Marie searched for the words to use to tell him that it wasn't just by chance that the media had lost interest. 'The thing is, Michael,' she swallowed and cleared her throat. 'I asked Lucas to get involved.'

'You did what?' Michael was incredulous.

'I went ahead and asked him to do me a favour, sort of kill the story, or at least spin it in such a way that it has nothing to do with us,' she blurted.

Michael's brow furrowed. In his memory, Lucas wasn't the type of guy that would go out of his way to help anyone, especially not him, not after he had warned him off nearly twenty years ago. He shook his head.

'Look, Michael, I know you don't like him…' Marie said. Michael never told her how he threatened Lucas to sling his hook and leave Marie alone all those years ago, he hadn't seen the point. 'But he was a good friend, once upon a time, and I really just wanted the story to go away.' She sighed. 'He was the best for the job.'

'Lucas,' He threw her a hopeless glance. 'The guy who was madly in love with you and begged you to leave me,' he said, his voice louder. 'For him,' he added. He fixed his wide eyes on hers in disbelief.

'We were just kids then, Michael, he was just worried for me,' she answered. 'You were ten years older than me, he…' She reconsidered. 'They,' she emphasised, referring to her entire college class, 'well, they were just looking out for me.'

'They might have been, Marie, but he definitely was only worried for himself.' He checked his rear-view mirror. 'For fuck's sake, Marie.'

'Look, he is quite good at what he does, and he can help make our connection to the story go away, you know he can,' Marie pleaded, she wanted to tell him the truth but couldn't. 'Just be pleasant to him, please, if you see him,' she added. She had no idea how the day was going to end up but with the connection to Lizzie and the Fitzpatrick family, she needed Michael to at least not do anything he would regret. 'He's doing us a favour.' She couldn't explain why it was so important to have the story managed, not without breaking the promise she had made to his mother.

'Pleasant to him, are you listening to yourself?' Michael said.

She had given Lucas as much detail as she could muster, the time of the funeral, the names of the old families and even the names of the detectives covering the case. Somewhere inside of the detail was the real personal story, the one that she promised to protect, and someone with Lucas's ability could surely spin a better story. Marie sat silently, the tension between them filling the air.

'Look, I know you don't approve, but I know what I'm doing,' she said, adamant that her decision had been the best one, in his best interest. 'It was more about damage control than it was about anything else, 'for Christ's sake,' she added slightly louder than she'd intended.

'Marie, it's not the principle of what you are trying to do, I just don't understand how you could contact him,' Michael said; his voice deliberately controlled, kept in time with the rhythm of the indicator as he pulled out into traffic. 'Of all people, seriously.'

'If I know, or knew,' she clarified, 'anything about journalism and the way sensationalism works, I know that this,' Marie spoke with her hands, 'me, ringing Lucas,' she glanced at his reaction to her mentioning his name, 'is a small price to pay to get the story buried, or if not buried at least controlled.'

'Jesus, are you listening to yourself, you sound like a campaign manager for Trump. When will you realise, it doesn't bloody matter what people think, it was nothing to do with us, Marie?' Michael said. 'We were just the ones that discovered it.'

'I know, Michael, I just didn't want the bad smell to be hanging around us for ever more. I know how these cretins work, Michael—'

'Lucas being the biggest cretin of all,' Michael interrupted her, a flicker of anger flashed across his face.

'I have no contacts in Ireland any more, Lucas has.' Her patience was growing thin and the plastic smile she had plastered on her face was beginning to wear. 'He knows how to play the game better than anyone I know. He'll be able to minimise the impact, bury the story, but most of all, at least, with him, the facts will be straight.'

'Who cares, Marie, seriously, why are you so bloody worried what others think, you'd swear you have something to hide.'

'Yes, Michael, but we live now in an information age,' she tried her best to justify her interference. 'If you don't act, you are at the mercy of these hacks who will knowingly print any story, just as long as they make money from it. If they can't find anything on us, they'll make something up, but they'll do it in such a way that we won't be able to answer them, it'll be by suggestion, innuendo. Please, Michael, trust me on this one.' Marie reached inside her bag to retrieve her phone that was vibrating. 'Regardless of what you may think, whatever is said now will stick. If your name, or mine or even the children's names are used in the same sentence as murder, it will forever show up on their Google search, even though it is complete fabrication, it's important, Michael, I know what I'm doing.' It was the best reason she could think of to explain it. She looked at her phone and noticed Lucas's number. It was reassuring to know that he was helping her protect her secret and if she was honest, it was lovely to have one of her oldest friends back in her life again but of all the times for him to ring, she thought to herself, there couldn't have been a worse one. She glanced apologetically at her husband.

'Answer it,' Michael said. She would have preferred not to but she knew he wanted to hear the conversation.

'Hi Lucas, how's things?' she asked. Trying her best to appear calm.

Michael was torn; he could see merit in some of what she was saying but he still wasn't comfortable with Lucas being back in his life, or more importantly, in Marie's. He glimpsed to the side, away from the midday sun that was pelting in from the driver's window.

'That's fine Lucas, honestly,' Marie continued to look forward as Michael manoeuvred the car through their electric gates; she checked her side mirror confirming the Fitzpatricks were behind them. 'No, no, you don't need to speak to Michael, really, he gets it.' Marie glimpsed back at Michael. She couldn't tell from his expression if he could hear Lucas clearly. 'Really, I'll ring you later, I must go now, we are having a bit of reception here at the house for the Fitzpatricks.' Marie slid off her seat belt as the car came to a halt. Michael parked the car. 'Look, can we discuss everything later; I don't really have time to talk right now…' Michael waited for Marie to end her call. 'I will,' Marie glanced at her husband again surprised, making it obvious to Michael that Lucas was referring to him. 'I'll tell him,' she said and hung up her phone.

'Tell me what?' Michael asked.

'Well, he says he wants to speak to you, when you have a minute, he says he can come up here, or if you prefer it, he's staying at The Park, you could go down to see him later?' Marie left the statement open, she had no idea why. 'Anyway, we have guests.' She smiled at the group standing in the courtyard and jumped out of the car to greet them before Michael had a chance to answer.

Chapter 29

Saturday Afternoon – 2016

'Wow, you are a dark horse, Mum. You never told me you were nobility.' Lizzie was in awe of the uninterrupted vista of rolling hills and magnificent buildings that adorned the entire Fitzpatrick Estate. No matter which direction she turned to, there was something to admire. It helped that the sun's golden rays beamed perfectly on the farmhouse. 'It is so impressive, Mum. Tim, I wish you had brought me here before,' Lizzie added.

Rose smiled warily in response. She clasped her spindly hands together to stop them fidgeting. She inhaled deeply trying to calm the rhythm of her heart. She only had young girl's eyes the last time she saw the farm and those eyes had been filled with sadness and torment.

'It didn't look like this in our day, guys,' Tim was quick to answer, guiding his sister and his niece with his long arms towards the house. 'There's Marie and Michael there now, come on, let's get inside.'

Rose remained quiet, the corners of her mouth twitched, searching desperately for words to use. Not once in the forty-six years since she had left the place had she ever imagined herself returning; she felt dizzy at the thoughts of stepping back inside.

She cleared her throat and with Tim's hand on her elbow, she turned. The fields seemed greener, cascading down the hill towards Mrs McGrath's farm and the sky, a beautiful shade of blue, framed the farm's edges. The grey ominous clouds of the Fitzpatricks' past were nowhere to be seen and, for once, there was not one rain cloud in sight. 'I don't remember it ever looking like this.' She managed.

'How much of that land is, or I mean *was* ours?' Lizzie stood with her back to the large grey farmhouse unable to keep her eyes from the view.

'Down as far as that house and hedge there.' Tim pointed to the array of green fields stitched together like an old patchwork quilt. 'Then there, where you see the darker green ditch,' he pointed down to the bottom of the fields, 'that's the start of McGrath's land, where Michael and George McGrath would have grown up.' The last time he was at McGrath's house had been the night Michael was born.

'Oh wow, so Michael literally came from the farm next door,' Lizzie exclaimed, oblivious to the connection.

Rose paused. The rolling fields down to McGrath's farm were now barely visible with the brightness of the sun glaring down. The steel gates and galvanised roofs of the working farm gleamed in the daylight. Modern garden seats and tables adorned the courtyard with Cath Kidston type fabrics on pillows and cushions. The house itself was bright and clean and alive with warmth and laughter. The discernible contrast made the whole place barely recognisable. It looked like time had healed the house after all.

Lizzie walked ahead up the three granite steps through the double fronted navy blue doors with Robert behind her.

'Shall we?' Tim squeezed Rose's arm tightly.

'Let's do this,' she asserted and followed Tim's lead.

A delicious waft of oven-baked foods drifted through the front hall and mingled with the scents of the Yankee Candles that were strategically placed on the hall tables. Marie had scrambled ahead to light them and make sure that the kids and George had arrived home in one piece. The scent of 'Fluffy Towels' was her favourite. The door to drawing room idled open, the last time Rose had been at that door, her mother had been on the other side of it. She pushed it open wider revealing an airy powder blue living room with the most luscious of velvet sofas freestanding in the middle of the parquet floor.

'There's Mum now,' Lizzie declared as she turned to see Tim guide Rose towards the kitchen.

'Rose, I'm really thrilled you are here.' Marie extended her hand to Rose and leaned in to kiss her cheek. 'Please,' she smiled. Knowing what she knew about Rose, she backed a little to allow her to catch her breath, she didn't want to overwhelm her. 'I hope you like what we've done with everything,' Marie said nervously. When Marie had first learned of Rose's story, her heart had broken and now that she was meeting her for the first time, her heart broke for her all over again. 'I'll just check on the food.' She turned as she walked away. 'Oh and Eve wants to give you a tour later, when you catch your breath, get your bearings,' Marie said. The letter that Mrs McGrath had given her, coupled with her mother-in-law's strict instructions '*You'll know when the time is right*' were dancing around in her head. She would tell Michael tonight, she decided. 'Eve has been practising all morning. She has poor Charlie tormented,' she continued. Charlie lifted his head from his bed at the mention of his name and when no food or belly rubs were forthcoming, he duly fell back asleep. 'Sorry Charlie,' Marie said under her breath. 'She might charge you mind, her daddy told her a short tour of the house was a fiver and a long tour should be a tenner,' she said.

Rose laughed at her charm, her nerves fading ever so slightly away.

'Oh, this is Eve now. The tour guide for the evening.' Marie ushered her daughter in front of her. 'She knows everything there is to know about the house.' Marie was twisting her daughter's ponytail in her hands as Eve's wide blue eyes looked up to her. 'Did you lose your brother? Where's Jack?' Marie smiled. 'Or did he lose you?' she said through the corner of her mouth, grinning.

'He's helping Daddy with drinks.' She smiled at her mum. 'Can I do the tour now?' she asked her mum expectantly.

'Have patience, darling, give everyone a chance to get in the door.' Marie looked apologetically to Rose.

'Its fine, Marie, honestly.' Rose looked at Eve, a lump forming in the back of her throat. She was like a mini-Lizzie. Blonde curls and wide-eyed. 'Hello Eve, it's lovely to meet you.' Rose crouched forward and held out her arm. Eve placed her hand in Rose's and they squeezed hello to each other. 'I'm really looking forward to the tour, you know, that's the best bit,' Rose said. It felt good to feel the size of a small hand in hers again. The simple connection was fulfilling. 'You'll have to show me your bedroom,' Rose said to her, playing into the child's excitement. 'Maybe it's the same one I had when I was a little girl,' she suggested as Eve beamed with delight. 'I hope you'll be able to answer all of our questions on the tour, though,' Rose warned. 'These three really love anything to do with houses,' Rose pointed to Lizzie, Robert and Tim as they listened to the conversation. It warmed Tim's heart to see their exchange. 'Tim draws houses for his job.' Rose's face was animated talking to Michael's youngest child. 'And Robert makes sure they are strong and safe.'

'I know, he's an engineer,' Eve said knowingly. 'My daddy told me.'

Marie wondered what else she might say and cringed, they really were going to have to make sure all doors were closed in future, if they were going to talk around her.

'And Lizzie here, she loves designing houses and decorating them and she knows an awful lot about old houses like this one,' Rose said. 'So I hope you have all the facts ready.'

'Is it your job too, Lizzie?' Eve asked, she was beginning to worry that she might not know enough to tell them.

'Eh, no,' Lizzie said. The glance that Tim threw in her direction gave her comfort. He had told her to follow her heart, which she didn't, but now, with the generous inheritance that both her mum and uncle had provided for her, she was closer than she ever was to doing it. 'But I hope to get a job doing it. Maybe you could give me ideas,' she suggested.

Eve was delighted with the vote of confidence from the beautiful woman at her party.

'I know all of the house's secrets, Daddy told me them all,' Eve answered.

'Well then,' Rose smiled, 'we had better get started.' The secrets about the house that Rose knew, would never be shared.

Lizzie, Robert and Tim followed as Eve gladly led Rose around the house.

'Seriously, Mum,' Lizzie spoke, her voice deliberately low so as not to be overheard, 'this place is utterly amazing, the restoration of everything is first-class.' She stroked the mahogany banister as she climbed the wide creaky stairs.

'It wasn't as nice then, love, as it is now.' Rose smiled at her daughter, grateful that she never had to know in her lifetime, grateful that Eve, the precious little child of her own son, her granddaughter who continued to hold her hand tightly, didn't have to know either. 'Very different times,' she added.

'Wow, everything just looks gorgeous,' Lizzie said as they followed Eve around. Modern pieces seemed to marry with the old restored floors and shuttered sash windows. The house wasn't overdone as she expected. 'Those cornices are beautifully restored,' she commented. 'And the Georgian paint colours were very well chosen,' Lizzie said, buzzing with excitement. 'Tim, look at the centrepiece.' Lizzie pointed eagerly to the ceiling.

Tim looked where she pointed, noticing the detail for the first time in his life. He had probably walked every inch of every floorboard when he had lived there but nothing looked or felt the same, and he was glad of that, content that there was nothing identifiable from the past that would jar with the happiness that now lined the walls.

'Oh, I love this stuff, I definitely missed my calling,' she said as they reached the top of the stairs.

'Watch the top step,' Eve warned. 'It squeaks,' she said. 'Daddy said that there are fairies living underneath and every time you step on their roof they squeak at you because they think it's going to collapse.'

Rose couldn't help but smile at her innocence; it had never occurred to her when she lived there to explain the squeak in such a fantastically magical way. Her House, Fitzpatrick House, the house that she vowed to never set foot in again, had been transformed from a house of horrors to a house where fairies lived, maybe coming back wasn't such a bad idea after all.

'Oh dear, I'm glad you told me.' Rose lifted her leg past the fairies roof and stood on the landing. 'I would have loved to have known the fairies lived there when I was small', she smiled, 'we would have been great friends'. Rose had wondered about Michael all his life, had he married, what was he like, was he happy, but in all the times she imagined his life, she had never been able to see him with children of his own and now, as she stood on the landing with Eve, she couldn't ever imagine him without.

Standing on the landing, Eve dashed to close all the bedroom doors. She was pleased with herself at the little game she had invented. 'You have to guess which bedroom is mine.' Impersonating a game show host she walked up and down the landing. 'Could it be this one, or maybe it's this one,' she implied as she waited for the adults to guess. They smiled and played along.

'I think it's this one,' Rose said with an air of seriousness, choosing what would have been Tim's old room.

'No, I think it's this one,' Tim chimed in, pointing to what would have been Rose's old room and Lizzie and Robert picked out of what was left.

'Is there a prize?' Lizzie asked before Eve revealed the correct answer.

'Em, yes,' she answered. 'It's chocolate cake,' Eve exclaimed, clearly enjoying the game. 'The guess that was right is…' Eve paused for effect, taking her role as quiz show host in earnest. 'The right guess is… this one.' She flung open Rose's old bedroom door.

'I win the chocolate cake!' Tim declared as Rose stood on the landing looking into her old room, frozen momentarily as a wash of memories drenched her on the spot. For a second she felt like a fearful fourteen-year-old again. Drawing deeply on her reserves, she shook away the overwhelming urge she had to run and regained her composure.

'Oh, it's so pretty, Eve,' Rose remarked as she noticed the pink, sparkly décor that festooned the space. 'It is so much prettier than when I had it.' Eve was delighted with herself. 'I think it was a yucky brown colour, with mustard swirls on the carpet,' Rose said as Eve scrunched her nose in disgust. She hovered by the doors of the rest of the rooms as the others continued on the tour. She couldn't bring herself to look inside. She had visited enough memories today. Stopping at the top of the stairs, she leaned against the wall and watched as Eve made her way ahead of them. Tim took her by the hand and walked her back downstairs. His grip all the support she needed, both physically and emotionally.

'How did that go?' Marie asked. It was Rose's response she was most interested in. Had it dragged up old unhappy memories or was it good for her to see it again, Marie couldn't tell from the enigmatic expression on Rose's face.

'Tim won,' Eve said. 'He gets the chocolate cake,' she added.

'Oh, well I'll see if we can find more cake for the losers then, shall I?' She curled Eve's ponytail again in her hands and watched as Rose looked lovingly on her. It wasn't hard to fall for the charms of Eve McGrath and by the looks of it, all four of them were smitten, especially Rose. 'The food is just ready.' Marie directed them to a seating area by the back of the house. I'll just grab some plates and then we are set.'

'Are you doing okay, Rosie?' Tim was curious. He would never have guessed that she would have willingly returned. He was the most surprised, out of all of them, that she had accepted Michael's offer.

'I'm fine, Tim, just…' Rose paused. 'I don't know, overwhelmed I suppose.' She looked around the room, Jack was like Michael's shadow, she hadn't really spoken to him yet, he appeared to be quiet and shy. 'But then it feels like the most normal thing in the world to be doing. I know I'm not making sense.' After a pause she continued, whispering, 'It is a little unbelievable. His beautiful little family, being back here after all these years. I don't know how to feel.' Tim rubbed her hand. 'He's happy, Tim, how could he not be.' Rose directed her gaze back to Michael and Jack. 'He reminds me of you,' she said, directing Tim's eyes to Jack. 'The quiet observer.' She smiled. 'And the little whirlwind, over there,' Rose said, her eyes filling up looking at Eve, 'full of life and mischief, so like Lizzie.'

'I thought that myself when I first met her,' Tim answered. 'Silver lining,' he added.

'Silver lining,' she repeated.

It had been forty-six years since she had left; half a century of changes, all of them, it would appear, for the better. Whatever the circumstances, in that moment, and for the first time in her life, she was happy to be at Fitzpatrick House.

'Rose, I'm so glad you could come.' Michael, temporarily finished with his drink topping-up duties, finally made his way around the room to mingle. He looked deep into her eyes and sat beside her calmly.

A frisson of electricity moved up her spine and she quivered in anticipation. She noticed the width of his shoulders through his open-necked cotton shirt; his tie abandoned on his drive back home. She found it hard to believe that this man was her son.

'Michael, it was a lovely idea of yours, so welcoming to invite us.' She smiled, giving Tim the look that told him she was okay.

Tim watched on in loving admiration as Rose spoke with her son, he had to pinch himself that it was really happening.

'You've done wonders with the place,' she offered, wondering what to say next. 'My daughter,' she paused, she felt almost guilty at using the word, 'Lizzie, really loved how you've done all the restoration and decoration, she loves all that type of stuff.'

'I can't take credit for that, I'm afraid, that was all Marie,' he said.

Marie overheard her name, the anticipation of Michael meeting Rose had overwhelmed her and now, as she saw them smile into each other's eyes, engrossed in each other's words, her own eyes glistened, how magnificent that they finally got to meet.

'She tends to have very good ideas, even if she does meet a bit of resistance along the way.' He scrunched his face, admitting his own stubbornness. 'She has plans to build chalets, small retreats in the field below.' He drew a deep breath, he wondered had it been a little insensitive to mention the digging in the field, it was because of the groundworks for the chalets that the body of Patrick Fitzpatrick had been found. 'The whole area of agri-tourism is booming down here,' he added. 'The government are throwing money at anyone who is mad enough to take it.' He chuckled.

'I heard that.' Marie floated by with a plate of cakes.

'That's fantastic, Marie,' Rose said. She could imagine the vision she had for the place. 'Artists and writers and all sorts of creative people would love that, not to mention the Americans, or city families, it's a superb idea.'

'Outside is more my area, though,' Michael added.

'Outside looks lovely too, the sheds have been rebuilt, by the looks of them,' Rose said. She watched Michael, the way his eyes widened in excitement when he spoke lovingly about his wife, the way the corner of his mouth curved enigmatically when he made a comical remark. She watched the sparkle in his eyes when he spoke about his kids, she was so relieved to see how fulfilled his life had become.

'A few new walls, new roofs, that type of thing, no major new builds, though. Although, there was an old cottage down below,' Michael smiled awkwardly. 'Who am I telling, of course you know there was an old cottage,' Michael added. 'I sometimes forget that people lived in this magnificent house before me, I never met any of you, you see, I was much younger than all of your generation, my mother tells me, I was God's doing, not hers.' He let out a laugh, the memory of his mother still warm in his heart. 'That was her dignified way of telling me I wasn't planned,' he said, grinning as the memory of his headstrong mother flashed into his head. 'My mother and Marie were very close, they got on like a house on fire.'

'I remember your mother well,' Rose said and cleared her throat. 'Mrs McGrath was one of life's angels.' Rose raked her stiff hands through her grey hair and a pang of jealousy curved its way into her heart fleetingly. She knew she had no right to be jealous. 'That's lovely that they were good friends,' she added. She had the pleasure of knowing the warmth of Mrs McGrath and both she and Michael were both the better for it. Michael was reared in love and warmth as one of Mrs McGrath's sons and Rose was spirited away from the drudgery of the Fitzpatricks on a make-believe scholarship to a wonderful boarding school in Dublin, close to her brother in college and faraway from all the harm that Fitzpatrick Farm could do to her. Even though they never spoke from that day she left for school, Rose knew the depth of love Mrs McGrath had for her and Michael, she would never be forgotten. When news had filtered through that Mrs McGrath had passed away, for one brief moment, Rose had considered coming back to pay her respects but didn't, it wouldn't have been fair, not to Mrs McGrath and not to Michael.

'That they were, I'd say Marie knows more about my mother than I or even George ever knew,' Michael answered. 'Mind you, I don't know if that was a blessing or a curse, there were times, they'd both gang up on me, they'd have me agreeing to all sorts of things.' He laughed.

They sat momentarily in silence, both remembering the woman that had meant so much to their very existence.

'You were saying about the old cottage?' Rose said eventually, reminding him, eager to establish if it was still there.

'Oh yes, I was saying we knocked it down, we plan to build a bigger milking parlour, state-of-the-art machinery onto the shed that's already there. We want to get the agricultural stuff on that side.' He pointed west. 'And then all the tourist stuff, chalets and food hall to that side.' He swung his arm around and pointed east.

'Oh, good idea.' Rose was content to know that it and all the evil that had seeped into the walls in the cottage had been levelled to the ground. Whatever it was about the house getting a new lease of life, she knew it would never have been possible with the cottage. Now, she knew, she could relax a little more. 'Eve brought us on a tour. She was very charming.'

'Ah, my Evie, she's a force to be reckoned with,' he smiled as an equally charming young boy stood by his shoulder. 'And this man here, is Jack.' His son had found him in the crowd like a magnet. 'Say hello to Mrs Fitzpatrick.' He smiled encouragingly at Jack.

'Actually,' she smiled, 'it's O'Reilly now, and anyway, call me Rose.'

Jack was the image of Tim when he was young, Rose couldn't pull her eyes away from him.

Chapter 30

Saturday Afternoon – 2016

It hadn't taken Louise long to order her usual lunch to go in the deli and with the paper wrappers scrunched on her lap and Kelly beside her having finished his, they made their way back to the station. Louise flinched as her phone buzzed for the third time since Kelly had sat into her car. 'Jesus Christ, can I just get a minute.' She looked at him exasperated. 'Why is it that as soon as I need a minute to myself, everyone else thinks they're more entitled to it than me?' She looked at the missed calls on her phone. 'It's the Inspector.' She sighed. 'I'll have to answer him.'

Kelly checked his own phone, mirroring her sentiments. 'Let's just sort this out, get him off our backs,' Kelly said, Louise nodded.

'Inspector, you were looking for me.' Quietly she got out of the car, throwing Kelly a knowing look. It was a routine that they had run many a time, she would make the call and get herself back into the office as though she had never left, convincing the Inspector that she was there for ages, and Kelly would take up the rear, locking the car, throwing coats on the back of chairs and readying the desks as though they had been there all day. It was familiar, reliable and dependable, just what their relationship had been, up until yesterday that was. She handed Kelly the keys as she left. 'Yeah, I'm in the station,' Louise answered, knowing McCarthy was on a mission to find her. 'What do you mean? I've been chasing you around the building for an hour now.' Kelly's footsteps caught up on hers as he took the steps two by two. 'Well, every time I go up to your office, you're not there.' Kelly smirked as he overheard Louise's stretching of the truth. She was brash enough to pull it off and clever enough to know when to stop. 'You must be in the lift, every time I go up the stairs, I'd say that's how we keep missing each other.' They both smirked at how she had just insinuated that the Inspector was lazy and got away with it. 'Right then, stay in your office now, I'll come to you, I'll bring Kelly with me and we'll finalise it then.' She looked at Kelly who had already left his jacket on the back of his chair to make it look as though he hadn't left and hung up the call. 'He wants us both up to discuss the Fitzpatrick case.'

'I told you that,' Kelly answered and they both grabbed their files and headed for the stairs. 'Shit,' Kelly remembered.

'What?' Louise asked.

'I meant to say. Just in case it comes up. Car trouble, just go with it,' Kelly whispered as Louise tapped loudly at the Inspector's door. Catching a glimpse of her reflection in the office window, she smoothed down her white blouse and stepped inside the room when they were bellowed at. She looked at him perplexed.

'Update.' The Inspector was as gruff in personality as he was in appearance. 'Seeing as you couldn't get back in time on Thursday.'

'As I said, sir,' Kelly threw a knowing glance at Louise, hoping that she had picked up on it, 'we were stuck on the N4 till around two a.m., bloody nightmare.'

'Yeah, bloody nightmare, sir,' Louise added, she wasn't sure what she was becoming complicit in but trusted Kelly enough to follow his lead.

'Yes, well, I waited here till one and when I got your text I headed home.'

'Yeah, sorry about that sir, bloody nightmare in Dublin and on the motorway. Kelly threw Louise a glance that said he would explain everything to her later. 'We did try and get into you yesterday too but, I believe you were off?' Kelly was deliberate in turning the fault back to the Inspector.

'Yes, which is why I'm here today'. The Inspector was less than pleased about having to explain himself to Kelly.

'Well, the update is…' Louise was always the first to speak and Kelly always trusted her to do so. She could articulate their intentions much more concisely than he ever could. 'We have the preliminary report, we have a suspect, the body identified.' She looked at Kelly for confirmation. 'And given the circumstance, although unsubstantiated, of the lives of both the suspect and his sister at the hands of this man, we have motive, what we don't have is a confession or statement or a guarantee that this was the event that killed him, the so-called, victim. Nor have we ruled out, Liam or Maeve Fitzpatrick, who are also deceased.'

'The so-called victim?' The Inspector raised his brown bushy eyebrows and narrowed his eyes.

'Well, he was a bit of a bastard, sir,' Kelly interjected, he could never have been as delicate with his words as Louise had been.

'That's coming from His Honourable Judge Kelly, is it? I wasn't aware of your appointment.' The Inspector was an inpatient man. 'Have we or have we not enough evidence to charge Timothy Fitzpatrick with the murder of Patrick Fitzpatrick in 1970? Simple question.'

'Technically, we have enough to charge him with Unlawful Killing,' Kelly said. Louise glared at him, he had an awful knack of saying the wrong thing at the wrong time. Kelly knew that arresting Timothy Fitzpatrick would serve absolutely no purpose other than to bolster the Inspector's profile, not that he'd admit to it. But if Tim was the man, or boy at the time, that put his uncle in the ditch for what he did to his sister, he sort of respected him for it.

'Right then, make it so.' The Inspector was eager to finish the case out.

'They are at a funeral today, sir.' Louise threw Kelly a look as though it was his fault. 'Of the so-called victim, who did in fact rape his fourteen-year-old niece, I might add, who just happens to be an old woman now.' Louise's composed edges began to fray and Kelly could sense it. 'I don't think they will be fleeing the country on a super yacht bought with the proceeds of their crimes, surely we could do it in the morning.'

'It will take me a few hours to catch up on the paperwork anyhow, so I might not get to him on time,' Kelly added, his partner instincts kicking in.

'This is really not good enough,' McCarthy hesitated. 'I don't want this dragging on any more.' He hawed in annoyance. 'I want an arrest before the weekend is over, clear?

'Right,' Kelly answered as he and Louise stood to leave the room.

'And Louise, can we keep the emotion out of it.' The Inspector started up his computer. His condescending words fell short before they reached her and she continued out of the room.

'I thought you were going to lose it with him.' Kelly waited until she had closed the Inspector's door. He was impressed by the way she had held her temper.

'It is infinitely more satisfying to stay silent when someone expects you to be enraged,' she said; her first foot on the top of the black covered stairs, Kelly was behind her.

'It's a pity then, you wouldn't stay more silent with me,' Kelly chided, he couldn't stand the atmosphere between them.

'Kelly, what are we doing, what is going on?' Louise stopped at the bottom, Kelly one step behind. She was still so annoyed. 'I think we need to seriously talk, don't you?' The hustle of phones and the bustle of voices could be heard inside the main door from the landing.

'Come with me.' Kelly stepped past her and placed his hand on the small of her back, guiding her past the second floor door. It was the first time they had connected since they had slept together. 'Outside.' Daringly, he kept his hand where he had placed it. He wanted her to know that he cared.

She let him guide her back to her car.

'Here, I still have your keys.' He reached inside his pockets and pulled her bunch of keys aloft. 'Actually,' he sidestepped her car and strode to the driver's side, 'I'll drive, get in before, anyone sees us.'

She liked Kelly, she really did and the connection between them excited her. She loved the way they worked together, instinctively knowing how to wade in to each other's situations or more importantly, how to wade out, she was finding it hard to understand why he would just leave.

'Kelly.' Louise waited until Kelly pulled out from the carpark onto the main road.

'Listen, don't say a word, I need to be looking at you when you are talking to me and I can't do that when I'm driving, just wait till I park.' Kelly said.

'Why, do you need to read my lips or something, is the old hearing gone that bad.' Louise couldn't help herself. A wide grin spread across her face, she couldn't fight it.

'Seriously, now you joke about my age.' He looked at her and couldn't help but smile back.

'Where are you driving to?'

'Jesus, Louise, would you just have a bit of patience, my god, you're a torment.' He pulled into a parking space outside his house a mere kilometre from the station. 'My place,' he said, knowing how significant bringing her inside for the first time would be to her. She didn't comment.

She followed him through the front door, realising that of all the times she had dropped him home or passed his door, this had been the first time she had been invited inside. He looked at her in silence for a moment as he closed the front door behind her.

'Coffee, or something stronger?' The interior of the small terraced house on Castle Street was not what she was expecting. He turned and walked through the short hall to the kitchen, she followed.

'Eh, coffee,' she answered, unsure of where to put herself. She stood just inside the doorway. 'I wasn't expecting this.' She unfolded her arms and relaxed her shoulders. The kitchen extension was white, bright and airy with ultra-modern white gloss units.

'Why, because I'm old?' He had always wanted to bring her home, but had never found a way to ask her.

'No, I didn't mean that.' Her voice was soft, she hadn't intended to be insulting. 'I mean I had no idea, how you lived, I just didn't expect it to be so sleek and well kept. Your house is actually lovely,' she added. She ran her hand along the white painted sideboard, it looked antique.

'In comparison to me?' he added, looking back at her. 'Sit down.' He pointed to the beige covered sofa that was positioned by the oversized windows overlooking the garden. 'I'll bring your coffee over.'

'Thanks.' It was all she could muster. She walked towards the sofa, her soft black pumps gliding quietly across the polished concrete floor. 'I just want to say…' Louise started, unsure of what it was she intended.

'Don't,' Kelly raised his hand in a stopping motion and smiled at her. 'Just let me start, if you don't mind.' He sat across from her and placed his mug on the coffee table in front. 'It's my mistake and I want a chance to fix it, if that's okay.' He was still unsure about the exact nature of what he had done wrong but he had a notion it was something to do with the way he'd left Dublin. It was only now on reflection he could see how it might have seemed.

'I suppose it's my fault.' He searched frantically to find the words to explain to her what had happened. 'I was actually trying to do the right thing, but I fucked up.' He lifted his mug and sipped. 'McCarthy wanted us both back in the station. That was him ringing when we arrived at the restaurant.' He scratched his chin. 'He was pushing for an arrest, he wanted to do it there and then, announce at some function or other that he was going to, that we had made an arrest. He wanted us both back in Kilkenny, he was going to meet us in the station at midnight.'

'And?' Louise was somewhat relieved that Kelly's disappearance could at least be explained. She supposed that it was a good sign too that he cared enough to try and explain but most of all she was interested in his reasoning, what would make him just abandon her in Dublin?

'Well, I suppose, I decided to go on my own, because when I went back in to the restaurant and I saw you…' He looked at her, his eyes pleading, she could tell that he was genuine. 'I saw you with Alex, and I thought, or made the decision, that you should stay with her; there was no need for both of our night's to be ruined.' He sighed and continued speaking before she could answer him. 'I know I shouldn't have made the decision for you, I know that it wasn't my decision to make, but I was trying to do the right thing.' He placed his mug on the coffee table in front of him. 'It's hot in here, I'm just going to open that window.' He rose and stretched to the window handle and unlocked it.

'I'm not annoyed that you made a call without consulting me, well I am but I'll come back to that. What's pissing me off is that you just sent a shitty text and pissed off back to Kilkenny, what was I supposed to think?' She made a mental note to come back to him on the 'making her decisions for her' bit.

'Louise, I'm not a total prick, I wanted to stay in Dublin, with you, I didn't want to come back but I thought I'd be able to hold McCarthy off, leave you to spend some time with Alex. You had just talked about how much you missed her and that you didn't see enough of her.'

'You could have said more in your text though, or why the hell couldn't you have just come back to the restaurant and told me to my face, for Christ's sake, you just disappeared, left me like a jilted sixteen-year-old.'

'Part of me knew you would have insisted on coming with me and I didn't want you missing out on time with your sister.' He fumbled with the window lock and gave up, opting instead to unlock the double back doors. A bracing breeze swirled in around them when he opened it, lifting a bundle of newspapers and scattering them across the room. 'Shit,' he said.

'Close the door.' Louise giggled as she leapt to gather up what she could. Sheets of paper fluttered around the room. 'Talk about throwing caution to the wind.' She laughed and Kelly joined her. 'There is so much wrong with what you have just said, I don't know where to start.' Louise bent in front of the table and scrunched up the last sheet that had blown away.

'Oh, I'm sure you'll find a way.'

'Well, for a start...'

'You see, I told you you'd find a way.' Kelly smirked.

'Will you shut up and listen, Jesus, you can be annoying,' Louise said. 'A mysterious text and disappearing act is not okay, not one hour after we have just spent the evening in bed, not ever.' Louise pointed to her first finger. 'Secondly, you don't get to make decisions for me, I do very well making my own.' She pointed to her second finger. 'The next time, you don't do either of those, wait, what was the story with McCarthy about the car then?'

'I was nearly back in Kilkenny and I still hadn't thought of a good reason to tell McCarthy why you didn't come back with me, so I pulled in and texted him from the side of the road, told him we'd be a bit late, that the car had broken down.'

'But why did he say then, that he waited and we didn't show?'

'Well I tormented him at bit.' He couldn't control the grin that formed on his face. 'I sort of kept the texts going and made him wait in the station for us, knowing I had no intention of showing up. I'd text him every half hour or so. He must have got pissed off around one and then went home.'

'Are you serious, well then why did you bother going down in the first place.'

'Ah, I only thought of it when I was nearly there, and besides, he might have called my bluff.'

'You are devious, taking advantage of the man's good nature.' Sarcasm came easy to Louise, especially when she spoke about the Inspector.

'Well he deserved it; he ruined my night, so I wanted to ruin his.'

'Well, I had to get a train from Heuston station because you abandoned me. In Dublin.'

'Abandoned you, what are you, a puppy?' Kelly couldn't help but laugh at her. His voice was much softer now as he realised the mess he had made of everything.

'Well, I still can't get over the fact that you decided not to tell me that McCarthy wanted me back in the station, that you were protecting me or something?'

'Seriously, does every argument have to turn into a sexist rant with you, I was just trying to do something nice for you, I wasn't trying to protect you, I promise.' His voice trailed off softly. 'So I don't want to protect you then, is that better.' He stepped a little closer to where she stood and placed the remaining three newspaper sheets down out of his hands.

'Well, I don't know.' Louise moved closer to him as she spoke. 'I think it's you that's going to need protecting.'

'Okay, then can we establish that it is you who will protect me if there is any protecting to be done.' Tentatively he reached for her, it had been torture not to be able to touch her.

She didn't push him away. 'Well, in the interest of fairness then, seeing as you protected me the other night, it's only fair that I protect you now.' Louise softened her body against his. He wrapped his arms around her waist and brushed the ringlets of black hair that had fallen from her ponytail back behind her ears.

‘I’m all yours for protecting,’ he said.

‘That’s the type of submissive attitude that I want to hear more of,’ she said.

He took her by the hand and led her upstairs. He stopped to kick off his shoes at the bottom step. ‘New carpets.’ He smiled and she slipped out of her shoes as well. She followed him up the stairs. ‘And if there are any more comments out of you about the style of my house or the type of décor that you just didn’t expect from me when you go inside my bedroom, I’ll put you out.’

‘Oh,’ she laughed. ‘I’m really excited now to see your bedroom, is it all silk sheets and velour pillows?’ She joked; he didn’t answer. ‘Would you really put me out though?’ she asked outside his door.

‘Well, maybe not straight away.’ He pushed back his bedroom door and pulled her inside.

Chapter 31

Sunday Morning – 2016

It took Rose a moment to remember where she was, when she woke. With the wall-to-wall damask curtains closed, the plush hotel room was in darkness. She concentrated on opening her eyes, flickering as a sliver of light crept through a parting at the top, casting an elongated ray over the foot of her bed. She closed her eyes again, adjusting to the brightness. The bizarre events of the funeral, meeting Michael and his family and returning to the hotel played on a loop in her head, like an old familiar advertisement, the accompanying jingle being the warm tones of his, her secret son's, deep voice. *Rose, I'm so glad you could come*, he had said. She was heady with joy, a feeling that she never thought she could associate with Kilkenny or anyone who lived there. She dissected every word that was spoken and every gesture that was made, every expression on his face, reliving the first time she had met her son, over and over again. A cesspool of murky memories drained, scrubbed and power-washed, and in its place the fresh sparkling waters of Michael, a reason for it all, a purpose for all her pain. She flicked her eyes open again, lasting a little longer this time.

Secretly allowing herself some of the credit, she thought about how handsome and strong Michael was and how relaxed he appeared, surrounded by his beautiful little family. She had listened carefully to Michael and Marie as they retold anecdotal stories of the events throughout the years, searching wildly for any clue of his life that might have been similar to hers or, dare she say it, because of her. She was fascinated by the man. He seemed cool, calm and collected. She wondered for a moment would it ever have been possible to be his mother. Would it ever have been possible for him to have known her as his mother without him having to get hurt? No matter how many times she wondered, she always came to the same conclusion. He was better off because she left him. They both were. Pragmatism couldn't be argued with.

Stretching, she pressed her foot against the weight of the woollen throw at the bottom of the bed and kicked down the crisp white linen covers. 'Bloody legs,' she said out loud, her mouth dry and tacky. She was becoming used to the dreaded sense of tiredness that she felt every time she woke, and like a tsunami, it descended upon her in slow motion, creeping stealthily through her body; her muscles refusing to work the way she wished them to, ignoring her commands. Her concoction of pills lay prepared in their individual compartments by the bed with a bottle of water. As had become the norm, she needed to take the blue ones as soon as she woke, to get the best effect for the day.

Rolling her heavy legs to the side of the bed, she urged her torso to sit up, helping herself by pulling at the sheets. Satin pyjamas, her secret weapon when it came to being able to move under sheets, helped her to slide her limbs across to the edge; her strength alone, not enough to move them. She was already exhausted. It was ten, she noticed from the clock on the TV.

She wished she could jump up and throw back the curtains and open the windows wide. She sat silently, listening for rain; she couldn't hear it. She heard the sounds of heavy doors swishing open along the corridor and the gentle clunk and thump as they closed. The patter of feet, both large and small drummed lowly on the mink wool carpet by her door and faint excited voices slipped through the keyhole as shadows peeked across the threshold. Tim and Robert would have already eaten breakfast, she suspected, and knowing Robert, he would have Tim out in the gardens by now. She smiled as she imagined Robert's exasperation at Tim's disinterest.

It had been surreal having both her beautiful daughter and her secret son in the old farm house on Fitzpatrick Estate. Lizzie and Michael in the same room, she could never have imagined it. The farm now owned by her son Michael. A question, no doubt that she would still have to answer, if Detective Kelly had anything to do with it. The extraordinary circumstances were almost implausible. However the stars had aligned, she didn't know, but the four-pound-sized hole in her heart had been filled. Not that she would, but if she told someone what had happened, they would never believe her.

She was glad she had decided to decline the breakfast invitation, knowing how long it would take her to get a shower and prepare for the day; she had taken the pressure off by bowing out of any morning get-together well in advance.

She steadied herself in a sitting position at the side of the massive four-poster bed; the morning dizziness rendering her momentarily immobile. Her first morning tablet would soon rectify that, she thought. It was her hands that let her down the most though, she noticed; once dexterous and strong, now frail and spindly. She fiddled, tediously with the stubborn water bottle top, screwed tight, defying what little strength she had. 'I should have poured a glass last night,' she rebuked herself, criticising her lack of forethought.

'Bloody hands.' Growing exasperated with the unopened bottle, Rose threw it on the bed. Frustrated, tears escaped from her eyes. With a deep sigh she resigned to lying back against the pillows. It wouldn't have taken much to use her phone. She could have called someone and they could have done it for her but she just didn't want to. She lay uncomfortably in silence as the waterworks continued down her cheeks, wishing that the heavy wall of curtains would disappear and her room would be filled with brightness and air.

'Right, I hear you.' She spoke again to the room. She liked to imagine Matt was speaking to her. He wouldn't have allowed the pity party. Determinedly, she tried the bottle again, still to no avail. 'Bloody thing.' The first tablet of the day was her lifeline, the pill that helped her with her blood pressure and helped dispel the dizziness, without it, it would take her an age to right herself. She attempted to sit upright at the side of the bed. It was always the mornings when she was at her worst and her symptoms the most pronounced, by lunch, she'd be a little more energetic, more like herself. Which is why, she supposed, she was able to keep it from Tim for so long. 'Right, this time.' She forced the bottle top with all her might, but she still wasn't strong enough. She closed the lid on her pill box, clasped it in her hands and neglecting her better judgement, she pushed herself to her feet, water from the bathroom tap would have to suffice. Her right foot slapped on the ground as she took the barefooted steps on the carpet, there were only seven to the bathroom door. She hoped she would make it.

A rush of pressure exploded in her head, her blood pressure plummeted, undermining her ability to continue. She lunged for a desk chair and sat with her head between her knees. There were only two steps left.

'Blooming nuisance,' she exclaimed as she felt the dizziness abate somewhat. As she sat with her head towards her lap, she could feel the pressure ease and a gentle tingling spark across her skin. She reached from where she sat and switched the bathroom light on. The door was slightly ajar and the extractor began to hum. Pushing the door with her foot, the light flooded into the room. The toilet seat was down, she noticed. She could reach the tap if she sat there.

Short of breath from her exertion, she pulled herself again to a stand. Her satin pyjamas clung to her clammy pale skin. Relentlessly, her blood rushed again from her head as though somebody had left a valve open in her toe. As best she could, she continued, her flat foot dragging on the ground. Feeling the cold tiled floor underneath her bare foot, she lunged to the toilet seat to try and sit down. The tingling numbness that started in her lips danced across her skin like a flame across paper, its heat searing her chest. A thumping pain of pressure rolled heavily from her head down her spine as she struggled, with all the strength she could muster, to pry open her eyes. Her vision made the ground sway and when the tiles rose up to meet her, her hands hung like heavy curtains, draped frozen by her side, her pills clenched inside of them. She screamed at them to move but they disobeyed her commands, immovable by desire alone. Slowly, she felt her body thud to the ground.

A warm wetness oozed around her legs as her skin prickled on the cold tiled floor. She opened her eyes and gasped for breath, like the last gasp of someone drowning. Pain pricked on her eyes like sandpaper, blurring everything in her sight, her focus skewed and irregular. Instinctively, she grasped to her face, her arm finally obeying the command her brain had sent moments ago. Everything felt wet, viscous. Her stomach began to retch, deep constricted strains in quick succession.

Bile erupted and flowed like lava from the corner of her mouth as she lay on her side; each surging spasm chucking out watery bile. Her eyelids grew heavy and a pungent smell drifted up her nose. A trickle of hot, viscous blood crept across the laneways of grout to the left and right. Tinged with yellow, the red liquid became brown and congregated in a pool just in front of her. Swallowing, she could taste it, almost metal like. Her eyelids flickered open and shut. Her body shivered, it was cold on the tiles. She allowed herself to drift asleep. She didn't feel any pain.

Chapter 32

Sunday Afternoon – 2016

A collection of papers were strewn across the sofas as Tim and Robert each sipped coffee from the hotel's mugs. They sat in contented silence at either end of the sumptuous sofas in a cosy corner of the lobby.

'Morning gorgeous uncles.' Lizzie leaned in, kissing them both in succession. 'Have you had breakfast?' she asked.

'Afternoon, you mean,' Tim stretched his cheek upwards. 'And yes, we have, you?'

'No, actually, I was going to meet a friend, if that's okay?' she said, reluctant to elaborate. She decided to meet Lucas at his hotel, just a short walk away. 'At twelve actually,' she added, looking at the large brass clock on the metallic silver wallpaper behind the reception desk. 'I was hoping to see Mum before I went though.' She looked expectantly at her uncles. 'She not down yet?'

'No sign yet.' Tim looked under his glasses as he creased the paper back into its folds. 'But, she did say she wouldn't be down for breakfast and we have a late checkout so there's no rush. We'll probably grab some lunch here before we hit the road.' Robert nodded in agreement.

'Any coffee left in that pot?' She reached to lift the silver pot to check its weight. 'I have ten minutes before I leave,' she said.

'Sure,' Tim said, watching her as she poured. 'What did you think of the house yesterday?' Tim noted the happy expression on her face.

'Oh, there are no words, amazing, I loved it,' she said. 'I wish I had known it before, you know, you and mum sold it, I could see myself, all lady of the manor, there', she smiled. 'But I don't think I could have stayed there full time, it would have had to be the country residence', she smiled.

'I thought you would have loved it, all right,' Tim said. He knew she had a passion for all things interior, especially design.

'Well actually,' she paused, 'I did want to do a little more research before I said anything.' She looked excitedly at Robert and then to Tim. 'But I was thinking I might,' she hesitated, 'go back to college in Dublin, maybe do a course in architecture, interior design, something along those lines?' she said, her insecurity evident in the tone of her voice. 'And Mum's been through so much this past year what with losing Dad, now this diagnosis, the more I think about it, the more it feels right.' Her face was alight with excitement. 'That's why I wanted to speak to Mum, see what she thinks,' Lizzie said. She glanced at the clock again. 'Actually, I'm surprised she's not down yet,' she said.

Tim turned his wrist to check his watch. 'Not like her to sleep in, although she is still getting used to the medication. The tablets have her all over the place,' he said. His expression changed. 'Hmm.'

'Maybe she had fallen back asleep?' Lizzie offered. It was so unlike Rose to be late. 'I'll ring her and see.' As Lizzie dialled her number, an ominous feeling came over her. 'No answer,' she said, slightly alarmed. 'I think I'll go up and see what's keeping her.' Already deciding she wasn't waiting for the call to be answered. She rushed to the lift.

'I'll come with you.' Tim already on his feet, behind her. 'Do you have a key for the door?'

'No,' she answered.

'You go. I'll get a key from reception. I'll follow you up.'

Lizzie took the lift and pressed the button for her mother's floor. She slithered in, just as the doors glided shut.

Robert gathered up whatever had been abandoned and met Tim at the reception desk. It hadn't taken long to convince the receptionist to call someone more superior. Tim managed to remain calm. He supposed that maybe he might be overreacting, but overreacted anyway.

'I can't give you the room key but I can use mine to enter if needs be,' the manager explained calmly. It was just past twelve, Robert noted from the clock behind the reception desk.

Tim, Robert and the manager made their way to the lift, none of them able to speak.

Lizzie stepped out onto the floor and quickened her step towards her mother's room, her face creased with worry. Her heart raced as she knocked on her mother's door.

'Mum, you in there?' The sound of her voice in the silence made her look around in awkwardness. Knocking again, more loudly and impatiently, she shouted, 'Mum, can you answer the door. Mum.' She banged the door as loudly as she could. Tim and Robert heard her as they ran towards her.

'Just open the door, man, there's something wrong.' Robert was dogged as he wrenched the key from its spring chain on the manager's belt. The manager didn't protest. Robert placed the key card in the slot and opened the door. The room was still in darkness except for the slice of yellow light that shot from the opening of the bathroom door.

'Ring an ambulance, Robert quickly.' Tim was insistent as he pushed past Robert into the foreboding room. Running to the bed, he found it empty. As he stood stunned, he looked to the light in the bathroom and saw Rose lying on her side on the bathroom floor. Her hair lay matted in vomit and blood. She was pale. He knelt by her side and checked her pulse.

'Is she breathing?' Lizzie was behind him, fear exploding inside of her.

Tim checked her chest. 'I think so. It's very shallow.' On the exterior, Tim was the epitome of calm, he knew that Lizzie would need him to be, but inside he felt as scared as he had been that night, forty six years ago when he had carried Rose to Mrs McGrath's house.

'Is that blood?' Lizzie cried. 'Oh my god.'

'Get a blanket,' Tim instructed the manager calmly as he held his sister's hand. They wrapped her in position and tried to heat her up. Shock enveloped their bodies as they stood watching Rose where she fell.

'We're here, Mum, it's okay.' Lizzie's tears flooded down her face. 'Tim is here and Robert too.' Lizzie looked at them individually as she said their names. She uncurled her fingers, took her mum's pill box from her hand and held her hands in hers, it was cold. 'She had her pills.' She passed them to Robert as he spoke to a dispatcher from the ambulance centre. 'She must have been trying to open them.' Lizzie wiped tears from her face with the heel of her other hand. She fell to her knees beside her mother and gently rubbed her back.

He placed them in his shirt pocket. 'Make sure her mouth is clear,' Robert said, relaying the message from the dispatcher on the other end of the phone. 'It is,' Lizzie said as she pulled open her mother's bottom jaw and peered inside. Robert looked around the room, Rose's clothes hung neatly on the hanger inside the fitted wardrobe and her case lay open on the rack, her shoes stood side by side by the table. Robert pulled open the curtains, her phone was on the table beside her bed and her water bottle lay unopened on her covers.

'Ambulance is coming, shouldn't be long', Robert finished his call and stood helplessly aside watching Tim and Lizzie as they sat where Rose lay.

'The ambulance is on its way. Are you awake, Mum, can you hear me?' Lizzie said.

Lizzie's plea was hard to listen to and a lump larger than rock formed at the back of Robert's throat. He picked up the water bottle and held it in his hand. He showed it to Tim.

'Bloody hands,' Tim repeated Rose's words for her. He remembered her asking him to open her bottle in the church. In his mind's eye he pictured her falling where she lay. He gasped when Rose moaned inaudibly. 'Rose.' He leaned in to her. 'Rose, hang in there, the paramedics will be here soon. Rose.' He wiped the side of her face with his hands. She didn't answer him.

Like a slide show, image after image of Rose's life flashed in front of her. The combine in the sun-soaked field and Tim, a young man, behind the wheel; Michael, her beautiful baby boy swaddled in blue on Mrs McGrath's bed; her soulmate, the love of her life, Matt, smiling by her side; her swollen tummy and Lizzie aged five.

'Mum, can you hear me, Mum?' Lizzie cried.

Rose tried to answer but nothing came out and the memories that played washed over her eyes and kept them closed as she scrolled through the images in her head. She wanted to revel in the happiness it brought, she willed for quietness so she could see them again. There was Lizzie smiling without her front teeth; Matt painting the kitchen duck-egg blue, there was more paint on him than the walls; Robert and Tim snatching a kiss. She saw Michael, handsome and strong without his tie, smiling, *so good of you to come*, he said and she saw Lizzie standing beside him. She tried to smile, she hoped Lizzie and Tim could see it.

'If one of you wants to come in the ambulance with us you can.' The paramedics manoeuvred the stretcher outside the bathroom door. Lizzie, Tim and Robert stood by the bed.

'I'll go,' Tim was first to answer.

'I'll go too,' Lizzie began to follow.

'Normally we'd only take one family member.' The paramedic turned to look Lizzie in the eye, 'But I suppose we can take you both.'

Lizzie was afraid that wasn't a good thing. Rules were only ever broken when they needed to be.

'Go.' Robert was calm. 'Both of you. I'll follow you there.' He looked to the manager. 'I'm sorry for ripping your key from your belt.'

Chapter 33

Sunday Afternoon – 2016

'They have her in the resuscitation room.' Lizzie and Tim met Robert at the swishing automatic door as he arrived. 'We have to wait in the family room.' Her voice trailed off anxiously.

Tim paced away silently on the blue vinyl floor, his head hanging heavily as he followed the lined pattern that snaked along the hospital corridor. His shoes squeaked rebelliously, defying the solemnity of his mood.

The swish and scrape of the swinging door from the resuscitation room silenced all three of them. Tim froze by the frosted window and craned his neck sideways to catch a glimpse inside, as the door crept closed. Like a vacuum, both Lizzie and Tim sucked in lungfuls of air as though that would be their last. But the door wasn't opened for them.

Inside the family room, brown leather sofas lined the walls and hospital chairs were dotted round small coffee tables. Sky News played on the small TV that hung on the wall. Used polystyrene coffee cups littered the tables and overflowed from the small bin beside the door. A small crucifix hung on the wall.

'This is serious,' Lizzie said.

'We don't know that yet.' Tim sat beside her, shooting Robert a resigned glance across the table.

'This room is only for families that they intend to give bad news to, there is no way that they'd have moved us in here unless it was bad,' Lizzie said, her soft grey eyes filling with tears.

'Let's not pre-empt anything. Rose is a fighter. She's in good hands.' Robert was the voice of reason for both of them.

'Now, a strong pot of tea.' A nurse peered around the doorway and introduced herself, Julie, she said her name was. 'A cup of sweet tea will keep you going.' She directed her instructions to Tim knowingly, identifying him as the family head. 'Is this all of you?' She looked to Tim for the answer as she bent over the coffee table placing the contents of her tray carefully and quietly on the table. 'Or are you waiting on anyone else?' She made it sound as though she needed to know if she needed to bring more cups, but Tim knew that wasn't the reason she asked.

'This is all of us,' Lizzie answered, but there was something about the expression that flashed briefly across Tim's face that made Julie think otherwise.

'Okay then,' she paused, 'I've let the team know that you are eagerly waiting for an update so, as soon as they can, they'll come find you.' Her smile was sympathetic. 'In the meantime, I'm just next door.' She looked at Tim's expression again. 'I might need someone,' her eyes fell to Tim's, 'to get more details for Rose's file, if that's okay.' Immediately Tim fixed to go with her. 'No, no, have your tea first.' She placed her hand on his shoulder reassuringly. 'Drop in to me when you are finished,' she said. 'Are you Mrs O'Reilly's husband?'

'No, her brother. Tim,' he clarified. 'This is her daughter, Lizzie, and this is Robert, her brother-in-law.'

'Grand, Tim,' Julie had a great memory for names. 'Finish your tea and come in to me then,' she said.

Tim wasn't able to drink and moved to the window, standing motionless, peering out. Darkness had crept stealthily from the sky and the surrounding city lights began to flare, softly at first. Footsteps scurried past their door and with every voice that weaved its way through, they paused, waiting to hear news of Rose, only to be disappointed that the activity wasn't for them.

'I shouldn't have insisted you all come to Kilkenny for that blasted funeral,' Tim scolded. 'If she hadn't have been here, she'd be at home in her own bloody house right now.' He stood staring out over the hospital grounds. 'Safe.' No one, not even Robert could comfort him. 'These walls are closing in on me.' Tim sighed. 'I need to stretch my legs.' He pulled back the door and propped it open. 'I'll go in and fill in the rest of the details, try and get an update,' he said, leaving his tea untouched, 'or do you want to do it, Liz?' he asked, knowing full well that she'd decline.

'You do it,' she said tearily and Tim left to see Julie.

'We should have gone up sooner.' Lizzie's balled tissue crumbled in her hands as she replayed every second of their morning in Kilkenny over and over again like a robot, analysing every detail of what she had seen. Robert took the tissue from her hand and replaced it with a clean one. 'We don't know how long she was lying there,' she said, her heart shattering as she spoke, the pain and torment constricting inside her chest. 'She could have been there all night,' Lizzie sobbed.

Robert sighed, there was nothing he could say. He moved to sit with her and placed his arm around her back.

'Julie,' Tim tapped on Julie's open door.

'Ah, Tim, come in, sit down.' She swivelled her chair from her desk and faced the seat that Tim had taken. 'I just need a few other details.' She pulled a green file from a pile on her tray.

'Is there any update?' Tim said anxiously.

'There is, I've just had word that they are just about finished in emergency and that the doctor is coming to see you.'

'Oh,' Tim could sense her reluctance to elaborate. 'Can you not tell me anything else?'

'Unfortunately not, the doctors must talk to you first,' she said. 'Protocol.' Her apologetic tone didn't ease Tim's growing unease. 'Tim,' she considered how best to forewarn him, 'is there anyone else who you need to call, at all?' Tim looked at her but didn't answer, his words were lost somewhere en route from his brain to his lips. 'It's just,' she continued, 'it might be a good idea to have people on standby, your sister, Rose, is still in a very serious condition.' Her words were weighted heavily but she knew that Tim could bear the load, for now at least.

'Ms O'Reilly's family?' Sloping around Julie's door, the doctor, still in his scrubs startled Tim.

'This is her brother, Tim,' Julie said, rising from her chair. 'The rest of the family are inside.'

Tim unfolded his hands and stood to follow the doctor inside, he needed to get to Lizzie.

'We have been working on your mother for some time and she is still in a very serious condition.' The doctor perched on the arm of the chair as he spoke directly to Lizzie. 'The injuries to her brain are quite severe so we have her sedated at the moment.' Pausing momentarily to allow the information to be absorbed, the doctor continued, 'Was she under any treatment at the time of the fall?'

'Well,' Tim cleared his throat, 'she was attending Vincent's, they suspected Motor Neurone Disease or one of the other neurological disorders.' Tim remembered the pills that Robert had taken. 'The pill box, Robert.'

Robert took the box from his shirt and handed them to the doctor.

'Thank you, we'll have a look at these.' He balanced the box on the file in his hand. 'There is a fracture in the skull and we are concerned about the swelling.'

Lizzie's body began to shake, she pressed her heels firmly to the floor and clasped her hands tightly on her lap, to make the shaking less obvious.

'Because of the swelling, there is immense pressure on her brain.' The doctor spoke with the perfect combination of calmness and information. 'So we need to make a small opening in her skull, what we call, a craniotomy, to release the pressure, reduce the swelling.' The doctor looked at the family to make sure the information was being heard. 'We are transferring her to Dublin, to Beaumont Hospital.' Lizzie glanced at Tim and back to the doctor. 'They will perform the craniotomy there.'

'A helicopter will transfer her in the next hour. There is no room for family,' Julie interjected. While the doctor was professional in imparting the medical knowledge, he couldn't match Julie for pragmatism.

'The next twenty-four hours are crucial.' The doctor stood, as though protecting himself from the grief that enveloped the family. 'But I must prepare you for the worst. Your mother is in a seriously critical condition. I must get back to her, but if you have any further questions, Julie can answer them.' He nodded to Julie to take over, said goodbye to the family and left the room.

'Can we see her before she goes?' Lizzie sobbed.

'I will bring you in briefly. I must warn you, she looks very swollen and will not be able to respond,' Julie began to speak. 'You will be upset when you see her,' she said, her expression emphasising her words. 'But, in my experience, patients can hear you and know you are there, so you must be strong,' she warned. 'Give her your strength, she's going to need it.' Julie was kind and considerate and skilled with people. She walked them through the corridor and waited while each of them disinfected their hands, then she gave them each a plastic apron to wear before they entered inside. 'Just through here.' Julie opened the door to the room where Rose lay. The plastic aprons they wore swished as they walked and the smell of the disinfectant hung in the air. 'Don't be alarmed by the beeps. They are monitoring her constantly,' Julie said. Rose's medical team, including the doctor that they had just spoken poured over her files at a computer to the side of her bed. 'Rose.' She walked to the bedside and placed her latex gloved hand on Rose's. 'Your family are here,' she said, momentarily glancing at Lizzie and Tim, encouraging them to move closer to the bed. 'They just wanted to see you before you leave.' She squeezed Rose's swollen hand, smiled at Lizzie and stepped away.

Lizzie was frozen, unable to touch her. A symphony of beeps filled the space and coloured lines jumped up and down on the screens. Vaseline shimmered on her lips and skin and tiny motors purred as they poured clear liquids in through her veins. A trickle of brown blood had dried at the side of her neck in a jagged line from her ear to her shoulder. Edging forward, Lizzie took her mother's hand. She stood there unable to speak.

'Rose, we are here with you, love,' Tim said, he moved to the opposite side of the flat bed. 'They are sending you up to a neurosurgeon in Beaumont.' He fought the urge to scoop her up and hold her, just as he had done the day Michael had been born. 'We'll be right behind you.'

'It's going to be okay, Mum,' Lizzie cleared her throat and wiped her wet face with the back of her hand.

'Rosie,' Tim's voice broke a little. 'You just concentrate on getting better. I want to see my fighting Rosie, you hear me.' He couldn't finish. His tears fell too hard.

'Tell your Mum you'll see her in Dublin.' Julie stepped forward. She put her hand on Lizzie's back and tried to guide her away. 'I'm sending them away now Rose,' she said.

'Love you, Mum,' Lizzie whispered as she pulled herself away and leaned across her mother to kiss her. 'See you in Dublin, Mum. Fight hard,' she whispered in her ear. Lizzie's tears wet her mother's paper-thin cheeks as she lingered hoping for a response. 'I don't want to leave her.' Lizzie was numb. 'I just can't believe this is happening.

'I know, love, I know.' Tim led her outside to where Robert stood waiting, already briefed by the nurse of the arrangements.

'I think you and Lizzie should get in my car now and get a head start on the road. I'll wait and see her off in the helicopter and then I'll head back for Rose's car and all our stuff.' Robert was Tim's rock. 'I'll get back to Dublin as soon as I can.' He looked at Tim and then to Lizzie. 'Just go, but don't speed,' he warned. 'One accident a day is enough.'

Chapter 34

Sunday Afternoon – 2016

'Michael.' Lucas stood from his table in The Park's sumptuous lobby as the lunch guests milled back and forth from the dining room. 'I'm glad you decided to come.' When his phone had beeped an hour earlier he had thought it was Lizzie messaging to say why she hadn't shown up, he was surprised to see that it was Michael.

'I'm here,' Michael answered, ignoring Lucas's extended hand. 'Can I get a coffee?' His tone was far more pleasant to the waiter who was passing by.

Lucas sat back down; he knew that Michael wasn't happy about him being there, but that was partly the reason he wanted to meet him. Especially now, with the information Marie had given him and his own connection to Lizzie. 'As you know, Marie rang me a few days ago, to see what I could do with *the story*.' Lucas attempted a smile, Michael didn't encourage it. 'So, since she called me,' he added quickly and turned his phone upright on the table, checking for the fiftieth time if Lizzie had texted, 'I've been digging around a bit and the angle that most of the…'

'Hacks, is that the word you are looking for?' Michael spat the words at him.

'If that's what you want to call them.' Lucas held his patience admirably, he expected nothing less from Michael McGrath, and if he was honest, he was distracted waiting for

Lizzie's phone call, she had said she would meet him at noon and it was already nearly two in the afternoon. He wondered had she decided to go back to Dublin, after all, just to avoid him. 'The hacks, as you call them.' Lucas shook his head at the irony of Michael's anger directed at him, if only he could tell him what he knew and what he had saved Michael from. 'These hacks, seem to be focusing on the whole Russian bog pilot comparison, body in a ditch for forty-six years, World War Two, et cetera, et cetera, I don't think they see a worthwhile story in just the murder investigation bit.'

Michael looked at him perplexed, he had no idea what the reference was but wouldn't humour him to ask. He'd Google it later instead. 'Yes, exactly what I told Marie would happen, so there was no need for you to come running.' Michael reached into his pocket and placed a fiver on the table as the waitress approached with his coffee. 'Thank you.' The smile he offered her was completely at odds with how he was feeling.

'Well yes, but I suppose, Marie wanted to make sure that nothing else was going to come of it, the story, you know, the background story.' Lucas sipped his coffee.

'So why ask me to meet you then, why the drama?' Michael's frown remained fixed to his forehead. His tolerance well and truly tested. 'And there is no background story, so what's the problem.'

'I suppose,' Lucas said, wishing just for one minute that he could throw back in his face that the reason there was no background story was because he had fed the other reporters the Russian pilot story. That stopped them digging any further and saved the secret that Marie was trying to protect. 'I asked, so that I could clear the air between us, make amends.' Marie had made him promise to keep the secret that she had told him, just as Michael's mother had done to her.

‘I think you’re mistaken, there will be nothing between us, no air, nothing, no fucking need.’ Michael’s already thin patience quickly evaporated. Curiosity had driven him to meet Lucas but anger was going to drive him to walk away.

‘Okay, I deserve that, I do, but what I wanted to say to you was that, yes, you were right,’ Lucas employed his first rule of social interaction, play to your opponent’s vanity. ‘I was a complete prick in college, I know that now.’ Michael listened, deciding how many punches he would love to bury in him. ‘But that’s just it, Michael, it was college, I was all of what, maybe nineteen, twenty years of age, I was an arsehole and I was utterly besotted with Marie, that’s the long and the short of it.’

‘You mean, my wife, Marie, the girl you hounded until she had to stop speaking to you, for her own safety. The girl who cried because she couldn’t understand what had got into you, her so-called *best friend*.’ His mocking tone would have been funny if he hadn’t have been so angry. ‘Give me a fucking break. Her best fucking friend, you know as well as I do that you were no more interested in being her friend.’

‘Michael—’

‘Don’t fucking, Michael me, you prick, you took advantage of her, she trusted you.’

‘I hear you, I did a lot of things that I shouldn’t have, I’m not proud of them.’ Lucas placed his cup back on its saucer and sat leaning forward on his elbows.

‘Tell me this much, Lucas, why does someone like you just drop everything and come running.’ Michael studied Lucas as he sat in front of him. ‘Are you going to beg her to run away with you?’ Michael exhaled as slowly as he could manage, he could feel his own anger overflowing. ‘Or tell her that you’ll kill yourself again if she leaves you?' Michael said, his voice getting angrier with each syllable.

Lucas dropped his head in his hands, the shame of his boyhood antics coming back to embarrass him.

'It's as well, you might drop your head in shame, you frightened the living daylights out of her, she was a wreck for days after you pulled that stunt, this is my wife we are talking about, the mother of my children, you stupid prick.'

'That's just it, Michael, you won, you got the prize, and I didn't kidnap her, she could have left any time, she knows that, or more like, she knew that, I told her to go, I did,' Lucas's voice trailed off.

'Yeah, I know all about it, what was it that you said, "If you leave me for him, I'll kill myself"?' Michael's eye's narrowed as he stared at him. 'I see you hadn't the balls to even see that through.'

'Look,' Lucas inhaled deeply, conscious that their argument was about to explode, 'it's nearly twenty years ago now, for fuck's sake, Michael.' Lucas rubbed his hands through his hair; his apology wasn't getting through at all. He had been besotted with Marie and he knew he should never have threatened to kill himself if she left him, he was just heartbroken. 'You asked, why does someone like me drop everything for someone like Marie?' He considered blurting out everything Marie had told him, but as much as he would have liked to have thrown a dig at Michael, he wouldn't hurt her, not a second time. 'It's because I owe her, plain and simple, I needed to make it up to her and when she rang and asked me for help, I'll be honest with you, I was thrilled, not because I thought that she wanted me back, or that I wanted her, but because I had a chance to prove to her that I wasn't the same fuckwit I was the last time she saw me. Simple as,' Lucas said. 'Besides,' he picked up his phone, quickly checked the screen and placed it in his pocket to leave, 'I have my own girlfriend, well at least I did, I risked everything with her to come here for Marie,' Lucas said, shaking his head at the irony of the connection now between him and Michael, a connection that wasn't up to him to tell him about. 'I just wanted to do the right thing by Marie,' he said. 'And you,' he continued. 'And I'll tell you that, yes, I was a prick, I was in love with Marie, your wife, but most of all, she was one of my closest friends, I realise that now and have done for some years.'

Lucas watched as Michael shook his head in disbelief.

'Whether you believe that or not,' Lucas stood, he had said his piece, 'I'm sorry for what I did all those years ago, I genuinely am, man,' he said. 'I'm leaving now for Dublin.' Lucas's resignation was palpable in his voice. Knowing that Lizzie hadn't shown was enough to defeat him, he didn't need any more reason to regret ever showing up in Kilkenny. 'Flight's tomorrow, stories are more or less managed, I'll email Marie. Job Done.' He gathered up his wallet, said goodbye and walked back towards the lift. Michael would probably never forgive him but maybe Marie would and if that was the only outcome, well at least he'd tried. He didn't turn but he felt Michael walk in the other direction for the front revolving door. He took out his phone and dialled Lizzie's number again.

Michael emerged from The Park's brass revolving door seething with resentment for the man he had left inside. The sun made him squint at the brightness. 'Bloody fool,' he said, staring past the hotel residents he shared the door with and searching the car park for his jeep. He tipped his sunglasses from his head to his face. He muttered under his breath, drawing the surprised eyes of a passer-by. He attempted a smile in response and quickly made his way across the manicured car park to his jeep, slamming the door behind him and banging his fists in temper off the steering wheel. He closed his eyes and exhaled slowly. He supposed he should ring Marie and let her know what happened.

'Well?' Michael knew she would be waiting for his call.

'Well,' he repeated.

Marie was anxious all morning. The meeting with Lucas was important on so many levels and Michael didn't even realise why yet. She felt somewhat disloyal to him not to have told him, but his mother had made her promise before she died. She was so conflicted.

'Well, yer man,' Michael said, folding down the sun visor to block the glare of sunlight that was beaming right onto his face, 'says he is sorry for being the biggest prick ever when you were in college.' He pressed the ignition button to start the air conditioning in his car. The heat was building inside the jeep. Marie smiled as she heard his tone soften. 'And exactly as I said,' he paused for effect, it was rare that he felt he was right and she was wrong, so he was going to enjoy it, 'there was probably no need for him to come and cover the story and that, most of the other journalists don't see much in it.'

'That's good,' Marie answered. She was satisfied that Lucas's involvement had been the catalyst that had kept the other journalist's away and she hadn't needed the satisfaction of Michael knowing it. 'At least that's done now.'

He could hear the relief in her voice and imagined the smile on her face. 'Oh, and he said, and I quote, that I "got the prize".' He laughed, knowing that her feminist flag would be flown within a matter of seconds at the derogatory reference.

'Did he, now?' Marie said, stockpiling the insult for a future conversation with Lucas. 'Anyway,' she paused, 'if anyone got the prize, I did,' she said, knowing he would at least smile at her joke. 'Are you on your way home then?'

'Actually,' Michael said, 'I was thinking I should call into Tim in his hotel and say goodbye, wish them a safe journey back to Dublin. It'd be the proper thing to do, wouldn't it?'

'Yes, probably. It would be nice,' Marie answered. 'Although, I'd like to see them myself, maybe you could drop out home first and we'll both go back in?' she suggested, hopeful that he would agree.

'Okay then,' Michael answered and headed out for home.

Chapter 35

Sunday Afternoon – 2016

'Right then. We may go do this arrest, try and get it processed before four o'clock and allow him to get a solicitor before it's too late.' Detective Kelly was unusually considerate, Louise noted as she looked at the clock. It was nearly half past two.

'Right so,' she answered. 'Did you tell McCarthy?' She knew that they couldn't stall much longer, McCarthy's deadline of, *before the end of the weekend*, was fast approaching.

'Yes.' Kelly glanced at the clock again and lowered his voice. 'I know that this is not the preferred outcome.' He was conscious of the lengthy conversation they had the evening before, now that they were in *a relationship*, as she put it. She desperately looked for an alternative to arresting Tim, but couldn't find one; she had exhausted every avenue she could think of.

'Really don't feel this one,' she said. 'But needs must, I suppose.'

'Needs must,' he repeated, the normal thrill of solving a case eluding both of them in equal measures. The adrenaline replaced with regret. 'We'll head to the hotel first and if they've left already,' they were both secretly hoping they had, 'well, maybe we'll follow them to Dublin,' he said, conscious of the other detectives overhearing them.

*

Robert finished packing Rose's belongings into her black Samsonite overnight bag and placed it beside his, Tim's and Lizzie's on the trolley in the corridor. 'That's everything, I think.' He nodded to the uniformed porter who took the luggage down the service lift to await Robert at the car.

Robert closed the room door behind him and padded his way towards the lift. He wasn't looking forward to the drive alone, his back was beginning to ache and his head was thumping. He couldn't begin to think how Rose must have been feeling when she collapsed. The lift doors opened and he crossed the lobby to return all three room keys.

'Robert.' Michael and Marie were at the reception desk. 'I was hoping to catch you guys before you left,' Michael said, enthusiastically. 'Are Tim and Rose around?'

'Em, Michael,' Robert signalled him to step aside. He ran his hand through his hair and exhaled deeply. 'There's been a bit of an accident.' His polite smile didn't reach his eyes. 'Rose is,' he cleared his throat and Marie placed her hand on his arm, directing him to the chairs to the right, 'on her way to Beaumont Hospital.' He paused. 'Helicopter transfer,' he added.

'Oh my God, Robert, what happened?' Marie asked as she sat Robert down on the chair beside her.

'She had a fall, we found her unconscious.' Robert shook his head as his eyes watered remembering the scene. 'Up in the room. I really have to get to Dublin. Tim and Lizzie have already left,' Robert said.

'Of course,' Marie said. 'Let us know how she is, won't you?' Marie couldn't believe the timing of everything, she had rooted out the letter that Michael's mother had given to her before she died and stuffed it in her handbag, she still hadn't decided what she was going to do with it. The words her mother-in-law had said to her 'you'll know when the time is right' had played repeatedly in her head over the past week and now they played so loudly that she couldn't ignore them. Is this the right time? She was sure there couldn't be a time more right, but maybe it was too late, maybe the right time was last week or even last year.

'I will,' he answered, eager to get on the road.

'I'll drive you,' Michael said, walking with him. 'I insist, I'll get you out of the city faster.'

'No, no there's no need, I'll be fine. She will be in surgery for a while anyway so I'll be fine,' Robert said. 'But thank you, really,' he said and left to Marie's relief.

'Michael.' Marie waited as Robert left and Michael returned his attention to her. 'I'll drive,' she added as they returned to the car park, taking the keys from him.

'Okay,' he said, her unusual behaviour confusing him. 'Is that Detective Kelly and Detective Kennedy?' he asked as he watched the familiar car, park opposite them.

'It is, do you think we should tell them?' Marie said.

'Mmm, I suppose,' he said. 'I'm sure they'd like to know.' He closed the passenger door and crossed the car park to speak to them.

'Detective Kelly, Detective Kennedy.'

'Michael, how are things?'

'Well actually, Rose Fitzpatrick is unconscious, apparently on her way to Dublin in the air ambulance. They found her this morning in the hotel.'

'Really, we hadn't heard,' Louise said, throwing a sideways look at Kelly. She knew now was not the time to elaborate as to why they were at the hotel in the first place. 'Thanks, Michael. Appreciate the info,' she said.

'No worries, sure I'd say they'd have more information inside,' Michael said.

'Probably, thanks then.' Louise smiled politely as he returned to Marie.

'Did they say why they were here?' Marie asked as Michael slid into the passenger seat.

'No I didn't ask,' Michael answered.

'Okay, listen to me for a minute.' Marie paused as she reversed from her parking spot. 'I think we should go to Dublin, I think you should follow up to see how Rose is doing.'

'What, why?' Michael said confused. 'We'd only be in the way, Marie, times like that are just for family.'

'I know but—'

'And anyway what about Eve and Jack.'

'I've just organised them, while you were over talking to the detectives, I phoned George and he is going to stay with them.'

'Really.' Michael scrunched his brow; he knew how unusual it would be for Marie to ask George to babysit.

'Just trust me,' she said as she pulled out onto the road. 'You need to get to Dublin, I'll explain everything as we drive.' Marie was adamant that now was the time that somehow her mother-in-law had expected and that it weighed on her shoulders to do the right thing. As soon as she reached the motorway out of Kilkenny city, she began to explain.

'You know how I looked after your mother and we grew very close before she died?'

'Yeah, and?'

'Well, she asked me could I do something for her, something that she said she didn't have the strength to do herself, something that she promised that she would never do.'

'What, Marie – what are you talking about?'

'She said, I'll know when to do it, that she trusted me and that she knew that what we had was real true love for each other.'

'What, Marie, you're freaking me out?'

'Well she said that because of our true love, I would only be able to do something out of love for you, so she asked me to hold a letter for you and only give it to you when I thought the time was right.'

'What letter?'

'It's in my bag there, if you pull it out, you can read it.' She paused. 'And then there's more to what she said after that.' She concentrated on the road as best she could and listened to Michael rattle her bag and retrieve the brown papered envelope inside it. She had reached into the back of the old dresser drawer that morning and pulled out the letter. It had sat for years under a stack of photo albums and yellowed Tupperware boxes that held photos and other bits of memorabilia that Michael's mother had entrusted to her when she knew she was very ill.

'Have you read it?' he asked as he traced his fingers over his mother's writing on the envelope.

'I did.' Marie thought for a second. 'She never actually told me not to, but I think she knew I would, I think that's why she said that I would know when the time was right. Read it,' Marie said. 'Read it, love.'

Marie's car whizzed silently northwards on the asphalt road as quickly as the speed limits allowed. She kept her eyes on the road as Michael concentrated on opening the envelope without damaging the fragile paper inside.

'What's in it?' Michael extended his hand for Marie to hold it.

'Just read it, Michael,' Marie said, taking her eyes from the road briefly so she could look at him.

'You do it.' He placed the paper on her lap. The sight of his mother's handwriting a poignant reminder of his loss. He wasn't expecting the jolt that came with it.

'Okay,' she said, noticing his watery eyes. 'I'll pull in up here.'

Marie unfolded the yellowing notepaper.

'My baby boy Michael,' Marie coughed, clearing the ball at the back of her throat. *'I have loved you since the second you were born and while I didn't know you were coming until the moment you arrived,'* Marie shifted so that she could see his face, *'I have been the luckiest mother ever since. You were born on my bed, as was your brother, and you slept in my bed all those first weeks of your life. I cradled you and loved you and gave you my best, then and always. I must tell you though there are some things that you did not know. You were born of my heart but not of my body and the circumstances of your arrival need to be explained.'*

Michael drew a bracing breath as he listened to Marie's voice speak his mother's words.

'You arrived on my doorstep on a Wednesday evening in September 1970 with another child. That child was an angelic little girl, from the farm across the way.'

Michael looked up from his hands and watched Marie's mouth as she formed the words. She continued reading, tears falling silently from her eyes.

'She had a horrendous childhood and while I did my best to help out, there was only so much I could do. The child's name was Rose and she was your fourteen-year-old mother. She was distraught and damaged and hurt beyond any reasoning and in a way, my small presence in her and her brother's life must have

meant something because it was me her brother brought her to when she needed someone. I was with her when she gave birth to you on my bed. She cried for you. You both cried. She was in so much danger, she had no choice but to leave you with me and to protect her and you, your father and I, promised never to speak of the circumstances again. She took the only option she had, which was to save you. I need you to know that what she did, she did for the love of you. She had a beautiful soul, you could see it in her eyes. Marie's voice faded as she squeezed his large hand. His tears fell hard.

'I have loved you all of your life and will continue to love you always. I will always be your mother and, in a way, so will she. I tell you now because it is yours to know. It doesn't make you any less mine or me any less yours. I will forever be yours, as will all of us. I want you to follow your heart always as your heart is so strong. I love you son. Mother.'

Marie gently folded the letter back into its creases and placed it carefully back inside the envelope. The heat emanating from Michael's cheeks radiated the car. His large hand shook as he lifted a bottle of water and gulped. The silence was only broken by the ticking of the indicator. Inhaling deeply he began to speak.

'She told you this?'

'Nope.' Marie took the water bottle from his hand and sipped, her mouth was dry. 'But she spoke to me as though she had known I would read it.'

'Why didn't you tell me?' Michael struggled to understand. It was something so life changing, he wondered how she had kept it all this time.

'Because she asked me not to, because she trusted me not to.' Marie had wanted to, so many times but stopped herself.

'Marie,' Michael rubbed his already red eyes as the water from his tears fell in lanes down his face, 'you should have told me, sooner, I should have known, my mother should have told me, Jesus Christ, this is unbelievable.'

'It's Rose O'Reilly, Michael.' Marie gasped as her sobs overtook her. 'Was Rose Fitzpatrick. I'm nearly sure. With everything your mother has told me and the details of the house and the estate, it all makes sense now,' she said. 'I didn't know this part,' she said, 'the part about Rose Fitzpatrick until this week, until the body was dug up and Timothy Fitzpatrick showed up.'

'Holy fuck.' Michael's heart thumped out of his chest. There wasn't enough air in the car. 'Are you sure?'

'As sure as I can be, your mother talked about instilling a love in you for Fitzpatrick Farm and arranging with the owners so that you could afford it eventually. That's why she was so supportive of you taking it over, so that you would feel connected in some way to it. It was deliberately made affordable to you so that you could inherit half of it without even knowing.' They sat in silence, neither able to speak.

'What am I supposed to do now?' It was all too much to absorb. 'Who else knows?'

'Just you and me,' Marie said. 'And Rose and Timothy Fitzpatrick of course.'

'And now she's in a coma.'

'She is,' Marie said, accepting that she might have left it too late. 'I'm so sorry, Michael, I should have told you sooner, I was going to do it tonight. After meeting Rose yesterday, I thought it was time, but I had no idea that she would have that awful accident. I'm so sorry, I wish I had told you sooner.'

Michael shushed her, he knew it wasn't her fault. 'I can hardly swan in around the hospital bed looking for a long-lost-son reunion. Can I?'

'I know, but if it's as serious as Robert says it is, maybe you should just at least be close by, you know, just in case.'

'Maybe,' Michael said.

Chapter 36

Sunday Evening – 2016

Rose lay flat in a white hospital gown. A hairband of staples arched from her left ear to her right, across her shaven crown. Her swollen head looked out of proportion with the small figure that barely made a dent in the mattress. Her complexion was ghosting white and her lips a grey blue. Lizzie sat in the chair beside her bed and Tim sat solemnly by her side.

'She looks so bad,' Lizzie whispered, as she rubbed her mother's listless arm. 'Do you think she is in pain?'

'No, not a chance she is in pain, love, with all that sedative being poured into her,' Tim said, as reassuringly as he could manage looking at the purring pumps as they hummed in the background. His sister's frail body was shrivelling before his eyes. 'Why don't you stretch your legs, get some food into you?' Lizzie didn't answer, she couldn't, so Tim continued. 'It'll be a long night, love, and we need to keep our energy up,' he said, rubbing her folded hands that she had clenched like vice grips on her lap. He was worried, more worried than he had ever been before. Rose didn't look as though she was fighting.

'I won't be long then.' Reluctantly Lizzie agreed and slipped slowly out of the room, her face stricken with worry and her shoulders heavily slumped. She walked into the eerily quiet corridor and turned towards the grey plastic chairs at the far end and sat down, she hadn't the patience to look for food nor the stomach to eat it. The busy vibe of the day had evaporated, leaving in its place, guarded whispers, pungent odours and muted lights. She jumped when her phone shrilled in the silence. She reached inside her bag and pulled it out.

'Lucas, hi,' she said quietly.

'Lizzie.' Lucas was relieved she had finally answered. 'I've been trying you all day. Are you okay?'

'Something's happened to Mum.' She hadn't figured out how to articulate what had happened yet and the words she used to explain her situation stumbled out of her mouth. 'In the hotel.' A picture of her mother lying on the cold tiled floor flashed by her eyes and took her breath away. 'She's had an accident.' It had seemed like a lifetime ago that they were in Kilkenny.

'What sort of an accident?' Lucas looked out of his airport hotel window. He had left Kilkenny, giving up any hope of seeing Lizzie and had already returned his hired car to Dublin airport.

'Oh Lucas, it's just awful.' She began to cry as she spoke. 'Mum fell, in the hotel,' she explained. 'She's in a bad way. She was unconscious when we found her. She could have been there all night. We don't know.' She was sobbing.

Lucas had picked up enough of her words to understand the gravity of the situation. 'Where is she now?' Lucas said, beginning to gather up his belongings. He always travelled light, so there wasn't much to gather. He stuffed his things into his travel bag as he spoke.

'She's in her room, she's just out of surgery.' Sniffling, she wiped her nose and her eyes with her sleeve.

'I mean what hospital?' he said, trying to get as much information as he could.

‘Oh,’ Lizzie shook her head, she was aware that she didn’t sound coherent. ‘They flew her from Kilkenny up to Beaumont hospital here in Dublin, to do the neurosurgery.’

‘Okay, I know it’s a stupid question but how are you doing?’ He could tell from the mention of neurosurgery, air ambulance and the lack of clarity in her voice that the situation couldn’t be any more serious for Rose O’Reilly. He opened his laptop and googled the location of the hospital. Ten-minute drive, it said.

‘I’m okay.’ She barely managed to say the three syllables between sobs. She hadn’t the energy to remember how angry she was with him, let alone that they had made an arrangement to meet that morning so that he could explain everything to her. ‘Listen,’ she noticed Robert looking for her at the other end of the corridor, ‘I’m going to have to go, I’ll call you later, okay?’

‘Lizzie?’

‘Yeah?’ She began to walk towards Robert, grabbing her bag as an afterthought.

‘I just wanted to say…’ He lost the nerve to say what was on his mind. Declaring his love for her in these circumstances would be all kinds of cheesy and he didn’t want the first time he told her he loved her to be anything but right. ‘Mind yourself, ring me later, okay?’

She agreed and ended the call, pacing quickly towards Robert as he signalled her with his hand. ‘There’s a doctor inside at the bed, just to give a brief update,’ he said.

‘I had just left, for a second,’ she said exasperated and dashed back inside.

‘We will be keeping her sedated so when you are speaking to her if you could do so softly.’ The junior doctor smiled at Lizzie as she entered. ‘I was just saying, don’t encourage her to wake up with your words. We need her to stay as still as possible for a while longer. We don't want her to get agitated.' The doctor opened Rose's file, shifting a white tub of lotion out of the way on the tray table and began to scribble. 'The swelling is still quite pronounced in the brain so we had no option but to remove some of the skull to relieve the pressure.'

'Is there any way of knowing how long she was unconscious for?' Tim asked.

'At this stage, no. We will be watching her closely and will keep you updated. I expect the entire team will want to have a proper family conference with you tomorrow, but for now, the first twenty-four hours are crucial.'

Lizzie's eyes glistened as she listened to the doctor speak. Flashes of the scene played in her head every time she closed her eyes, even if it was just to blink.

'I'm on all night, so if you think of any questions, you can ask me the next time I come around.' The doctor smiled. 'I just want to do some tests, so if you wouldn't mind, you can wait in the family room across the corridor, I'll have the nurse ring the room when you can come back in.'

Tim, reluctant to leave, led Lizzie and Robert to the waiting room. He had turned over and over in his head whether or not he should break his promise. He couldn't decide what was for the best or who the best was for. Would Rose want to have her son with her after all these years or would she be happy to keep the promise she made? How would Lizzie feel, finding out that she had always had a brother that she had so dearly wanted when she was younger? And what would Michael say, to find out at forty-six years of age that the woman he thought was his mother wasn't his mother after all? The weight of the problem began to tell on Tim's face. Robert squeezed his hand letting Tim know that he was there.

'Robert, we'd be lost without you.' Tim placed his hand on Robert's shoulder affectionately and extended his other arm around Lizzie's shoulders. 'You are a rock of strength.'

It was heart-warming for Lizzie to be part of. 'You are our rock, Robert,' Lizzie agreed and reached her lips up to his cheek to kiss him.

Robert, a man of few words, nodded in acknowledgement.

'I think we need to plan our night.' Tim took a seat at a table and Lizzie and Robert followed. The blinds were open but the night sky had grown dark outside. An aroma of percolating coffee wafted around the small room and Robert stood to pour them some. 'The more quiet time the patients have, the better, or so the nurse says.' Tim sipped the freshly brewed coffee in between speaking, it was time to breathe and fill his lungs with more than just gasps of air. 'I don't think they'll let us all stay in the family room, its one person per patient,' he added. 'I think you could go home, Lizzie, get a few hours rest.' He looked at Robert who weighed in on his plan willingly. 'Robert could go with you,' Tim said, 'and then when you guys come back in, I'll go home then.'

Robert knew there was no way that Tim would leave the hospital without his sister but played along. The dimly lit waiting room provided cover for their puffy reddened eyes.

'I don't know, I don't want to leave her,' Lizzie said.

'I'll wait and see her when they let us back in and then I'll think about it,' Tim said.

She nodded in agreement just before the door opened and Lucas walked in.

'Lucas.' Lizzie sat in shock. He was the last person she expected to see.

'Lizzie, I'm sorry…' He looked at Tim and Robert, both of whom he had identified in his surveillance at the funeral. 'I'm sorry for barging in, I really am, I just wanted to check on you, see if you are doing okay.' He stepped closer to their table, both Tim and Robert stood up, they figured by his English accent, who he was. 'Sorry, I'm Lucas, Lizzie's, eh, friend from London,' he introduced himself and shook both their hands.

'Nice of you to come over, for Lizzie,' Robert said.

'Lucas,' Tim looked at Lizzie to gauge how he should react to him. He wasn't sure that she was happy to see him. 'Nice to meet you.'

'I was at the airport when you called, Lizzie.' He looked back to her, 'So I just thought I'd call out and see you, if that's okay?' Lucas stepped closer to her and she stood to greet him.

A wave of uncertainty washed over her as she remembered his reason for being in Ireland in the first place and gave in to an awkward hug.

'I thought you had gone back?' she said.

'No, tomorrow,' he said, throwing a sideways look at Tim and Robert. 'I thought I might just see you, maybe take you downstairs for something to eat.' He looked awkwardly at Robert. 'That's if it's okay to leave?'

'That's a good idea,' Tim said. He was suspicious as to how he had got to the hospital so quickly but was too distracted to ask him. 'She hasn't eaten all day. See if you can get her something in the cafeteria downstairs.'

Lizzie threw Tim a disgruntled look. 'I'm not five.' She raised her eyebrows just enough to remind all three of them that she was quiet capable of making her own decisions; besides, she wasn't hungry and if her uncle had known the real reason why Lucas was here, he sure as hell wouldn't be encouraging him. But now wasn't the time. 'Okay, then, come on.' She grabbed her phone from the table, irritated. 'Ring me if we are allowed back in,' she said, throwing her uncle daggers.

'Lizzie.' Lucas placed his hand on her hip as he walked beside her along the hospital corridor. She didn't shirk it away. 'Can I hold you?' He didn't wait for the answer and scooped her into his chest. 'I don't know what to say, Lizzie, I wish it wasn't happening to you, to your mum,' he murmured into her hair. 'I'm such a fool, Lizzie, but believe me, I know it's not the time, but I did what I did for a very good reason, I owed it to someone and maybe, when everything works out with your mum, you'll let me explain it to you.' He shook his head, he didn't know how he was going to tell her what he knew, but he knew he had to. 'I know you don't feel like trusting me, but I'm begging you to trust me so that I can be with you.'

She pulled away from his embrace and looked at him, it was his eyes that convinced her to give him a chance.

He reached for her hands, it was then that he noticed Tim looking on.

'Lucas,' Tim coughed as he stood away from the closing family room door. He hadn't intentionally followed them to overhear how this Lucas guy would treat his niece but he was glad he had. 'I just came out to tell you, the cafeteria is closed, so you won't get anything down there.' Lizzie wiped away the latest tears that had fallen. She looked so like her mother used to. 'Lizzie, I think Lucas should take you back home, what do you think?'

'I don't know, Tim, I just don't want to leave her.'

'I know you don't, but it's necessary, you'll be no good to any of us tomorrow if you don't.' Tim looked behind him as the family room door creaked open again. 'I could do with Robert staying with me, if it's okay with you, Lucas?'

Lizzie wasn't fooled by her uncle's feigned neediness and her brief smile let him know as much.

'Sure. Absolutely.' Lucas was delighted to be asked. He let go of Lizzie's hand as though he was a schoolboy that had just been caught kissing his first love. 'That's fine.'

'But,' Lizzie gave in; she was exhausted, 'only after I get to see Mum.'

*

It was an hour later when Lucas parked Rose's car underneath the old oak tree that stood for years shadowing the front of Rose's house. Lizzie had seen her mother as she had wished, before she allowed herself to be brought home. She only intended to stay at home for as long as it took her to take a shower, charge her phone and maybe grab an hour or two's sleep.

Lucas gathered the bags from the boot, where Robert had placed them and followed Lizzie along the gravel path around the side of the house to the back door. 'Where do you want these?' he asked Lizzie as she entered the code for the alarm from memory and flicked the kitchen light switch on.

'Oh, anywhere there,' Lizzie pointed out into the hall. 'Some of them are Mum's. I'll unpack them later.' She watched as he stacked all the bags, including his own, in the hallway and returned to the kitchen where she stood. 'I can't believe you are here.' She walked towards the double lounge doors and turned the lamps on inside. Lizzie was close to tears again. Having Lucas in her family home in Ireland felt so surreal.

'Where else would I be, Lizzie, I want to be with you.' He moved to hold her but she dodged him, unspoken answers jumping around in her brain, still niggling at her in the background.

'I'll make some tea,' she said.

'I could make you something to eat,' he signalled to the fridge, looking for her permission to open it. She nodded for him to go ahead. There were cold cuts of meat, limp lettuce and a jar of gherkins – he knew she didn't like them. 'I'll make some toast.' he said, wishing she was as comfortable with him now as she had been when he held her at the hospital. 'You doing, okay?' He opened the bread bin and found the last few slices of a batch loaf.

'I don't know how I am, Lucas, I haven't the strength to think,' she said, waning by the second.

He could tell that she was still unsure of how she felt about him being here and the reason why he decided to come. It would take her some time to trust him again, he accepted. 'Why don't you jump in the shower, I'll have this ready for you when you come back down,' he said; being as supportive as he could was the only option he had until he could tell her the truth. She gave him a hug, a promising start, he thought, and went for a shower.

The smell of toast wafted up the stairs and mingled with the fresh lemon scents of her body wash, a pang of hunger shot through her and she waded down the stairs in her bare feet, tying her dressing gown around her waist. It was already one a.m.

'I've locked the back door.' Lucas said handing her a plate of toast. He had buttered it straight away so that the butter would melt, just like how she liked it. In the twenty minutes she had been upstairs he had cleaned away the kitchen, figured out how to lock the back door and made her toast. He'd had a chance to take in a few of the family photographs that were dotted around the walls and sideboards. She looked exactly the same in the old photos as she did now, fresh-faced with long hair tumbling down her shoulders. If only he could make her smile like she did in the pictures.

'Thanks', Lizzie nibbled on the first slice of toast, as hungry as she had felt, she hadn't the stomach to finish it.

'What time do you want to go back in for?' Lucas held his phone to set his alarm.

'Six I suppose, when they are doing their rounds.'

'Perfect, I'll set the alarm for five, so.' He swiped his alarm app and placed his phone back in his pocket. 'And where…' he dropped his eyes awkwardly. It was unreal to be so close to someone one minute and then to have to ask permission for being with them the next. 'Where do you want me to sleep?'

She closed her eyes momentarily, it was strange to be in this position with him.

'I would like to, sleep with you,' Lucas said awkwardly. 'I mean…' He scrunched up his face as soon as the words came out. 'Sleep in the same bed as you, hold you, in case you want me, is what I mean, Jesus, this would be funny, if it wasn't so sad, Lizzie.'

'Just turn off the lights, Lucas,' Lizzie grabbed her phone and charger and headed up the stairs. Lucas flicked the switch and followed her. She opened the door to her bedroom and turned to allow Lucas in. It was so personal to have him in her house and now that he was standing in her childhood bedroom, decorated with fluffy clouds and pink love hearts, it felt as though she was revealing a part of her soul.

He stepped inside in his stocking feet, his shoes already abandoned at the bottom of the stairs. He took his phone from his pocket and placed it on the bedside table beside the softly lit lamp and unbuckled his belt, exactly as she had seen him do it every night she had spent with him in London. Next, he unbuttoned his jeans, shook them off and laid them over the chair, he sat in his T-shirt and boxers at the edge of the bed.

Lizzie hung her dressing gown on the back of her door and as she reached up for the hook, the hem of her nightshirt rose just enough to expose to rim of her bum, Lucas pretended he didn't notice.

'You ready?' he asked, his hand poised over the lamp.

'Yes,' she answered, fixing her pillows on her side as he flicked the switch.

He reached over for her in the darkness and pulled her close to him. He could feel the tension briefly leave as she relaxed her body against his. Pushing back her hair from her face, he wiped the wetness from her cheeks. 'It's okay, I've got you,' he whispered as her body squirmed in despair, sobbing for her mum. His heart broke for her. He held her tight until her breathing slowed and her body softened.

Chapter 37

Monday Morning – 2016

Michael sat soundlessly for hours on his hotel room chair; he had no idea what he should do next. Marie had suggested driving to the hospital but Michael wanted more time to think and that was what he had been doing ever since, as she slept on the bed beside him. He replayed the letter, word for word, in his head, a world of secrets that he couldn't begin to understand. Secrets, so profound that his own mother, Mary McGrath was unable to tell him. He wondered how she felt for keeping the secret and what had made her break her promise in the end. And then there was Rose, a child herself when she had him, *an angelic little girl*, his mother had said, only three years older than his own handsome Jack was now. What had gone through her head, when at fourteen years of age, she had to leave him behind? What had been the *danger* that she had to *save* him from? What had *damaged her beautiful soul*? His mother's words swam around his mind creating more questions than answers and perhaps the most pressing of them all, if Rose had been his mother, who was his father? And then there was Lizzie, Rose's daughter, a sister, something he had never had, and an uncle, or two if he counted Robert, that he would have to welcome into his life. He wondered how George would feel when he told him.

He watched soundlessly as the dawn tiptoed over the Dublin city scene, extinguishing the street light chains and, as if by magic, turning the navy blue shadows in to brighter shades of grey. It was already four a.m. He lay back down beside Marie and waited for the morning to come. He would go to the hospital for seven, he decided, it was the right thing to do. He closed his eyes, finally content with his decision and drifted off to sleep.

*

The silence of the house began to lull Lucas asleep as he held Lizzie close. Gentle snores escaped as his sleep became deeper.

Lizzie moved, her sleep disrupted by the unfamiliar sound. Carefully, she turned and moved his arm, it didn't wake him. Reaching past the lamp, she located her phone. Pressing once, she checked the screen, it was four a.m. She couldn't believe she had already slept for three hours. Stealthily she slipped out of bed, watching the rhythm of Lucas's breathing as she tiptoed around the bed and crept across the landing to her mother's room.

Small warm tears trickled down her eyes as she sat on her mother's bed. She wondered had her mother been lonely here since her father had died. The room was neat and fresh as she always remembered her mother's room to be, but the house seemed so silent and eerie to her now. She opened a door to a wardrobe, noticing her late father's suits still hanging. Sadness washed over her. *Time and tide wait for no man*, she could hear him say. She climbed under the covers on her mother's side and lay back on her pillows. She could smell her perfume.

*

Tim had sat like a sentry beside his sister's bed throughout the night. He watched the team as they glided with certainty around Rose. Bottles were hung and needles were placed, monitors binged and motors hummed. Muffled moans from other beds drifted through the curtains and hushed, lonely family members tiptoed to their loved ones' bedsides. Family beds lay empty as the mums, dads, brothers, sisters, husbands, wives, sons and daughters sat with trepidation, hoping for a miracle, perched on the hard grey chairs reaching for a lifeless hand. Afraid to leave in case their loved one woke, or worse still, in case they didn't.

'Tim, we need to change the picc line. We'll call you when you can come back in.' The nurse was small and young and purposeful as she laid out her sterile tray on Rose's statue-like legs.

'Okay,' he mouthed, and left the room.

Robert dozed on the family room chair, waiting for Tim to return.

'Any change?' he sat up straight as Tim came in, his voice hoarse with tiredness.

'I can't see any fight in her.' Tim sat with his head in his hands. 'It's just not like her to be so helpless.' For the first time since he arrived in the hospital, tears dropped unashamedly from Tim's eyes.

'They have her sedated, Tim, she's not going to be able to fight through that. The doctors said they needed her as still as possible. Its early days.' Robert himself was worried, but reassured him none the less.

'You know, there's something on my mind.' Tim sat across from Robert and leaned forward on his knees. Reaching inside his jacket pocket that Robert had hung on the back of the chair he pulled out his phone and placed it facing up on the table.

He padded his chest for his glasses and found them on his head. Taking a deep breath, he explained to Robert why he had an important phone call to make to Michael. He detailed the hidden history of Fitzpatrick Farm for Robert; everything from his mother' reclusiveness to his father's violence and his uncle's depravity. He told Robert of how he tried to protect his little sister by giving her a whistle so that she would always be able to call him. He explained how they left for Dublin and, because of the promise they made, never looked back. He knew that Robert had figured out some of it, but he needed to say it all, out loud.

Robert sat quietly, letting Tim talk, it had been an age bottled up inside of the man he loved, relieved that he finally felt able to speak about it. Most of it he had suspected, but the harrowing detail had left him dismayed.

'I think it's the right thing to do, Michael needs to be here.' Robert was sure. The image of the whistle that Tim had given to Rose played over and over in Robert's mind.

'My only concern then is for Lizzie and how she might take the news,' Tim said.

'You and your sister, as much as I love you both,' Robert widened his eyes in a reprimanding way, 'have underestimated what that woman, and yes, I mean woman,' Robert was only too aware that Tim still thought of her as a teenager, 'is capable of, she is strong, and resilient and capable, just like her mother; she is more than able to handle this.'

'Okay, I hear you.' Tim rubbed his face in his hands. 'I'll ring Michael then as soon as it's a decent hour.'

'But before you do,' Robert picked up Tim's phone, 'I have been fielding some of your calls.' He held Tim's phone in his hand. 'Detective Kelly was looking for you, a few times yesterday.' Robert had mulled over when would have been best to tell Tim, but it hadn't been a priority, till now. 'He wanted you to come in voluntarily to Kilkenny Garda station.' He paused. 'He thinks that if he has to arrest you, that it would look better for you that you came in voluntarily.'

'Fucking hell.' Tim's shoulders dropped; this was all he needed. 'So they are going to pin it on me.' The murder investigation, the interviews in Harcourt Street and the past week's events were a vague and insignificant memory for him. 'Well, they'll have to drag me out of here, because I'm not leaving here without Rose, simple as.'

'That's what I said to him,' Robert answered. 'And in fairness, he sort of accepted it, I told him where we were and that if he wanted to speak to you it would have to be in the Intensive Care Unit of Beaumont Hospital. By the tone of him, I'd say he might just work with you and give you a little time, but I don't know that for sure.'

'So be it,' Tim said. There was nothing more he could do.

'For what it's worth, Tim,' Robert reached across and held Tim's hands, 'What you did...' Robert said. 'What you did for Rose...' Robert blinked, stemming the tears that were queuing up to fall down his face. 'For Rose, for yourself, what you did was nothing short of heroic, no two ways about it.' He wiped his cheek with the back of his hand. 'You are a fucking hero,' Robert's voice trailed off, the lump in his throat making it impossible to continue.

Tim wiped his own tears from his face. He felt a weight lift off him as Robert took half of his load. 'I just wish she had the whistle now, so she could call me, and I'd come running, faster than ever.' Fat bulbous tears landed on the ground in front of him as his mind floated back to when they were young. 'I just want to help her, I wish it was me in there.'

'You can't think like that Tim', Robert sighed.

'Look, you need to ring Michael,' Robert glanced at the clock, it was nearly five. 'I think Lizzie should be here when Michael arrives, so I'll ring her and check to see what time she is coming in for, it's better that they are both here with Rose.' He paused. 'Just in case,' he added.

'Okay then, I'm going to walk outside, get a blast of fresh air and ring him.' Tim said as he headed outside.

'I'll ring Lizzie.' Robert wasted no time and dialled her number. 'Lizzie, love, everything's okay,' Robert was quick to ease her fears.

'Oh, okay.'

'I was just checking on you; did you get any sleep?'

'I did, about three hours, I'd say, did Tim sleep?'

'Not a wink, but we knew he wouldn't.' The familiarity between them was comforting to them both. 'What time do you think you'll come in for?'

'I'm going to leave here in the next half hour.'

'Perfect, tell me this much, did your mother ever mention anything about a whistle to you?' Robert was nothing if not sentimental, he thought that Tim could do with a token of their past, something to focus on.

'Yeah, there's something familiar about that all right, was something to do with that if she needed Tim on the farm, she was to blow the whistle?' Her memory of the story was buried deep. 'God, I haven't heard that story in years.'

'Would you be able to find it, do you think?' Robert was hopeful. 'It's just, Tim has mentioned it and I thought it might be nice for him to hold onto it for a while.'

'I'll have a look, knowing Mum she has it safely categorised, boxed and colour-coded.' They both giggled. The comfort they both felt in their familiarity was short lived as they both wondered would Rose ever be able to colour code or categorise again.

'Thanks, love, see you in a while,' Robert said and ended the call.

Lizzie pushed back the covers and stretched her legs, she wasn't convinced that she would find the whistle with so little time to dedicate to the search, but she decided she would give a cursory look anyhow. She leafed gently through the bedroom drawers and ran her hand over shelves, but nothing jumped out. It was then that she remembered the drawers in the console table in the hall, it was there that all sorts of treasures were hoarded over the years. Quietly, she made her way downstairs and began to root for the whistle inside.

Lucas rubbed his eyes and reached for his phone, he could tell by the light diffusing through the curtains that it was morning. He reached across to look for Lizzie, but she was gone. 'Lizzie,' he said out loud, pulling himself upright; she wasn't in the room.

'Unbelievable,' Lizzie said as she reached past a bundle of envelopes and pulled out the whistle she was looking for. To Lizzie and Matt, the drawer had been a junk drawer; to Rose it was a treasure trove. She pulled the whistle, bringing with it a bundle of envelopes that tumbled out and fell to the floor. As she bent to pick them up, she heard Lucas's footsteps upstairs.

'Morning.' Lucas arrived on the landing, pulling his T-shirt over his head. 'Why didn't you wake me? Are you awake long?'

'No, just an hour I'd say.' She placed the whistle in her dressing gown pocket and straightened up the envelopes and placed them distractedly back on the table. 'I was going to head to the hospital in the next half hour, if that suits, or you can stay here, you don't have to come.'

'Of course I want to come, I'll drive you,' Lucas said. 'Can I take a shower?'

'Oh sure, work away. I'm coming up now to get dressed.'

'Is that a whistle I saw you put in your pocket, or...' He raised his eyebrows and smiled. 'Or are you just happy to see me?'

She always enjoyed his humour. 'Very funny,' Lizzie said, allowing herself a small but significant smile. 'It's a long story.' She pulled the whistle out of her pocket and dangled it in front of her on its string. 'I've to bring it into Tim. That drawer,' Lizzie was already on the third step on her way back upstairs when she turned to look at the table, it was then that she noted her name on the top envelope on the pile, 'is like Mary Poppins' bag, the deeper you dig in the more you will find.' She stepped back down into the hall and reached for the letters and carried them upstairs. 'That's weird.' She was speaking to Lucas as he stripped naked in front of her with the bathroom door half open.

'How does this work.' He reached for the silver dial and pulled the shower lever and the water began to flow. 'Never mind, I think I have it,' he called to her as she made her way past the bathroom door and into her bedroom. She sat on the edge of her bed studying her name written by her mother's hand.

'What's weird?' he called, the water temperature finally regulating.

'It's my mum's handwriting, and there's an envelope addressed to me,' she said loudly so he could hear her.

Lucas rinsed the shampoo from his hair and the suds from his body. He dried himself with the towel she had used only a couple of hours before.

'Open it,' he said, walking into her room.

'What on earth?' Lizzie couldn't believe what she was seeing as she pulled the crisp white printed paper from the envelope. 'There are three others here too, one addressed to a Michael,' she looked perplexed at the name, 'and another addressed to Detective Kelly.' She showed Lucas the envelopes in her hand. 'And one for Tim. What on earth?' she said, anxious to find out what was inside of them.

Lucas wrapped his towel around his waist and sat beside her. He had a feeling that the information that was in the letters was the same as the information he was guarding from her.

Her heart began to race, her breathing became shallow. 'I can't read it. You read it to me.'

Lucas could feel Lizzie's small body tremble beside him. He took the letter from her shaking hands and started to read the letter out loud.

'Dearest Lizzie,' Lucas cleared his throat and continued. *'I have loved and have been loved beyond my wildest dreams, for this I am eternally humble and blessed. Know that I am happy and always have been, I will always hold your heart in my hands, until you find a love that is capable of holding it as softly as I do. When you do find the love of your life, which I know you will, I will hold both your hearts together'*. Lucas paused, grasped her shaking hands and held them both tightly in his.

'When you get married, I will dress you on your wedding day as I did on your christening day. The only difference is I will use your hands to do it, not mine. These old hands are too stiff now anyway, I'd rather work with yours. This awful disease will not get the better of me, not yet anyway.'

A loud sob escaped as Lizzie gasped for air.

'I will lovingly fix every strand of your hair before I place your veil on your head and your father and I will walk side by side

with you down the aisle when you get married. You will always know I am with you… I will never leave you.

'There is a special person that should be part of your life and I would like you to find him. When you do, tell him I love him as much as can be, always have. He is your older brother,' Lucas cleared his throat as though he was trying to remove himself from any prior knowledge.

'I was only fourteen when he was born and although I would have loved nothing better to keep him and love him like any mother would, given the circumstances of my life at the time and the danger we both would have been in, I had no choice but to let him go. It was a different time then but there has not been a day since, when I haven't thought of him. His name is Michael McGrath. He was born in Kilkenny and he now owns Fitzpatrick Farm. I promised his mother, the lady that reared him for me, that I would never come back and I haven't, but life is too short and I wish for you to have a loving big brother as I did. A brother that will protect you as Tim has done for me. A brother that will be with you when you need him.

'Trust your instincts always and when you are not sure, listen to your heart, it will tell you what to do. I know because I have heard your heart speak with compassion and love. Know your limits, but test them often. Allow yourself to be sad; allow yourself to be happy. Just don't be either exclusively. Everything passes, Lizzie, whether it is good or bad, so it will be no time till we meet again. Look for me; I will be the one smiling. And in case I can't tell you then, I tell you now: I love you with all my heart. I want you to listen to our song often and when you get the choice to sit it out or dance, I hope you dance. I am and always have been in awe of you, Lizzie. Always and forever. Mum.'

Lizzie was speechless. How her mother had the foresight to write such a letter she would never know. Lizzie grabbed back the pages that Lucas was holding. 'This can't be real,' she cried. 'How could I not know this?' Her body turned cold. 'Let me read it again, properly.' Unable to stop her hands from shaking, she placed the letter on the bed in front of her and read it again.

Lucas dropped his towel and pulled on his boxers, T-shirt and his jeans as quick as he could.

'It's Michael McGrath.' She lifted up the letter with his name on it. 'I need to tell Tim, Lucas, quick.' She flung her nightshirt over her head and pulled on her clothes. 'I just can't believe this,' she said, shocked at what she had just learned.

'Lizzie,' Lucas paused, 'I think...' Lucas carefully selected the words he was about to use. His involvement in the Fitzpatrick family business hadn't been of his own doing and the last thing he wanted was for Lizzie to take it out on him, especially now, since he had just been allowed back in. 'I think Tim knows,' he said, screwing up his mouth uneasily.

'What?' Lizzie pulled her white vest top over her head. 'What do you mean, he already knows, how would you know?' She opened her old wardrobe looking for a pair of jeans.

'It's complicated; I can explain it all on the way in in the car, if you like.' Lucas was anxious that he was true to his word but even more anxious that he eased some of Lizzie's confusion.

'Your fucking right it's complicated.' She pulled her trainer socks from the travel bag on the chair. Her mother hadn't tidied them away with the other stuff. 'Tell me what you know and how?' Her brow was rutted with curiosity. She gathered up the letters and made her way downstairs. She found her Converse in the hall, sat on the first step and pulled them on.

'This is part of what I learned when I came over to look into the story.' He sighed. 'This is why, Marie...' He paused, waiting for a backlash that never came. He followed Lizzie into the kitchen and watched her search for her keys. '...Asked for my help.'

'Who's Marie, Marie McGrath?' Lizzie asked.

'Yes, Marie McGrath, Michael's wife. She was the one that asked me to help out with the story about the body.'

'Marie McGrath.' Lizzie was confused. 'What, what do you mean?'

'I didn't get a chance to explain everything to you but I know Marie from college.'

'Michael McGrath's wife, Marie,' she clarified. 'How does she know everything?'

'Michael's mother, that is Mrs McGrath,' he said, correcting himself, 'told her about Rose and the fact that she was a scared fourteen-year-old who had nowhere else to turn to.'

'And why ask you to cover the story? What, to reveal all the sordid details of my mother's life?' She pressed the on button on the alarm and opened the back door to leave. She checked her bag for her keys, her wallet and the letters. It was hard to put a shape on all the questions bouncing about in her head. She was confused, not knowing what to feel. Why hadn't her mother told her sooner, had she not thought that Lizzie could have handled the news and what was the danger that her mother was in? With so much upheaval, Lizzie didn't know what to do.

Lucas followed her outside. 'On the contrary, Marie was afraid that the secret would get out when the reporters started to look into the story behind the body that was found and she wanted to protect Michael. She was trying to keep the secret, not expose it.' He held his hand aloft for the keys. 'I'll drive.'

She handed them to him without argument and jumped into the passenger seat of Rose's car. 'And why you, why drop everything and go to her, against my wishes?' Lizzie said exactly what she had wanted to say for the entire week. 'Why do you keep saying you owe her?'

Lucas reversed the car from Rose's drive, crunching quietly on the gravel and pulled out on the road. 'It's not so much as I owe her, but I do need to make amends with her. I was a right prick to her in college; not because I cheated on her or anything.' Lucas was quick to rule out infidelity. 'But I sort of became obsessed with her and wanted her all to myself, which she didn't take to very well; I even told her that I'd kill myself if she left me for the guy she was seeing.'

'Were you an item?'

'Only in my imagination,' Lucas ran his hand through his hair; he was glad he was facing forward and that she couldn't see the embarrassment that had flared on his cheeks. 'And her then, boyfriend—'

'Michael?' Lizzie said, utterly shocked.

'Yes, Michael,' he threw her a flinching glance, 'well, he gave me a warning, I will sort of never forget.' He raised his eyebrows in regret. 'And when I realised what a prick I had been, it was too late, and I didn't dare go back looking for her.'

Lizzie was amazed. She had known that he had gone to college in Ireland but never in her wildest imagination would she have thought this could happen. 'Oh, Lucas.'

'Yeah,' he grimaced, 'talk about fucking up royally. She really was the sweetest girl; I just didn't know my arse from my elbow back then.'

'Back then?' Lizzie couldn't help herself.

'And so when she asked me to help, I knew she must have been in trouble, so that's why I came.'

'And Michael?'

'Well he hasn't quite come around yet, but I hope he will, in time.' He cleared his throat and rolled his shoulders back. 'Especially when he realises…' He swallowed hard, it was now or never, he thought to himself, she would either be delighted he would say it or kick him out once and for all, 'Especially when he realises that…' He looked to his side and she looked back at him. He checked the road briefly and looked back into her eyes, 'That I'm in love with his sister.'

Chapter 38

Monday Morning – 2016

'Morning Michael, I hope I didn't wake you, its Tim Fitzpatrick here.' Tim was anxious as he dialled Michael's number, he wiped the morning dew from the wooden bench to the side of the entrance and lowered himself down; his sciatica always flared whenever he sat in the one position for very long and sitting silently beside Rose's bed all night hadn't done him any favours. Tim knew that Michael deserved to know, he just felt compromised not being able to discuss his decision with Rose first.

'Not at all,' Michael wasn't surprised to see Tim's number flash on his phone. 'Sure I've half the day behind me,' Michael joked politely. 'How is…' he hesitated, he was uneasy saying her name out loud. 'How is your sister doing now?'

'She's still the same. Michael, I was ringing…' Tim paused; he tried desperately to find the correct words to use. The morning was so still and fresh, in direct contrast to how he felt inside. 'You sound as if you are driving, am I interrupting you?' Tim said.

Michael looked at Marie and then back to the road. 'I am driving, not too far away from you actually, I'm in Dublin.' Michael paused; he hated talking on hands-free in normal circumstances, never mind in situations such as this.

'Oh,' Tim said, curious about his visit to Dublin. 'I see.'

'I'm five minutes away from you now; I was going to call in,' Michael said. The early hours had dragged relentlessly for Michael and when he couldn't take any more waiting he and Marie had decided to go to the hospital.

'Right.' Tim thought it unusual. 'I'll see you soon then.' Tim's voice croaked a bit from tiredness.

'Okay.' Michael indicated for the hospital entrance, 'I'm literally driving by your road right now.' He paused and heard Tim hold his breath.

'Okay, great,' Tim said. 'Good timing, I see Lizzie arriving there now too.'

Lucas dropped her at the entrance and she sprang out of the car. She closed the door, flung her handbag over her shoulder and scooped up her hair into a band.

'Lizzie, over here,' Tim waved. 'Michael, I'll meet you in reception when you park.'

'Tim,' Lizzie said, walking towards him as he finished his call. 'Any change?' she asked, the tension in her voice matching the stiffness in her shoulders.

'No, love. Afraid not.'

'Tim,' she sat beside him, 'I've found something at Mum's.' She fumbled with her zip and rummaged inside her bag.

'Before, you do, there is something I need to tell you, love.' Tim knew that Michael would arrive any minute and he had little time to spare. The only saving grace was that the concrete, overpriced carpark was a good five-minute walk from the entrance.

'What?' Lizzie held the envelopes in her hand impatiently. The rate of her breathing increased as she waited eagerly for him to speak.

'It's about your mum, when she was just a child,' he began, 'she had a baby, which she left in the care of someone else.'

Lizzie bit her lip and dropped her head, closing her eyes. She stayed silent while he spoke.

'The thing is, with your mum being so critical, I was thinking that we should let him…' His mouth was dry. 'Her son, know that she is in a bad way.' Tim's hand stretched across his mouth and the scratch of his greying stubble sounded as he rubbed his chin. He reached his hand across to hers. He couldn't begin to understand what it must have been like for her to hear about her mother's secret, especially in these circumstances.

Lizzie's eyes remained closed as she shook her head. It was a moment before she could speak. 'Tim, I know.' She paused. 'I found these letters in Mum's drawer,' she said and showed him the letters in her hand, one with Michael's name on it. 'But only since a couple of hours ago.'

'Oh my god, did she leave it for you, how'd you find it?'

'I was…' It wasn't the time to explain that she was looking for her mum's whistle for Robert, that was a detail that she could add later, she decided. 'I was looking for something else and these,' she fanned the other envelopes in her hand, 'fell on the floor.'

Tim took the envelopes from her and traced his sister's handwriting with his hand. 'So she wanted you to know, she wanted Michael to know?' Tim ran both his hands through his hair and inhaled deeply. He was utterly relieved that Rose had come to the same conclusion as him; it wasn't sitting easy with him that he was about to break her confidence.

'Tim, what did Mum mean, when she spoke about the danger, she and the baby would have been in if she had kept him?' The words her mother had used sent shivers down her spine.

'It was a different time, then love, things were different, families were different and if our father had known about Rose's pregnancy, well, there was no telling what he would have done'. Tim hoped it was explanation enough, he didn't know how he was going to answer the question if she asked about the father.

'Lizzie, there's something else,' He decided it was better to warn her. 'I think I might be arrested today, for the murder on Fitzpatrick Farm.' Tim felt his heart thumping in his chest as he heard himself say the words out loud. 'This, Detective Kelly thinks I had something to do with the body of Patrick Fitzpatrick ending up in the ditch.'

'Tim,' Lizzie cried.

'I'm not worried, love, but if it does happen, you just concentrate on your mum, she's the priority; Robert will be with you, I just don't want you to be unprepared.'

'Tim—'

Tim saw Michael in the distance. 'Lizzie, the baby that your mum had…'

'I know, Mum explained it in her letter.'

Tim wasn't sure what Rose had explained or how concise she had been with the detail so he waited for her explanation.

'It's Michael McGrath, from the farm,' she said.

'It is, love, thing is, I rang him, he happened to be in Dublin and he is here just now.' He signalled with his eyes as Michael and his wife Marie approached.

'Does he know?'

'I haven't told him but something tells me he is not in Dublin at five in the morning on a whim.'

'I'm going in to Mum.' Lizzie stood to leave, she needed more time to process the information before she was able to see or speak to Michael.

'Lizzie, are you okay with this?'

'I'm fine, Tim, like you said, Mum is the priority.'

'You are so like her, Lizzie, you really are.'

She left, tears welling in her eyes; she didn't know what to think.

'Michael, nice to see you again.' Tim shook his hand. 'Lizzie has just gone in to see her mum.' Tim watched as his niece scurried through the entrance to avoid talking to them.

'I'm just going to get some coffee,' Marie made her excuses and left.

'How's Rose now?' Michael said, taking the seat beside Tim.

'She's not doing too well, to be honest, Michael. The doctors are not very hopeful that she'll pull through.'

'How is Lizzie holding up?' Michael listened as Tim spoke, feeling as though he was looking at himself from the outside in. His mind wondered over the images of Rose as she smiled at his children in Fitzpatrick House. If he had known yesterday, what he knew today, he wondered what he would have said to her.

'She's strong, like her mother. She'll be fine.' Tim didn't know how to continue.

'Could I see her, Rose, while I'm here, do you think, or is it just…' Michael couldn't bring himself to say family. He coughed instead to mask his discomfort.

'The thing is, Michael,' Tim's heart threatened to rip clean out of his chest, 'I don't know how to say this to you.' Tim hesitated and waited for the words to materialise in his head. 'Oh.' Distractedly he waved to Lucas as he went by. 'That's Lucas, Lizzie's boyfriend from London.'

'Lizzie's boyfriend?' Michael asked, in shock at the connection.

'You know him?'

'I used to, long story, another time.'

'The thing is,' Tim restarted, 'Lizzie found a letter, a letter with your name on it. In Rose's house.' He checked the bench beside him, but Lizzie had taken it with her. 'It's the same reason I called you this morning.'

'I know, Tim, I received a letter from my mother last night too.' Michael spoke slowly and quietly as though he was being overheard. 'Marie had been sworn to secrecy, she had been keeping it for me, on the instructions of my mother.' Michael looked at Tim, both of them as overwhelmed by the power of the women they were surrounded by as each other. 'It seems that the women had their own plan.' He managed a sad smile. 'Her instructions were that Marie would know when the time was right to give it to me.' Michael stood, the energy inside him making him move, the muscles in his back needed stretching to alleviate the unease. 'It turns out my letter,' he sat back down and leaned forward with his elbows on his knees, 'had Rose Fitzpatrick's name in it.' Tim's hands instinctively rose to cover his face.

'Unbelievable, Michael, so your mother's letter told you about Rose?' Tim was relieved. The burden of breaking the secret was lifted, both mothers, Mrs McGrath and Rose, deciding to break their promise at what seemed to be the same time.

Michael's sadness was etched on his face. He couldn't look Tim in the face. His gut wrenched as it became real for him.

'And that is why you are in Dublin this morning?' Tim pressed.

'Yes.' Michael's eyes filled. A ball stuck in his throat as he fought hard to contain his sadness. 'I didn't even get a chance to know her,' he whispered through blurry eyes, not trusting his own voice.

'I'm so sorry, Michael.' The tragedy was unbearable; Rose would have loved to know him as much as Michael would have loved to know Rose.

'Anyway. I'm here now.' Michael feigned composure as he wiped his eyes and blew his nose. 'Is she in any pain?'

'The doctors say no. Her coma is induced so she shouldn't feel anything through it.'

'At least that much.' Michael's heart was heavy. 'So Lizzie knows about me?'

'She does.' He couldn't begin to understand what the man must have been feeling since he found out last night, nor what was going through Lizzie's head for that matter. 'I think we should go up.' Tim was eager to get back to Rose. 'We can talk about everything else later, if that's okay?'

'Of course.' Michael followed Tim's lead. 'Tim, there is just one quick thing.' Michael was unsure of how to ask. The question had been hovering around in his head unable to land since his mother's revelation came in his letter yesterday and there was no one else who would know.

'Yes, Michael.'

'Do you know, who my father is, or was?'

'I don't, Michael,' Tim cleared his throat and looked ahead. He was afraid that Michael might see his eyes. 'Rose never told me.' It was a secret that Rose wanted to keep and Tim had vowed to keep it for her; Michael would never hear it from him.

'Okay.' Michael accepted Tim's words.

*

Lizzie stood up from her seat and nervously watched as Michael opened the hospital room door. Adrenaline galloped around her body, rendering her muscles jellylike and weak. Her heartbeat sprinted and a wave of tears exploded from her eyes.

'Michael.' She shook her head, opened her arms and met his strong grip.

'Lizzie, I'm so sorry for Rose, for all of this,' he spoke, conscious of the medical staff in the room.

'You're here. She'd be glad you are here.' She held him close and couldn't let go, he was like a connection, a frayed link to her mother, another piece of her alive.

'I am,' he whispered as he dried his face with his sleeve.

'Come in closer, tell her you are here.' Lizzie pulled him by the hand and stood by Rose, Michael frozen by her side. 'Mum, it's me,' Lizzie whispered. Gently, she rubbed her mother's cheek with the back of her hand. 'Michael is here too, Mum. I found Michael like you asked me to in your letter.' She glanced at Michael, 'Although it was him who found us.' A deep sob escaped from Lizzie as she uttered the words. Michael exhaled heavily and stepped closer to Rose. 'I have your letter here too.' She reached inside her bag and handed it to him.

'Rose.' Michael walked to the opposite side of the bed. He reached tentatively towards her hand. 'It's me, Michael here.' Awkwardly, he spoke. He looked across the bed at Lizzie who was sobbing into her hands. 'I've just spoken to Tim.' He smoothed down the plastic apron in front of him to keep it out of his way. He tried to catch the rogue tears as they escaped down his face. 'The funny thing is, my mother, Mary, left a letter for me too and thanks to the instructions she gave my wife, I only got it last night.' His voice cracked as he tried to hold his resolve. He lifted his head and offered Lizzie his saddest smile, 'I always wanted a sister.' He wiped the drips from his nose and sniffled. 'Said no man, ever,' he added under his breath, making Lizzie smile in return. He swallowed the lump of sorrow back down to his gut, reached for Rose's frail hand and took it in his. 'I know she can look out for herself, but I suppose I may look after Lizzie now, seeing as I'm the big brother.' Lizzie smiled through her tears. He stifled his sobs as he turned from the bed. 'Rose,' he paused, 'we are all rooting for you.'

'It really is too much stimulation for the patients to have so much going on. Can I ask you all to leave for a moment?' She turned to her folders and began to record her data from the monitors.

'You didn't get long with her,' Tim remarked as Lizzie and Michael returned to the corridor outside.

'They are doing something with her,' Lizzie explained. Lizzie nodded to Lucas and smiled at Marie. 'I see you have all found each other.' It felt right that Lucas was there and as she looked at him, the words that he had used earlier registered with her for the first time, did he really just say *because I am in love with his sister?*

The table in the family room was strewn with empty cups and spoons and Marie busied herself gathering empties for the trash. Papers had collected unfolded and scattered and she smoothed them over and piled them neatly on the table. They didn't have to wait long for the consultant to enter.

'Your mother, as you know, has had a traumatic brain injury. It's quite severe,' she warned. A vacuum of air formed as Rose's family drew a collective breath. Tim cleared his throat. 'We are concerned by the lack of brain activity on the tests and as of this morning we have her on a hundred per cent oxygen. Without the ventilator, she would not be able to breathe.' She waited till the family processed the information. 'All the signs are discouraging at the moment, I'm afraid.' The consultant paused as she surveyed the room. Tim sat stoically without averting his eyes. 'We must prepare you for the worst.' Michael could feel Lizzie's body shake beside him. He grabbed her hand under the table. 'We don't expect that Mrs O' Reilly, your mother…' The doctor directed her gaze at Lizzie. 'will last the night, although it is very hard to put a time on it, in our experience, it is very close.' She hadn't used the words *the end* but they all knew it was implied. 'You will need to make a decision in relation to resuscitation' The room was silent. 'Did you know your mother's wishes?' The family shook their heads. 'We do need to know, as a matter of urgency, to what extent you want us to intervene.' Lizzie stared down at her lap, she couldn't meet the consultant's gaze. 'She is comfortable, not in any pain,' she assured.

Time stood still in the room. Michael held Lizzie's hand tightly, she sat, trancelike, absorbing the words.

'I'm so sorry'. The consultant added. Lizzie nodded her thanks.

'And she's not in any pain?' Lizzie asked again.

'No, I can assure you we are keeping her comfortable, she is not in any pain'. The consultant waited for any more questions they might have had. 'You should go, be with her, is there anyone else to come?' She asked.

'No', Tim answered. 'This is the entire family.' He looked at Lizzie and then at Michael, All of them silently acknowledging the significance of his words.

'Well, if you need anything, we'll be right inside.' She rubbed Lizzie's shoulder as she left.

'I'm going back in to her,' Lizzie said and Tim and Michael followed.

They watched as Rose lay motionless in the bed. Her fragility portrayed in her waiflike frame that barely created a shape in the bed. Tim noted it all, the beating of her heart as the lines scrawled across the screen, the rhythm of her breaths as the tubes forced air into her lungs. Her numbers looked worse now than they did before. Her blood pressure leapfrogged from high to low and back to high again. It was staying at low just now. Tim could see that her body was giving up. It made sense to him now as he re-ran the doctor's comments in his head. He had been blinded by hope before.

'I'm here, Rose. It's okay.' He rubbed her arm lovingly, he felt helpless. Wishing for the umpteenth time that there was something he could do. Noiselessly he moved closer to her side. 'I have everything under control here, you know,' Tim spoke softly to her. Michael and Lizzie listened. 'If you need to go, it's okay.' He lifted his head and looked directly at Lizzie and Michael. 'I'm sure Matt is waiting for you. We'll all be fine.' His whispers betrayed the shakiness in his voice. His eyes glistened with tears as he spoke. 'You know, Rosie, you have been the light of my life,' He shook his head; her smile would have lit a million hearts. 'You are the bravest person I know.' He put his head in his hands and his body shook as he cried. 'I'll miss you, but…' Tim knew she was listening, he could feel her in the room. 'But it's time for you to go. I love you, Rosie.' Tim held his breath in an attempt to hold his tears from falling. He wiped his face in the side of her sheet. Pulling himself to her side, he reached in and kissed her cheek. 'You don't need to fight any more, Rosie, you made it.' He was sure he saw her smile.

'Let's get you more comfortable, Rose.' The nurse was brief as she busied by the bedside. Quickly she adjusted the dials and restarted some pumps. There were eight medicine pumps in motion at the same time. 'I'm just going to check your pupils, Rose,' she announced as she forced open her eyelids, one by one, and shone her pencil torch at them. Her pupils were uneven.

Tim stepped away as the nurse began to work. 'Do you need us to go?' he asked.

'No.' The nurse looked at him knowingly. 'You should stay with her.' The tone in her voice was understood. 'The chaplain is outside, would you like him to say a few prayers with you for Rose?'

Tim looked to Lizzie and Lizzie shrugged. Rose had long since turned her back on the Church but she believed in God and they both thought it would have been something she would have liked.

'Maybe, just a blessing,' Tim offered and moved to the other side of the bed to allow the Chaplain some room.

Lizzie moved towards her mother and rubbed her arm as the chaplain anointed her forehead with oil. 'She's cold,' she said, pulling the sheet around her closer as soon as the chaplain left. 'She would have hated all this fuss.' She looked at Michael, sorry for all the insights to Rose's life that he wouldn't have known. 'She was always giving out about drama, there was no need for it, she'd say.'

'Didn't do the whole crocodile tears thing at all,' Tim offered. 'Stoic, strong, I've yet to meet anyone with her strength.' He waited for the nurse who gathered her tray and went to the back of the room. 'She would have loved to have known you, Michael.' Tim swallowed hard. 'I didn't get a chance to talk to her properly after the funeral, but the smile on her face after we came away from your house said everything I needed to know. It made her day, meeting you, Marie, the kids.'

'I'm so glad now that I got to speak to her.' Michael sighed.

'And I am so glad I came home from London, Tim, thank God, you made me come,' Lizzie added. She brushed her fingers through her mother's hair. 'She looks different.' Lizzie moved to her side. 'More relaxed.'

Michael stood behind her, he had been in the room when his mother had passed away and he could tell that Rose's end was very close. The nurse walked around the bed and silenced the alarms that had begun to sound more frequently. Tim watched her. He knew her body was giving up.

'I'm just going to make her more comfortable,' the nurse said.

Michael placed his arm around Lizzie's shoulders.

Lizzie bent towards Rose in the bed. 'Love you Mum,' she said and laid her head on her mother's shoulder.

Tim moved towards his niece and held her hand. He watched, as her children, Lizzie and Michael, finally united, cried inconsolably by their mother's side. He studied Rose's chest as it rose up and down briefly gasping for air and then stalling, then he scanned the monitors for tell-tale signs.

'It's okay, Rosie,' Tim said, the sadness in his heart dripping out through his eyes. 'We are here.' He glanced around the room, 'Lizzie's here, Michael's here, I'm here.' Robert slid behind the curtain followed closely by the nurse. 'And Robert's here,' Tim said contentedly. Collectively they held their breath waiting for her to gasp once more, but she never did. 'I think that's it.' He spoke solemnly. 'I think she's gone.'

Michael and Lizzie stood motionless, unable to move, holding each other for balance, the light in Lizzie's life as she knew it, extinguished.

Chapter 39

Monday Morning – 2016

'Detective Kelly.' Robert recognised him as he strode into the family room, Detective Kennedy walked behind him. 'True to your word, I see.' Robert's tone was far from welcoming. He had seen through the glass panels detectives Kelly and Kennedy arrive and discreetly left Rose's bedside to intercept them.

'Have we met?' Kelly asked.

'No, but we spoke yesterday.'

'Ah, Robert.'

'Yes,' Robert answered. 'This really isn't a very good time.' Robert shook his head in disdain. 'Rose has just passed away. Tim needs to be with his sister.' He swallowed hard as he choked back his own emotion.

'I see.' Louise stood closer to him. Her reluctance to even come to the hospital had caused her to question why she was in the force in the first place. 'We are sorry to hear that.' She placed her foot slightly in front of Kelly's, her body language enough to tell him to retreat. 'Really we are.'

'Can I get you guys coffee or anything?' Marie stepped forward from the kitchenette; she had busied herself as much as possible since she arrived. 'I've just made a pot.'

Both of the detectives declined. Kelly was curious as to her presence there.

'So Timothy is inside with Rose?' Kelly asked.

'He's with Mum.'

The detectives turned to see Lizzie entering, her eyes puffy and red. It had been nearly too much to bear to see her uncle break down after her mother had finally passed, it was then that she remembered the whistle, she had decided to nip across to the family room to remind Robert to give it to him.

'This is Detective Kelly, Lizzie, and this is Detective Kennedy,' Robert introduced them.

'Oh,' she answered and walked past them to the table where her bag was. She rummaged in her bag and pulled her mother's whistle out for Tim. She showed Robert what was in her hand and smiled. 'I thought I'd get Tim this, I forgot to give it to you earlier.'

'Good girl,' Robert said.

She blinked as she recognised the name on the last envelope in her bag. 'Detective Kelly, did you say?' It wouldn't have occurred to her to give it to him had she not just heard his name.

'Yes.'

'Well, this is for you then.' She pulled the envelope from her bag with Detective Kelly's name on it. 'I found it this morning, when I was looking for something, in mum's stuff.' She handed him the envelope.

'Okay,' Detective Kelly answered, holding out his hand. 'Thank you.'

'I'm going back into Mum, okay?' She looked at Robert as she spoke. 'Will you come back in with us, Robert, Tim needs you.'

Robert followed, much happier to walk away from the detectives than he was to stay. 'Is there not too many of us in there?'

'It doesn't really matter at this stage,' Lizzie answered. 'The nurse has said for us to take a few moments until the doctors come to do their final observations and then they'll ask us to leave and then we've to go back in, when they have taken away all her tubes and everything.'

'I see.' Robert's sad eyes glossed over. 'What do you think is in the letter?' He motioned his head in the direction of the family room that they had just left.

'I don't know,' Lizzie answered as she pulled back the door to the room where her mother lay. 'But she was never one to do things by halves,' Lizzie answered, she couldn't help but be proud of her. She wished she had known her mother's secret sooner, it must have been a heavy burden for her to bear on her own. She was the strongest, most loyal person she knew and for that she loved her. 'Here.' She unclenched her hand and showed Robert her mum's whistle inside. 'You give it to him. It was your idea.'

Robert rubbed her back, he was so lucky to have her.

Back in her mother's room, she stood behind her brother and placed her hand on his strong shoulders. 'Michael, I meant to give this to you earlier, I just wasn't thinking straight.' She placed her mother's letter in his hand. 'It's the letter Mum wrote for you.'

Michael opened his envelope and began to read.

Dearest Michael,

You do not know me and sadly I do not know you. You are my first-born child. I became pregnant with you when I was fourteen years of age. When you were born, I named you Michael and I left you with a guardian angel, the woman you called your mother. I could never have looked after you and your mother, Mary McGrath, saved us both, the night you were born. You were so strong for someone so small. You insisted on coming before your time, but I had to leave you, for both our sakes. There was no one better for you than Mary. You were born on her bed, as her other son, George, was. She loved you as her own. She loved me, she loved us.

All my life I have thought of you. Especially on your birthday. That is the day that I feel closest to you. I close my eyes and imagine your life. I have missed you. There is a massive hole in my heart where you should be. The pain and loss that I feel will always be there. It is bearable only because I know that you do not feel it. It wasn't the goodbye that hurt the most, it was the knowing that there will never be a hello.

I have no doubt that you are a wonderful person as your mother would have raised you to be. I wonder sometimes would she have tried to tell you the truth. We both promised that we would never speak of it again and although I wished for nothing more than to telephone or write or even call to your mother's house, I didn't, it wouldn't have been fair. I remember your piercing eyes and tiny body and find it hard to imagine you as a man, the compassionate and strong man that I know you would have grown to be. I wish nothing but the best for you and I have always had a place in my heart for you, Michael. Know that I have always loved you. What I did, I did for the love of you. Your precious innocence deserved it. You have a beautiful younger sister, Lizzie. Please find her and hopefully you will both fill the void that I have left in your lives with each other.

My love always,

Rose x

Michael couldn't speak. He bowed his head and cried, holding Rose's hand.

'Tim,' Lizzie had seen Robert, from the corner of her eye, hand Tim her mother's whistle. She watched as Robert dried her uncle's tears. 'Detective Kelly is outside looking for you, is there anything we can do?' she asked.

'Leave it to me.' Tim stood and placed the whistle in his pocket. He bent close to Rose and kissed her cheek. 'There'll never be anyone like her, that's for sure.' He placed both hands on Lizzie and Michael's heads as he passed them by. 'She'll be delighted she has you both together.' He left them with a smile. He smoothed down his shirt and stretched out his neck and left.

'Detective Kelly.'

'Timothy.' Kelly refolded the paper that was in his hands and stuffed it back into his inside pocket. He had left Louise talking with Marie in the family room moments earlier to read the letter in the corridor. 'I'm very sorry to hear about Rose, I don't know what to say.' He sighed.

'Thank you,' Tim managed.

'Do you want to take a walk?' Kelly asked, he looked over Tim's shoulder suspiciously.

'I don't really want to be far away from Lizzie, that is unless I have to,' Tim answered.

'Well, just come down here a little further, would you.' Kelly glanced back towards the closed doors once more.

'Okay.' Tim followed him.

'Thing is, I was here to arrest you this morning. I have the warrant here.' He patted the breast pocket of his jacket.

'And?'

'And I was just handed a signed confession for the murder of Patrick Fitzpatrick, well, self- defence if I'm right in picking up what happened.' He cleared his throat and pointed to a vacant seating area further down the corridor. They sat opposite each other.

Tim looked at him inquisitively. 'What on earth do you mean?'

'The thing is, if I take this confession at face value, you are completely off the hook.' There was a suggestion in his voice that he thought the confession was questionable.

'I don't understand.'

'Here, read it for yourself.' Kelly handed Tim the piece of paper from his pocket.

Tim noticed Rose's writing on the envelope. 'From Rose?' Tim remembered Lizzie showing him the letters earlier that morning. He hadn't thought about it since.

'Read it,' Kelly instructed again. He folded back the creases and placed it back in his hand.

'*Dear Detective Kelly,* I see it's dated last week,' Tim noticed. '*In 1970, I was the victim of rape at the hands of my uncle, Patrick Fitzpatrick...*' Tim began reading aloud but reduced his volume to a whisper as his eyes scanned over the words. '*...On the family farm in Kilkenny. I was fourteen when the abuse happened, and due to my naivety, I didn't realise I had fallen pregnant by him. Times were different then, we were not as advanced as teenagers are today.*' Tim's nostrils flared as the buried anger bubbled inside of him. He thumped the seat beside him. *When my then seventeen-year-old brother, Tim, realised what was happening to me, he did what any brother worth his salt would do and confronted him. You see, we had the type of upbringing that involved us bringing up ourselves. We* *couldn't have told our parents, my mother was frail, weakened by the physical violence her husband, my father, had subjected her to and also by the sexual violence she suffered at the hands of Patrick Fitzpatrick. Patrick bragged about what he did to my mother to me, so you see, she couldn't have helped, she wasn't able to help herself.*

Tim and I would never have told my father, it would have angered him more, and God knows who he would have taken his anger out on: me, Tim, my mother, we just couldn't be sure, so Tim confronted Patrick himself, and after they fought physically, Tim warned him to leave, to never come back and as far as we were all concerned, that's what he did, disappeared like the coward he was.

However, what Tim doesn't realise is that I was so worried that Tim would get hurt that I followed him the night he set out to find my uncle. I hid in the bushes while they fought and when it was over I watched Tim leave. My uncle was still very much alive. He stood from where Tim had left him, steadied himself and began to make his way home. When I noticed he was drunk, zigzagging back and forth on the road repeatedly, I decided that I should get home too, thinking that he wouldn't notice me if I left my hiding place, but he did and he grabbed me on the road, just across from the ditch from where you found him. I tried my best to get away from him but he was just too strong. I knew by the way he was unbuckling his belt that he was going to rape me again and I had had enough. I believed that my uncle would kill me that night. I was afraid that if I screamed that Tim would hear me and he would come running back and he would end up getting killed too. And when he pushed me to the ground, held my throat and lay on top of me … Tim closed his eyes and swallowed hard. Streams of tears erupted down his face. He fought hard to stop the anger that was rising from his stomach and choking him. …*I reached behind me, lifted a rock from the ground and hit him as hard as I could on the head. It was then that it stopped.* Tim lifted his head from the letter to look at Kelly. *I rolled him off me into the ditch and ran as fast as I could for home.* Tim sat stunned into silence. *It is my wish that the detail of my encounters be used solely and purposefully for the reason of establishing the truth and should in no way be taken out of context or out of the confidence of the law in so far as is possible. My reasons are to protect my children, both Lizzie and my son Michael, who should never know who his father was.*

'Fucking hell Rose,' Tim said, wiping his mouth with his thumb and finger. 'Can she do this?'

'She just did,' Kelly answered. He rewound the scene in the family room when he arrived and remembered Marie McGrath offering him coffee. 'The Michael,' Kelly pointed to the letter in Tim's shaking hands, 'is Michael McGrath, from the farm.' Tim nodded. 'Which answers why he was able to buy the farm at half price.'

'The proceeds of the sale then were put in a trust for Lizzie,' Tim said. 'That's the way Rose wanted it.'

'Makes sense, half and half,' Kelly said. 'Did Michael know?'

'Not until an hour ago,' Tim said.

Kelly nodded. 'As far as I'm concerned,' Kelly stood, 'if Rose's account can be believed…' He looked at Tim, he had his suspicions that Rose may have fabricated the story to save Tim from the consequences, but he admired her for it and now that Rose had passed away, none of them but Tim would ever know whether it was true. 'The case is closed.'

Tim's head fell into his hands. He wiped his sweaty hand in his trousers and met Kelly's as he stood.

'I admire what you did, Timothy.'

'But that's just it, Kelly, I didn't do anything.'

'Well,' Kelly accepted Tim at his word. 'Well, here's to Rose who, at the age of fourteen, had the strength to bring that bastard to justice.' For curiosity's sake, he would have loved to know, was it Tim protecting Rose, or was it Rose protecting Tim. Either way, he believed that justice had been done, not that he could have admitted that publicly though. He stood to leave extending his hand to Tim. 'I suppose, the only two people who will ever know the truth is you and Rose and I'm okay with that, what you did, what you both did for each other has my full respect. You won't be hearing anything more from the Gardaí.'

Tim sat back down in silence as Detective Kelly moved away. He watched as patients shuffled by and staff sprinted past. He listened as high-pitched beeps bounced from the ceilings and doors swished open and closed. Muffled voices trailed along the walls, falling inaudibly on his ears. He sat forward, his elbows landing on his knees, life went on without her, it wasn't fair. He reached inside his pocket and held her whistle in his hand.

'Tim.' Lizzie sat beside him and placed her hand in his. 'You doing okay?'

'I am, love,' he said. 'You?' He squeezed her hand tight. She nodded, her voice unable to lie. 'God, Lizzie, what will we do without her.' Tim studied Lizzie, the sorrow in his eyes second only to hers. She screwed up her mouth and bit the inside of her cheek, just like her mother did.

'She wrote you a letter too,' she said and handed him the last envelope. 'I'll leave you to read it.' She kissed her uncle on the forehead, squeezed his shoulder and stood to leave. 'Come up to the family room, when you are ready.' She walked away, knowing how hard it would be for him to read it.

He emptied his lungs slowly, scratched his head and unfolded the paper, his hands shook.

My Darling Tim,

For you, my brother, are the light of my life.

Tim, what you did for me, how you protected me, will be forever engrained on my heart. I was only strong because you were there and I am strong now because I know you will always be.

I cannot begin to tell you how you have saved my heart. You have given me the strength to love, by teaching me that love conquers all. In the face of fear, you are the bravest soul I know. Because of you I can face whatever this life can send me, these muscles may not do what I tell them to but my heart will and because you have shown me that there is something inside so strong, I have lived a wonderful, blessed life.

Thank you for bringing me to the McGraths all those years ago and helping me to leave Michael in their home. I still believe that he is where he belongs but I can't shake the feeling that he belongs with us too. I wish for you all that you find each other, if this stupid illness has taught me anything, it's that life is too short, find each other and love each other and then when you've done that, love each other some more. The greatest wish I have is that Lizzie will have a brother like I had.

Robert, lovely Robert, is the kindest man I know and tell him from me, since he arrived into your flat with his bell-bottoms and beard all those years ago, I knew he would never leave. He will always have a piece of my heart.

It is unimaginable to think that someone as kind-hearted as you could be treated as though you have done something wrong. In my eyes you are a hero, the man who saved me. With my last breath, I promise you that Patrick Fitzpatrick will never cause any trouble for us again. I love you my brother, my light, my life.

Your Rosie. X

Epilogue

Fitzpatrick Estate Christmas 2016 – 6 Months Later

Eve watched in anticipation as the amber lights of the cars on the road below, whizzed by. With each passing car, she was becoming even more disappointed. The motorised snowman hummed as he bowed slowly, tipping his hat every thirty seconds to the background Christmas tunes that Jack had play listed for their mum on his iPad.

'Aww,' Eve sighed. 'That's not them either.' Her red velvet dress swished as she twirled around the drawing room and the bow that she had chosen with her daddy, that day, pulled her beautiful blonde curls from her face. 'When will they be here?' She had been ready for an hour already and there was no sign of her party guests.

'Soon, love, soon.' Marie smiled as she straightened the stockings she had hung on the marble fireplace. There were nine hanging this year, a family record for the McGraths. She had all their names embroidered on each one and Eve and Jack had filled them with the gifts they had chosen at the school Christmas fair. Marie left the drawing room to check on the oven. 'Why don't you help me set the table?' she called back to Eve, whose excitement had been bubbling over all day.

'Can I sit beside Aunty Lizzie, Mum, please?' Eve pulled the plastic wrapper from the Christmas crackers and set about lining them up in front of each place.

'Sure, darling.' She was nearly as excited as her daughter, it wasn't often that they had a reason to entertain and now, with their new-found extended family, she pictured herself doing it all the time. 'I'd say Uncle George will want to sit with Uncle Tim and Uncle Robert, don't you think?' She handed Eve nine silver napkin rings from the dresser and a pile of carefully folded linen napkins.

'Ooh, the giant's wedding rings,' Eve said, making her mother smile; the only use her Newbridge Silver had ever seen up till now was in Eve's imagination. 'Jack will want to sit beside Lucas, I'd say.' Eve threw her eyes upwards and gave a dramatic, animated sigh. 'Technology.' She nodded her head and placed her hand on her hip as though she were the adult.

'True for you, Eve, true for you.' Marie laughed.

'Can we not use these Mum, these are nicer?' She waved the Christmassy paper napkins in front of her mum instead, stashing the old Irish linen back on the dresser. They were red and green and had funny-looking reindeer on.

'Maybe use both?' Marie answered. 'Actually, maybe put Dad with Lucas and Jack as well, we don't want him to feel left out, do we?'

'I suppose not.' Eve's face was radiant in the twinkling lights of the Christmas tree and the roaring log fire in the drawing room had made her cheeks glow.

Marie checked her watch, an early but extravagant present from Michael; he had wanted her to have it for Christmas Eve and had given it to her in bed that morning. She slipped out of her slippers and stepped into her heels that she had placed in the hall. They sparkled, just like she hoped her first family Christmas Eve party would. 'I think that's someone arriving there now.' She kissed Eve on her head and scooped up her slippers from the rug. 'Michael, they're here,' she called up the stairs. 'Jack, come down and say hello.' Her shy, but smiling son bounded down the stairs as he was told to do.

'Lizzie, oh,' Marie kissed her sister-in-law on the cheek and did the same with Lucas. 'You look even more radiant than usual.' Marie ushered them both inside. 'Eve has been waiting patiently all day. We all have.' She giggled. A blast of cold December air swirled around the hallway and scents of cinnamon and log fires greeted her first guests inside.

'So have I,' Lucas said, raising his eyebrows to Eve who was watching them unbutton their coats impatiently. You could smell the cold from them. 'Someone,' he pointed deliberately at Lizzie as Eve giggled, 'couldn't decide…' He placed their overnight cases to the side and stacked the Hamley's bags that were overflowing with Christmassy wrapped gifts, deliberately on top of them. '…Which present to get their favourite niece and nephew, so…' he bent down to Eve's ear and placed his hand to his mouth to whisper, 'she bought them all.'

'I heard that,' Lizzie said as she shook the droplets of rain from her hair. 'But he is right you know.'

Her wide happy eyes made Michael smile as he watched his sister from the landing. The past year had been the most bizarre he had ever known, a dead body on his land, a letter from his dead mother, another letter from Rose, a mother who he had never known, and Lizzie, a sister, who just happened to be the light of both his and his family's lives. He was delighted Marie had talked him into hosting Christmas this year. But then again, he smiled as he visualised her in the bed this morning, she was usually right about most things.

'I did actually buy them all,' Lizzie said, ignoring the exaggerated look that Marie was giving her. 'What, I'm their aunty; I can do reckless and irresponsible things.' She lunged for Eve and Jack and ran away from Marie as she swiped for her with a tea towel.

'I'll throw the bags up, will I, out of the way?' Lucas said.

'Good idea, Lucas,' Marie said. She was as sure as she could be, that the old Lucas, the friend that she loved in college, was the Lucas who was now in love with her sister-in-law and as much as Michael had revolted against it, he was warming up to the idea of Lucas being back in their lives. And if she was truthful, she felt a little smug that her judgement hadn't been totally askew after all. 'I've put you in the back, Lizzie's favourite room.'

'Great.' Lucas smiled. He snatched up the bags in his arms. He hadn't stayed here with Lizzie the few times that she had stayed over, but from the numerous tours that Eve had made him take on his day visits, he was sure he knew which one Marie meant. 'Merry Christmas Marie.' He smiled at her widely. 'I appreciate you and Michael inviting me, I really do.' He grabbed as many handles as he could and bounded up the stairs.

Michael was standing on the landing waiting for him. 'Lucas.' He held out his hand and Lucas placed down a bag to shake it.

'Michael, Merry Christmas.' Lucas's hand was much smaller than Michael's. 'Lovely to see you again.'

'And you,' Michael said, holding his grip a moment too long. 'You know,' he smiled, finally letting go of his hand, 'I've been warned…' Michael's smile was warm and wide. He took a slight step backwards as though to appear less threatening. 'I've been warned by my wife and my sister to be nice.' He couldn't help but grin. When Lizzie and Marie got together lately, they were a force to be reckoned with.

'I like the odds of that.' Lucas laughed and exhaled. It was only then that he realised that he had been tense for the entire journey down. It had taken him some time to dispel the awful isolated impression Michael had of him. But he still hadn't won him over completely. 'If I had to pick a team…' He raised his eyebrows just enough and threw a glance back down the garland decorated stairs towards Lizzie and Marie. 'I'd want it to be the two of them.' Michael and Lucas laughed together. It was the first time they had agreed on anything.

'I'm glad to have you here, Lucas,' Michael's chest relaxed. 'I actually am.'

'What, just so you don't have to listen to the girls on your own?'

'There is that,' he smiled. 'How has Lizzie been doing?'

'She has good and bad days, but mostly good, she misses her parents so much, mostly around now, of course. I try and get over at least every weekend and she gets back to London when I can't get here.'

'I saw your piece in the Indo. Leaving investigative journalism behind for the opinion pieces?' It was a surprise departure for Lucas but he had jumped at the chance when the editor of the Irish Independent had asked him to do it. They placed the bags on the carpeted floor and Michael moved to pull the curtains.

'Well, I'm hoping to make that a more permanent feature, that was only as a guest piece, but if the talks I have lined up for January go well, the paper might take me on more permanently.' Michael listened. It was a good sign that Lucas was making moves to be in Ireland more full time, especially since Lizzie was tied up with the interior design course in Dublin. Michael worried about her being lonely in Rose's old house.

'That would be good,' Michael said.

'Yeah,' Lucas added, 'especially now.'

Michael heard the crunch of the gravel on the driveway. 'Let's get back down, they'll be waiting to see which one of us has the black eye.'

'I'll just throw these inside the room', Lucas said and like two rugby full backs, larger than life, Michael and Lucas stepped back down the stairs, dependable agile characters ready for the ball to come their way.

'Well there's something you don't see every day.' Tim pushed back the door and stood dripping in the hallway. The sight of Michael and Lucas coming down the stairs together made him smile. 'Maybe you are more like your old uncle than you thought you were.' His innuendo made Michael grin from ear to ear, it was a joke that only the four men in the hallway appreciated.

'Tim,' Michael shook his head drolly at his uncle's joke, 'you just can't help yourself, can you.' He punched his uncle playfully on the arm. 'Robert, welcome.' He took Robert's coat.

'Good to see you.' Robert reached up and hugged him, slapping his back.

'Your brother George is just behind us. Either that,' Robert braced himself as he saw Eve make a run for him, 'or Santa clause is arriving early by tractor.' He scooped Eve up as she jumped into his arms. 'Marie, what's the smell, I'm starving.' He carried Eve back into the kitchen, high-fiving Jack as he walked by.

'Nearly ready,' she announced as she fanned the steam that erupted from the open oven door. Aromas of garlic and thyme wafted through the kitchen and the sound of glasses chinking and logs cracking and laughter filled the room.

George came in through the back door.

'Just in time, George,' Marie said as she kissed his cheek.

'Sure wasn't I watching for smoke signals.' He laughed. 'I hope it's not as cremated as last week's.' He winked at Jack, it was their private joke.

'Sit down, George.' Marie laughed and Michael patted him on the back; the bond between them as brothers as strong as it had always been, still the same McGrath men, both born on their mother's bed and raised by the same amazing angel.

Marie lifted the roast tray from the rack with her oven-gloved hands and placed it on the countertop to cool. 'Michael, will you mash the spuds?'

He touched her discreetly on her side as he passed her to help.

Tim watched contentedly as the people that he loved, hugged and laughed beside each other as though they had always done so. It was Rose's legacy, a legacy that he was proud to be part of. A family that, without her, would not be together.

Marie placed the silver platter of carved meat on the table and began to serve. 'I got a card from Louise the other day. They are on a Disney cruise at the moment and will be till New Year's.' She passed the large bowl of roast potatoes across to Tim. 'They've taken Kelly's sister, Annie, on a holiday.'

'Sorry,' Tim asked, 'Kelly's sister?' He wasn't sure who she was referring to.

'Detective Kelly,' Marie confirmed. 'He has a sister, in her fifties with Down syndrome,' she added. 'And she loves Disney.' Marie and Louise had become quite good friends in the past six months and Marie had been kept abreast of all the romantic developments between Louise and Kelly.

'Detective Kelly and Louise are together?' Tim said.

'Yes, they were while they were working on the case.' She didn't need to give the details.

'I'm all on for seizing the day.' Tim lifted an empty glass. 'The best of luck to them.' If Tim had learned anything this past year, it was that life was for living and it was best to do it while you had the health and the strength to do so.

'Oh, sorry, guys, it was my job to fill the glasses.' Michael jumped to his feet to retrieve the Prosecco. Quickly he opened it and began to pour. 'Will you do the honours, Tim.' He reached over Tim's shoulder and filled his glass first.

'Him, toast, he doesn't really like to be the centre of attention.' George smirked as he chided Tim who sat across from him. On Tim and Robert's frequent visits to the farm, George, Tim and Robert were fast becoming good friends.

'If you insist.' Tim waited until all nine glasses were full, including the grape juice that Eve and Jack had been poured. He reached inside his pocket and pulled out a navy velvet bag. 'I was going to do this later.' He untied the silk strings. 'But now is as good a time as any.' A brief flash of sadness flickered across his eyes, everyone at the table felt it. 'I was trying to think about what I'd do with it and I couldn't decide.' Robert fiddled with the stem of his wine glass in his hands, he had given Tim several suggestions as to who might appreciate it most. 'But this is something that sort of has a bit of meaning to me and my baby sister, Rosie.' He took his wallet from his back pocket opened it and unfolded the letter from Rose. Since Lizzie had found it and given it to him that day at the hospital, he hadn't left it down. 'So I tried to think of how I would give this to all of you.' He lifted up the velvet bag and dangled it in the air and in the other hand held the letter that Rose had left for him.

'What is it, Uncle Tim?' Eve was like a puppy waiting for a ball.

'In a minute, Evie,' he answered. 'So I thought,' Robert coughed comically, looking for his attention. 'Sorry, we thought,' he nodded his glass in his partner's direction, 'that maybe the best place for it was somewhere that we all could see it and we could use it whenever we needed.'

'How about on the Christmas Tree?' Eve suggested, she still didn't know what was inside the velvet bag but to her the Christmas tree was the most obvious place.

'You know, Eve,' Tim laughed a hearty, warm laugh, 'that's not a bad idea.' Eve was as proud as punch and Jack smiled across the table at her. 'Which brings me nicely to the toast?'

'Finally,' Lizzie said comically.

'To Brothers and Sisters,' he raised his glass as a flash of Rose's smiling face sparked across his eyes.

'To Brothers and Sisters.' A chorus of toasts chimed around the room as they all remembered Rose in their own unique way.

'Can we do the bag now, Uncle Tim?' Eve couldn't wait to see it any longer.

'You can, my love.' He put his fingers inside and pulled out Rose's whistle. Its tattered string had been removed and in its place, a purple silk ribbon had been tied. Attached on a loop was a small sterling silver tag. Tim had had it engraved.

'Ooh, shiny,' Eve said as she left her seat to touch it. 'Can I put it on the tree now?' she asked. 'Jack will help me.'

'Show me,' Michael said as his daughter skipped it over. 'It's lovely, Tim, it really is.' He handled it in the palm of his hand and noticed the engraving on its side. The story of the whistle had touched all their hearts and will forever be known in the family's history. 'It's engraved.' He flashed a look at Tim, looking for his permission.

'Read it.' Tim's voice was low. He was beginning to well up inside. Rose would have loved to have been at this table. But he was sure she was around somewhere, it wouldn't have been like her to miss a party. 'Please.' Tim nodded.

Michael cleared his throat. He looked to Marie and in the glimmer of the table candles he could see her embracing smile. He knew he was a lucky man. He watched Lucas as he tenderly rubbed his sister's back, another lucky man, he smiled, and finally, he admired Robert as he stretched a masculine arm across the back of Tim's chair. There were a lot of lucky men in the room, he decided. He cleared his throat and began to speak.

'For Rose,
She stood in the storm,
And when the wind did not blow her away,
She adjusted her sails.'

Gently he placed the whistle back into his daughter's hand, overwhelmed by the words. He could only imagine what Lizzie and Tim were feeling right then, because he was floored. 'There you go, guys, hang it on the tree.' He watched as his son Jack lifted his sister Eve as high as he could manage and decided he needed to do something the same to mark it. He took Lizzie's hand and dragged her reluctantly up from the table.

'What are you doing?' Lizzie laughed. 'You nut.'

'I'm not sure I'll be able to lift you as high as Jack can lift Evie.' Michael laughed, gulping back the remainder of his glass. 'But I'll give it a try.' Laughter erupted from the table as Michael pretended to hoist her up to help put the whistle on the tree.

'Actually,' Lizzie whirled around in front of them, 'I might be a little heavier, than normal.' Her beautiful eyes glinted with tears as Lucas drew a deep anticipatory breath. He had wondered how she was going to tell them. She immediately pressed on the corner of her eye to stem the flow. She placed both her hands on her stomach and lovingly caressed it. 'Because,' she beamed with happiness from ear to ear, 'there are two of us to lift now.'

'Are you serious?' Michael held her hands wide, looked at her stomach and drew her in for a hug. Lucas's earlier comment made sense to him now. 'Especially now, you said earlier.' He looked at Lucas knowingly, finally realising what he had meant. 'This is amazing, guys, a cousin, Jack, Evie, a new little cousin for you.' Michael bounded around the room with excitement for Lizzie, and if he was truthful, for Lucas too. He hugged her once more and whispered into Lizzie's ear as he twirled her. 'To Brothers and Sisters.'

We hope you enjoyed this book!

Adele O'Neill's next book is coming in spring 2018

More addictive fiction from Aria:

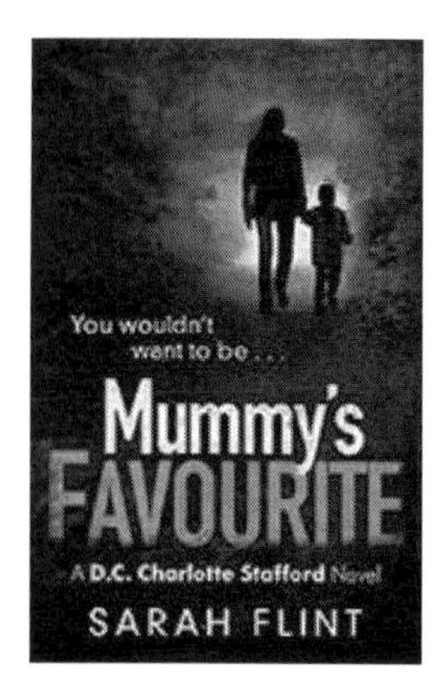

Find out more
http://headofzeus.com/books/isbn/9781786690692

Find out more
http://headofzeus.com/books/isbn/9781784978969

Find out more
http://headofzeus.com/books/isbn/9781786695451

Acknowledgements

An idea to write a book is all very well and good until you realise that the idea alone, will not get the book to the hands of readers and so I must, with the humblest of hearts and a depth of gratitude, give thanks to the patient people who helped turn my idea into the novel it is today.

As an emerging author, the name of the game is to get your book into the hands of someone who believes in your novel and your characters as much as you do, so a special word of thanks to my very special friend, bestselling author Carmel Harrington, who not only championed my writing from the beginning but held the spotlight on me so that my agent, Tracy Brennan could find me. A special word of thanks to Tracy for guiding me along this journey.

To my editor, Caroline Ridding, whose wonderful emails and amazing forensic insights into my characters, have transformed my novel into what it is today and to all the team at Aria, Head of Zeus for their unwavering support and amazing book knowledge. As bad as it sounds, I love hearing that I make an office full of people cry!

I am overwhelmed with the lovely people who share their expert knowledge so generously to writers looking to make their characters as real as possible so a massive thank you to Doctor Liam Farrell who was invaluable in making sure the medical elements made sense, however this is a work of fiction so all medical inaccuracies are my own.

To all the committee at Wexford Literary Festival who work tirelessly to promote writers and reading. Their support has been invaluable to me throughout this process.

To all my online bookish friends and #WritersWise buddies, you make tweeting an especially funny and unmissable experience.

A thank you also to Lorna Sixsmith for her insights into all things agricultural, again all agricultural inaccuracies are my own.

To Madeleine Keane for her insights into the world of journalism and for sharing her world of knowledge.

Special thanks to my amazing brothers and sister, without whom I would not have been able to write about the depths of love and loyalty there is between siblings (or know what Detective Kelly's curse words mean).

And lastly but most of all, to the other three A's, Alan, Alannah and Ava, I owe you three everything, none of this would mean anything without you 'When you get the choice to sit it out or dance, I hope you dance.'

About Adele O'Neill

Having lived and worked in the UK and Dublin since college, ADELE O'NEILL now lives in her home town of Arklow, Co. Wicklow on the east coast of Ireland, with her husband and two teenage daughters. She writes overlooking the Irish Sea and is an active member of the Wexford Literary Festival committee.

Find me on Twitter
https://twitter.com/adelesbooks

Find me on Facebook
http://www.facebook.com/AdeleOneillBooks

Become an Aria Addict

Aria is the new digital-first fiction imprint from Head of Zeus.

It's Aria's ambition to discover and publish tomorrow's superstars, targeting fiction addicts and readers keen to discover new and exciting authors.

Aria will publish a variety of genres under the commercial fiction umbrella such as women's fiction, crime, thrillers, historical fiction, saga and erotica.

So, whether you're a budding writer looking for a publisher or an avid reader looking for something to escape with – Aria will have something for you.

First published in the UK in 2017 by Aria, an imprint of Head of Zeus Ltd

9 7 5 3 1 2 4 6 8

A CIP catalogue record for this book is available from the British Library.

ISBN (E) 9781786696786

Aria
c/o Head of Zeus
First Floor East
5–8 Hardwick Street
London EC1R 4RG

www.ariafiction.com

Printed in Great Britain
by Amazon

Seven Sisters

New Quilts from an Old Favorite

American Quilter's Society

P. O. Box 3290 • Paducah, KY 42002-3290
FAX 270-898-1173 www.AmericanQuilter.com

Located in Paducah, Kentucky, the American Quilter's Society (AQS) is dedicated to promoting the accomplishments of today's quilters. Through its publications and events, AQS strives to honor today's quiltmakers and their work and to inspire future creativity and innovation in quiltmaking.

EDITORS: BARBARA SMITH & SHELLEY HAWKINS
GRAPHIC DESIGN: LYNDA SMITH
COVER DESIGN: MICHAEL BUCKINGHAM
QUILT PHOTOGRAPHY: CHARLES R. LYNCH
(UNLESS OTHERWISE NOTED)

Library of Congress Cataloging-in-Publication Data
Seven sisters : new quilts from an old favorite / by American Quilter's Society.
p. cm.
Summary: "Seven Sisters quilt block is showcased in the annual international challenge, New Quilts from an Old Favorite, sponsored by The Museum of the American Quilter's Society. Eighteen finalists share their tips, techniques, and patterns"--Provided by publisher.
ISBN 1-57432-875-1
1. Patchwork. 2. Quilting. 3. Stars in art. I. American Quilter's Society. II Title.

TT835.S454 2005
746.46'041--dc22

2005000395

Additional copies of this book may be ordered from the American Quilter's Society, PO Box 3290, Paducah, KY 42002-3290, call toll-free 1-800-626-5420, or online at www.AmericanQuilter.com.

SPONSORS

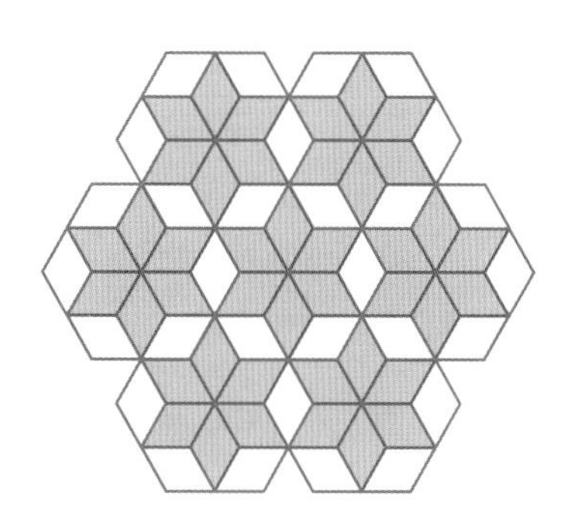

Thanks to the following sponsors:

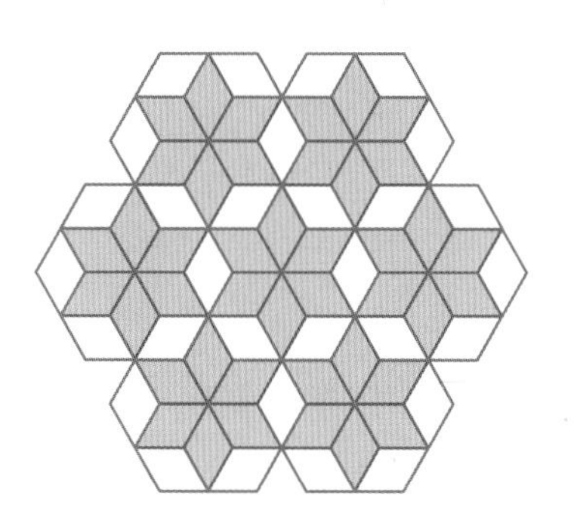

Dedication

This book is dedicated to all those who view a traditional quilt block and see within it a link to the past and a vision for the future.

The Museum of the American Quilter's Society (MAQS)

An exciting place where the public can learn more about quilts, quiltmaking, and quiltmakers.

Through collecting quilts and other programs, MAQS focuses on celebrating and developing today's quiltmaking.

Whether presenting new or antique quilts, MAQS promotes understanding of, and respect for, all quilts – new and antique, traditional and innovative, machine made and handmade, utility and art.

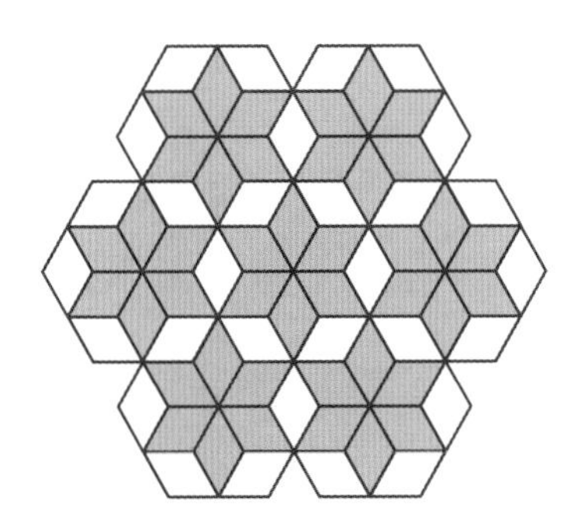

Contents

Preface

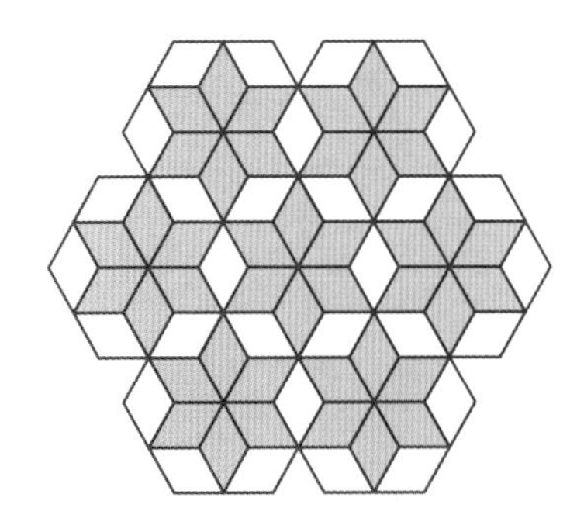

While preservation of the past is a museum's primary function, its greatest service is performed as it links the past to the present and to the future. With that intention, the Museum of the American Quilter's Society (MAQS) sponsors an annual contest and exhibit called *New Quilts from an Old Favorite*.

Created to acknowledge our quiltmaking heritage and to recognize innovation, creativity, and excellence, the contest challenges today's quiltmakers to interpret a single traditional quilt block in a work of their own design. Each year contestants respond with a myriad of stunning interpretations.

Seven Sisters: New Quilts from an Old Favorite is a wonderful representation of these interpretations. In this book you'll find a brief description of the 2005 contest, followed by a presentation of the five award winners and the 13 finalists and their quilts.

Full-color photographs of the quilts accompany each quiltmaker's comments – comments that provide insight into their widely diverse creative processes. Full-sized templates for the traditional Seven Sisters block are included to form the basis for your own rendition. Tips, techniques, and patterns contributed by the contest winners offer an artistic framework for your own work.

Our wish is that *Seven Sisters: New Quilts from an Old Favorite* will further our quiltmaking heritage as new quilts based on the Seven Sisters block are inspired by the outstanding quilts, patterns, and instructions in this book.

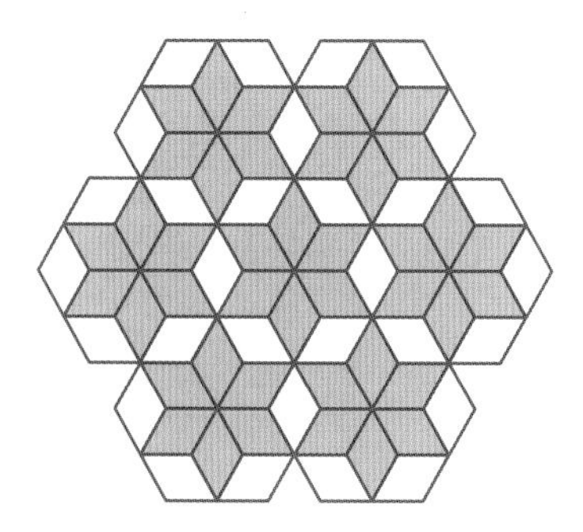

The Contest

Although the contest encouraged unconventional creativity, there were some basic requirements for entries:

- Quilts entered in the contest were to be recognizable in some way as being related to the Seven Sisters block.
- The finished size of the quilt was to be a minimum of 50" in width and height but could not exceed 100".
- Quilting was required on each quilt entered in the contest.
- A quilt could be entered only by the person(s) who made it.
- Each entry must have been completed after December 31, 2001.

To enter the contest, each quiltmaker was asked to submit an entry form and two slides of the quilt – one of the full quilt, and a second of a detail from the piece. In the *Seven Sisters* contest, quiltmakers from around the world responded to the challenge.

Three jurors viewed dozens of slides, deliberating over design, use of materials, interpretation of the theme, and technical excellence. Eventually they narrowed the field of entries to 18 finalists who were invited to submit their quilts for judging.

With quilts by the 18 finalists assembled, three judges meticulously examined the pieces, evaluating them again for design, innovation, theme, and workmanship. First- through fifth-place award winners were selected and notified.

Each year the *New Quilts from an Old Favorite* contest winners and finalists are featured in an exhibit that opens at the Museum of the American Quilter's Society in Paducah, Kentucky. Over a two-year period, the exhibit travels to a number of museums across North America and is viewed by thousands of quilt enthusiasts. Corporate sponsorship of the contest helps to underwrite costs, enabling even smaller museums across the country to display the exhibit.

Annually, the contest winners and finalists are included in a beautiful book published by the American Quilter's Society. *Seven Sisters: New Quilts from an Old Favorite* is the eleventh in the contest, exhibit, and publication series. It joins the following other traditional block designs used as contest themes: *Double Wedding Ring, Log Cabin, Kaleidoscope, Mariner's Compass, Ohio Star, Pineapple, Storm at Sea, Bear's Paw, Tumbling Blocks, Feathered Star,* and *Monkey Wrench.*

For information about entering the current year's *New Quilts from an Old Favorite* contest, write to Museum of the American Quilter's Society at PO Box 1540, Paducah, KY, 42002-1540; call (270) 442-8856; or visit MAQS online at www.quiltmuseum.org.

Seven Sisters Block

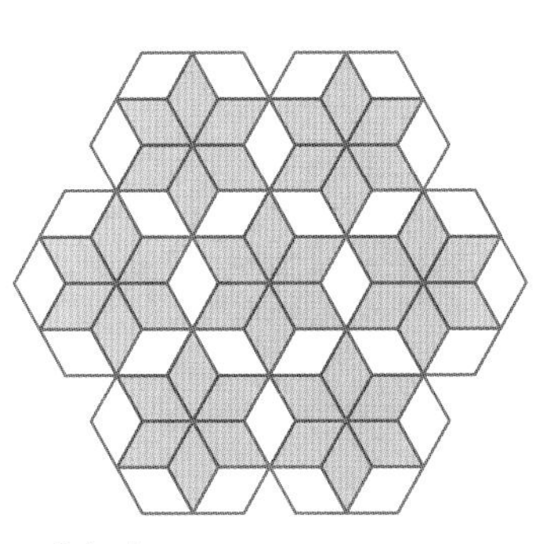

The Seven Sisters patchwork pattern is based on a diamond and may possibly be derived from early nineteenth-century English paper-pieced hexagons. An early American example of Seven Sisters dates from 1845, and the related Tumbling Blocks pattern appeared in *Godey's Lady's Book* in 1851. These diamond-based designs are frequently found in silk quilts from the late Victorian period, and a Seven Sisters mail order pattern was sold by the Ladies Art Company in 1898.

During the Depression era, mail order quilt-pattern companies flourished. Mrs. Donner's Quilts published a Seven Sisters pattern and *Capper's Weekly* included the same construction but named it Seven Stars in a Cluster. The pattern lends itself to scrap print fabrics on a solid background in much the same way that Grandmother's Flower Garden quilts of the period were sewn.

In Greek mythology, the Seven Sisters were called the Pleiades, daughters of Atlas and Pleione. In the Northern Hemisphere, the star cluster known by this name is found above and to the right of the constellation Orion. The Pleiades are in the constellation Taurus and figure in the mythology of most ancient civilizations. In the United States today, the term Seven Sisters refers to the seven traditionally women's colleges that are comparable to the male Ivy League schools. Two of the Seven Sisters schools and all of the Ivy League colleges have become co-educational.

Just as those schools have changed, quilt blocks may change. When challenged by the intricate construction of this design, today's quilters rose to the task. They curved seams, pieced flower diamonds, stretched shapes, made holes in their quilt, used chenille thread, and exploited the entire color palette. The Pleiades stars may have been visible since the dawn of mankind and the Seven Sisters quilt block born in the nineteenth century, but the block has come of age in the twenty-first century through the exceptional creativity of these quiltmakers and their quilts.

Judy Schwender
Curator of Collections and Registrar,
Museum of the American Quilter's Society

Yoshiko Kobayashi

Osaka, Japan

"The most wonderful part of quiltmaking is that I can pursue my own possibilities."

I started making quilts in 1988 after becoming inspired by a quilt exhibition. I continued my quilt work after studying quiltmaking for four years. My mother was a dressmaker and loved fabrics, and I always loved to draw and enjoyed making various handicrafts. Now I'm wholly absorbed in sewing fabrics, as my mother was, because of my encounter with quiltmaking.

I'm honored to have four quilts that have been finalists in the MAQS contests: WWW Navigator's Compass in the Mariner's Compass contest, Early Spring Wood in the Kaleidoscope contest, Ancient Mirror Came from across the Sea in the Storm at Sea contest, and now this Seven Sisters quilt, Joy of Gardener. The MAQS contest always provides a good chance for more quiltmaking and more inspiration.

Inspiration and Design

Here in Japan, the pattern Seven Sisters is not well known. I first saw the pattern name Seven Sisters in the contest announcement then found "Seven Sisters" on the Internet. I also found that the pattern is popular in the United States. I wanted to make a quilt with this pattern by all means.

Joy of Gardener

69" x 69"

Fig. 1. Original sketch

Since my family moved into our house three years ago, it has been a great pleasure for my husband and me to design and care for our little garden. I imaged a flower garden from the pattern shape of Seven Sisters and designed and redesigned this quilt with my favorite flowers, trees, and plants in mind.

For the shaded part of the quilt, I wanted to use fabric from an old kimono, which had been presented to me by an acquaintance. Even though it was polyester, it had a dark blue and bamboo grass design that I liked very much.

JOY OF GARDENER was made with paper-foundation piecing and was machine appliquéd. The fused appliqué pieces were free-hand cut.

Fig. 2. Trial color

DESIGNING JOY OF GARDENER

I started by drawing little sketches (fig. 1). Then to firm my idea, I made some simple drawings on paper and colored them (fig. 2).

This quilt is square, but the hexagons are a little longer than they are wide, making the construction quite complicated. So, I created an assembly plan and made an actual-sized drawing of one-fourth of the quilt.

After transcribing each pattern on tracing paper, I drew the piecing lines on the tracings and used the foundation method to piece the fabrics. I continued cutting and piecing, referring to the construction plan again and again. Still, I made some mistakes. This quilt was hard work for me, so if you decide to make a quilt like this, it would be better to use a hexagon with equal sides.

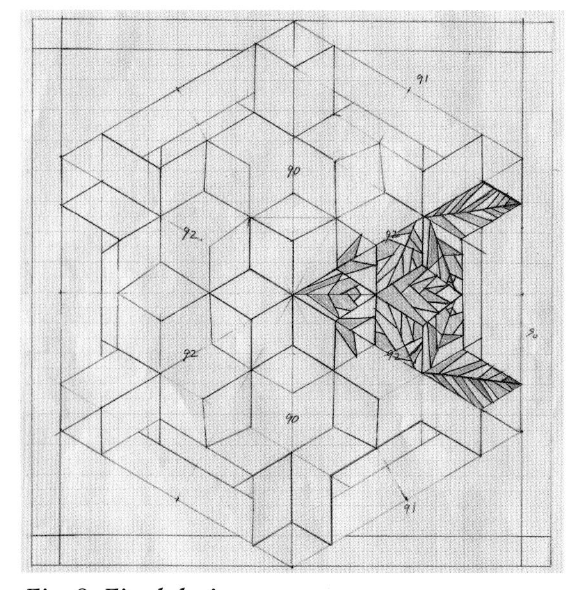

Fig. 3. Final design

The original part of the design with grass plants was changed because the work required would be too difficult and it would not be effective. I put in more pots instead of grass and decided to fill the pots with flowers or trees, like those in our garden (fig. 3).

Appliqué Patterns

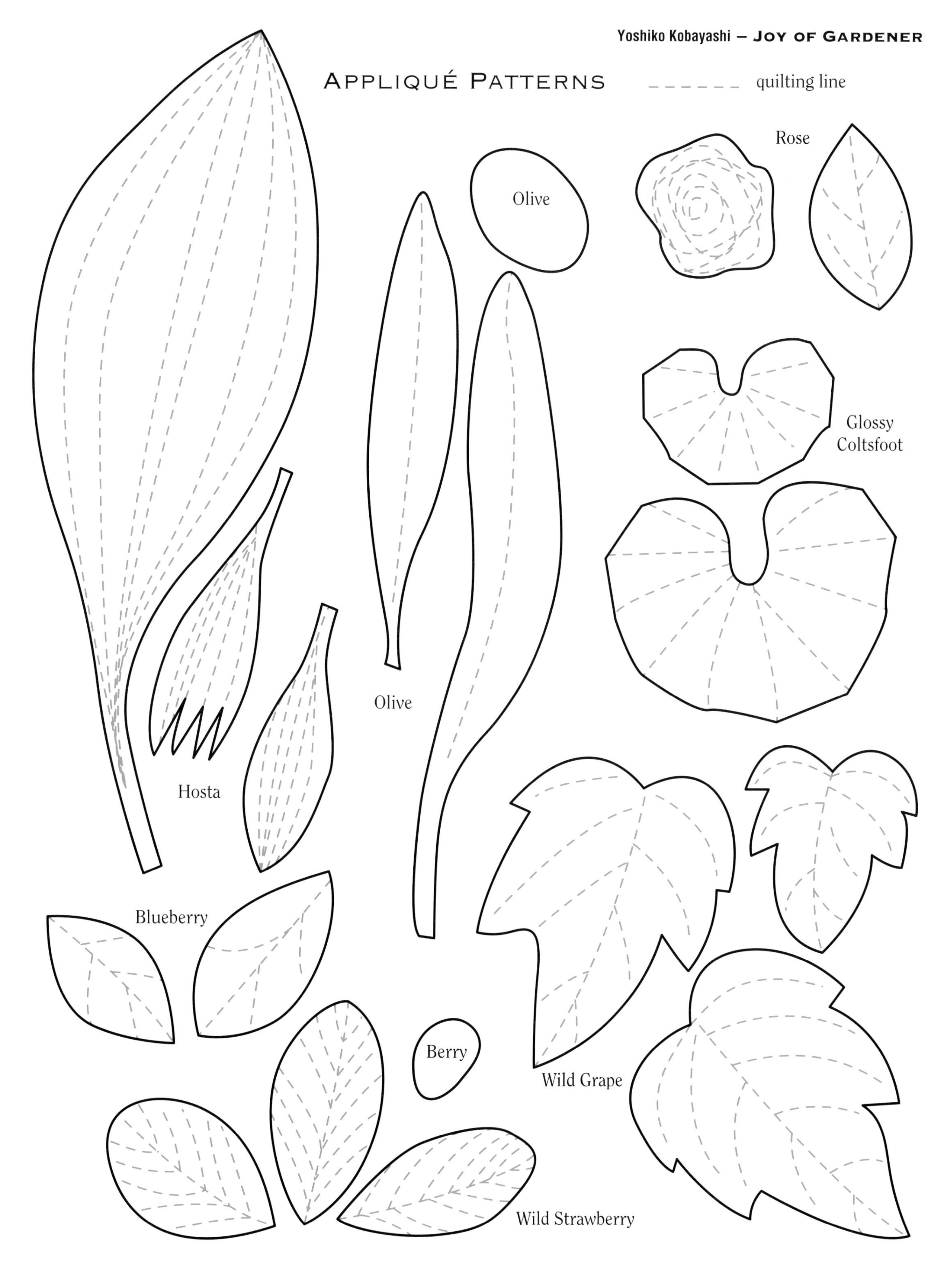

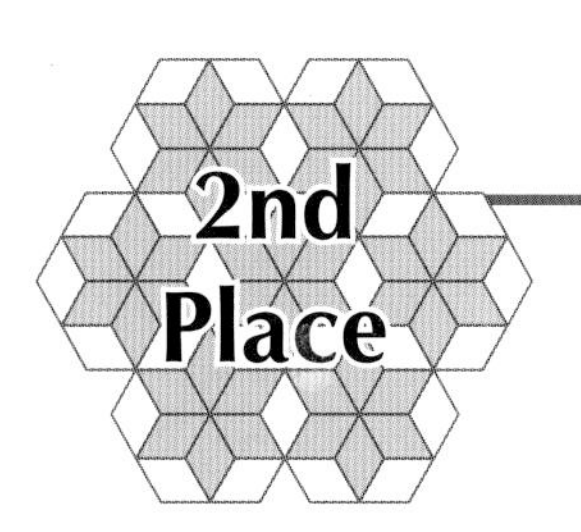

Kathy Parker

Albuquerque, New Mexico

"My goal is to make quilts that I have not seen before by using techniques and designs that I have not done before."

Throughout my life, I have enjoyed sewing and handling fabrics. As a small child, I remember keeping a collection of hair ribbons under my pillow so that I could play with them when I was supposed to be napping.

I liked little embroidery projects and gradually learned to sew clothes. My first quilt was made in the early 1970s for my three-year-old son. Ten years later, I made a biscuit quilt for my daughter. In the 1980s, I made a coral and brown Log Cabin quilt from all sorts of different fabrics but did not finish the quilting until 20 years later.

Serious quilting started about 12 years ago when I bought a new sewing machine that had all the nifty embroidery stitches and free-motion quilting features. I bought the machine for general sewing purposes, but the quilting was so much fun that I was really hooked on that alone.

At the time I bought the sewing machine, I was working full time as a speech-language pathologist in the Albuquerque Public Schools so I had to fit quilt projects around my family and work schedule. I taught myself to quilt by watching programs on television and by reading every quilt book and magazine that I could find.

I started with a couple of lap quilts then made larger quilts for my mother and my husband's mother. I used patterns designed by the teachers on television and followed their directions to learn

Kathy's photo by Patrick Ware

Los Platos

85" x 75"

machine quilting. As my love of quilting progressed, I read a booklet by Irma Gail Hatcher that included her secrets of quilt design. From that point on, I began thinking I should design my own quilts. At about the same time, I thought it would be fun to enter a quilt contest.

My first design was inspired by a magazine quilt contest. Although it took most of my summer vacation to finish the small quilt, I actually got it done on time and was thrilled to find out it had won second place. Since then, I have designed one other small quilt for a competition. Although the quilt did not win a prize, it was included in a tour.

Now that I have retired from my job, I have done a lot more quilting. I find that the design challenges are the most stimulating part of the quilting process, but in my case, it can be pretty chaotic. The construction and sewing stages are more manageable, and I like to structure my newfound time around these activities.

I have amassed a considerable library of quilt books and refer to them often for technical help and inspiration. I enjoy studying all the quilts in the books, but the quilts that attract me have traits such as an exciting setting, a good mix of big pieces with a lot of little pieces, circular shapes, or anything else that moves.

I like novelty and want to expand my repertoire of quilting skills. I have just begun my first Southwestern quilt, and I am now trying to figure out how to apply heavy hand embroidery in a way that does not distort the background fabric. I also bought a quilting hoop so that I can do hand quilting while away from the sewing machine.

Inspiration and Design

The inspiration for Los Platos came from several Mexican collectors' plates that are displayed on my fireplace mantel. I purchased the plates while on vacation in Puerto Penasco, Mexico. To me, the attraction of the plates is the uninhibited use of the bright tropical colors with a variety of detailed designs. The designs, which are organized into four or eight sections, resemble Four- or Eight-Patch quilt blocks from a distance. The different sections are filled with large, painted flowers or uneven grids, which are mixed together with cobalt scrolls.

Since buying those plates, I saw the similarity to quilt blocks and thought about making a quilt to look like them. The New Quilts from an Old Favorite contest caught my attention at about the same time, so I put the two ideas together, although I had never seen Seven Sisters nor stars on a Mexican plate.

I wanted the quilt to have colors like the prettiest plate, so all the large areas of the quilt were made from bright fabrics in purple, lime green, orange, and blue. I also used several cobalt fabrics and extended the terra cotta color to include rose. Although I like bright, clear colors, I was definitely not within my comfort zone in choosing the fabrics. I remember telling the lady in the quilt shop that, most likely, I would be creating a disaster.

I always seem to do everything wrong before I get it right. I revise everything. That is exactly what happened when I designed Los Platos. I wanted the quilt to include cobalt scrolls, black-and-white grids, and flowers. I needed to integrate these elements with the Seven Sisters block. Every morning, I had new approaches to the task and drew out the quilt themes on hexagon graph paper. Eventually, I gave up on the graph paper because I could not get an adequate idea of how the smaller details would work within a larger framework without taping a lot of graph paper together. No way!

I then decided to start with just one large star. I cut colored paper into different sizes of scrolls, hexagons, and stars, then moved them around until the arrangement was satisfactory. I layered the different sizes of stars and turned the hexagon into a circle with scrolls moving around the center stars.

For several weeks, I tried to integrate the large star design within a medallion setting but could not find suitable border options. Because I really like the movement created by six stars surrounding a center star, I used the Seven Sisters block itself as the setting.

Once the large framework of the quilt was in place, I started on all the fun fabrics and finishing details. Because I love scrap quilts, I wanted the inside of each plate to be different. I went to my fabric stash and pulled every fabric that looked like stucco, plaster, tiles, or tropical foliage. I even found a fabric that looked like a Mexican blanket, which I used to fussy cut the small center stars.

A black-and-white grid fabric was used for the small stars on the outside of the plates. The large central star was emphasized by using the bold combination of cobalt and orange, and I added circles surrounding the stars on the outside edges to suggest a border made from flowers. Outlines of red stars were topstitched to some of the circles to continue the Seven Sisters theme.

The quilt designs in the large orange areas of the quilt were replicated from wrought iron gates typical in the Albuquerque region.

Drafting the Star Plate Block

Necessary materials include rulers, a mechanical pencil, a compass, and drawing paper. Before you use any of your drafted patterns to cut fabric pieces, remember to add ¼" seam allowances.

Large Star

Fold a 20" square of paper in half horizontally and vertically for an 18" circle. Mark the fold lines with a pencil.

Set the radius of your compass at 9", which is half the diameter of the circle (fig. 1, page 16). Place the tip of the compass in the center point and construct an 18" circle. See Making a Compass, page 17, if your compass isn't large enough.

Label the point at the top of the vertical line where it crosses the circle as number 1. Label the point at the bottom as number 4 (fig. 1, page 16).

Put the compass tip in point 1 and draw an arc to the right, intersecting the circle. Label this as point 2.

Put the compass tip in point 2 and draw an arc at point 3. Point 4 is already in place. Draw 5 and 6 as you did 2 and 3, using point 4 to start (fig. 2, page 16).

Draw lines between the points to construct the hexagon (fig. 3, page 16). Each side of the hexagon should measure 9". Correct any inaccuracies.

Using the 18" drafted hexagon, draw a line from the center to point 2 (fig. 4, page 16). Use this 9" equilateral triangle as a pattern to make the large star tips.

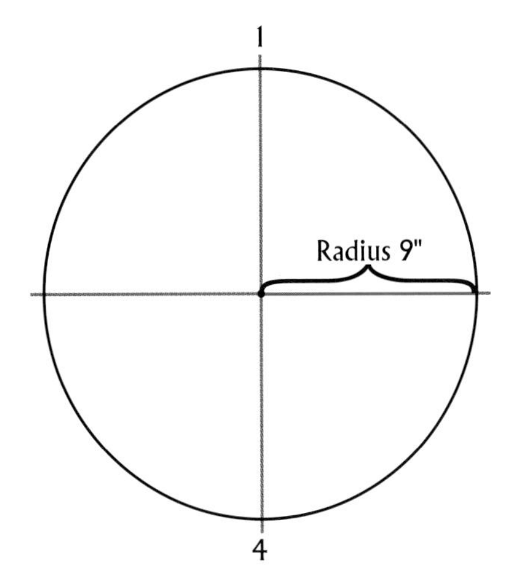

Fig. 1. Draw an 18" circle with a 9" radius.

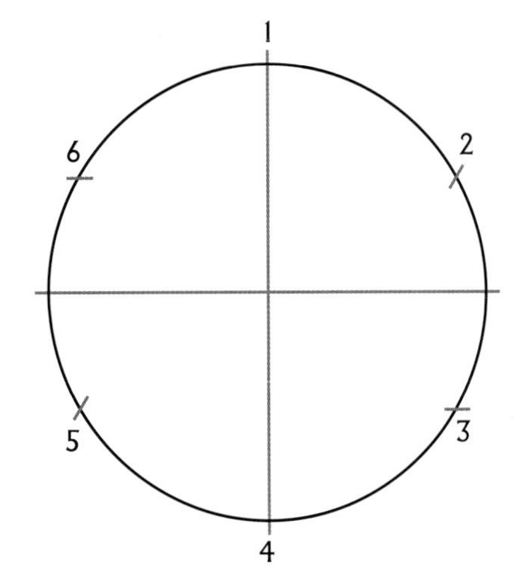

Fig. 2. Using a 9" radius, draw arcs intersecting the circle.

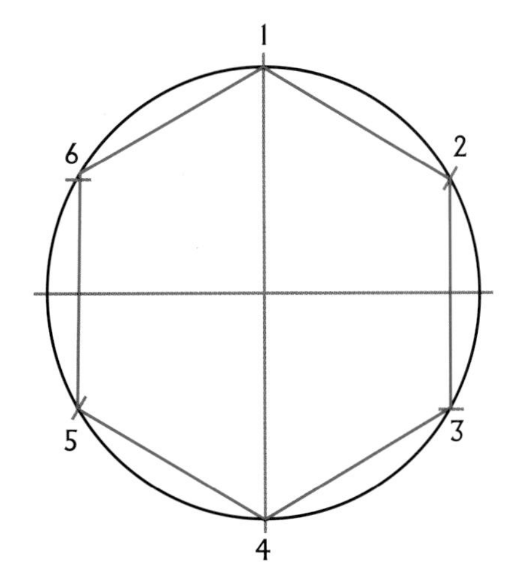

Fig. 3. Connect the points.

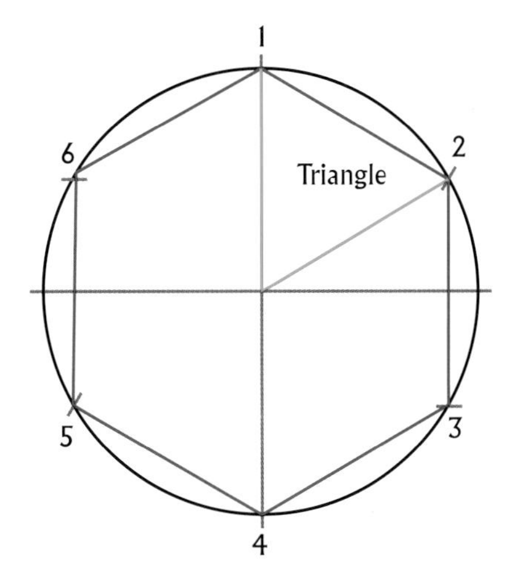

Fig. 4. Use the triangle for star points.

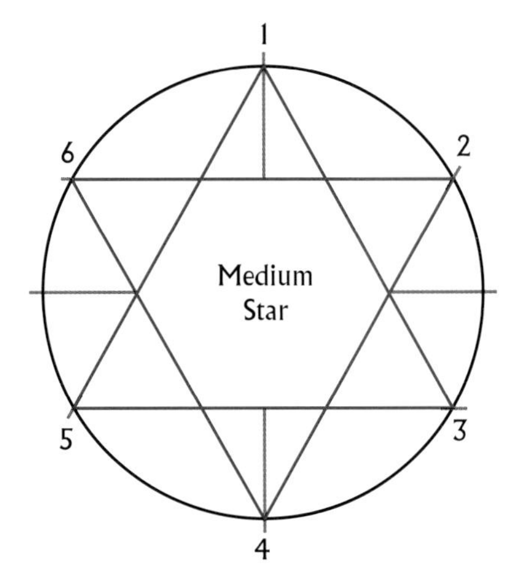

Fig. 5. Connect the points.

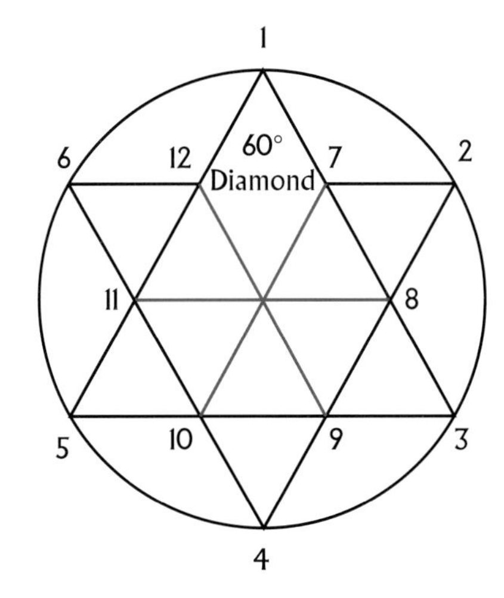

Fig. 6. Connect points 7 through 12.

I used the 18" hexagon to cut a piece of foundation fabric. The large star tips were sewn to the foundation fabric. The circle for the plate was machine appliquéd on top, and the foundation was cut away.

Medium Star

Set your compass radius at 6½" and follow the previous directions to make a 13" circle and mark the six points.

Draw lines between the points, as shown in figure 5.

Small Star

Follow the previous directions for making the medium star but use a radius of 1¼".

Label intersections 7 through 12, as shown in figure 6.

I traced the diamonds on freezer paper so I could fussy cut the fabric. I then hand pieced the stars, using the freezer-paper edge as a sewing guide. I used a light box and ruler to position the seven stars on top of the medium star and took out the paper after the stars were appliquéd.

Tiniest Star

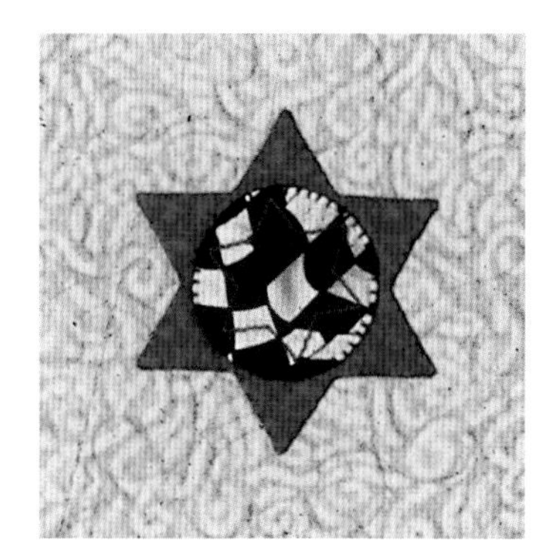

Follow the directions for making a medium star but use a ½" radius.

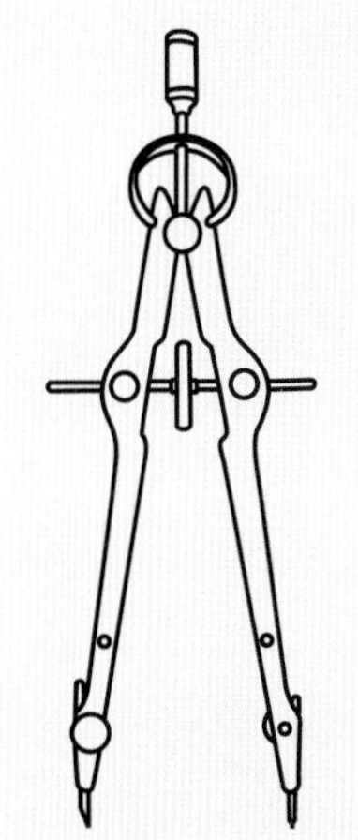

Making a Compass

My compass does not extend to 9", so I used the following method to make one:

Cut a 10" strip of template plastic about 1" wide.

Use a quilt pin to poke a hole in the strip, about ¼" from one end.

Poke a second hole 9" away (or equal to the radius of the circle you want to draw).

Put a thumbtack in the first hole to act as a compass tip, and place it at the center point of your circle.

Put the lead of a pencil in the second hole and draw the circle.

Helen Remick

Seattle, Washington

"I want to bring viewers into my work, play tricks on their eyes, and add dimension to flat surfaces through design alone."

My great-grandmother quilted until she died at age 96. I still have one of her quilts, though it is worn beyond use. My grandmother was a seamstress, and my mother sewed but not enthusiastically. It was up to me to revive sewing in our family. Doll clothes came first. Four-H offered me instruction in sewing and an outlet for my creativity. I did well at the county fair and twice won the Alameda County dress review. For many years, I made almost all of my clothes.

In the early 1970s, I made two comforters with intricate piecework, both designs inspired by op art. I switched my creative energy to knitting for a number of years, finding ways to translate Escher-like designs into sweaters. One of my designs was published in *Family Circle* in the late 1970s.

In 1994, my friend Laura Saunders suggested that we take a quilting class, and I haven't stopped quilting since. We took a class on color from Joen Wolfram. She later included my second quilt, which is red, black, gray, and white, in her book *Color Play*. After my first three projects, I shifted from bed-sized quilts to wallhanging/lap-quilt size.

I approach each quilt as a learning experience and explore something new in either color or design. I have not shown my work until recently. In 2004, I entered two of my quilts, BLAZE ON BRIDGET and TANGLED WEB, at the Pacific Northwest Quiltfest and both were accepted. The MAQS contest is the first one I have entered.

Helen's photo by Lisa D. Brown

Ma, Why Does She Get All of the Attention?

56" x 62"

In my work life, I am the assistant provost for equal opportunity at the University of Washington, where I have worked for almost 30 years. My job is a demanding combination of policy and numerical analysis on the one hand and intense interpersonal interaction on the other. Quilting provides an excellent means of relaxing when I am not at work. I have read that the repetitive nature of handwork has a meditative quality. I certainly find it to be a stress-reducer.

Handwork is portable and quiet. It can be done around others, in airplanes, and at conferences. I find machine sewing to be enjoyable but far less relaxing. Most evenings, you will find me doing handwork while I keep Jack, my partner of 41 years, company. Jack is a writer who has many artist friends. He and they have been essential in helping me find myself as an artist.

My daughter, Elizabeth, also quilts. She is a professor of Chinese politics at Tufts University in the Boston area. Elizabeth and I have scouted out quilt stores from Oregon and Washington to Massachusetts and Maine. Elizabeth brings me silks from her trips to China, and I expect to be doing more work with silk in the future.

Inspiration and Design

I am drawn to geometric designs and graphic arts more than representational designs. I love the work of M. Escher. The op artists of the 1960s and 1970s, especially Bridget Riley, produced images that have stayed with me and shaped my artistic vision.

Mathematical shapes intrigue me. I like starting with a traditional design. I ask myself, what if? What if a hexagon is projected into a rectangle, what if the center of the design is moved to another position within the square, what if the square is changed into a rectangle, what if straight lines are curved? I stay within the traditional quilt patterns yet make them my own. When I saw the MAQS contest, I knew this challenge was for me.

I have been collecting red, black, and white cotton fabrics for ten years. I have many other colors in my stash, but find that the intricate designs I love are more visible with this palette. I am also drawn to gradations in color and to values ranging from light to dark. I ask the viewer to do some of the work, so I shade from light to dark, using only black-and-white prints of different ratios and scales.

The six-pointed star and hexagonal designs resonate with me. I find the angles more pleasing than those in the eight-pointed star. I made a hexagonal quilt but discovered it is hard to hang, because the narrow top quilt edge cannot handle the weight. I put the star in a circle, which is even harder to hang. I was puzzling about how best to put the star in a rectangle when I saw the advertisement for this contest. It was the push I needed to create hexagonal shapes that would hang well.

An idea may percolate for quite some time, even years. I will change design midstream if I don't like the result, or change techniques to fit a particular part of the quilt. I will also combine techniques, though it can be challenging to ensure that the pieces will fit together.

This was the first quilt I had made under a fixed time limit. My original design had been even more complicated than the final version, but to meet the deadline, I had to rethink the project. I switched from hand to machine piecing and redrafted the six outer stars. I have always done hand quilting, but after quilting for three hours and seeing how little was finished, I ripped it out. It was time to remember what I could from a machine-quilting class and to get out my machine-quilting books. Part of a weekend was spent practicing techniques before I took a deep breath and began quilting for real.

Hand Piecing

My first quilting class was from Nancyann Twelker. Nancyann loved handwork and taught Laura and me a wide variety of techniques. I especially liked the English paper-piecing method, in which one makes a postcard-weight pattern, bastes fabric to the pattern, then whipstitches the pieces together. The technique is precise though a bit time consuming. Nancyann also showed me traditional hand piecing; that is, how to trace around a template then sew on the traced lines. I could not imagine ever using this technique, which for some reason I saw as more work than the English paper piecing.

In my first attempt at a hexagonal star with curved lines, I used English paper piecing as I had previously when making stars with uniform diamonds. While using this technique to make one ray of the star, I learned an important lesson. It is best used when all of the pieces are the same size.

In previous projects, when the pieces were all the same size, they fit together well at the end of the project, even if the finished size of the whole piece was slightly bigger or slightly smaller than projected. However, when the pieces are not of a consistent size, variations in the assembly angle and stitching tension affect how the pieces fit together.

In the contest quilt, the largest pieces in the star rays are several inches across, and the smallest are less than ½". As I sewed the pieces together, the areas of the quilt with large pieces stayed fairly true to scale, but the areas with small pieces, and therefore many seams, did not.

So, I pieced the central star by hand but used traditional hand piecing instead of English paper piecing. This method still requires care with size because tracing around a template results in a slightly larger outline, but allowances have to be made for the fabric folding into the seam. You will need to experiment with your own stitch tension and tracing ability to find where you should be stitching relative to the line you have drawn.

Color and Value Placement

I like drafting by hand. I make small sketches, then, for tops as complicated as this one, draw full-sized models of the various components. I give each piece a row and column indicator so that I can keep the original orientation (figs. 1a and 1b, page 22). The labeling system is important for shading as well (fig. 2, page 23).

For this quilt, to get the three-dimensional effect with the central star, the diamonds vary in size from large in the center to small on the outside. The black-and-white prints also vary from light in the center to dark on the edges, and the red prints range from a saturated orange-red for the largest piece to dark red and black prints on the edges. I also used bolder black-and-white prints on the rays than on the large diamonds surrounding the star.

I began by sorting my black-and-white prints into five piles from lightest to darkest. I sorted the ray pattern pieces as well; I matched the darkest fabrics to the outside pattern pieces in each ray. The remaining pieces went into the next darker pile, etc., until only the big red piece remained. I fussy cut that piece from a fabric with a pattern that added to the "bursting" effect of each ray. A similar technique of sorting went into the diamonds surrounding the star to create the gradation from white to black.

The six outer sisters are made from reds ranging from mediums to dark, with the ray of each star being a different fabric. In drafting the six sisters, I kept as many angles as possible at 60 and 120 degrees to echo the original design. Thirty and 90 degrees were my next choice, and only a couple of angles are outside of these four.

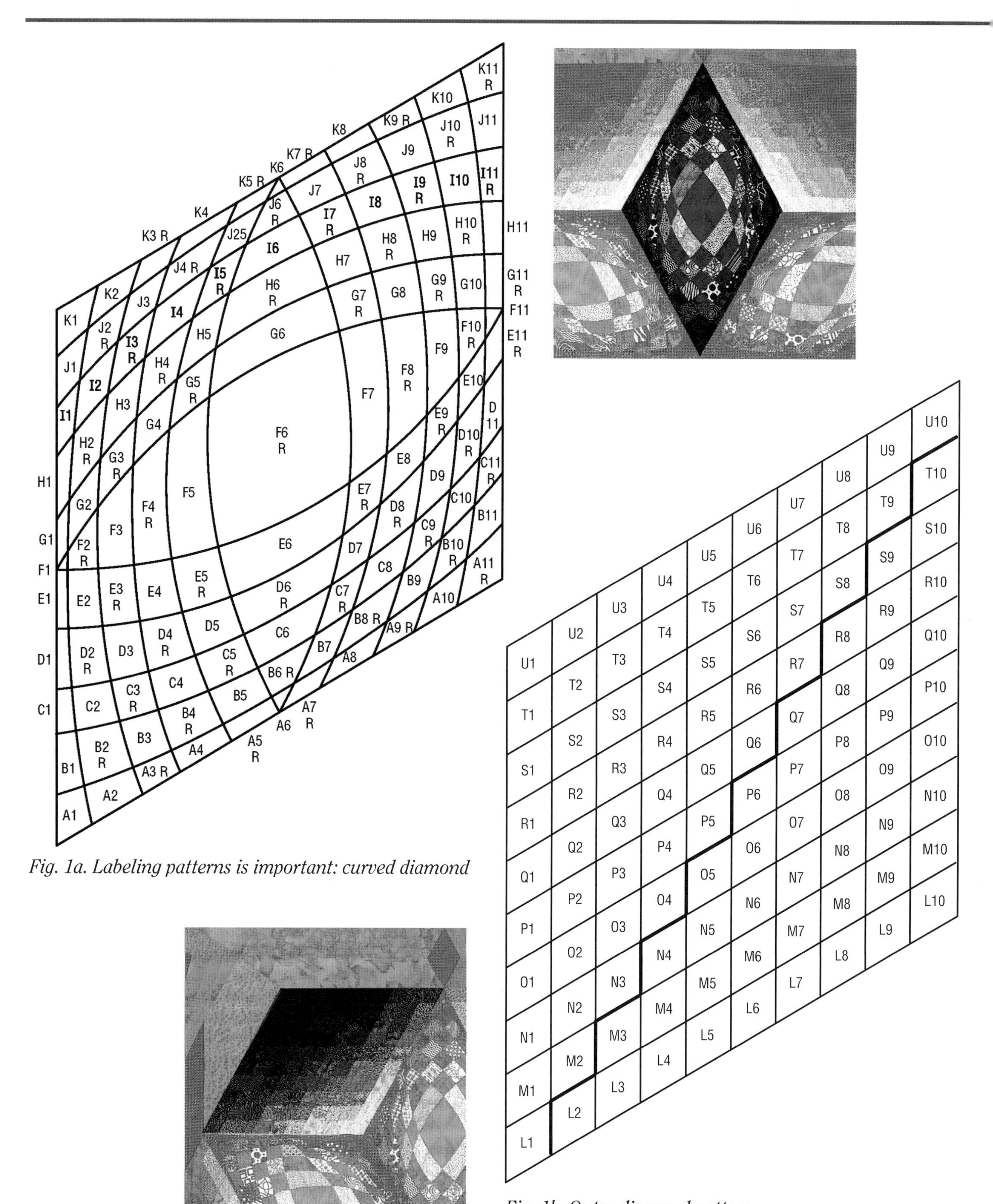

Fig. 1a. Labeling patterns is important: curved diamond

Fig. 1b. Outer diamond pattern

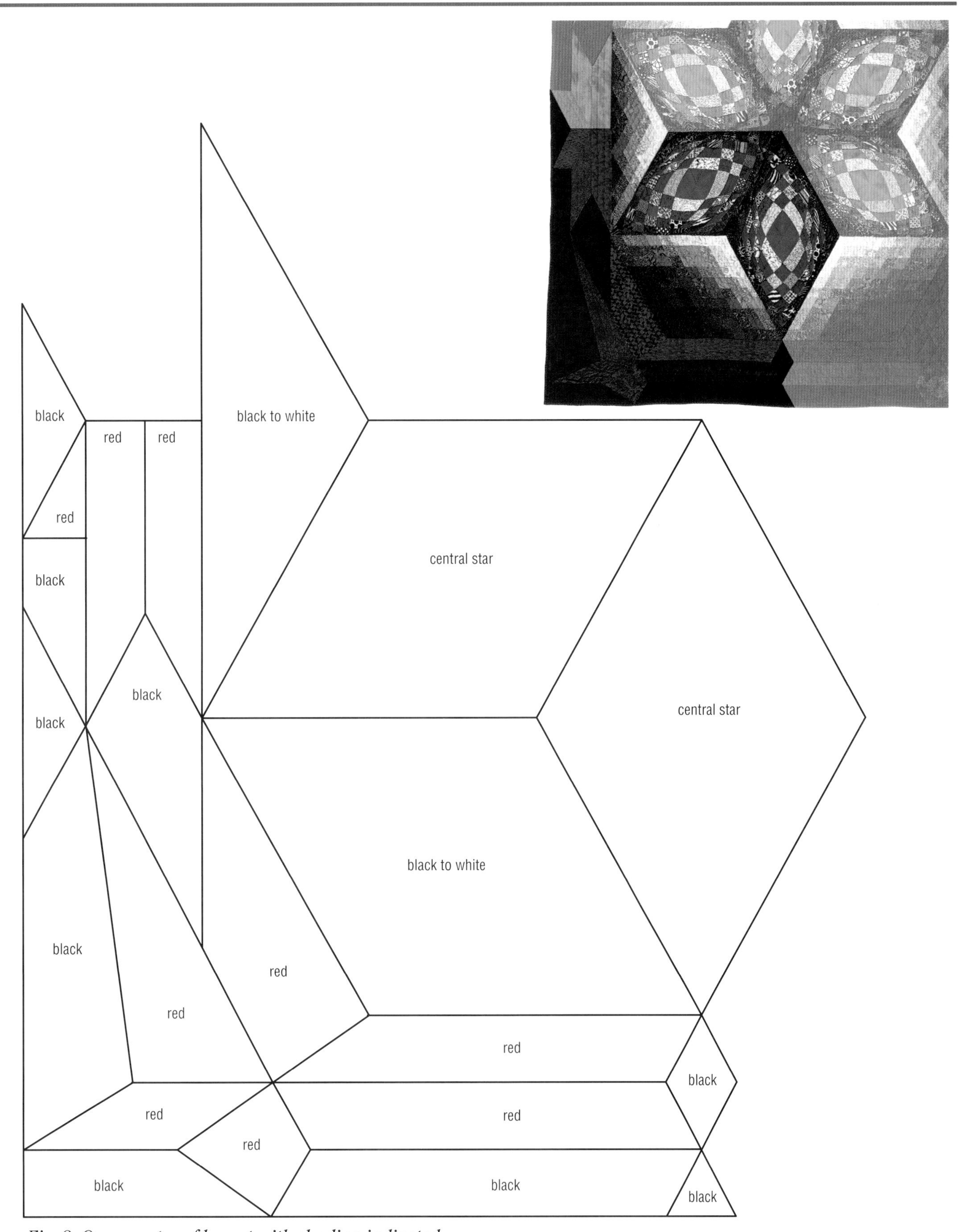

Fig. 2. One quarter of layout with shading indicated

Scott Murkin

Asheboro, North Carolina

"I do most of my machine quilting without marking first. It is a more productive use of my time, and it allows my creativity to flow more smoothly."

In 1994, I was beginning my final year of a family medicine residency, my daughter was two years old, my wife was pregnant with our son, and Grandma died after a long struggle with emphysema. My daughter needed to move out of her bed so it could be converted back into a crib. Feeling sentimental, I decided that she needed a quilt for her new "big girl" bed, and with Grandma gone and a wife and mother who didn't sew, it was up to me. Ten months later, my daughter had her quilt, the beginning of a grand adventure for me.

For the next four years, I hand pieced and hand quilted about two pieces a year. I was steadily improving my workmanship, working largely in isolation and making quilts as family gifts. I was completely oblivious to the larger quilting community. Then in 1997, I saw that a local group was having a quilt show. I contacted them through our local arts association just in time to help finish up that year's raffle quilt. I was badgered into putting some of my quilts in the show, and my life has never been the same.

Through my guild, I quickly learned about quilt books, magazines, shows, new techniques, rotary cutters (yes, I was still using templates and scissors), sewing machines, and stash! In no time, I was machine piecing and machine quilting. By now, I could make quilts for 12 years from the fabric I own, and my quilting and design library hovers around 700 volumes.

Warp Holes

71" x 68"

I currently teach quilting, appraise quilts, do some occasional custom work, exhibit widely, write and design patterns for magazines, and judge quilt shows as a National Quilting Association-certified quilt judge. A full-time medical practice, family commitments, home-schooling our two children, and community involvement mean that I have to be frugal with my time. Because I'm not willing to give any of it up, I'll just keep making it work.

INSPIRATION AND DESIGN

Inspired by quilts uncovered during state quilt-search projects, I researched all the project books to find quilts based on the Seven Sisters pattern. After looking at the many traditional variations, I designed the center hexagonal medallion on Electric Quilt 5. By changing the construction lines, I made the design easier to piece (no set-in seams), and by altering the color placement, I created a secondary star design with the background fabric. I liked the idea of using seven sets of the seven-sister unit to create another analogous, larger seven sister.

I considered many options for the large hexagons between the "sisters," including "Why do you have to have anything there at all?" Then the title WARP HOLES presented itself to me. I liked the connection to the other meaning of Seven Sisters, the constellation, and from that point, I was determined to make it work.

I considered using a placeholder fabric for the holes and cutting them out later, but couldn't see how to make that work. So, the top was constructed with the holes already in place, but they were not put in the batting or backing until after the quilting was completed. I considered alternate edge finishes for the holes, but wanted the hard line of an applied binding, which would also be visually compatible with the outer edge binding. The machine quilting was done without marking, but it was quilted fairly heavily, contributing to the proper hanging of the quilt.

QUILTING DESIGN

I believe that the integration of the quilting design with the overall quilt is essential to creating an extraordinary quilt, and I put the same amount of care, thought, and attention into deciding how a quilt should be quilted as I do into the design of the top. I believe that the quilting should never be an afterthought.

I begin thinking about quilting designs for a quilt from the moment I begin planning it. During the selection of patterns, colors, and specific fabrics, I realize that I am creating something three-dimensional, even though one dimension is rather small, and that I will need quilting designs to create that third dimension. The converse of this is that I don't make final decisions on the quilting designs until I'm ready to mark or quilt. At times I have been so enamored with a quilt design that I've used it even when it turns out not to be the best choice.

Rough sketch of central quilting designs

While most of my machine quilting is done without marking, I was having trouble eyeballing the center of the hexagons. I solved this by using a white chalk pencil and a medium-sized button to mark a circle in the center of each hexagon. The circle gave me a visual landmark to keep things looking smoother.

When planning your quilting designs, consider the dual functions of the quilting design. The first function of the quilting stitch is structural, holding the three layers together to create the little air pockets that make a quilt so comforting to wrap up in. It is important for the quilting lines to be close enough together to hold the batting in place through usage and washing, or hanging, in the case of wall quilts. Also, the amount of quilting needs to be distributed fairly evenly across the quilt surface so that the quilt does not become distorted. Quilting stitches also take stress off of the pieced seams, and while many quilters hesitate to quilt across seam allowances, especially by hand, I actually look for opportunities to do so to soften some of the hard edges in my piecing.

Because quilts are no longer made primarily for warmth, the second aspect of quilting, the design, has taken on new importance. The quilting design can emphasize some point you've made in your quilt top, subtly change the focus of the quilt, or merely provide support for a busy surface design. I would like to emphasize a few design points that have been the most helpful to me.

Keep an open mind. You can find quilting designs everywhere you look, nature being my personal favorite. Once you start looking at the world around you as a source of inspiration, it's hard to stop. If you come across something particularly appealing, trace it or make a quick sketch so you will have something to work from later.

Don't try to use everything you have in one quilt. Find a few compatible designs and use multiple variations and scales of them to create unity in your final design. Always keep in mind proportion and scale. A quilting design needs to be balanced with both the space it fills and the overall size of the finished piece. Quilting motifs should be carefully sized to avoid crowding a space or floating in vast fields of unquilted fabric.

Never skimp on background quilting. It may be boring, tedious, and under-appreciated, but it will make the rest of your quilting designs sing. It's one of those thankless jobs that is only noticeable if you neglect it.

Focus on the design unit rather than the construction unit when you quilt. We often piece quilts in a certain way to make the construction easier, but the unit of design covers multiple pieces of fabric. Always quilt these units as a single element so as not to draw attention to your methods of construction. Quilts with strong secondary designs where the blocks join together can really be enhanced by quilting to emphasize these new designs. For each quilt design you are considering, ask yourself if it is helping the viewers to see what you want them to see or if it is drawing attention to some lesser aspect of the quilt that doesn't need to be emphasized.

In machine quilting, never use a straight line where a curvy line will do. Curvy lines are forgiving of minor irregularities. I will quilt straight lines when they are the right choice, but I have to be convinced that they are the best option.

Always think about your quilting design. I had decided to use the outer corners of Warp Holes for elaborate quilting in a lighter thread that would break up the large field of color. The more I thought about it, I knew this would not work. Because formal, marked quilting designs would be incompatible with the free-form designs I had in mind for the rest of the quilt, I auditioned multiple options before coming up with the final corner design that met all of my needs. Had I not been thinking about quilting designs all along, my final quilt would have been very different.

Nadine Ruggles

Gerlingen, Germany

"Even when I'm not in my studio quilting, my mind is sometimes subconsciously working on a project. The best ideas will appear at the oddest moments throughout the day."

I began quilting in 1991 with a Bargello wall-hanging. I've been a somewhat compulsive quilter ever since. I work on something quilt-related every day, sometimes as long as eight hours a day. My perfect day would begin with coffee in my studio, continue on with very few, very short breaks for food, and end with quilting late into the evening (or early morning) hours. Yes, it is my obsession. I can live with that. Quilting is my passion and my relaxation. It's easy for me to shut everything else out and let myself be consumed by my work.

I have no formal art or design training and am mostly self-taught. I read and study quilter's books and occasionally take classes. I really enjoy the trial-and-error method of learning, just doing what might work, seeing if it is successful, and if it isn't, trying something else. That's really the best part about quilting. There are no rules, so if you think it might work, try it, and if it doesn't, try another approach. Working through and overcoming design challenges becomes easier as you gain experience.

My work is a collection of many different styles. Some quilts are decidedly traditional, while others are more innovative or in the art-quilt genre. I design most of my current work, and prefer to start with an idea, then let the design lead me where it may. I tackle design challenges as they happen, then plan the next part of the project. While my hands are working on the more repetitive parts of a project, I try to let my mind think ahead to the next activity.

Material Marquetry

87" x 97"

I teach quilting classes for two small shops serving American military families in southern Germany, as well as classes with local German and American quilt guilds. I frequently exhibit my work at quilt shows. I would like to author books, and dream of seeing my work in the permanent collection of the Museum of the American Quilter's Society someday.

INSPIRATION AND DESIGN

MATERIAL MARQUETRY was designed and made specifically for the New Quilts from an Old Favorite contest. I experimented with variations of the Seven Sisters design, on paper, with the computer, and in fabric. I envisioned that the stars, in many different colors, twirled a bit. The stars became seven dancing sisters, twirling on a patchwork floor, each of their skirts a different color.

Using various computer programs, I drew an enlarged Seven Sisters block, in which each of the seven stars was twisted slightly to add movement and interest. I've always admired Jinny Beyer's work and the way she uses many gradations of different colors. I used her method of dividing each curved star point into seven wedge-shaped pieces to provide the opportunity to blend many fabrics and colors for each star. To select the color palette for this quilt, I chose the border print first.

The star and background sections were pieced on foundation paper for ease and accuracy. The paper was removed before the stars and background pieces were assembled. I had no solid plan for how the quilt design would be finished when I started. I really enjoy the challenges presented when making it up as I go along. The early plan was for a wall quilt. The design had other ideas. I decided to complete the inner medallion with a wide border set, incorporating the border print and more six-pointed stars.

This medallion then needed a large background space between it and the outer border, not only to provide some quiet space in the design, but also to make the quilt rectangular. The three inner borders are graduated in size and varied in color to provide a division between the interior of the quilt and the border print. One final narrow border was added after the border print.

I was looking forward to filling the large open spaces beyond the center medallion with extensive feather quilting but was a bit intimidated by all the blank space waiting to be filled with my own designs. The border print provided some ideas for design elements, and I drafted the feather quilting designs to fit the available space. As in the border print, I allowed the feathers to wrap around straight column-like elements and added feathered hearts and ovals to fill in other areas. Anita Shackelford's Infinite Feathers Quilting Design Template was invaluable in the design process.

The feather quilting designs were traced on the background areas of the quilt by using a light box and a blue washout marker. The feather designs on the darker fabrics were applied, just before the quilting, by using stencils and chalk pencils.

After it was quilted, I wanted the quilt to look as if it were carved marble. To support this illusion, the quilting thread is a shade or two darker than the background fabric, and the background is heavily stippled, making the foreground feather designs stand out more effectively.

I initially saw seven dancing sisters, with skirts twirling, and thought of a few names for my quilt based on that vision. When the quilt was complete, however, none of those names seemed to fit. My mother, who is a wonderful wordsmith, and I did some brainstorming and decided that the design was reminiscent of marquetry designs in wood; hence the name MATERIAL MARQUETRY.

PIECING STARS

To construct each star for the center medallion, you will need six foundation-pieced A units (page 32). For the most definition and interest, use a different fabric, in values from light to dark, for each wedge in the star point.

When preparing the star-point foundations, use a ⅛" punch to make a hole in each corner (fig. 1).

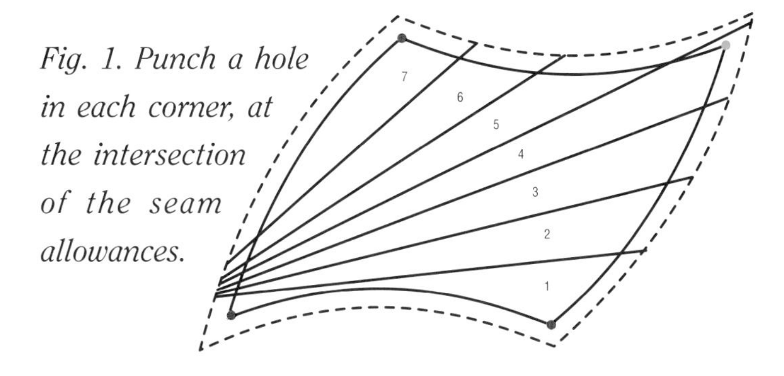

Fig. 1. Punch a hole in each corner, at the intersection of the seam allowances.

After foundation piecing each section, press it well and trim off the excess fabric. Using a chalk or graphite pencil, mark each corner point through the hole in the foundation, to use in matching points while sewing.

Sew three star points together, matching the center and outside points carefully and pinning well. Stitch the seam, backstitching at the points. It is important not to sew through the seam allowances at the points (fig. 2). Press seam allowances toward the first piece in each section.

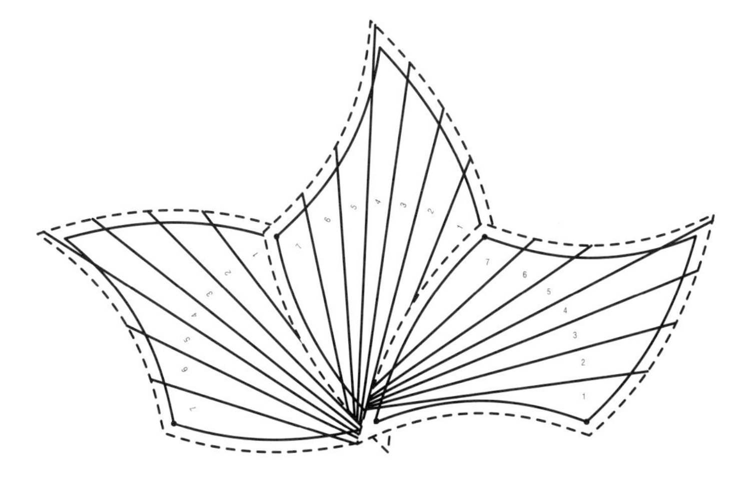

Fig. 2. Sew three star points together.

Make two half stars then sew the two halves together, matching center and outside points carefully (fig. 3). Press the center seam allowances open.

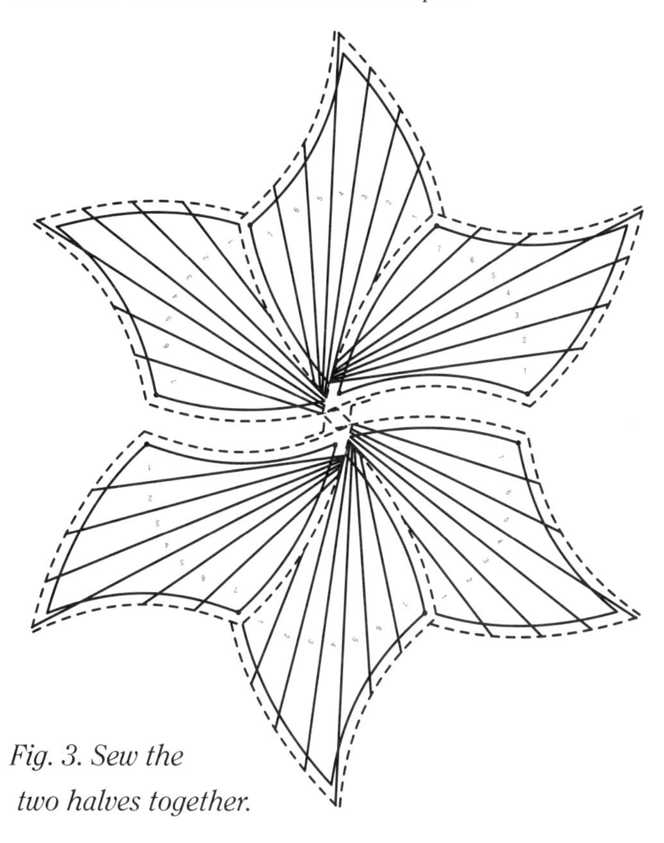

Fig. 3. Sew the two halves together.

Make six star points exactly the same for each complete star. Make seven stars, each in a different selection of fabrics, if desired, for the complete medallion.

For the background pieces, make 12 of section B, six of section C, six of section D, and six of section E (pages 32–33). The sections can be pieced with many different fabrics for more textural interest. Piece and trim each section in the same manner as the star points, making sure to mark the corner points on each section.

Lay out the stars and background pieces, positioning each background piece so that fabric piece 1 on the foundation-piecing diagram is toward the center of the medallion. Sew each seam carefully, matching the corner points and backstitching at all points.

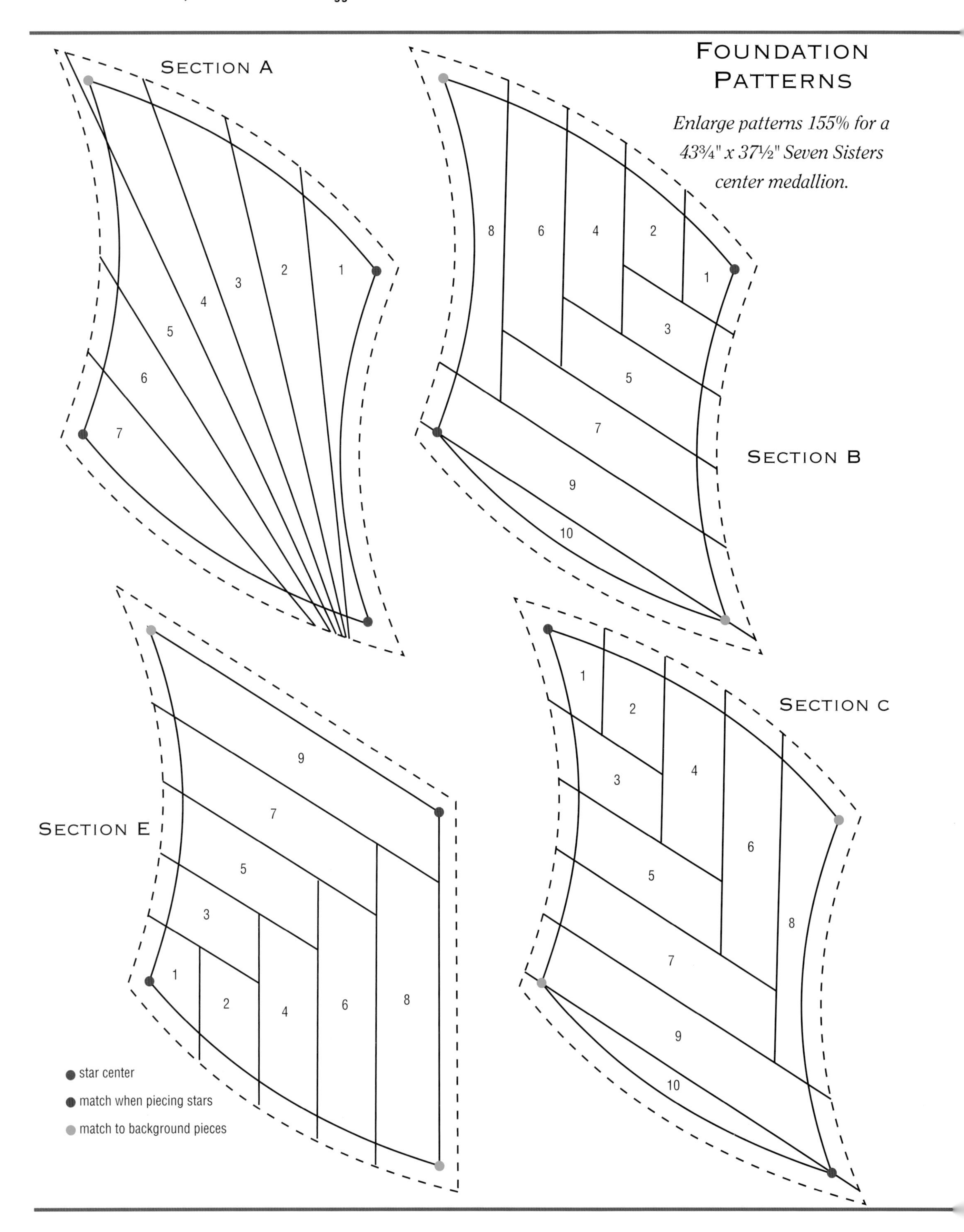
SECTION A
1
2
3
4
5
6
7
FOUNDATION PATTERNS
Enlarge patterns 155% for a 43¾" x 37½" Seven Sisters center medallion.
8
6
4
2
1
3
5
7
9
10
SECTION B
SECTION C
1
2
3
4
5
6
7
8
9
10
SECTION E
9
7
5
3
1
2
4
6
8
star center
match when piecing stars
match to background pieces

Enlarge patterns 155% for a 43¾" x 37½" Seven Sisters center medallion.

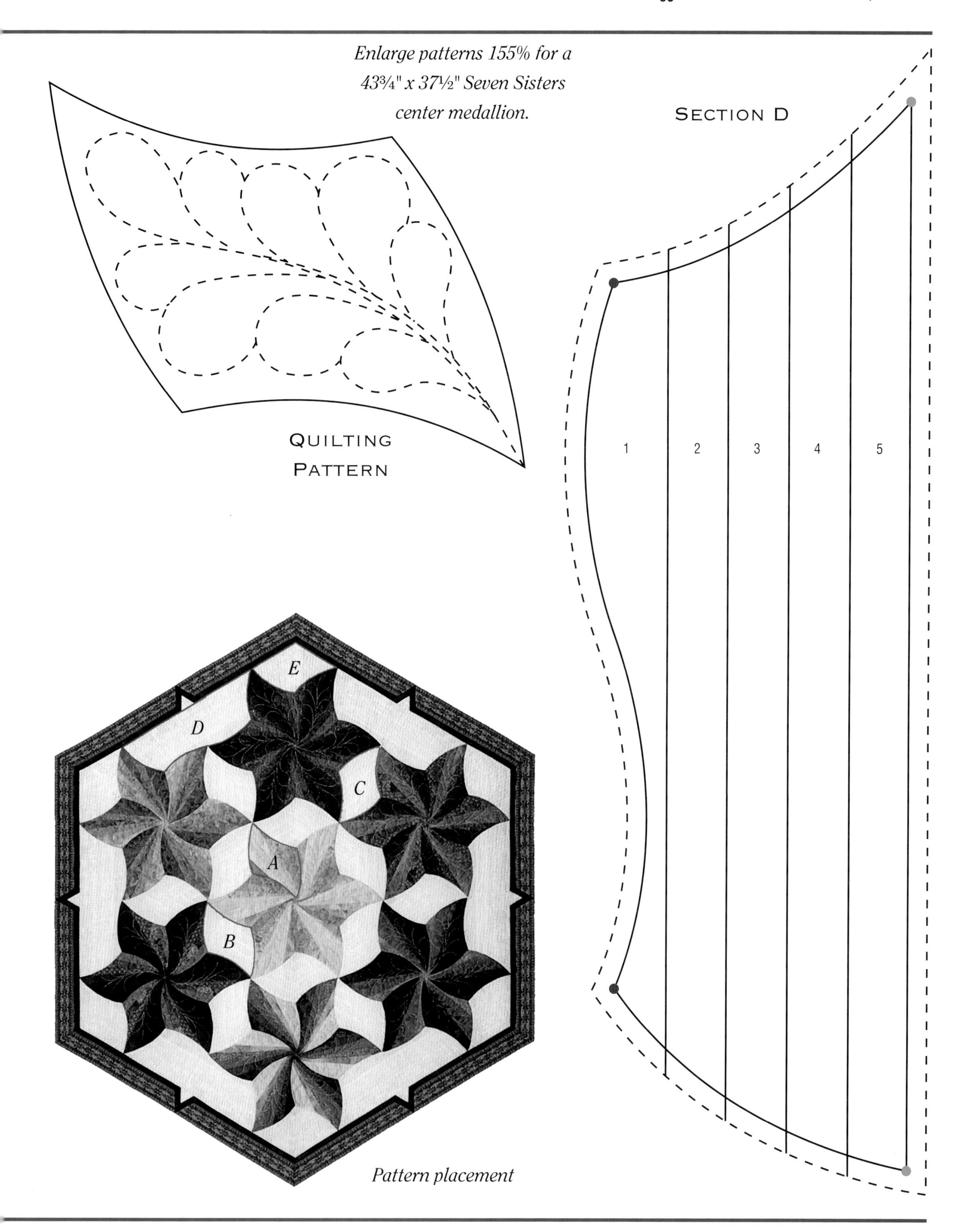

Pattern placement

BARBARA CLINE

Bridgewater, Virginia

"I was blessed to participate in a recent mission trip to Albania to teach native women the art of quilting and piecing as a self-help program."

Family and fabric have always been of great importance to me because I was born the seventh sister in a family of eight children. Around age 10, I embarked on my first sewing project, which was a simple dress. I learned the importance of precision and perfection because my mother insisted on picking out the pleats, mistakenly stitched into the sleeve tops, and replacing them with gentle gathers. She taught me never to be satisfied with poor workmanship and to persevere until perfection was achieved.

My first quilting lessons came, in my early teens, from my deaf grandmother, who was an expert quilter. The first session resulted in a whole evening of labor and only six inches completed. Perseverance again paid off, and I was soon able to quilt a few feet and have since learned to thoroughly enjoy quilting.

My interest in fabric and quilts expanded when my parents purchased a small fabric store, named The Clothes Line. As I gained experience, I became a clerk, Bernina® sales person, and teacher at the store.

When I married and had children, I stopped working at the store and so had time to explore quiltmaking at home. My husband has been a great source of encouragement to my quilting as well as supplying helpful suggestions on color selection and combination.

Barbara's photo by Oren Heatwole

Spinning Sisters

98" x 98"

Sewing quilt tops to sell and enjoying five small children made each day an adventure. I returned to the store, now called Patchwork Plus, when the children were all in school. Teaching quilt classes has kept me up to date with new methods and fresh ideas and has inspired me to market a few of my own patterns.

The character of the lady in Proverbs 31 challenges me. My aim is to bless my husband and children as I work with my hands and my beautiful fabric. I also satisfy my desire to help the needy by donating quilts to a local relief auction.

Inspiration and Design

Because I'm the seventh sister, I felt inspired to create a quilt for the Seven Sisters contest to symbolize our family. My sister Julia Graber is also a finalist in this contest. Each color represents a sister and how she has inspired me with her own life. The quilt is woven together in a design to represent our close relationship.

An annual sewing retreat is held by my family. My mother, sisters, sister-in-law, and any interested nieces meet for a week. During this time, we share our sewing projects, ideas, and the deep places of our hearts. We consider this time of togetherness a highlight in the year. At this retreat, I began creating Spinning Sisters. As I displayed my carefully selected fabrics, two of my sisters voiced their opinions on the color selection. With their input, I could see that I needed to change some fabric color to create the value needed. I hurried back to the fabric store. Then, with new fabrics, I was ready to begin sewing.

Quilt Construction

Spinning Sisters began as a triangular unit with curved lines. Each unit is divided into four curved pieces. Each swirl is made with six units, and each spinning sister includes seven swirls.

During the design process, I discovered that, by drawing different lines inside my unit, different effects were created (fig. 1). I kept working until I liked the design (fig. 2 38and pattern, page 38), then chose seven different colorways and developed color placement (fig. 3, page 37).

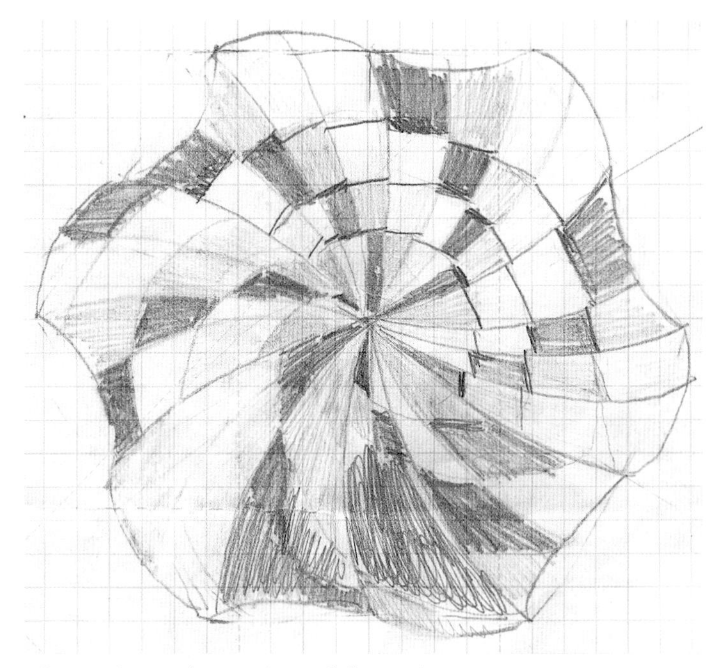

Fig. 1. An early version of the unit

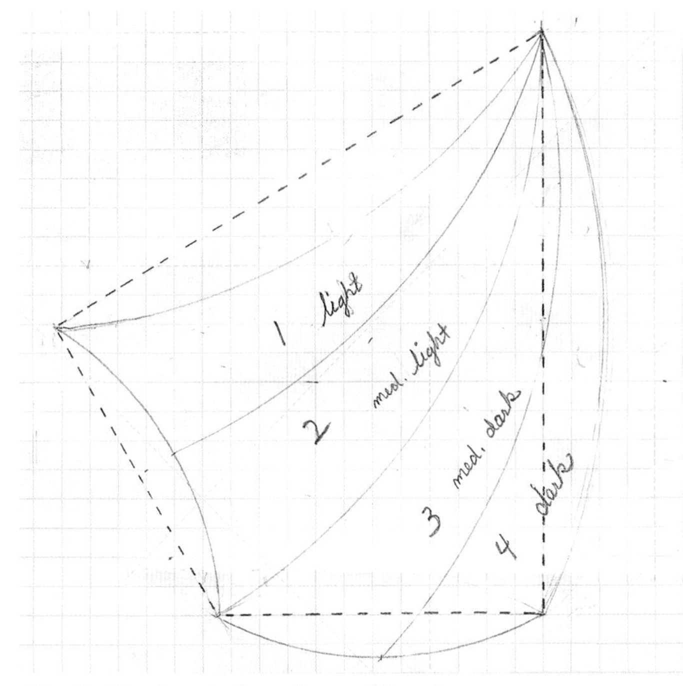

Fig. 2. Final unit, based on a kite shape

Fig. 3. Developing colorways

Because each spinning sister is composed of only one unit, the quilt was constructed by sewing three units into triangles and then rows (fig. 4).

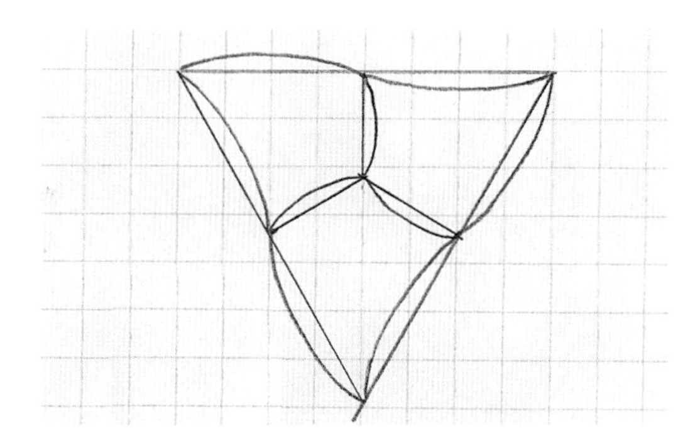
Fig. 4. Joining units

The original design did not include the center circle in each swirl. I discovered the center to be too bulky with 24 seams coming together. This was remedied by appliquéing a small circle and trimming the seam allowances underneath.

The center background is comprised of black and gray stripes. I used a large hexagon shape then gently appliquéd the spinning sisters on top. The quilt was accented with a border of each different fabric pieced in small rectangles and placed on the corresponding corners of the hexagon.

The final gray background was added next, but a finishing touch was needed. Black piping and a bias rainbow binding were just right. I created the binding by cutting strips from each different fabric and sewing them in rows. These were cut at a 45-degree angle, 2¼" wide (fig. 5).

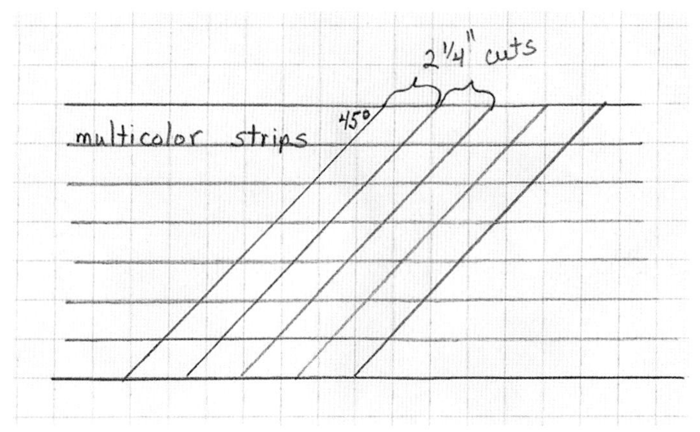

Fig. 5. Rainbow binding

MACHINE QUILTING

Because the quilt is 98" x 98", I began quilting with batting and backing in the center section only, to reduce bulk. I basted the layers with safety pins and pins, then free-motion quilted the center section. Each swirl was quilted with a free-motion design in alternating pieces (pattern, page 39). I repeated this process of layering and quilting to finish the right and left sides of the quilt.

The large gray background was bland, so I used metallic thread and a trapunto look to bring it to life. This trapunto technique includes cutting small hexagon-shaped pieces of batting. These were inserted into the quilt on top of the regular batting. I then quilted the design through both layers to create the puffy, three-dimensional appearance. I also used stipple quilting to accentuate the nearby design.

KITE-SHAPED FOUNDATION UNIT

Pattern placement

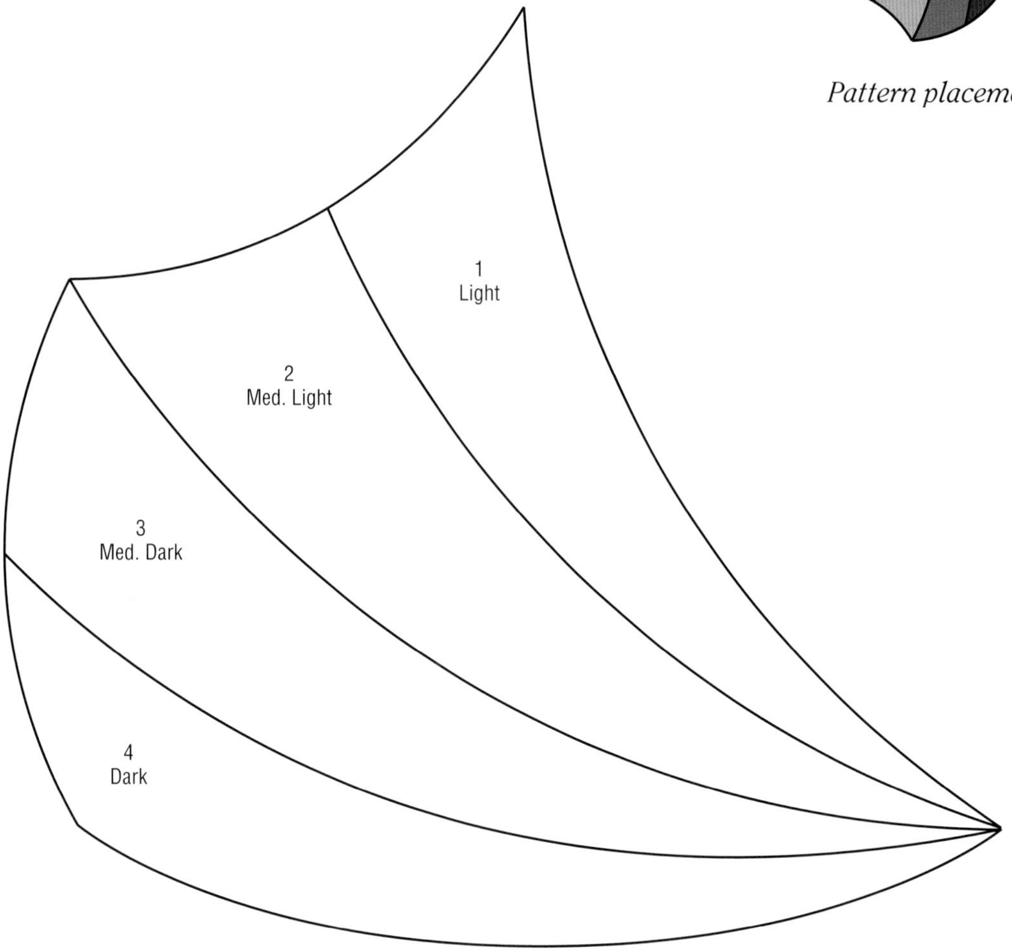

1
Light

2
Med. Light

3
Med. Dark

4
Dark

FREE-MOTION QUILTING PATTERN

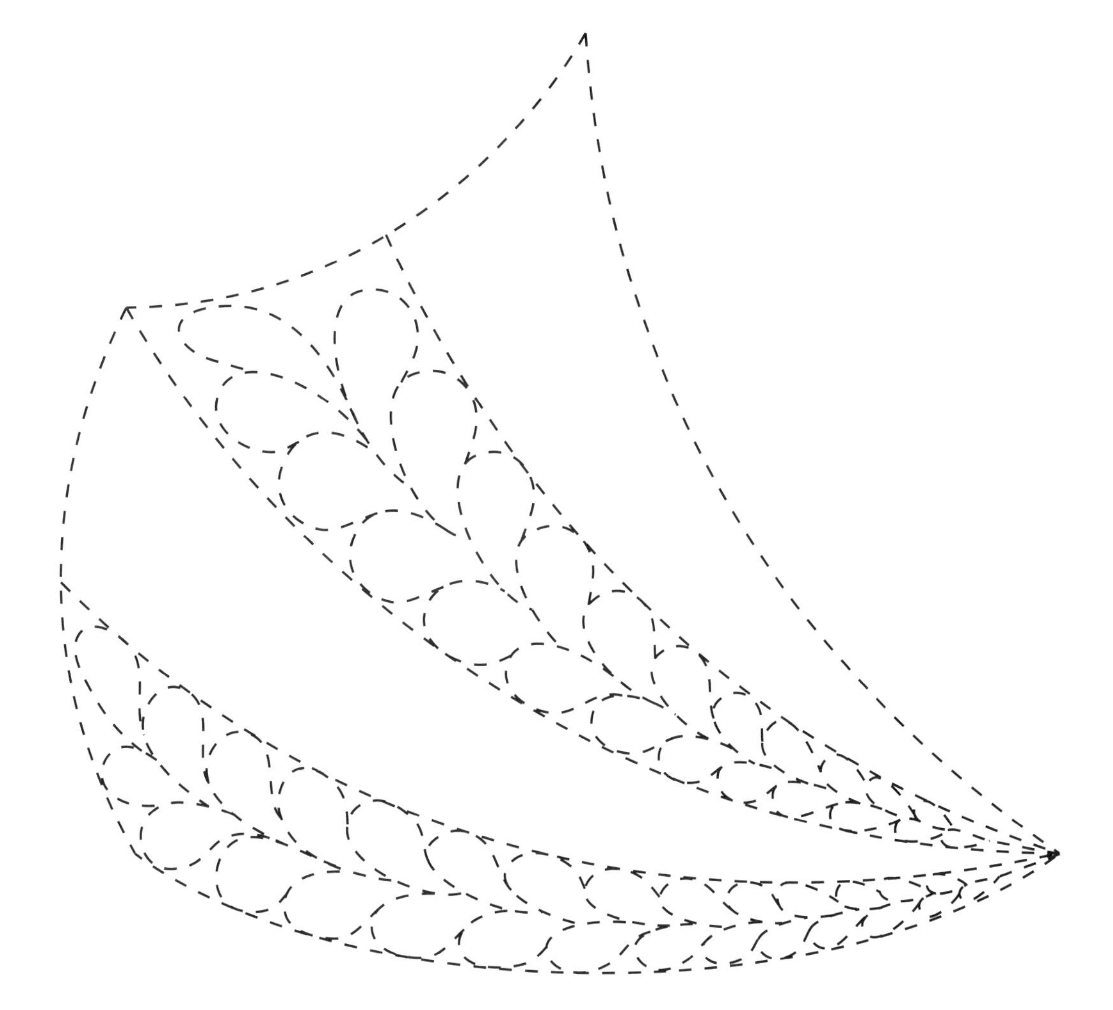

Sherri Bain Driver

Centennial, Colorado

"I usually choose fabrics early in the design process to be able to draft patterns sized for specific motifs in the fabrics."

I've been quilting for more than 18 years, and quilting plays a huge role in my life. I'm an editor for a quilting magazine and spend much of my free time in quilt-related activities. I have written two books and designed scads of patterns, and I am a quilt judge, certified by the National Quilting Association. Most of my friends are quilters. Many of my vacations are planned around going to quilt shows and checking out quilt shops. I even dream about quilts. In my eyes, a day without quilting is like a day without sunshine.

There's something about working with fabric that really speaks to me. I love the colors and textures. I especially love ikat fabrics and have a ridiculously large collection of them. Hand-dyed fabrics make wonderful companions to ikats. My friend Janet Jo Smith, who is also a finalist in this contest, dyes gorgeous fabrics. I often dash to her house with a handful of my ikats, and I can usually find some fabric she has already dyed that looks great with mine. Sometimes I get her to dye something special for me.

Fabrics are usually the inspiration for my quilt designs. I used to set aside my best and most beautiful fabrics for a quilt I imagined making in the distant future when I came up with the perfect design. I finally realized that the perfect design might not come, and my beautiful fabrics could become another generation's car-washing rags. I'm sure nobody else loves these fabrics as much as I do, so I decided it was my duty to preserve them by making them into quilts.

Sherri's photo by Kathleen A. Powloka

Sol Sisters

51" x 51"

INSPIRATION AND DESIGN

I remember using a compass in elementary school to draft simple geometric shapes. It was really fun and seemed like magic. Drafting six-pointed stars begins by drawing a circle, so when I started thinking about an innovative interpretation for Seven Sisters, it seemed natural to use circles and curves in my design. I imagined the Seven Sisters cluster of stars in the center of a larger star.

I drew the center, the traditional Seven Sisters, on equilateral-triangle graph paper then traced it onto blank paper. I wanted to see what would develop if there were no extra lines on the paper to influence my decisions.

I chose a few absolutely favorite fabrics, then added others that would still allow my favorites to shine. I wavered between drafting my pattern and selecting fabric, and often asked myself, "Where can this fabric go?"

I hand pieced the Seven Sisters for the center of the design then set it aside while I drafted the rest of the quilt. I taped together sheets of freezer paper to make a big piece the size of the finished quilt. A couple of folds were used to mark the center lines, and I taped the huge freezer-paper piece to the cement floor in my basement. Several days were spent drafting the full-sized pattern by using a yardstick compass for the curves.

I selected a group of fabrics that I thought would make a striking and dramatic large star. To use the fabrics to their best advantage, I referred to them as I drafted pieces to fit specific designs in the fabric. I checked and rechecked each measurement before I went on to the next step.

When I was sure that the pattern was what I wanted, I labeled each pattern piece with a number and drew registration marks across every line. Once a pattern is cut apart, it can be difficult to reconstruct, so these labels and marks are crucial. I used the freezer-paper pieces as patterns, some for foundations, others for conventional piecing.

I made the large star as a separate piece and appliquéd the hand-pieced Seven Sisters on the center. I pinned the cluster of smaller stars over the center of the large star, covering the raw edges with an appliquéd bias strip.

When I finished the top of SOL SISTERS, the inner edge of the circle that pierces the star points was nearly the same value as the adjacent yellow bias strips. I had envisioned stronger definition to visually separate those two fabrics. When I finished the quilting, large areas of rust-colored background were too plain and boring. How was I to solve these problems on a nearly finished quilt?

Familiar with couching, I thought that might do the trick. Interesting threads in compatible colors provided the perfect solution. To couch the threads, I just placed the yarn on the quilt and zigzagged over it with monofilament thread. The yarn ends were threaded through a large-eyed needle and buried in the batting layer.

JOINING BINDING ENDS

When joining strips for bindings or bias trim, I like to use diagonal seams and press the seam allowances open. This reduces bulk and makes the seams almost invisible. We probably all know how to join the lengths smoothly, but joining the strip ends can present a challenge. I want the final seam, the one that connects the beginning and the end, to look just as smooth and flat as the other seams; so it also needs a diagonal seam with the seam allowances pressed open. After a lot of experimentation, I've devised a simple and foolproof way to join these ends. I've been using this method for 15 years.

Cut the number of strips needed to bind your quilt then trim both ends of each strip at a 45° angle, making sure that all the cuts are angled in the same direction (fig. 1).

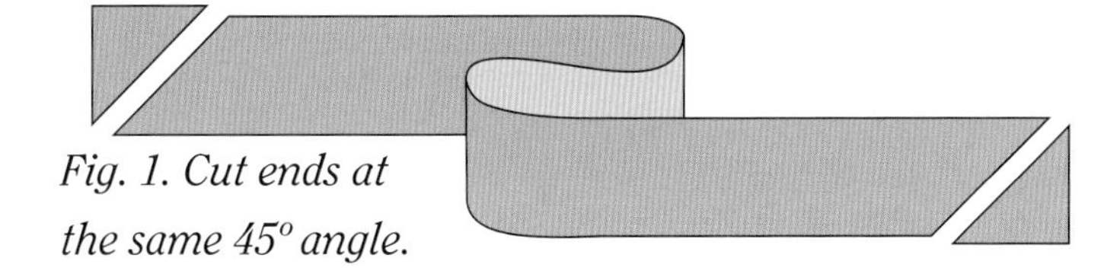

Fig. 1. Cut ends at the same 45° angle.

With right sides together, and using a ¼" seam, join the strips. The points will be offset a bit so the strips match ¼" in from the edge (fig. 2). Press these seam allowances open. (There are other methods for joining these strips, but this method is great practice for the final seam.)

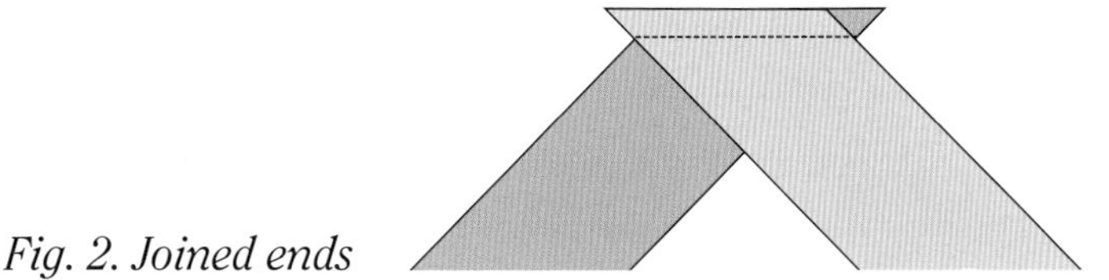

Fig. 2. Joined ends

Starting in the middle of a side and leaving loose at least a 6" tail of binding, sew the binding to the quilt (fig. 3). Wide bindings require that you leave a longer tail.

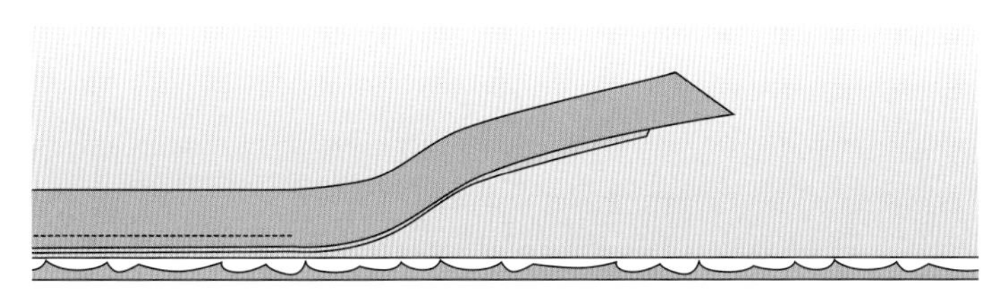

Fig. 3. Leave a 6" tail.

When you get back to the first side of the quilt, leave at least 12" of the quilt edge unbound. On a flat surface and with the binding folded open, pin the ending tail along the quilt edge (fig. 4).

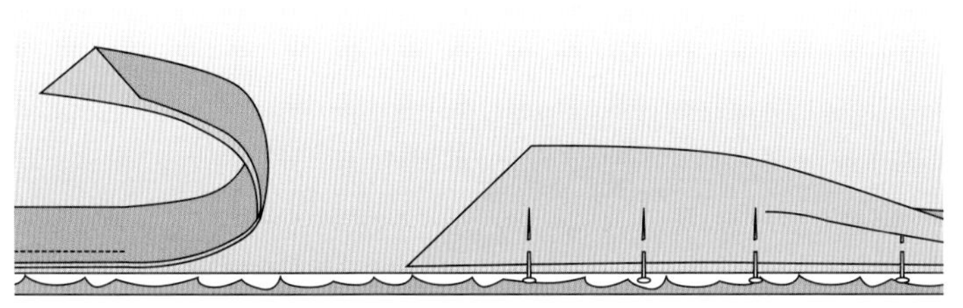

Fig. 4. Pin the ending tail in place.

Smooth the beginning tail over the ending tail. Following the cut edge of the beginning tail, draw a line on the ending tail (fig. 5).

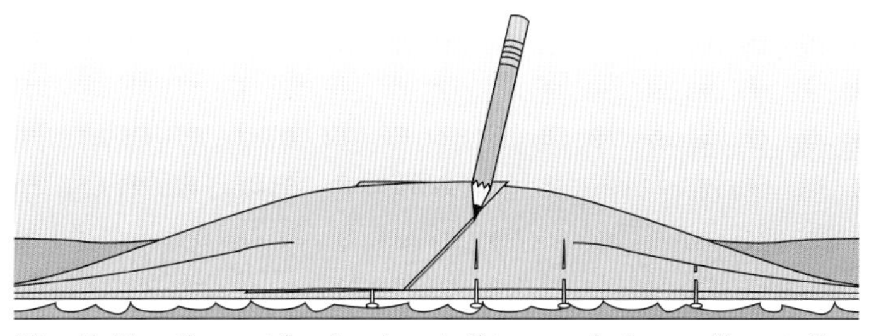

Fig. 5. Use the cut beginning tail to mark the ending tail.

Fold the beginning tail out of the way and draw another line ½" to the left of the first line (fig. 6). The second line is a cutting line.

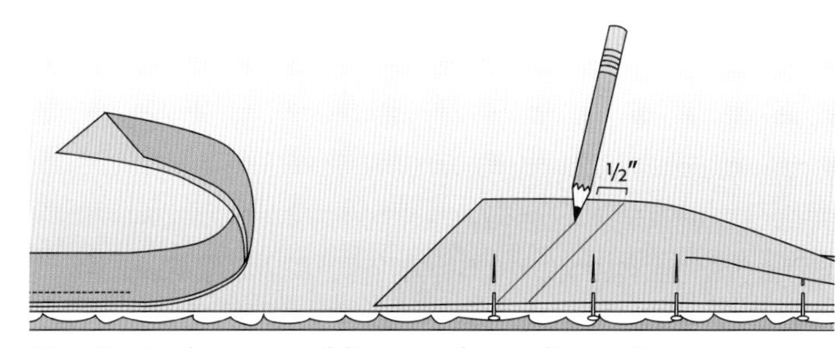

Fig. 6. Mark a second line on the ending tail.

Cut along the second line (fig. 7), join the ends as before, and press the seam allowances open. Finish sewing the binding to the quilt.

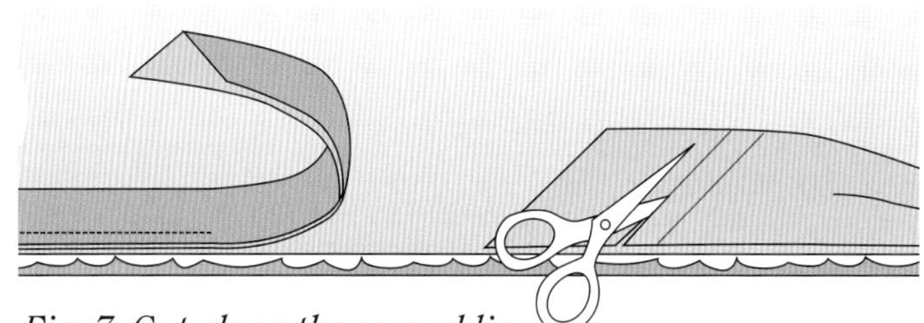

Fig. 7. Cut along the second line.

In Sol Sisters, I used this method to make smooth connections in the binding, accent piping, and the bias strip that covers the center star edges. I also used it to splice together several striped strips when I ran out of fabric.

Margo Ellis

Key West, Florida

"Living in Key West with the profusion of tropical flowers and trees year-round stimulates my creative juices and fuels my color choices."

I am a third-generation quilter. My grandmother, May J. Dunn, lived with us throughout my childhood. She used to lay out pieces for Dresden Plate and Grandmother's Fan blocks that she had cut from fabrics of the 1930s, '40s, and '50s, which were scraps leftover from dresses. I remember the doll quilts she completed, which she loved to arrange and piece on her treadle sewing machine. My mother, Margaret Zittel, taught me how to sew and make my own clothes. I got my first Featherweight® machine when I was 13 because she was tired of sharing her machine with me.

When my grandmother moved into an assisted-living facility in the '70s, mom brought me her box of scraps and unfinished objects (UFOs). I used them in my first attempt at quilting, which was a crazy quilt on muslin foundations. The layers were tied with string. Because of the false starts and dead ends, the project took two years, but I was hooked on a new craft. I already had a fiber passion: sewing, embroidery, knitting, and crocheting. Quilting took the place of all of these in my heart and in my closets and cupboards and on windows and walls. My husband even suggested I make a house cozy when we lived in Maine.

I enjoy all the different quiltmaking techniques, but my favorites are handwork, piecing, appliqué, and quilting. I teach children with behavioral issues, so it is nice to come home to a peaceful evening of handwork. I can share time with my husband, Rodger, and three dogs and still get some quilting done. He is always supportive of my

Margo's photo by Gerald Adams

Sassaman's Sisters

60" x 60"

habit (obsession) and tolerates the baskets, pins, threads, and other detritus of quilting.

I like to enter challenges. Last year, I won first place in the Marcus Brother's Aunt Grace's Challenge. Challenges give me a starting point for creating. I seldom have a drafted plan and prefer to see how my work progresses and how the fabric inspires me.

I get my inspiration for quilting from many sources. I began dyeing my own fabric after an article by Vimala McClure in *American Quilter* magazine (Vol. XI, No. 3). I also took fabric-dyeing classes from Carol Suderland. I enjoy mixing the hand-dyed fabrics with beautiful commercial fabrics. Our guild, Paradise Quilters, has been bringing national teachers to the Florida Keys for several years. I have learned new techniques from these classes as well as from our members. I often make samples to hang in my local quilt store, the Seams Shop. I teach classes there and at Ben Franklin to encourage more people to take up quilting.

It is not always easy to find time to quilt while working full time, but I do a little every day while watching television. As a teacher, I have the summers off and spend them working on projects I have dreamed of through the year. The Key West summers are the opposite of Maine winters where I used to live, but the result is the same for me. I spend a lot of time inside with the air conditioning on, instead of the furnace, while quilting and listening to books on tape. I always have several hand projects to work on and even carry one in my purse for long waits at appointments and meetings.

Teaching and watching others fall in love with quilting keeps me expanding my own skills. My fabric stash grows out of proportion to the small home we have, but I always seem to find room for a little more fabric. Sometimes I think that the selecting, coordinating, and handling of the fabrics brings as much joy as the actual quilting. My dream is to retire soon and to be able to quilt full time, funding my retirement with teaching, designing, making contract quilts, and expanding my skills. Then living in Key West really would be paradise!

Inspiration and Design

I saw the New Quilts from an Old Favorite: Mariner's Compass exhibit in Venice, Florida, a few years ago. I hand pieced a Mariner's Compass wallhanging after seeing that exhibit and thought about entering competitions, but I didn't seriously consider entering until recently. When I saw that the theme was Seven Sisters, I went online searching for samples and ideas. My inspiration came from photos in *Quilt Camp in the Pines*, July 15, 2002. Marti Mitchell is shown displaying some Seven Sisters quilts, and I was thrilled with several of them. I drafted my own hexagon and points with a compass and ruler, taking into consideration the required size of the finished quilt (fig. 1).

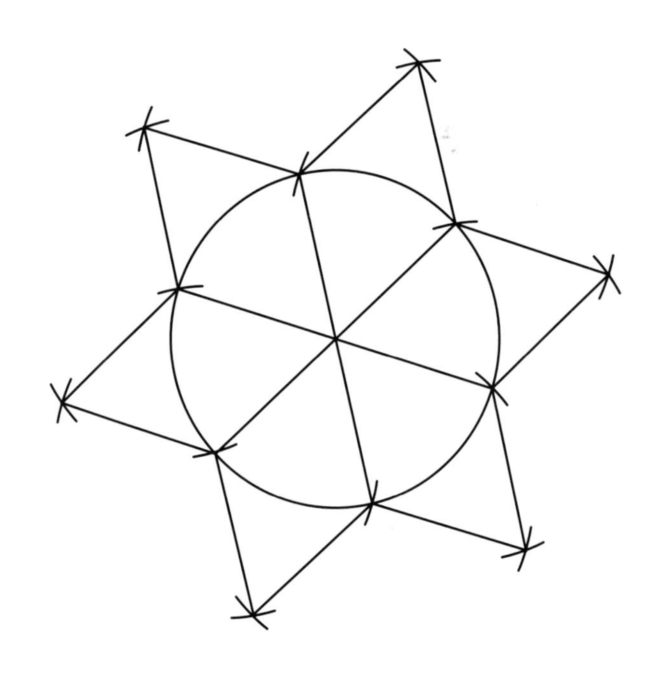

Fig 1. Draft of a hexagon star

I like to use the patterns in fabric to create new designs, and found Jane Sassaman's Floral Fantasy line just the ticket for fussy cutting and hand piecing the sisters. I selected seven different patterns from this line as well as the coordinating polka dots to use as background.

I began the quilt last fall as soon as I received the fabric in the mail. I began by piecing seven stars from one fabric, varying my cutting and placement to be sure each was different. I was thrilled with the results and knew I had picked the right fabric. When my dad, Redfield Zittel, died last November, I packed my handwork to keep busy. I spent many hours piecing and reminiscing about him.

Once the "sisters" were finished, I began arranging them on my design wall to see how they looked best. I didn't have a final plan in mind and got stuck once I had done the central part. I couldn't seem to figure out how to finish it and put on borders. It kept getting larger as I added more and more triangles and time was running out. I tried a border of all triangles, but it was too busy. I tried plain borders but it was too "blah." I finally settled on a mixture of the two and was thrilled when the fabric for the last border fit exactly right, with the flowers at the corners of the hexagonal shapes.

Mitering the binding was tricky because the angles are not 90 degrees, but I managed to do it fairly successfully. When the lower triangles didn't quite fit, I decided to just have them flow into the border as an extension of the design.

Many of my designs evolve as I work, and this one really changed from my first idea. I machine quilted around all the sisters and hand quilted within them to accentuate the fabric patterns. If I had had more time, I probably would have done more quilting and some embellishments, but with the deadline fast approaching, I had to get it finished.

FUSSY CUTTING

I think the most important technique for this quilt was the fussy cutting of the diamonds. I used template plastic to trace around the selected portion of the fabric design. I marked the wrong side of the fabric at the points of the diamonds with a permanent, fine-tipped pen. I then removed the template and used a ruler and mechanical pencil to connect the points for the sewing line. I cut the shapes about ¼" outside the drawn lines.

For each of the other five diamonds, I laid the first fabric piece on the fabric so it disappeared into the pattern. I used pins to mark the four points through the top diamond. I marked where the pins were on the back with the pen and drew lines to connect the points as before.

I ran out of some fabrics because of the fussy cutting, so I used two different fabrics in some of the sisters rather than cutting six identical diamonds (fig. 2).

Fig 2. Some of the seven sisters feature stars made of two different fabrics.

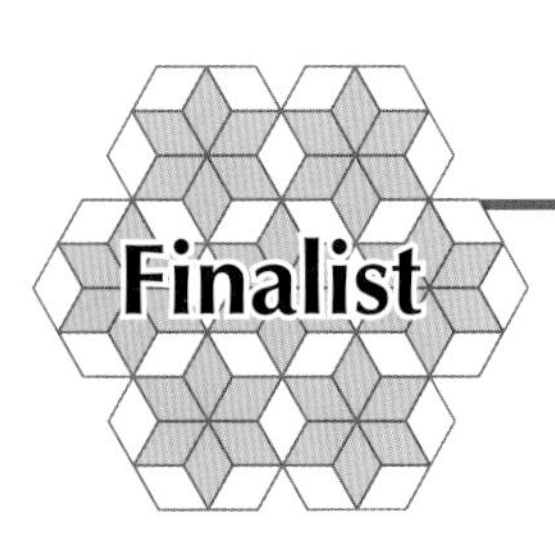

Ann Feitelson

Montague, Massachusetts

"Two thirty-year friendships are embodied in this quilt. I am so grateful for these friends."

Inspired by the 1971 groundbreaking exhibit at the Whitney Museum, Abstract Design in American Quilts, I made three quilts, combining calicos with eye-popping psychedelic prints. I moved on to painting and knitting, my mother moved on to weaving and pottery, and the stash we had accumulated through years of sewing clothing languished, unused, rumpled. Eventually, with my permission, my mother donated it to a friend. I was sure I'd never see it again, let alone want it. But...

When I came back to quilting five years ago, I began to pine for that stash. My 1970's quilts continually reminded me of it, and of its loss. On my behalf, my mother contacted her old friend to ask for its return, but the friend said she was using it up, slowly. I understood that the answer was no; after all, how could she possibly find any of what had been given to her 20 years before? I resigned myself to having forsaken that wealth of fabrics.

While working on this quilt, however, I couldn't help but think of that stash some more, especially the green fabrics that had been in it. I'm nothing if not persistent. I called my mother's friend myself and asked if she still might have any of those green fabrics and if

Ann's photo by Leah Gans

Seven for the Seven Stars in the Sky

55" x 83½"

she would be willing to part with them. This time, the answer was yes. I was so thrilled when I got them in the mail: fabrics on a 30-year journey from my mother and me, to her friend, and back to me. The fabric that I am especially thrilled to have back is a Kelly green with a white-rope lattice.

Another old friend of my mother's and mine (these women are in their eighties now) spontaneously reconnected with me during the past year. This friend had been an inspiringly avid knitter when I first knew her in the 1970s, and she later turned to quilting. We visited. I told her of my need for many, close greens for this quilt. She, too, sent me fabrics. Some are vintage fabrics – one is green with white pin dots – and many are contemporary.

Inspiration and Design

I have an idea of green, a pure, glowing, vivid jade green, as deep as the cosmos – an unearthly color, almost neon, yet tender. And this idea is connected to a beloved counting song, "Green Grow the Rushes O!" The quilt's title is taken from the song. Green represents a life force, as in Dylan Thomas' poem, "The force that through the green fuse drives the flower."

When I started this quilt, I had been working with an architect painting scenery for community theater, and every flat we painted was founded on the unifying principle that "the light comes from the upper left." I was interested to see if I could transfer that principle to this quilt. So, sunny yellows and yellow greens are at the top center.

The top-left diamond in each large star catches the "light." Its colors have the highest contrast. The opposition of low contrast and high contrast is critical to the structure of the quilt. The background of the large Seven Sisters constellation, indeed, of the whole quilt, is low-contrast green stars within green diamonds.

Each large star has a suite of colors that relate to each other. Each star is composed of two color triads, two sequences interwoven, more or less. The top center star is yellow and purple. The next large star, clockwise at two o'clock, is pink and green. The next is turquoise and purple. At bottom center, the star is red and green. At eight o'clock, the star is red with purple. At ten o'clock, the last star is pink with yellow-green. The group of colors in one star stays within that color idea. Still, I try to stretch those limits to keep the color lively and unpredictable. I also like to combine symmetry with asymmetry. Notice that the large central star is not in the center of the quilt.

The Seven Sisters configurations are in four different sizes. The large central star has 6" sides, and a cropped Seven Sisters cluster at the upper left has 2" sides. Below that, there is a cluster with 1½" sides, and at the bottom right, in dark green, another cluster has 1" sides.

A mysteriously ugly, yet beautiful fabric became a key focal point to lead the eye around the quilt. It has a bristly web of mint green dots over celadon bricks, a preposterous combination. I can't imagine what the designer had in mind. I had only a 10" square of it, so it was strangely precious.

When I was almost finished piecing, I was surprised to find a batik similar to this fabric, with dark green background, a green grid, and green dots. It is in the upper left in several places. I'm interested in a dialogue of similarity and differences between fabrics.

Star Design

I've probably developed a unique method for piecing six-pointed stars. I had valuable guidance from two knowledgeable mentors, but while making hundreds of stars, I questioned every step and possibility, asking myself with each star whether I could find a more accurate way to sew them. I machine piece with 60-weight thread, which gives more precision than heavier threads. When pressing, I line up the edges along a straight line on the ironing board. I press only from the right side, and never with steam. I prefer fabrics with a tight weave and fine threads, such as batiks and poplins. They distort less than coarser weaves. I don't bother to starch, because I don't want to have to wash it out.

For a star with 1" sides, I cut strips measuring 1⅜". With templates, I cut diamonds from the strips. I chain piece the diamonds, always opposing a bias edge with a straight-grain edge for stability (fig. 1). The stitched line indicates the stopping point at ¼" for all future seams, so I don't have to do any marking. When necessary, I unsew a few stitches to free the piece to rotate it to sew a subsequent seam.

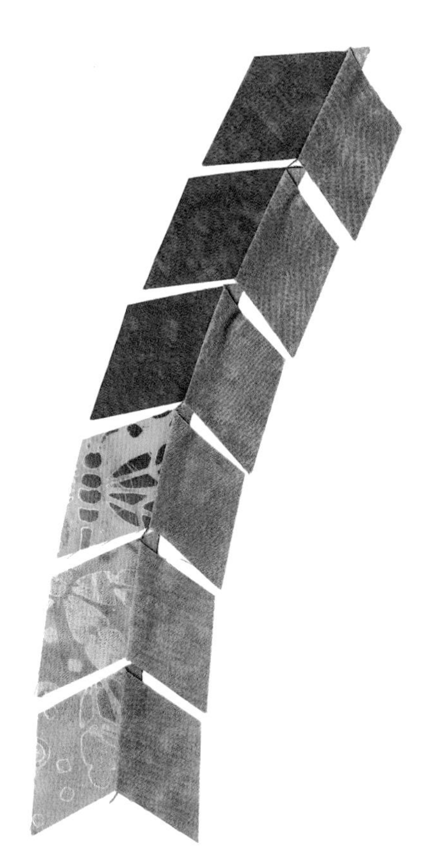

Fig. 1. Chain-pieced diamonds

The chain-pieced diamonds are pressed, then arranged in a star shape (fig. 2). The first pair of diamonds is joined. I sew edge-to-seam when possible, seam-to-seam otherwise. Another pair is joined to the first pair, making a half star. The two halves are joined with a 2" seam across the centers. The centers of the stars are fanned when pressing (fig. 3).

Fig. 2. Chain-pieced diamonds arranged to form a star

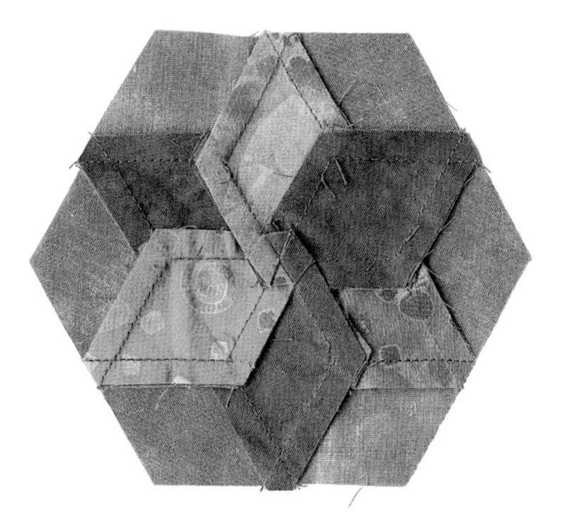

Fig. 3. Back of sewn star

A Seven Sisters configuration builds from there. Whenever matching points, I sew across two diamonds, but otherwise it's single seam by single seam, which is tedious, but nevertheless I love doing it.

Julia Graber

Brooksville, Mississippi

"I find quilts to be so much more than articles of beauty. They have gone from simply something to cover up with at night to objects of expression."

My interest in quiltmaking was sparked in my early twenties while working as a clerk at my parent's fabric store, The Clothes Line, in Dayton, Virginia. I learned to sew in home-economics classes in eighth and ninth grade. From that early beginning at the sewing machine, I learned to make my own clothes. While working at the store in the evenings, I'd see all of those fabrics and dream of putting quilts together.

I began making utility-type quilts – not the art quilts that I've learned to enjoy now. I pieced and tied several of those before I married. After marrying, I began to experiment more and more, with each quilt becoming more challenging than the last.

In time, I joined a few of my sisters in a round-robin quilt project. We each made a quilt center and passed it on to the next sister to add to it. In the end, we each had a quilt. Next, I taught a class of high-school girls how to piece quilt blocks. Those two events taught me a lot about quiltmaking. I began to spearhead projects for my church's sewing circle, which involved making quilts for charity. I have also taught several quiltmaking classes in my home, and my love for the craft has grown with each quilt made.

I come from a family of seven sisters and one brother. One of my sisters, Barbara Cline, also entered this Seven Sisters contest, and she is a finalist as well. Each year, we have a retreat that not only includes the seven sisters, but also our one sister-in-law, our mother, and

Seven Sisters – Leaving Home

77" x 83"

some of our daughters. For an entire week, we sew and quilt, make baskets or scrapbooks, and talk and laugh together late into the night having the best time. We take our current projects and work on them, learning and gaining inspiration from each other. Our grandmother was a very creative quilter, so the tradition is being carried on. It thrills us now to see some of our daughters take up the craft. I feel so blessed to be part of my family.

Quiltmaking has opened my eyes to the intriguing patterns and color in our world. My husband is involved in missions in Romania. While traveling there with him, I was intrigued by the terra-cotta roof tiles of the village houses and the interesting patterns on the courtyard gates. These images are stored in the back of my mind, and one day, I hope to try them in a quilt.

I've been involved in counted cross-stitch and other crafts, but quiltmaking has taken center stage among my hobbies. I like the feel, color, and designs of fabric. I used to make traditional quilts that looked nice on a bed, but what I enjoy making now involves bold, brassy colors that fit together in a scheme. SEVEN SISTERS – LEAVING HOME fits a scheme that means a lot to me personally. My siblings have all followed distinctive paths in life, yet common ties connect us all.

INSPIRATION AND DESIGN

The annual New Quilts from an Old Favorite contest books inspired my quilt. Because I'm number three of seven sisters, it only seemed right for me to enter this contest.

We have a strong family unit and one-by-one, we got married and left the family nest, which is represented by the brightest cluster of stars near the center of the quilt. The bright stars flinging out from the center represent each of us going in different directions, creating a larger world for our family.

When thinking about a design for this quilt, I started with a traditional Seven Sisters pattern, but wanted the design to include stars swirling away from the center. I wanted to use the Stack-n-Whack® method to make the stars, so I chose a large, brightly colored floral fabric on a black background.

As the quilt came together, I discovered that some of the stars were very bright, while others were more subdued. The brightly colored stars symbolize my sisters and myself, and the darker ones symbolize extended family. As a puzzle there is one cousin sister with a broken arm. Can you find her in the quilt?

The entire quilt is comprised of equilateral triangles, so I had to place them strategically to make Seven Sisters. I learned that by turning the triangles within each star, an entirely different effect was created (fig. 1). I liked the way the emerging design kept my eyes moving.

Fig. 1. Arranging triangles within each star

ARRANGING THE STARS

To begin the piecing process, I drew the pattern on isometric paper. Because there are only six stars on the outer edge of the Seven Sisters block, my first sketch had only six stars blazing trails across the design (fig. 2, page 55). I had to rearrange the star paths to accommodate a seventh trail (fig. 3, page 55).

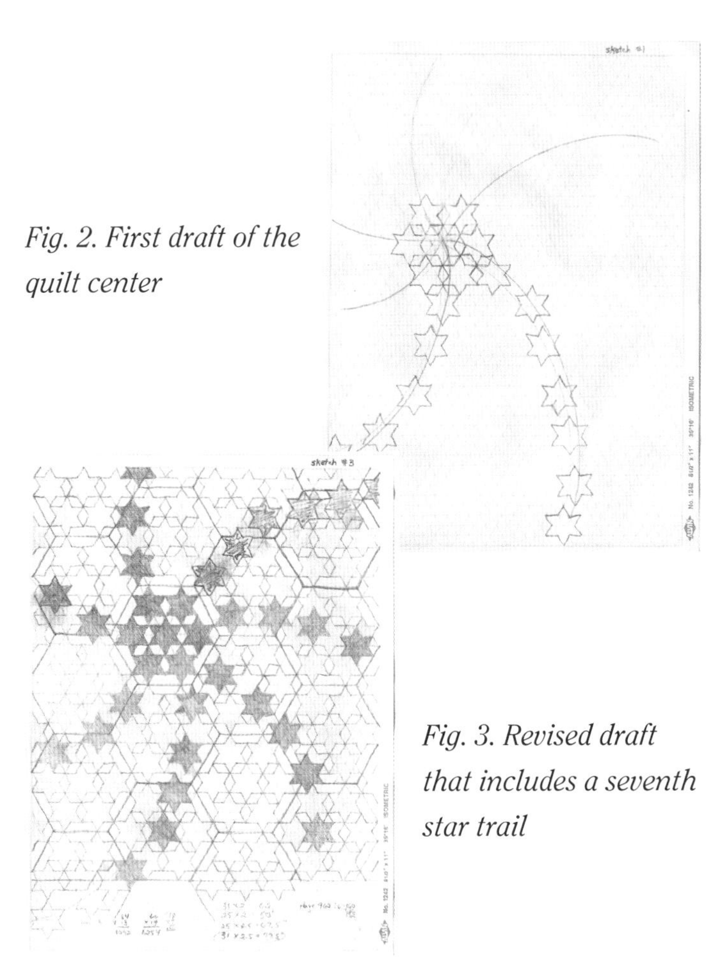

Fig. 2. First draft of the quilt center

Fig. 3. Revised draft that includes a seventh star trail

Fig. 4. Arranging the quilt on the design wall

Fig. 5. Preparing strips of triangles for sewing

The fabric pattern repeated itself about every 18". Using the Stack-n-Whack method, I cut six strips from the floral fabric, each one laid over the identical flower designs as the one before. Then I cut the strips to get six identical triangles from each cut. These were arranged in a variety of ways to create the floral effects of the stars.

To make the design phase easier, I leaned two folding tables against a wall and placed a fuzzy blanket over it to form a design wall. Solid black triangles were placed between the floral stars to clarify the clusters (fig. 4). The arrangement of the stars resulted in long rows of triangles that were sewn into strips (fig. 5). The challenge was to keep the points of the triangles turned the right way. It was easy to get them mixed up and turned around. The design wall helped immensely to keep things straight.

Because the design was more in the use and placement of the fabric, I knew the quilting stitches wouldn't show up much. I machine quilted the black pieces in black thread and used gold-colored thread within the stars. A zigzag stitch around each cluster of Seven Sisters in colorful decorative thread helped define them (fig. 6).

Fig. 6. Decorative zigzag stitch around Seven Sisters clusters

Diane Powers Harris

Monroe, New Hampshire

"Little did I realize that this quilt would have a mind of its own ... kind of like the man for whom it was being made."

In November 1979, my family and I attended a local vintage-airplane fly-in. After looking at the planes on the field, we decided to see what was going on in the exhibit hall. It was a wonderful event called The Harvest, put on by the South Florida Historical Association. There were vintage automobiles, craft vendors, food, live demonstrations of early life in Miami, music, and wonder of wonders ... quilts. There were new and old quilts piled high waiting to be purchased and quilts on display, hanging from the ceiling in a judged competition.

I talked to a remarkable lady at the sale table, and she persuaded me to sign up for a class at the local quilt shop. I did so, and life has never been the same. I took my first quilting class in the spring of 1980. To help quench some of the thirst for quilt knowledge brought to life in that beginning class, I worked for about a year in the quilt shop.

In 1985, with the encouragement of my mentor Irene McLaren, the remarkable lady from The Harvest, I established a National Quilting Association (NQA) chapter in Miami, known today as the Ocean Waves Chapter. I served in many capacities, holding various offices and committee chair positions.

For several years, I organized the quilt competition for The Historical Association in conjunction with Ocean Waves at that same local event, The Harvest. During the late 1980s, I served as the area

Diane's photo by M. Katherine Rodimon

BEWARE THE BLACK HOLE

72" x 86"

coordinator for Dade County (Miami) for the Florida Quilt Heritage project. Because Florida is largely a migratory state, this project's main goal was to document how quilts arrived there in the first place. Additionally, I organized several quilt symposia, including the 2001 NQA show.

I'm happiest when designing and selecting the fabrics for my newest quilt. For most of the years that I've been quilting, my time has been spent as an organizer of quilting events, which leaves little time to actually quilt. The last few years have been devoted more to creating quilts than event planning, and I love it. I've had two quilts accepted at the International Quilt Festival in Houston, Texas.

Inspiration and Design

I'm sure my move to northern rural New Hampshire will have a profound effect on my future quilts. The small town where I live is primarily a dairy community with wonderful views of the Connecticut River and the mountains of both Vermont and New Hampshire. In observing my neighbor's cows in the fields and on their journeys to and from the barn, I have discovered that the placid front they present covers personalities friendly, frolicsome, comical, and dare I say it, a bit mischievous. Who knew that cows have a sense of humor? So I do foresee a couple of quilts featuring cows in ways that you might not envision, but that is so true to their life and curious nature.

While inspired to create something for the MAQS contest, I made this quilt primarily for my husband Harold's fiftieth birthday. While attending a local quilt show in south Florida, I came across a tessellating template. Inspiration struck and I knew what to make for my star-gazing husband.

I love selective cutting and designs that make a kaleidoscope pattern. So, for the center star of each of the four blocks, as well as the "black holes," I used fabrics that, when fussy cut, created swirling secondary designs. With the exception of the border fabric, all the fabrics came from my stash and are a mix of 100 percent cottons, batiks, and glitzy cottons. The star fabrics were selected with a taste for the masculine. All of the background fabrics have stars on them.

Because of a small miscalculation of template size on my part (okay, it was a large miscalculation), what was originally planned as a nine-block wallhanging grew and grew until it was crawling off my design wall onto the floor, and it was way too large for the challenge requirements. Oh what to do! The quilt whispered, "Turn me into a four-block quilt." By the time the border was added, the quilt had become double-bed sized. This fit within the size requirements and made a quilt that could not only be admired but actually used by my tall husband.

From the beginning, I knew that a feeling of motion was needed for this piece. Each of the seven stars in each of the four Seven Sisters blocks is quilted in a different pattern with metallic thread. These patterns are derivatives of each other, but each is slightly different — like sisters, similar but different.

After 210 hours of machine quilting, it was done, or so I thought. But no, it required more! The quilt needed sparkle. After all, it is a star quilt. My first thought was beading, but then someone mentioned Swarovski® crystals. They catch the light beautifully, adding so much interest and shimmer. I had never worked with these crystals, but found them fun and easy to apply. They have a heat-reactive glue back and are put on with a special heat gun. Once attached properly, they are permanent.

When I presented my husband with his birthday quilt, Harold's comment was, "Wow, this is a really great quilt, but I've already seen it – we've been sleeping under it all summer!" The summer had been unseasonably cold and wet. Because everything we own is still packed, it was the only thing warm that was readily accessible. Even though it was under construction, it was unstinting in its enveloping warmth, for which we were thoroughly appreciative.

BEWARE THE BLACK HOLE

The quilting for this piece began shortly after my move to New Hampshire. Once the stitching in the ditch around each piece was done, everything came to a screeching stop. Not sure what direction to take, I knew only that a feeling of motion needed to be achieved. Hanging my quilt to get a good visual was imperative, and there was no place in the house to do this. So with quilt in hand, I went to a local quilt shop, introduced myself, and asked the owner if she had a design wall where I could hang my quilt. She immediately grabbed my quilt, led me to her studio, and proceeded to hang it on her wall. Her suggestion for an amoeba-shaped design was the springboard for my creative imagination

I haven't been able to master free-motion quilting, but through trial and error, I have achieved good results with even complex curved designs by drawing on Golden Threads paper, pinning it in place, and stitching. The paper, which comes on long rolls, tears away nicely and leaves little residue under the stitching line. Of course, like everything else, the paper was packed, but I did locate some white pencils among my supplies.

Using these pencils, I drew the spiraling fingers for the central "black hole" and stitched along that outline. Upon completion, I realized further thought was required before going forward. To give myself time to think, I did heavy random background quilting around the black hole, using a variegated machine-quilting thread. The random quilting was accomplished with much back-and-forth stitching, using the reverse button on my machine.

Once the black holes were completed, the stars were next. With an idea in mind, I jumped in, trying to create motion in the whole star. Quickly realizing this wasn't working, I ripped out the stitching. At this point, I had to concede that planning was required, so out came the pencil and paper. I drew the basic star unit (fig. 1) on several sheets of paper and started doodling.

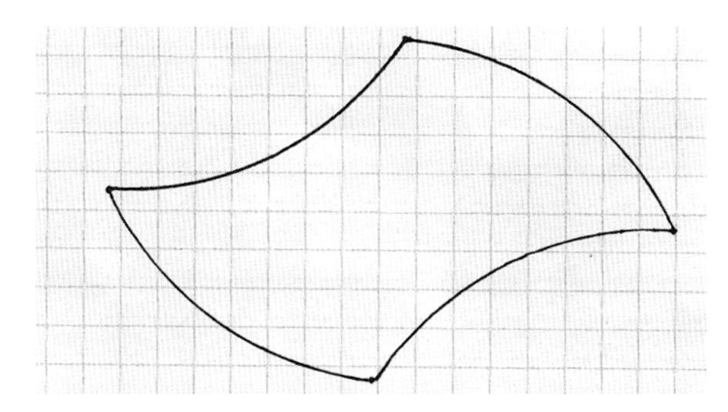

Fig. 1. Star unit

I did not want to mark the quilt, so the designs needed to be easily stitched yet look complex. Following the curved edges of the individual units seemed to work the best. After exhausting the various designs in the whole unit, subdividing the unit seemed to be the next logical step: first in half in each direction, then in quarters (fig. 2).

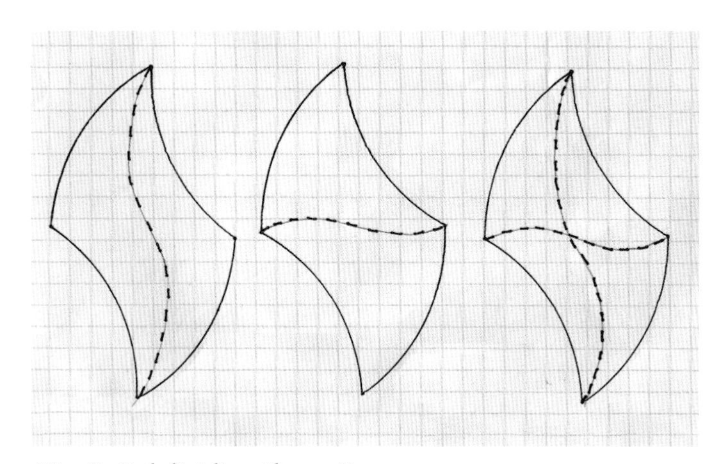

Fig. 2. Subdividing the unit

These subdivisions were done with a gentle curve. This did require a minimal amount of marking on the quilt, but I discovered that the subdividing lines could be extended across two units at a time, eliminating two starts and stops of stitching (fig. 3).

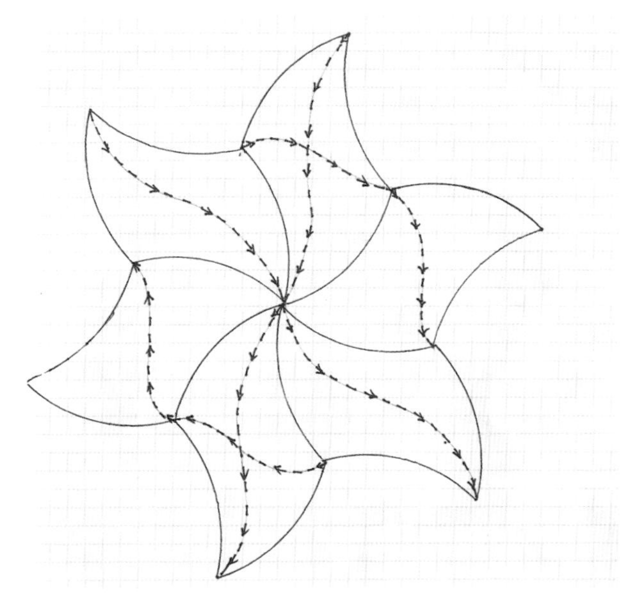

Fig. 3. Quilting lines extend across two units.

Then I began to doodle within the subdivisions. Varying where the line started changed the look of the design, ensuring a myriad of possibilities (fig. 4). As an added benefit to this manner of design, it created a kaleidoscope pattern, greatly enhancing the feeling of motion.

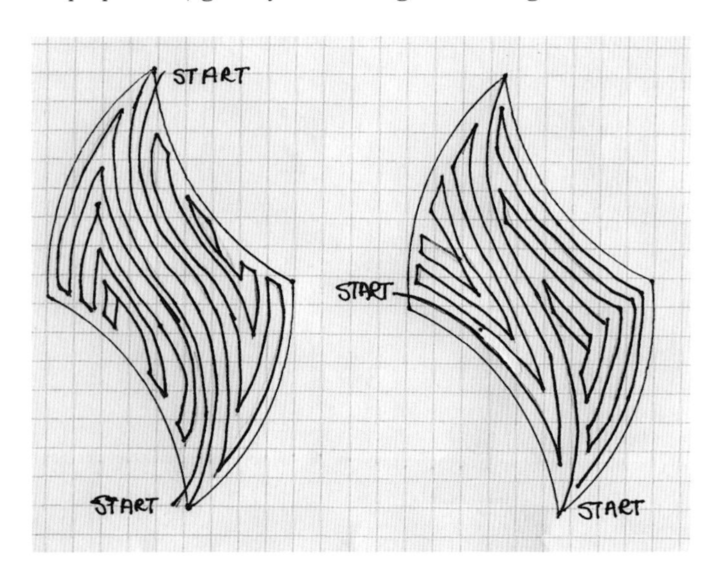

Fig. 4. Changing the starting place changes the design.

After some trial and error, I realized that it was easier to stay within the same section of the design for each of the six points of the star (fig. 5). Once each portion was completed, I moved to the next segment. In this manner, the quilt required little turning to have it facing in the proper direction for the next segment.

Fig. 5. Quilt the same subsections first, indicated in red.

For the background designs, I wanted to continue the illusion of motion and to give the feeling of spatial distance. Again, sheets of paper were filled with line drawings of the individual units. I found these units also needed to be subdivided from corner to corner. To achieve more of a navigational feel, straight rather than curved lines were used (fig. 6). To keep the design consistent, I mathematically subdivided along these straight lines (fig. 7, page 61).

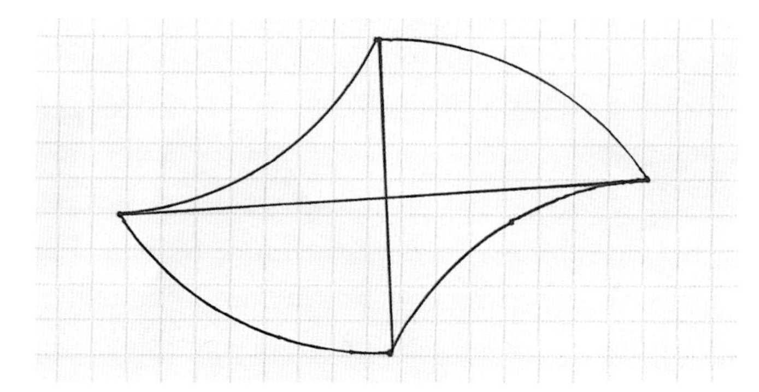

Fig. 6. Straight lines subdivide the background units.

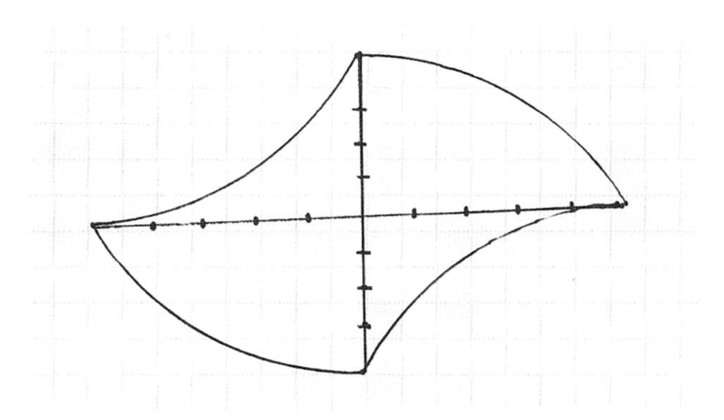

Fig. 7. Subdivisions can be further divided.

When creating the grids within the units, I came to the conclusion that what looked good on paper did not necessarily work in fabric because too many lines could become lost. So I simplified the design to a point at which the original intent was not lost (fig. 8). This was definitely a case of less is more. The first version looks good on paper, but there are too many lines.

The next version eliminates the center line and widens the space between lines.

The third version opens the center a bit more and keeps the grid lines equidistant. This one is almost right.

In the final version, the center is more open, creating the illusions of contour. The grid lines are still equidistant but a little farther apart.

Once all the quilting in the body of the quilt was complete, the central black hole still needed finishing. I had come to the conclusion that the quilting needed to be ethereal, almost not there. To attain this end, a charcoal metallic thread was brought into play. This offered a hint of sparkle and mystery, and at the same time issued the warning, BEWARE THE BLACK HOLE.

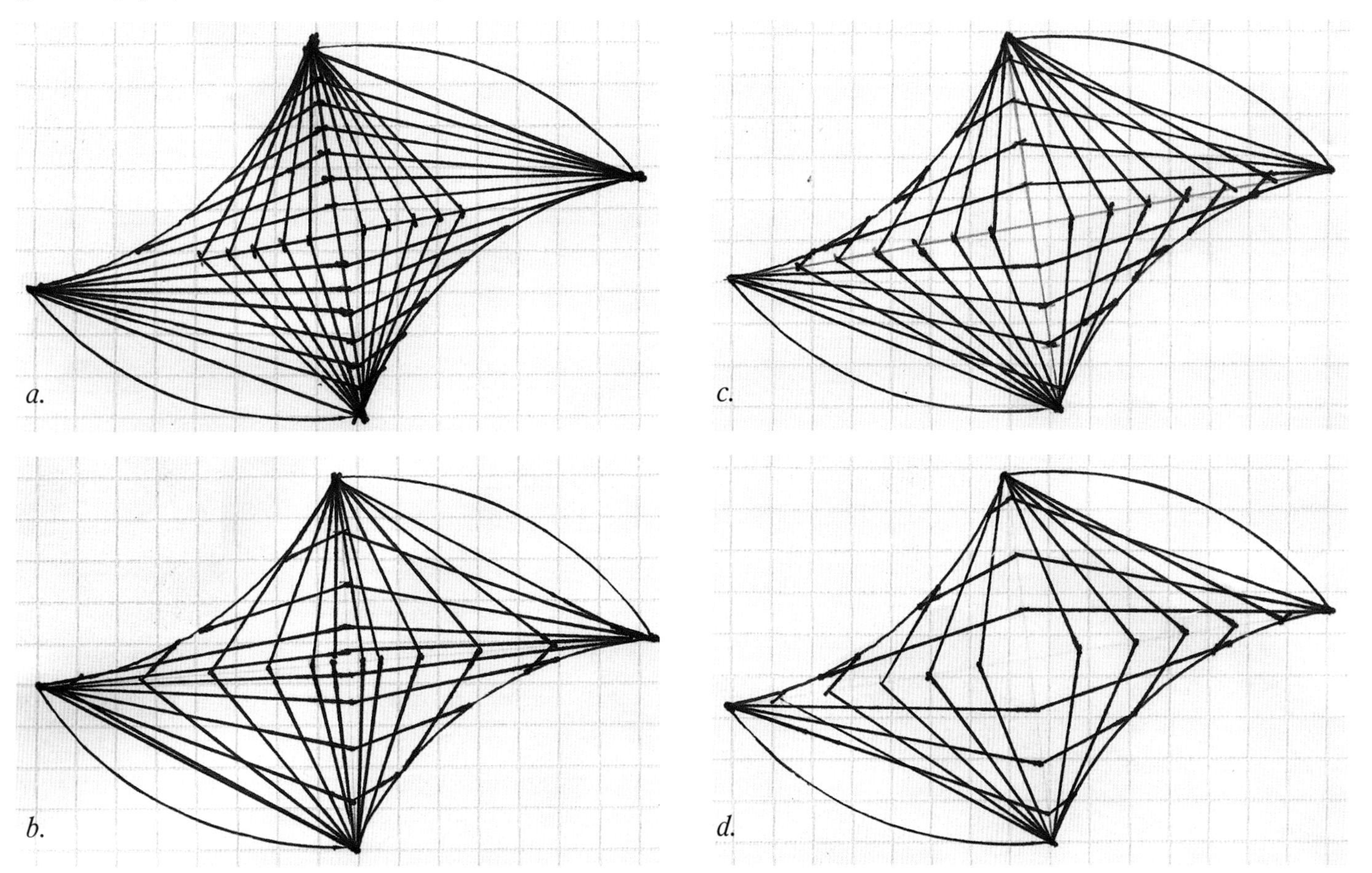

Fig. 8. Design simplification: too many lines (a), no center line (b), equidistant grid lines (c), and the final version (d).

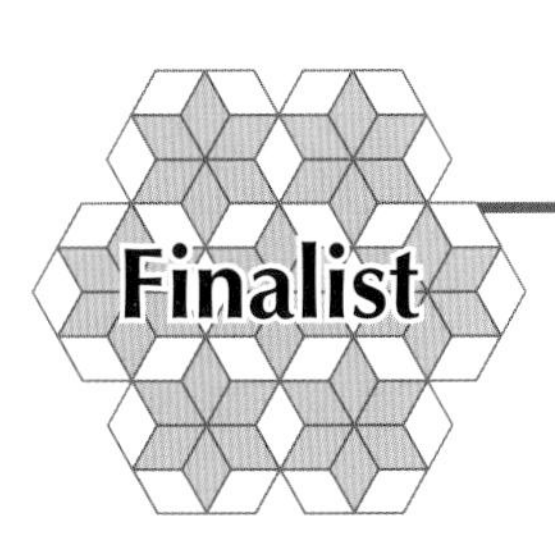

Marie Karickhoff

South Lyon, Michigan

"I put a huge amount of time and energy on accurate cutting and piecing, neither of which would bear much fruit if the pressing stages were neglected."

"Mon pays c'est l'hiver" means "my country it is winter." My country, my homeland, is Quebec. It would appear that the word Quebec is symbolic of cold and snow, which inspired my quilt.

For a while, I had wanted to make a blue-and-white quilt, inspired by the flag of Quebec, adorned with its glorious fleur-de-lis. The Seven Sisters pattern would become a perfect platform to feature the six-sided snowflakes, which are omnipresent elements in my native Quebec's winter landscape. Like nature's snow crystals, my stars' six arms would be identical, but each snowflake would inherently be different from the others. As in a real kaleidoscope, the components creating the patterns remain the same, but the perspective varies, thus creating different images.

Inspiration for this quilt came to me 20 years to the day that I met my husband, and I sewed the label on the day of our twentieth wedding anniversary. It is a fitting tribute to the man whose hard work provides for us and our three children, and whose patience and tolerance have allowed me to indulge in my other passion: quilting.

Although I have always loved to create traditional quilts with a twist, it is only in the last six years that I started making quilts for challenges. Upon request from my guild, adhering to set guidelines, I designed a raffle quilt. The constraints of a challenge foster

Marie's photo by Naomi Oldford of Poi Photo

Mon pays c'est l'hiver

56" x 65"

growth within one's craft. I now love to participate in guild challenges and quilt show contests.

I make a fair number of larger quilts, but my true love is miniature quilts. They are no less time consuming because I usually hand quilt them. I do not have a preconceived idea on whether hand or machine quilting is better. Each quilt calls for its own technique.

I genuinely enjoy hand quilting and detest free-motion machine quilting. The process fills me with anxiety, although I will resort to it when appropriate ... it is often appropriate. I used to call myself the Queen of Quilt in the Ditch. Two of my more successful quilts were quilted in the ditch, which I like because it conserves the crisp graphic lines of a sharply pieced top. I still do it, most often on charity quilts, because it is quick, easy, and good-looking.

These last couple of years, I have used a much smaller fabric palette than I used to, which makes finding and harmonizing fabrics more difficult. I love to create intricate bindings. This quilt has 36 pieces of binding, cut and mitered to match the adjacent fabrics.

In each new project I tackle, I often try to introduce myself to an element of quilting with which I'm not familiar or comfortable. That forces me to expand my technique repertoire and develop my artistic ingenuity. I truthfully enjoy tedious piecing, especially the miniatures. I much admire Sally Collins' work.

My next project, which could be on the drafting board for 6 to 12 months, will be a sampler, medallion, miniature quilt. I've done neither sampler nor medallion quilts before. Just because I like to complicate my life, I'll throw in one more element of difficulty: irregular angles.

Inspiration and Design

In a quilt for the AQS 2002 Nashville show, I used a technique called shaded kaleidoscope six-sided stars. It borrows its roots from Bethany S. Reynolds' Stack-n-Whack® method. I really enjoyed the challenge. In fact, in the past three years, I have made three hexagonal quilts. All three were major milestones in my quilting career.

I absolutely love the 60-degree triangle and the 60-degree diamond, with their innumerable setting possibilities. I was thrilled with the thought of designing a Seven Sisters quilt for the MAQS contest. However, it took until August 1, 2004, for inspiration to finally erupt.

The initial drawing was quickly drafted with pencil and graph paper. I then drew the quilt on Electric Quilt 5 to yield a clear colored image. I judiciously positioned two values of blue on stars and teeth so that the design flowed seamlessly from large to small stars, but would flip-flop where the small stars met.

This quilt was designed as a whole, the small stars filling the spaces between the large stars, all separated by sawtooth sashing. There were no individual blocks. The initial task in making the quilt was to determine the actual perimeter of a workable block. Three possibilities quickly emerged: a triangle, a diamond, and even a rectangle. All three of these block outlines had a major flaw. They would require me to piece the center seams of the stars' arms last or nearly last. I wanted to piece them first because the fabric print needed to be impeccably matched. That put a massive constraint on creating a naturally occurring block.

During August, I crisscrossed southern Michigan in search of the elusive two sets of twin fabrics I needed for the quilt. My design scheme required that I find two prints, one small, one large, both in two different colorways that would coordinate, both in hues and values. I wanted to use blue – blue like the flag of Quebec, blue like a blue-ribbon at the fair. The fabrics also had to be suitable for the Stack-n-Whack method.

I thought I had found them until, quite along in the construction of the top, I realized that the print I had selected for the large stars was very wrong. The stars were neither shaded nor kaleidoscope-like. With the deadline looming, I sadly had to settle for a more generic pair of prints. The original large stars were used on the back of the quilt. The small stars turned out just as I had planned, with subtle but distinct variations.

Contemplating Quilting Designs

In the past, I have adapted commercial quilting designs. For example, I'll take a design meant for a square block and convert it to fit a hexagonal block. I always extend the drawing into the neighboring blocks' open areas, crossing over the seams. That way, I avoid the lumpy channels that are created at the seam lines when blocks are quilted to within ¼" from the seam lines. I will often redraft a quilting pattern to have some of the lines cross over the exact center of the block, so that the thick center, often made of 8 to 12 converging seams, doesn't pop out, looking like a circus tent peak.

Whereas a complex quilt top design can emerge in my mind and be drafted in less than an hour, I agonize for days over which quilting designs to choose. An improper design can ruin an otherwise magnificently pieced top. I copy, modify, redraft, recreate, enlarge, reduce, rotate, and flip until I come up with something that I can live with (fig. 1). For this project, I decided that I would create my own design from scratch. It turns out that it took me no longer to create a brand-new design than it would have taken me to modify one.

I wanted to use a fleur-de-lis, the emblem on the Quebec flag. To create my design, I drafted the exact outline of the large stars, including their adjacent "teeth," to be quilted with one of three designs used in the quilt. The small star would contain another, and its white background, yet a third. All three are continuous-line quilting designs.

Fig. 1. Evolution of a quilting design

For the first design, the challenge was to fill the entire space, without spilling into the white portions, because a different thread color would be used there. Unable to squeeze six fleurs-de-lis agreeably into the large stars, I removed the top sections of three alternating fleurs-de-lis designs and replaced them with tulips, representing Michigan, my current home state. Refer to the large star quilting pattern on page 67.

The small stars are quilted with a simple pattern composed of what's known in the Midwest as pumpkin seeds. I like to call them by their Southern name, orange peels, to represent my three children, all born in Florida. Both the small and large stars are quilted with smoke-colored nylon monofilament thread. I always use invisible thread for this type of quilt. I like that it doesn't blur the overall color and print effects created with the Stack-n-Whack technique.

The white portions around the stars are quilted with white cotton, in a wreath-like quilting design composed of a string of tulip cups, lopsided chalices, and orange peels (fig. 2). All three elements are borrowed from the two stars.

Fig. 2. Small star quilting pattern composed of tulip cups, chalices, and orange peels

LARGE STAR QUILTING PATTERN

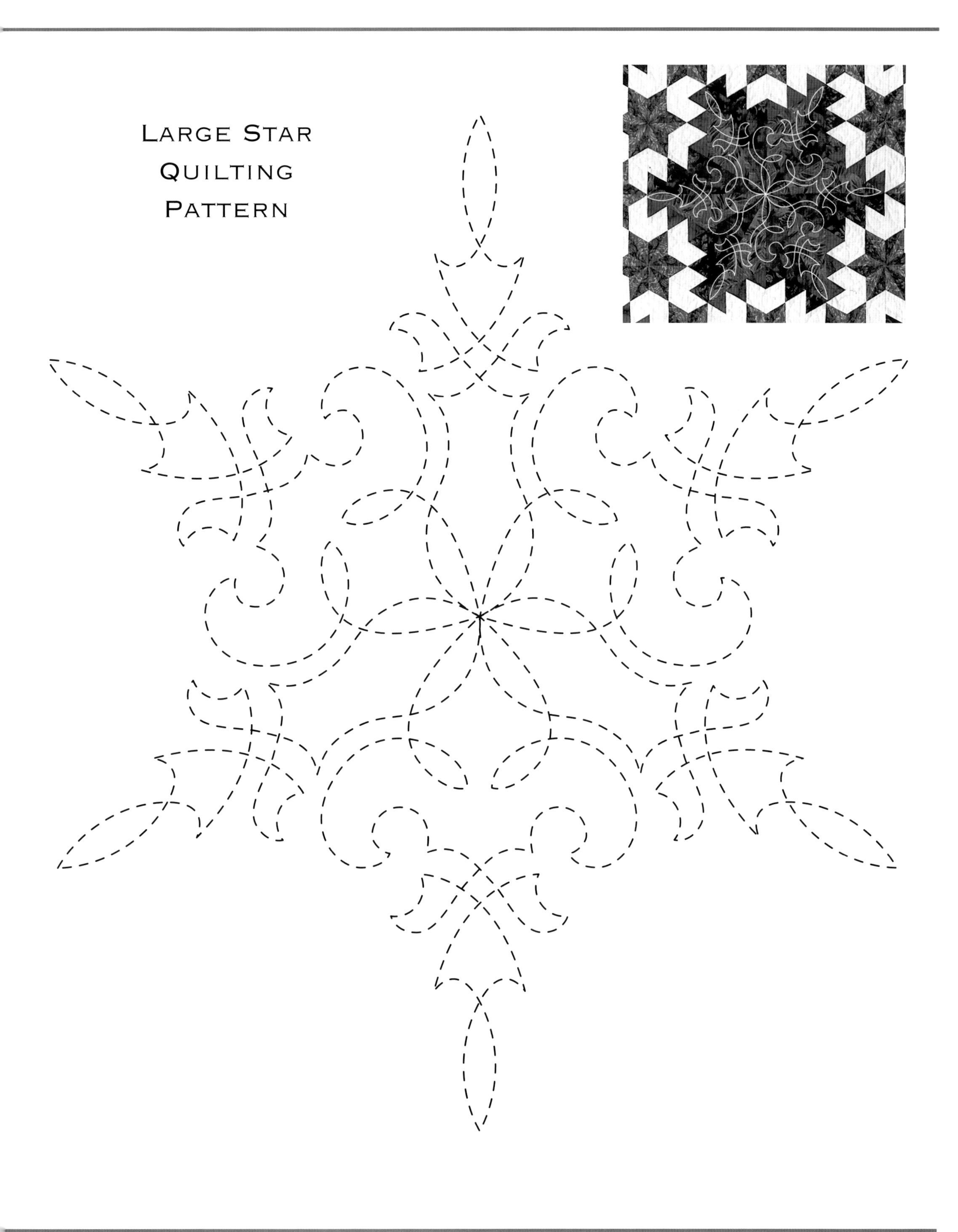

Vicky Lawrence

Overbrook, Kansas

"Without the help and urging of many friends and others, such as the enthusiasm of the copy-center man, this quilt would still be a drawing on my bulletin board."

My husband and I were both raised on farms, and when we got married, we started saving our money to buy a farm in rural Overbrook, Kansas. We still live there with cats, dogs, sheep, goats, horses, and chickens. I have been a weaver and spinner for years, and at the farm, we have sheep and angora goats for the fiber.

Then quilting took over my life when we purchased an old iron bed. It needed refinishing, which my husband did, and it needed a quilt, which I attempted making. Knowing little about quilting wasn't a problem, because I didn't even know if I was doing something wrong. Since then, I have learned from classes and other quilters what a mess that first quilt really was.

Quilting fills my time, leaving little time for the other fiber arts. I teach classes and have always learned as much from my students as I had hoped to teach them. Their questions and suggestions continue to lead me into finding new ways and techniques to use in my quilting. I now own and design for my pattern company, Prairie's Edge Patchworks. I believe that each quilt is a learning experience and hope this attitude will continue giving me new ideas to use.

Vicky's photo by Margaret Carrero

Pleiades Seven Brides

67" x 62"

INSPIRATION AND DESIGN

For several years, I have wanted to make a Seven Sisters quilt. When the shop in the town where I live wanted a design to use in their shop book, I designed a Seven Sisters quilt with long points on the outer edges. This quilt had spiky flowers in the large spaces outside the stars. However, this design was never used because the book required a quilt that could be made without templates. I liked the Seven Sisters idea so well that the drawing for this quilt was pinned to my bulletin board, and it stayed there for several years.

Usually, there is quite a lot of time to get to know and discuss things with your students during a daylong class. During one such class, we were talking about different contests and challenges. I mentioned that I wanted to enter the Seven Sisters challenge. I told them about the drawing on my bulletin board and that it involved a lot of appliqué, which is my least favorite technique. A student said that, knowing me, she thought that I would come up with some other way of jazzing up the design.

Armed with her confidence in me, I went home and began working on my design once again. This time I drew it with long, outer bent points to give the illusion of a spinning constellation. With that in mind, the spiky flowers were eliminated. Who has ever seen flowers floating in the sky? After the flowers were eliminated, I couldn't wait to work on the quilt.

Next came the fabric choices. At first, after eliminating the flowers, I thought I would do the quilt in bright fabrics. It soon became apparent that it was turning into a quilt with only primary colors. So that idea was tossed aside. Because searching for fabrics is my favorite part of the process, I gladly started again, and eventually the colors were chosen.

I then drew my design on graph paper. By doing this, I can be sure that the points are the same length and bent in the same curve. Then I took it to a copy center in a larger town. I told them I wanted it increased 400 percent and left for the hour they said it would take. When I got back, my copies weren't done because there was a problem. So the manager came out to explain that their copier wouldn't go large enough to increase it 400 percent. He said to do it, they would have to make it in two halves to get the complete pattern and he didn't think I would want that. I said that two halves would be fine because I was going to cut it apart anyway. So he started making the copies himself. Then he laid it out on the floor of the store, positioned it together, and began asking questions about the process. His grandmother had been a quilter, and he was interested in my technique.

I sewed the quilt together in five sections, then sewed the sections together. As you can see, the points on some of the stars reach out over the borders. These were left free until after the borders were sewn. Then they were appliquéd (the "A" word) down to the borders.

Metallic, rayon, and cotton threads were used for the quilting – whatever would help the design. I had to be careful with the border because I had used the fabric on the bias to get the desired effect. I didn't like the geometric design on the fabric when I laid it on the straight of grain beside the quilt body. When the fabric was turned on the bias, it fit in well with the turning of the stars, and it wasn't as apparent that it was a geometric design.

I bound the edges before beading the quilt. This kept the strings and batting from shedding during beading. It also helped to keep the bias border from stretching during the handling while beading.

ENLARGING DRAWINGS

Draw your quilt design on graph paper. The paper used for PLEIADES SEVEN BRIDES was hard to find because it was 60-degree graph paper. It is designed especially for quilts.

Take the graph-paper drawing to a copy center and increase it in size to get the size needed in the final quilt.

If more than one copy is needed for larger designs, tape the copies together. Then tape together freezer-paper pieces to make a sheet the same size as the photo copy.

With a fine Sharpie®, redraw the whole quilt on the shiny side of freezer paper. When doing this, you have to be careful to let the lines dry before putting your hand or arm on top of them, or you will have fuzzy lines on your drawing and ink all over yourself.

Put hash marks on the seams to match them when sewing them together.

Pin the original copy to your design wall. I have a small sewing space and have taped together two heavy ceiling tiles to create a 4' x 4' design wall.

As you finish each section of the quilt, pin it to the original copy. By doing this, you can see where you are going and if you are happy with the results as they unfold.

Quilt design drawn on graph paper

Sharon Norbutas

Camarillo, California

"I had spent 10 years exploring the uses for bias grain in quilt blocks, and I knew that the curves would be perfect for defining the nature of the 'sisters' and their relationships."

One day, in the late 1970s, while searching a closet, I found a box. To this day, I have no recollection of how or why that particular box followed me through many years and several moves. The box contained two completed quilt tops ca. 1930. I determined that my mother as a teenager had pieced one of the tops, a version of Sunshine and Shadow. My mother had always hated sewing in any form, so I knew she must have labored over every stitch. The result was a shape that was concave on all four sides. I immediately decided, with impish glee, to complete the task and return it to her, almost 50 years after she had made it.

As a child, I had found an old treadle machine in our attic. Somehow I learned to make it run. This led me to a career of 30 years, teaching clothing construction at a local college. So, how hard could it be to finish this quilt? At the time, I did not know any quilters. I headed to the library to get some directions. The few books available all seemed to end the same – "Now quilt it." I ordered a quilt frame from the Sears catalog and proceeded to stitch the layers together. The joke was on me. I became hopelessly entranced by quilting in every way, shape, and form.

The advances made in the last 30 years astound me. While I wield a rotary cutter through layers of fabric, I think of when I traced a cardboard template with a pencil. I recall when orange and purple were rare among the tiny calico prints. At the time I began to quilt, there

Sharon's photo by Marilyn Volan

Sisters – Similarities, Differences, Relationships

70" x 86"

were only two ways, a right way and a wrong way. Anything that works is correct today. Now, with hundreds of books to choose from and speakers coming monthly to our local guild, my options seem endless. There is never enough time to try everything that beckons me.

While I love every aspect of quilting, I am most intrigued with techniques. New tools, new products, new methods, new patterns, new ideas ... all of these call for problem solving, and I welcome the challenges. I take a wide variety of classes from others and never fail to learn something new. I am always on the lookout for a better way. Then there is the fabric! It is sometimes comforting and calming. Other times it is exciting and inspiring.

I have learned why people have more than one machine. I now have several, each for specific techniques. Generally, I do piecing in the daytime and hand quilting at night. Occasionally, I am drawn back to appliqué. It is exciting to work on a show quilt, but I find peace in the construction of quilts for our community outreach. Then, there are all the quilters around me. They teach, they inspire, they comfort. My quilt world is a safe haven. How fortunate I was to find that box in a closet. I can hardly wait to start the next new project!

Inspiration and Design

Seven Sisters was one of the first quilt patterns to fascinate me when I began quilting more than 25 years ago. The announcement of the 2005 contest was the perfect challenge. The "sisters" come in different shapes and sizes. Each has traits in common with the others, but none are alike. They have various connections to each other and the family group.

When I first began quilting, I had a background in textiles and clothing. After mastering some basic quilting techniques and unlearning some old sewing habits (like pressing all seam allowances open flat), I was free to apply my previous education to my new infatuation. All the "what ifs" and "why nots" began to surface. The most frequently recurring subject, for me, was that of bias. For centuries bias has been used to enhance cling, drape, and flow of garments. Surely I could find some use for bias in quilts. The first clue I found was from June Ryker's *Dance of the Logs* (Possibilities, 1995). Bias strips were used to make one gentle curve. I began to experiment with multiple curves.

SISTERS is the fifteenth piece in a series. I began with a tiny drawing of distorted diamonds. The first step was finding a tessellation, then enlarging it to a workable size. I did this with a sheet of paper, pencils, ruler, and a lot of math. I found eight separate diamonds within the design. After setting curves along the edges, there were 11 templates – some of the reverse templates are not true mirror images because of those curves.

Each curved diamond was hand drawn on paper (see figure, page 75). The lines within the outline were drawn freehand and were different for every piece. Bias strips of fabric were applied in the manner of string piecing. The technique is tedious, time consuming, and sometimes downright dangerous, because it requires sewing over pins, and it takes some practice to make the fabric stretch or ease for the amount of curve. My goal is always to have no tucks or gathers. Perhaps the greatest challenge when bending bias is the patience it requires. Once a block is constructed, there is no way to change one single strip. An error made in selection or sewing means remaking the block.

It is difficult to plan just how a set of bias blocks will look. Drawing all the tiny segments of the design is almost impossible. When working on a bias quilt, I generally take a leap of faith and am often surprised by the results. While working on this quilt I began to think I was making the twenty-first-century version of the postage-stamp quilt. Another difficulty encountered is in the basting process. The bias fabric strips tend to cause the shape of the piece to shift, and careful measuring and readjusting is required.

After spending five years on this quilt, the last two quite intensively, it was impossible for me not to give the sisters personalities. The yellow family is a close and loving group. They are held together by one sister, who is strong and works hard to keep them close. Two of the sisters are very much alike, close in age and interests. They have formed a bond somewhat tighter than the others. Even the shy, retiring one has been kept within the family circle. Their yellow color is indicative of warmth.

The red sisters are a political bunch. They run the PTA, the city council and assorted other organizations. Because they all share this trait, they are spread out, so as to allow each to operate within a territory. Their red color signifies their dynamic and authoritative positions.

The blue sisters are philanthropic. They love to do good deeds and quietly are on call whenever there is a need. They are somewhat closer together, as they assist each other often. Blue signifies their strength of mission.

Are you wondering about the purple sisters? They are a dysfunctional family ... lost in society and often overlooked. One sister, slightly more colorful than the others, has taken her own path in her own direction, breaking the chain of communication within the family.

USING BIAS

The method I have devised for using bias is a cross between string piecing on paper and paper piecing. It is a slow procedure and requires a bit of practice. I begin with a straight-line drawing, then develop the curves. The amount of curve and the width of the fabric strip are codependent. The width of any strip is limited by how much bend can be achieved: the tighter the curve, the narrower the strip of fabric.

Here are some suggestions for making a practice piece: Begin with a piece of paper to use as a foundation. Small, tight curves require stiff paper, while large, flowing curves can be done on lighter weights.

Draw the main shape on one side of the paper, filling in the inner lines, then trace the lines on the back of the paper. A lead pencil may soil the fabric, so consider a non-smear marker. Leave extra paper around the edges of the piece.

When selecting fabric, be aware that there will be waste. It is better to have too wide of a strip than too narrow of one. I generally find that a 1⅛" wide strip is quite workable.

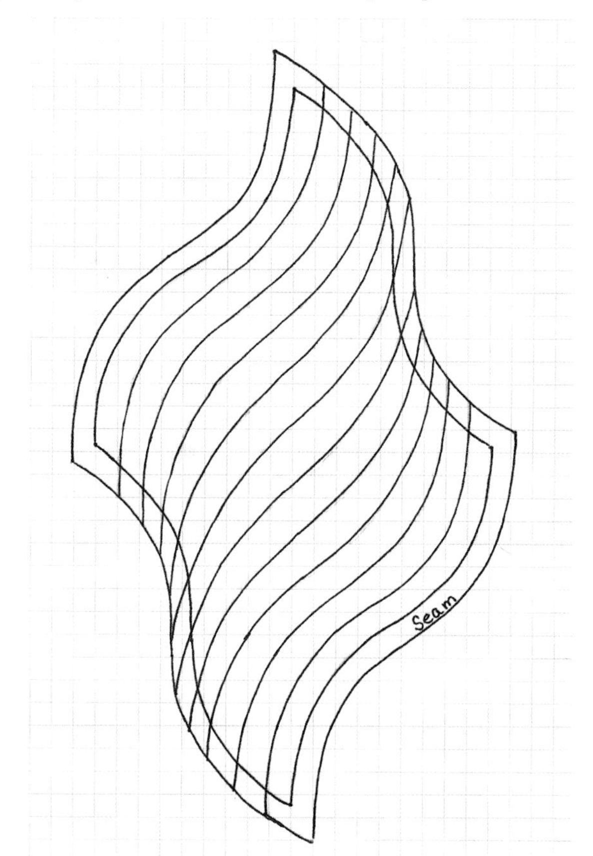

Practice diamond drawn on graph paper

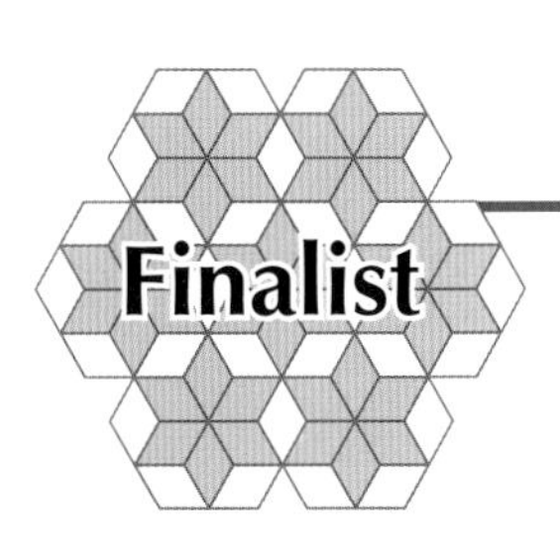

Lucy Silliman

Fort Scott, Kansas

"My pieces should not be called quilts, but fiber art ... They simply must be hung on a wall and enjoyed from a few feet away."

I have been making quilts for about 15 years. In 1995, I tried something new when I made some baskets around a large feathered star. I filled them with my originally designed two-toned ruched flowers and real pheasant feathers, sprayed with hair spray to make them more durable. The quilt show judge was horrified and said the feathers would never hold up when the quilt was used to cover a bed. Only then did it occur to me that maybe quilts needn't always be used to keep us warm but could be used to hang on the wall as objects of art.

I am also beginning to accept the fact that my family and friends can never use all of the pieces I make, so I'm beginning to sell some of them. This year marks my second two-person show in a gallery. In addition, I am the only fiber artist to show in an art gallery in a city near my home. I now think of myself as an artist, searching for new expression in my original designs. I look forward to drawing regularly and finding new design solutions for old ideas.

Lucy's photo by Gary A. Palmer of Captured Images

The Pleiades: Seven Sparkling Sisters

75" x 80"

Part of this new image is the result of redesigning my work space. I used to crawl over a bedroom set to get to my design space. That furniture is now gone, and my official studio now has a cutting table made from an old dining table, my machine is built into a cabinet, and one wall is completely devoted to a design space. When I enter my new room, I immediately have a new sense of creativity. I can hang interesting pieces of fabric or a painting to inspire me. I now try to "let the fabric do the talking" while I step back to listen.

Another important part of my emergence as an artist is my participation in a group of other fiber artists. I drive 120 miles each way once a month to exchange ideas and friendship with this small group. We encourage each other to work in our own style while being able to understand some of the frustration we have in walking a different path. Our discussions of goals, marketing plans, and professional development, as well as new products and techniques, make each one of us excited to keep experimenting and growing. We are now developing a plan to show our work as a group, and who can tell where this may lead.

At this point, I find myself working on many ongoing series of pieces at once. I work best when I find unusual images that inspire new ideas. Then I draw, revise, and find the fabrics to fit the ideas. In each piece, my aim is to increase my level of skill in design and to find new approaches to convey my ideas to the viewer. I want the viewer to sense a dynamic tension in my work. Hopefully, my pieces are not described as beautiful, but as striking and interactive. With this in mind, there will always be room to grow and develop into the artist I am becoming.

Inspiration and Design

Stars, both in quilts and in the skies, have always fascinated me. When I was in college, I took astronomy to fulfill the physical science requirement. That has fueled my interest in the celestial objects as well as the calculations and myths of early people, who predicted major life-sustaining decisions based on their observation of the heavens.

In doing research for my quilt, I began with a search on the Internet of the "Seven Sisters." According to Greek mythology, the star cluster Pleiades, in the larger constellation Taurus the Bull, was also known as the Seven Sisters. As told in Greek lore, these sisters were the daughters of Atlas and Pleione. One day, they were traveling with their mother, when they met the handsome hunter, Orion. Stunned by their great beauty, he fell in love with Pleione and her seven daughters. He began to chase them, trying to win their affections. Eventually, Zeus came to the aid of the seven sisters. He transformed them into doves so they could fly away from Orion's lust. The doves then flew into the sky to become the stars we see today.

Modern science tells us that Seven Sisters is a rather young star cluster, only about 50 million years old. It is embedded in a reflection of cold gas and appears as a blue hue. Astronomers call it M-45.

When I looked at the stars in the traditional Seven Sisters quilt block, I imagine the sisters in the Greek myth. Why not incorporate their images into the design? Therefore, I removed the center star from the traditional block and filled it with a sister's face.

The background for the stars had to be the night sky. I pulled out all my black fabrics looking for the ones that depicted swirls of light and twinkling stars. I strip pieced them and used the nine-degree wedge ruler to cut the strip-sets into 40 pieces. These were then placed off center in the background.

The blocks themselves were pieced in seven different sizes to achieve the illusion of depth. They were also placed approximately in the same configuration as the actual stars in the cluster. Then they were machine appliquéd to the background. Gold tulle and beads were added to fill blank areas and give more sparkle to the night sky.

With the background completed, the real challenge of making the faces began. Because I have never taken a drawing course, my ability to draw faces is rather limited. I tried silhouettes and some drawings of faces by one of my friends, but there was either not enough or too much detail to interpret in machine embroidery. I finally discovered that the simple outline of the face with a minimum of features worked best. As they say, "Less is more." I used my scanner/printer to size the faces to the star blocks.

The same tulle as in the background was used to outline the hair flowing away from the faces. I wanted to make it appear as if it were blowing softly in a solar breeze. To give each goddess her own personality, each was given a different color for her star and hair. Yarns and beads were sewn into place, and the seven sparkling sisters finally came to life.

Making Faces

Making a face is easy and fun, and the size of the face can be easily changed by using a scanner/printer. To begin, use a light box to trace the outlines of a face very lightly onto fabric. Muslin is too light and gives a ghostlike feeling. A washy print without a definite pattern in a slightly peachy beige is what I found worked best. There are also shades of solids made specifically for flesh tones. Remember to trace lightly because these lines are only guides. You will always vary slightly from them as you sew. This is *not a mistake,* but your own unique touch!

Put a layer of cotton batting behind the face fabric and use machine embroidery to outline the face and facial features. I used a satin stitch and black thread. Be sure to taper the stitch width as you come to the ends of the eyelashes, lips, and any other place where a line ends in space. I also found that stitching each of the lines twice added depth to the satin stitch. The second stitching should be slightly wider to cover the first.

When the features are complete, put the design face down on another piece of the face fabric for the backing. Sew around the whole head with a short stitch length. Be sure you sew outside your first stitching line. Slash an "X" in the backing fabric and carefully turn the piece right side out. Lightly press.

For the hair, I used two different yarns from the same color family. The yarns can be the color of real hair, or you can use fantasy colors. There are many wonderful yarns that have a built-in variation in color. Real hair has many different shades, so try to find a variegated yarn. If this isn't possible, twist two or three different shades of yarn together. Sew the yarn in place with invisible thread, going straight down the middle of the lines, then fill as needed.

Use tulle shapes for the hair that flows away from the faces. I cut these freehand with my rotary cutter. Cut more than you think you will need. Then arrange the shapes coming from behind the face. Sometimes turning the tulle upside down will make it the perfect shape. Cover the outside line with yarn as in the hair section, and fill in the center. Add beads if desired.

Finally, sew the face by hand over the tulle/yarn strands. If there are any spaces on the front edge of the faces, use a permanent pen or marker to touch up anything lost in the fabric turning.

Janet Jo Smith

Morrison, Colorado

"The in-and-out, 'now you see it, now you don't' aspect of this design depends entirely on value."

Recently, I needed to purchase some insurance for my little cottage-industry, quilt-related business. After all, I have a nice sewing machine, yards and yards of fabric, and quite a few quilts. With all the forest fires we have in the Colorado foothills, I was concerned. During my phone conversation with the representative, she asked, "What do you do?" She became confused as I listed all my activities – dyeing fabric; designing, making, and patterning quilts; and teaching, lecturing, and free-lance editing. It was too many jobs. They denied coverage. After two phone calls and a bit of convincing, I eventually got coverage.

It's the same when I meet someone new and they ask what I do. I always pause. I know what's coming. "I'm a quilter," I respond. They promptly say, "A what?" During the six years that I worked for a quilting magazine, I would answer, "I'm a magazine editor." They always asked, "Oh, what magazine?" When I said *Quilter's Newsletter Magazine*, they would wrinkle their brows and say, "What newsletter?" How can I explain who I am?

I made my first quilt in 1976. I was a single mother of two young children, working full time and going to college in the evenings. I

Vanishing Stars

67" x 60"

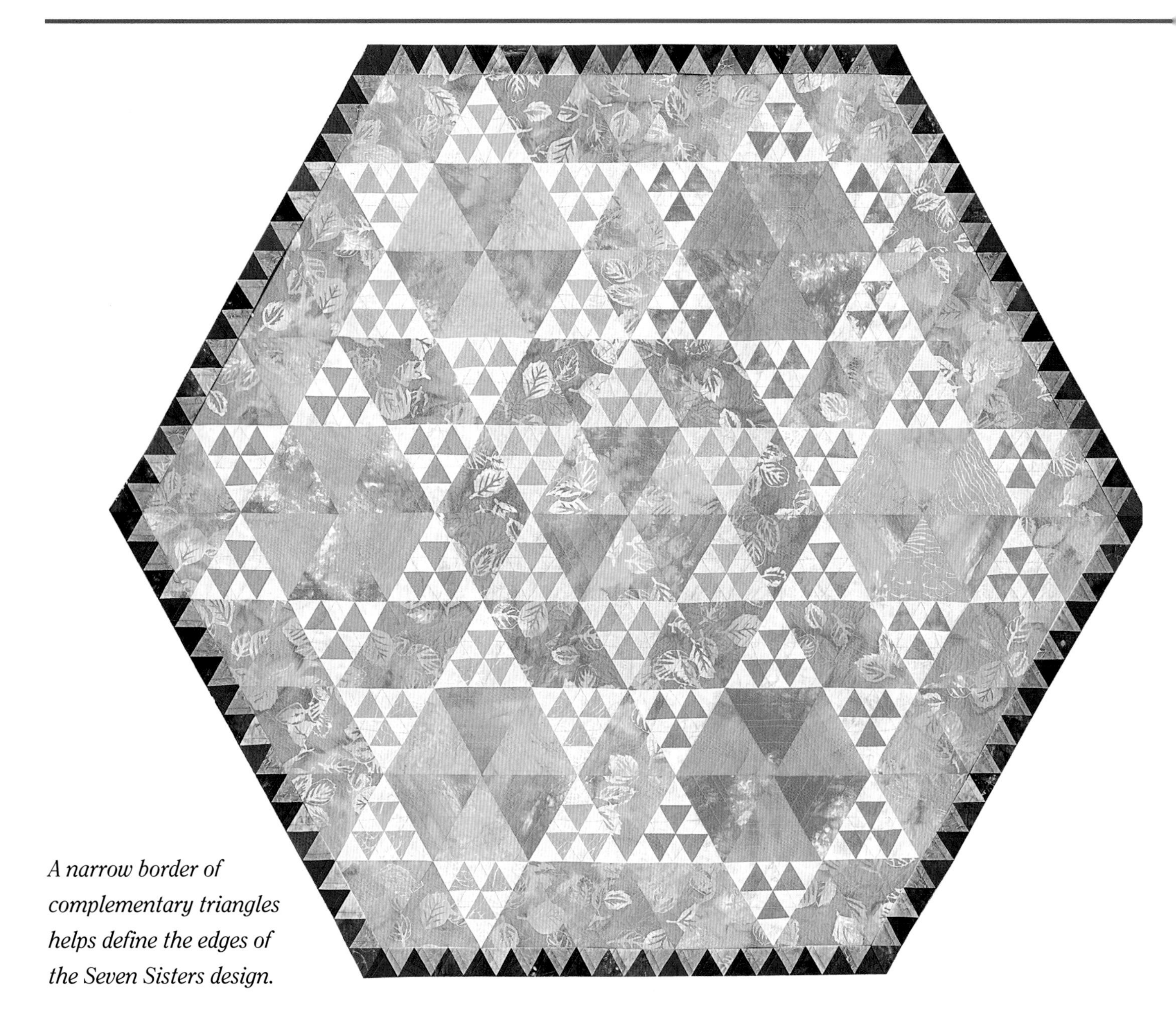

A narrow border of complementary triangles helps define the edges of the Seven Sisters design.

was busy. I enjoyed embroidery on my free evenings and picked up a set of cross-stitch blocks at a local craft store. Once they were finished, I found a book and made a quilt top. My mother and Aunt Louise came to my home for a weekend, and they helped me put the quilt in a homemade frame of one-by-twos and C-clamps that rested on the backs of the kitchen chairs. I became a quilter!

I finished college, raised my children, remarried, and even went to law school, but never stopped quilting. Eventually, after joining a quilt guild, a weekly bee, serving on several guild boards, and taking a few classes, I was in so deep that I made a career of it. Now I have a studio, a machine, yards and yards of fabric, a lot of quilts, and insurance coverage for my quilt business.

Inspiration and Design

I love making quilts for themed exhibitions. It gets my creative juices flowing to face a new challenge. However, when I learned that the Seven Sisters design was the focus of the current MAQS contest, I wasn't so sure. The pattern isn't square, and it has a lot of diamonds, meaning set-in seams. However, once I realized that the quilt could be constructed from equilateral triangles, I got busy.

I'm not so good at planning on paper. Working on a design wall is best for me. It helps to see the actual colors and values as I go. I love the idea of tradition with a twist. VANISHING STARS is essentially a one-block quilt, made large and broken into smaller units. My goal was to have the seven stars visible, but at the same time, have different areas of the block move in and out of dominance as the viewer looked at the quilt. By cutting a lot of large and small triangles and arranging and rearranging them on the wall, I eventually got my design.

Often, a single fabric makes me itch to get stitching. With this quilt, it was the batik fabric in the background that begged to be used in a quilt. Combined with other batiks from my stash and hand-dyed and hand-painted fabrics I had made, the center of the quilt went together quickly.

A problem emerged at the corners because I was running out of the red and purple batik. I knew I wanted a narrow final border to frame the design, but there wasn't enough to fill in the whole space. Work ground to a halt until I found another fabric, this time a stripe, to fill in those square inches. It also helped define the edges of the design. Sometimes, running out of fabric is a happy accident.

Choosing Fabrics

Although I have been dyeing and painting fabric for many years, when making quilts for an exhibition, I had always used commercial fabrics. Finally, my friend Sherri Driver told me I should be making quilts with my own fabrics. I decided that she was right. In VANISHING STARS, my inspiration fabric was the purple and red batik used in the background. With that in hand, I went to my stash and pulled out hand-dyed and hand-painted fabrics that could be featured in the large areas of the block. A variety of other batiks were also chosen that fit into the color scheme.

As I select fabrics for a project, I don't like for them to be too complementary. For this red-and-purple quilt, I used all hues of the basic colors. Some reds are scarlet while others are more fuchsia. The purples range from blue to red-violet. Because purple is red plus blue, I put in quite a few blue fabrics even though this color isn't in the inspiration batik. I intentionally chose fabrics that had a tinge of green, a hint of yellow, or a spot of orange. By having all parts of the color wheel represented, even in minute amounts, the finished quilt has more sparkle and the primary colors are enhanced.

Apart from color, my other consideration in choosing fabrics is value. The hexagons in the center of the stars are all dark and relatively solid fabrics. The star points, however, are light values of tan and cream. To mix things up a bit, I chose medium tans for the points of the center star. The medium tans are repeated in the inner pieced border of triangles that surrounds the block. To emphasize the center of the quilt, I used the darkest triangles of the red-purple batik around the star.

Ultimately, the success of a quilt design depends on thoughtful use of color and value. So whether the fabrics are calico, plaid, hand-dyed, or a combination of types, I try to use all the colors of the rainbow and include light, medium, and dark values as I design.

Kristina Chase Strom

Glendale, Ohio

"There was the sense that making any kind of art was a grand adventure filled with limitless possibilities. This spirit both informs and inspires my quiltmaking."

I come from a long line of strong women who have led incredibly busy lives, but have always found, sometimes demanded, the time to express themselves through the work of their hands. The unspoken credos were "if you're not going to do something well, it's not worth doing," and "a day in which you have not created something new or made a difference in some way, no matter how small, is a day wasted."

Seemingly strict and potentially crippling, these expectations were delivered with gentleness and a silent conviction that whatever was dreamed could be achieved. Best of all, especially while I was growing up, working on a creative project took priority over such menial tasks as cleaning that could always be done tomorrow.

Though I have never taken a formal class or participated in a workshop, I don't consider myself to be self-taught, but rather home schooled. Shop owners and fellow customers are exceptional resources. Connecting with them is invaluable.

My personal life and professional commitments preclude my active involvement in local quilting groups, a void that the wonder of the Internet has filled. Around six years ago, I discovered a group of America Online® quilters who meet online every Saturday at midnight – a guild meeting at a time that fits my schedule. The Quilting by Moonlight members are generous and enthusiastic, and our exchanges run the gamut from silly to serious. I remember more

Dancing with the Pleiades

52½" x 56½"

than one night that my entire household was awakened by laughter. Friendships have been forged there that transcend time and space.

Of the myriad art forms I have explored, quiltmaking resonates to me in a way unlike any other. Finding words to briefly describe the depth of this resonance is a struggle. I drive a road-weary but reliable and well-loved minivan. The license plate reads RTQUILT, which stands for romancing the quilt. Perhaps that says it all.

INSPIRATION AND DESIGN

The inspiration for DANCING WITH THE PLEIADES came about while observing the magnificent star cluster Seven Sisters on a frosty full-moon night in autumn 2003. While I thoroughly enjoy living in a metropolitan area, I am a nature girl at heart. On retreats to my land in the Appalachian foothills, all the cares of the city are left behind and my perspective is restored.

Over time, I have come to realize my design process for the MAQS challenge mirrors that of the seasons. Late autumn and winter are spent on contemplation and study, planning, and dreaming. Spring is a time of abandon and play, for sketching rudimentary ideas. Summer is when the design takes final form and the actual work of construction begins. And early fall is the herald of completion.

My initial image of a quilt celebrating the Pleiades was abstract and contemporary, consisting of flowing and pulsing forms. However, my thinking about traditional blocks took me traveling on an imaginary journey through time. Alternative names for this block are Seven Stars and Seven Stars in a Cluster, signifying a period in which people were more connected with and conscious of nature, when the movement of a specific stellar configuration had such direct meaning that warranted documentation in a quilt. Thinking further back in history brought a vision of petroglyph carvings on stone and in wood made for the same reason. I realized that quilting is a similar language of symbols universal in nature, and my quilt design was conceived.

A preliminary design was drawn on isometric graph paper (fig. 1), then archetypal symbols were experimented with (fig. 2) and eventually rearranged to reflect the sister angle of the theme. My friend Marilyn Rose described this perfectly: "The seven central stars are all related but not the same, sort of like real sisters. Opposing stars have similar outsides but different insides. The three pairs surround the center star, which contains elements of all the others."

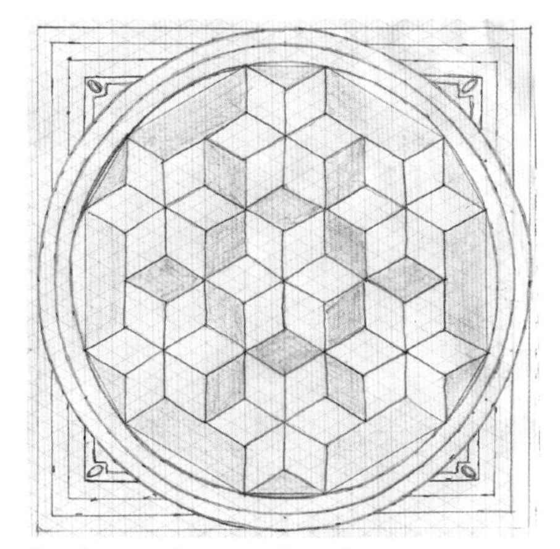

Fig. 1. Preliminary design sketch

Fig. 2. Initial arrangement of the archetypal symbols

The quilt was to consist only of this enlarged block, but it felt incomplete. In early summer, I took another moonlit walk to reconnect with my inspiration. The

Pleiades were out of sight, but remained clear in my mind's eye. I remembered the many other stars of the cluster radiating and softly sparkling in the night, dancing around the central stars. I literally ran back to my chalet, grabbed a piece of scrap paper, and scribbled a new layout. At last I was ready to work.

Solving a Construction Dilemma

The miniature circular Seven Sisters blocks were tackled first. I was so surprised when the hand-dyed batik fabric overprinted with gold resisted precise piecing on this scale, both by hand and machine, even after repeated washing. The next attempt was paper piecing, which worked satisfactorily, but the surface did not have the desired textural depth. I finally used an old art school maxim as a solution. When you are having trouble capturing the positive space (in this case the hexagonal stars), render the negative space and the positive will take care of itself.

Templates were made for the background shapes, cut from batik, and needle-turn appliquéd to a square of the deep blue-purple. Though the technique worked beautifully, the time involved was prohibitive. The entire process took nearly ten hours for one block.

Just playing, I traced all the background shapes onto a sheet of 8½" x 11" paper. A rectangle of batik fabric was treated with a solution for preparing fabric to receive printed images. The next prescribed step was to iron the treated fabric to freezer paper cut to size, but I was in a mood of careless abandon and starched the thing until it was stiff as paper and fed it into my printer. Amazingly, this method worked (fig. 3).

The pieces were cut out individually with a ⅛" seam allowance. To streamline block production, the seam allowances were turned under, finger pressed, and held in place with miniscule dots of fabric glue applied with a hypodermic needle. To ensure accuracy of placement, I went back to the printer, this time armed with the discarded paper-piecing diagram. A copy was made into a transparency that was taped at the top to a manila folder. I slipped yet another rectangle of the deep blue-purple fabric under the clear film and lightly glued each background segment in place. The pieces were then machine appliquéd with invisible polyester thread and a small buttonhole stitch.

The next step was cutting out the 1" circular sashing for each block, so I drew freezer-paper templates with a compass. For some serendipitous reason, I checked to see what remained of the dark fabric because it was no longer available. There wasn't much. I quickly calculated the amount needed for the central stars and sashing, as well as the border, and set all that aside. There was no way that six circular sashes could be cut from what was left. As a last effort, I sliced the template in half and managed to squeeze out 12 semicircles. The dilemma was solved, so I continued my joyous dance with the Pleiades.

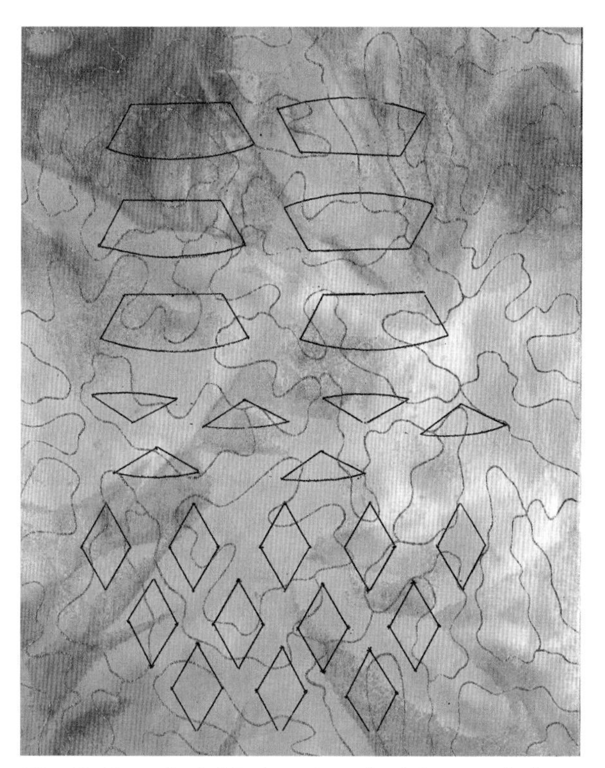

Fig. 3. Starched fabric printed with traced shapes

The Out of Towners

Tennessee

"The energy and bright colors of the fabrics we chose represent a wonderful future for our continuing collaboration."

The Out of Towners formed in 1997 as a group of artists wanting to encourage each other in making art quilts. A contest in a national magazine brought us all together to discuss design ideas and critique our different quilts. Out of the four quilts, three were completed and entered in the contest, two were finalists, and one received honorable mention.

We were definitely encouraged to try another contest and found one with a fabric collection we fell in love with, a much-needed deadline, and a design we were anxious to try. The results were favorable, so that was the start of our group of four designers working together on one quilt.

Keeping the group in stitches, Patty S. Ashworth of Oak Ridge, Tennessee, always has fun with her quilt themes. Quilting for nearly 20 years, she has quite a collection of fiber art and a growing clientele for her hand-quilting business. With a husband on an oilrig in the Gulf of Mexico and a son in college, she has time to volunteer for various positions in the group.

The Out of Towners group photo by Gary Heatherly

Quilt assembly photos by Bridget Matlock

Twist and Shout

72" x 91"

Originally from Norway, Tone Haugen-Cogburn of Maryville, Tennessee, is married to an east Tennessean. They have two very active girls and a large group of visiting relatives and friends from around the world. Her mother-in-law taught her to quilt in the early 1990s and Tone hasn't slowed down yet. Her work changes from traditional to innovative on one piece to the next.

Bridget Wilson Matlock of Alcoa, Tennessee, has done everything from hand stitching to machine quilting and is in charge of quality control in the group. Bridget is a postal carrier by day and a mother and grandmother to her girls by night. Her work is branching out to include several computer-generated photos and computer-drafted designs.

From White Pine, Tennessee, Candace Tucker is the newest to quilting in the group. She has been a fiber artist since the late 1960s, but more in the surface-design area than in quilting. Candace is a fabric store manager and shows her work at two art galleries in the Knoxville area.

Today, our group makes both art and traditional quilts. The only two rules we have are that no one person owns the quilts and that the quilt goes to contests or competitions and is sold. This pays for our habit. Each of us still does our own work and has taught workshops. One thing that remains the same from that first contest quilt is that we still have a million design ideas and so little time to create.

INSPIRATION AND DESIGN

Between the four of us, we have six sisters and many, many sisters of the heart. We dedicate this quilt to them. We enjoy working with the diamond shape, and achieving movement in the design is exciting (fig. 1). This is our third quilt made with the diamond block.

Fig. 1. The diamond shape is a group favorite.

Because we have four schedules to work around, it becomes a challenge to set up workdays. When we decide on a design, one member usually sketches it on graph paper or on the computer, while the rest of us jot down our ideas and bring the notes to a design session (fig. 2). In the meantime, we all start collecting a palette of fabrics. For this quilt, we started with fabric from our stash.

Fig. 2. The design is brought to life.

The design wall is an essential part of the process for us. We start cutting and sewing, placing the elements on the wall for approval or disapproval before we go on to the next step (fig. 3). None of us is shy about letting others know if the design is working and letting the quilt talk to us, which sometimes leads us down another path from where we began.

Fig. 3. A design wall brings everyone's design visions together.

We discuss changes and design ideas while rotary cutting, sewing, pressing, and generally solving all the problems of our small world and the big world around us. We exercise a lot of "what ifs" as we work (fig. 4). During this planning, there is a continual patter of title suggestions flying around the room. Sometimes the name-calling gets out of hand.

Fig. 4. Alterations are easily made with friends.

When the design seems to be stalled, it's time for lunch. This recharges the brain cells and we come back to the design wall with clear eyes and more ideas. We then solve any problems we may have had before lunch and continue working until one of us has to pick up a child or whatever. Lunch is not usually planned in any way, but comes together like our quilts with a little bit of this and lot of that. One of our last salads is on its way to becoming a small quilt. We never know where creativity may take us (fig. 5).

Fig. 5. A group effort came together beautifully in the finished quilt.

SEVEN SISTERS BLOCK
5" WIDE

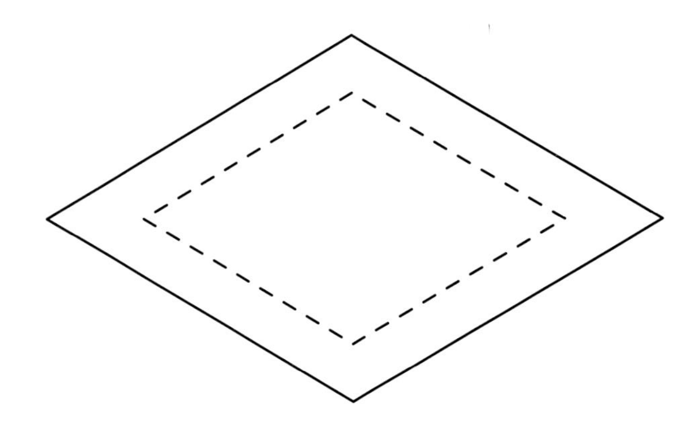

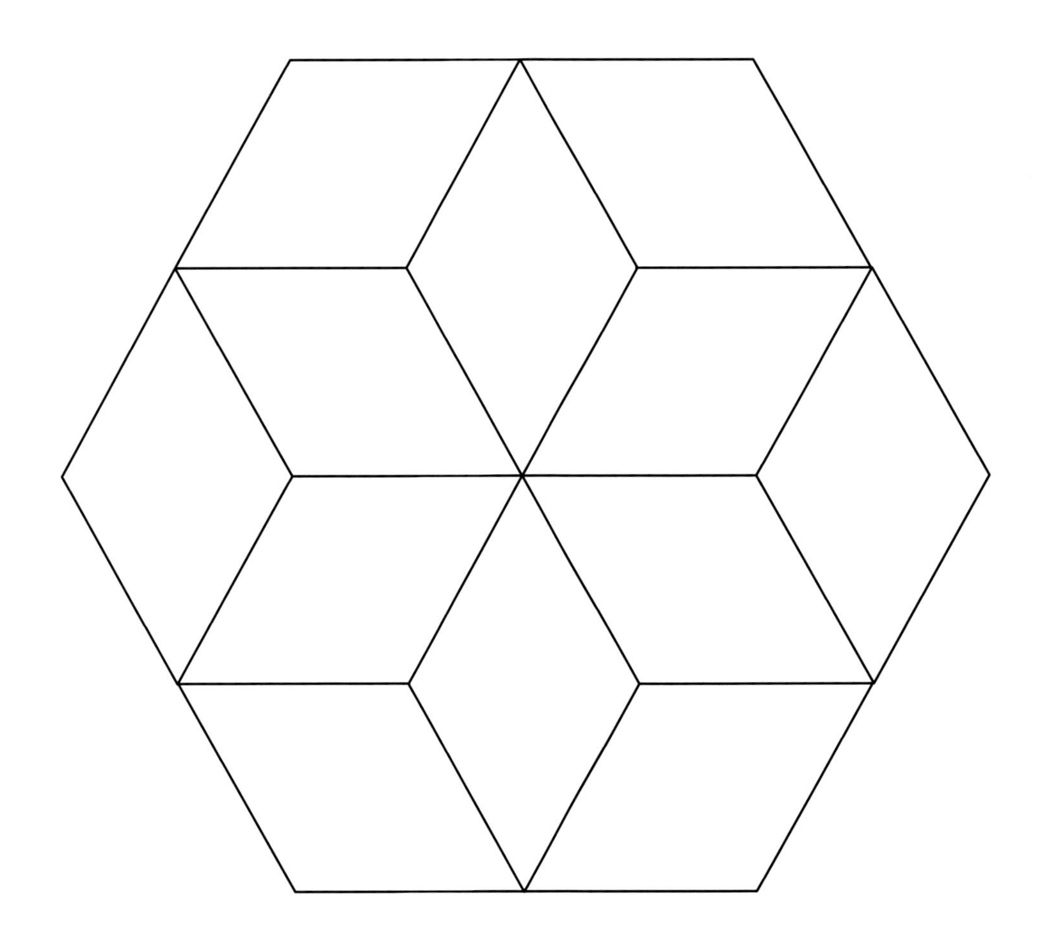

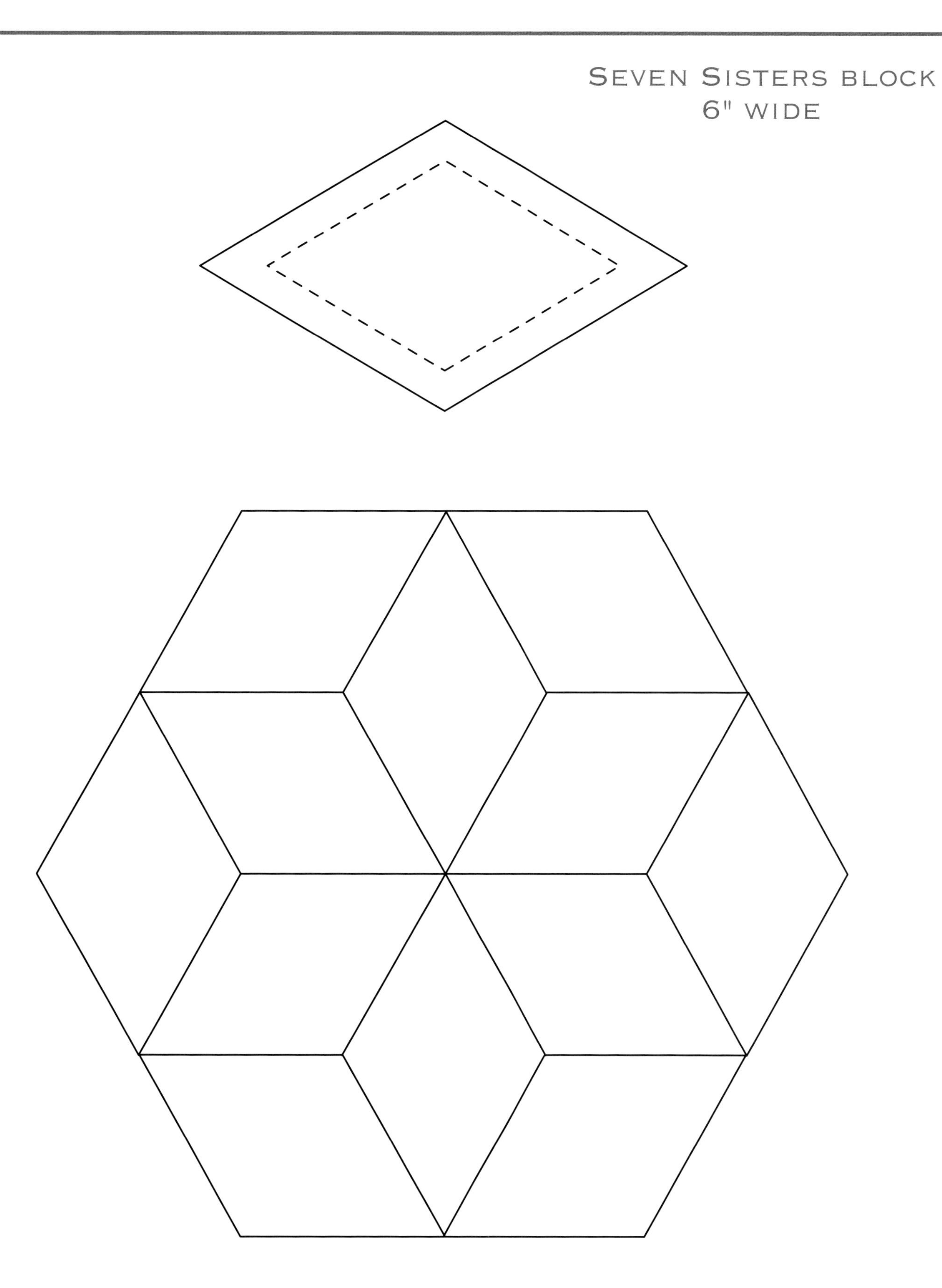
SEVEN SISTERS BLOCK
6" WIDE

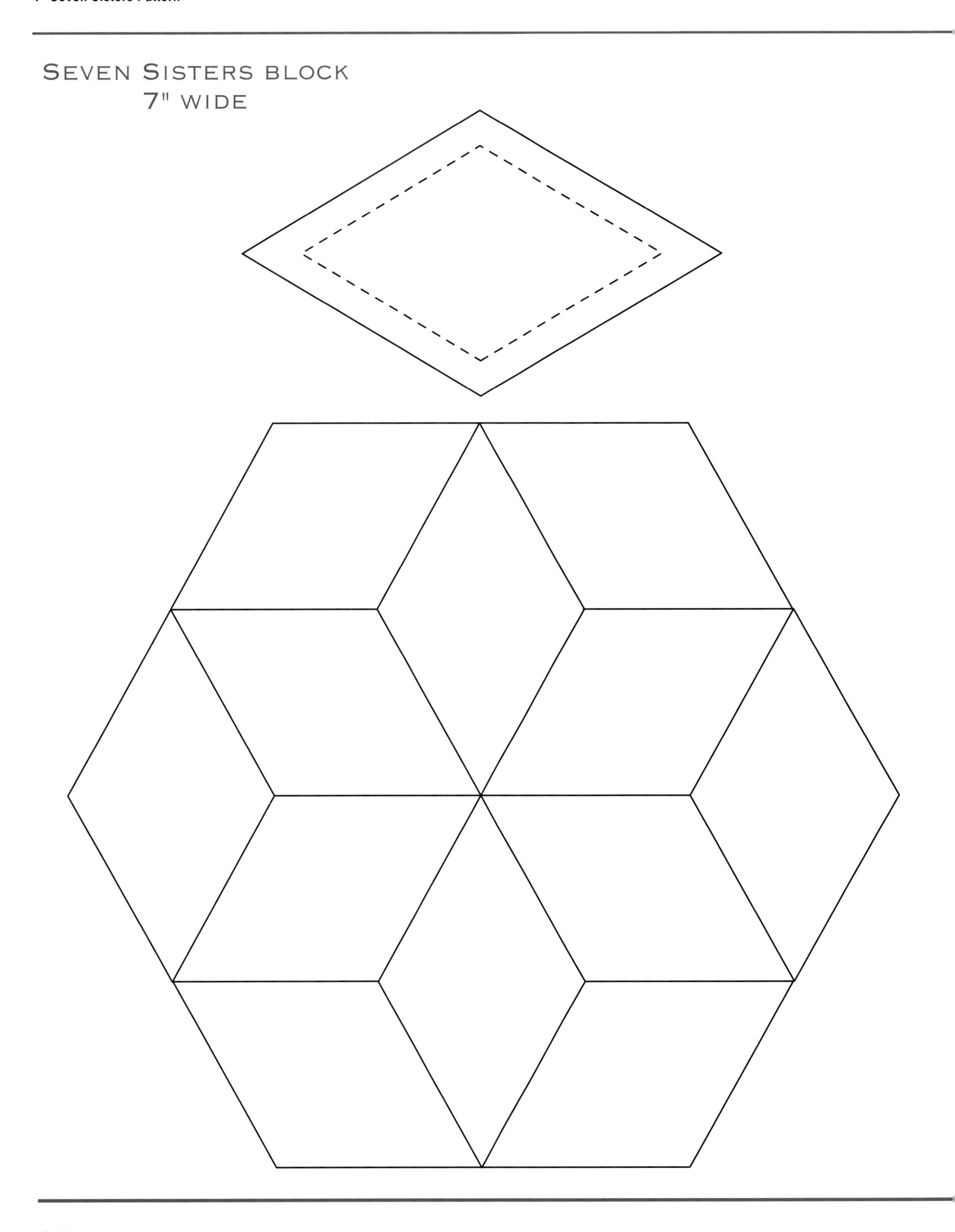
SEVEN SISTERS BLOCK
7" WIDE

The Museum

The Museum of the American Quilter's Society (MAQS) is a truly exhilarating place to learn more about quilts, quiltmaking, and quiltmakers. It is the world's largest and foremost museum devoted to quilts and the only museum dedicated to today's quilts and quiltmakers. Established in 1991 by AQS founders Bill and Meredith Schroeder as a not-for-profit organization, MAQS is located in a 27,000 square-foot facility. It was designed specifically to display quilts effectively and safely. Three expansive galleries envelope visitors in color, exquisite stitchery, and design.

The highlight of any visit is The William and Meredith Schroeder Gallery, which displays a rotating installation of quilts from the museum's permanent collection of over 200 quilts. Before MAQS opened, the Schroeders had acquired a private collection of remarkable quilts. In addition to being a source of wonder for the collectors, the collection came to recognize extraordinary contemporary quilts and their makers. Through the Schroeders' generosity, the nucleus of the museum collection was formed. In addition, the permanent collection includes award-winning quilts from the annual Quilt Show and Contest. Educational programs offered in three well-equipped classrooms serve local and national audiences. Specifically, MAQS offers an annual schedule of in-depth workshops taught by master quilters. Children and families can participate in hands-on projects. Exhibitions developed by MAQS, like New Quilts from an Old Favorite, travel to other galleries and museums, helping educate and inspire a wider spectrum of viewers. The MAQS shop and bookstore offers very special quilt-related merchandise as well as fine crafts by artisans from this region and beyond. One of the largest selections of quilt books anywhere can be found in the shop.

Located in historic downtown Paducah, Kentucky, MAQS is open year-round 10 A.M. to 5 P.M., Monday through Saturday. From April 1 through October 31, it is also open Sundays from 1 to 5 P.M. The entire facility is wheelchair accessible. The Museum programs can also be sampled on the Web site: www.quiltmuseum.org. For more information, e-mail info@quiltmuseum.org; call (270) 442-8856, or write MAQS, PO Box 1540, Paducah, KY 42002-1540.